PE?

PEER

HENRIK IBSEN (1828–1906) is often called 'the Father of Modern Drama'. He was born in the small Norwegian town of Skien and made his debut as a writer with the three-act play *Catilina* (1850). Between 1851 and 1864 he was artistic director and consultant for theatres in Bergen and Christiania (later spelled Kristiania; now Oslo), and contributed strongly to a renewal of Norwegian drama, writing plays such as *The Vikings at Helgeland* (1858), *Love's Comedy* (1862) and *The Pretenders* (1863). In 1864 he left Norway on a state travel stipend and went to Rome with his wife Suzannah. This marked the beginning of what would become a 27-year-long voluntary exile in Italy and Germany. Ibsen experienced a critical and commercial success with the verse drama *Brand* (1866); this was followed by his other great drama in verse, *Peer Gynt* (1867), the prose play *The League of Youth* (1869) and his colossal *Emperor and Galilean* (1873), a 'world-historical play', also in prose. The next decisive turn in Ibsen's career came with *Pillars of the Community* (1877), the beginning of the twelve-play cycle of modern prose plays. Here he turned his attention to contemporary bourgeois life, rejecting verse for good. This cycle would include *A Doll's House* (1879), *Ghosts* (1881), *An Enemy of the People* (1882), *The Wild Duck* (1884), *Rosmersholm* (1886), *The Lady from the Sea* (1888), *Hedda Gabler* (1890), *The Master Builder* (1892), *Little Eyolf* (1894), *John Gabriel Borkman* (1896) and, finally, *When We Dead Awaken* (1899). By the time Ibsen returned to Norway in 1891, he had acquired Europe-wide fame, and his plays soon entered the canons of world literature and drama. Following a series of strokes, he died at home in Kristiania at the age of seventy-eight.

GEOFFREY HILL, the son of a police constable, was born in Worcestershire in 1932. He was educated at Bromsgrove County High School and at Keble College, Oxford. After teaching for more than thirty years in England, first at Leeds and subsequently at Cambridge, he became Professor of Literature and Religion at Boston University in Massachusetts, where he was also founding co-director of the Editorial Institute. In 2010 he was elected Professor of Poetry at the University of Oxford, and in 2012 he was knighted. His collection *Broken Hierarchies: Poems 1952–2012* was published in 2014.

JANET GARTON is Emeritus Professor of European Literature at the University of East Anglia, Norwich. She has published a number of books on Scandinavian literature, including *Norwegian Women's Writing* (1993), the edited letters of Amalie and Erik Skram (3 vols., 2002) and a biography of Amalie Skram, *Amalie – et forfatterliv* (2011). She is a director of Norvik Press and has translated several works of Norwegian and Danish literature, including Knut Faldbakken: *The Sleeping Prince* (1988), Bjørg Vik: *An Aquarium of Women* (1987), Kirsten Thorup: *The God of Chance* (2013) and Johan Borgen: *Little Lord* (forthcoming).

TORE REM is Professor of British Literature at the Department of Literature, Area Studies and European Languages, the University of Oslo. He has published extensively on British and Scandinavian nineteenth-century literature and drama, including the books *Dickens, Melodrama and the Parodic Imagination* (2002) and *Henry Gibson/Henrik Ibsen* (2006), as well as on life writing, the history of the book, reception studies and world literature. Rem has been Christensen Visiting Fellow at St Catherine's College, Oxford, was director of the board of the Centre for Ibsen Studies and is a member of the Norwegian Academy of Science and Letters.

HENRIK IBSEN

Peer Gynt
and Brand

In versions by
GEOFFREY HILL

Introduced by
JANET GARTON

General Editor
TORE REM

PENGUIN BOOKS

PENGUIN CLASSICS

UK | USA | Canada | Ireland | Australia
India | New Zealand | South Africa

Penguin Books is part of the Penguin Random House group of companies
whose addresses can be found at global.penguinrandomhouse.com.

Penguin
Random House
UK

First published in Penguin Classics 2016

008

Translation of *Brand* © Geoffrey Hill 1978, 1981, 1996 and 2016
Translation of *Peer Gynt* © Geoffrey Hill 2016
Introduction © Janet Garton, 2016
Other editorial materials © Tore Rem, 2016
All rights reserved

Published with the support of the Norwegian Ministry of Foreign Affairs

Every effort has been made to trace copyright holders of quoted passages.
The publishers are willing to correct any omissions in future editions.

Set in 10.25/12.25 pt Adobe Sabon
Typeset by Jouve (UK), Milton Keynes
Printed and bound in Great Britain by Clays Ltd, Elcograf S.p.A.

ISBN: 978-0-141-19758-6

www.greenpenguin.co.uk

MIX
Paper from
responsible sources
FSC® C018179

Penguin Random House is committed to a
sustainable future for our business, our readers
and our planet. This book is made from Forest
Stewardship Council® certified paper.

Contents

Chronology   vii
Introduction   xv
Further Reading   xxxi
A Note on the Text   xxxv

BRAND   1

PEER GYNT   165

Afterword: Translating and
    Recreating Ibsen: An Interview
    with Geoffrey Hill   343
Notes   353

Chronology

1828 Henrik Johan Ibsen born to Marichen and Knud Ibsen, a retailer and timber trader, in the town of Skien, 100 km south of Oslo (then Christiania).

1833 Starts school at Skien borgerskole (*borgerskoler* were schools for the bourgeoisie of the towns).

1835 Knud Ibsen is declared bankrupt. The family's property is auctioned off, and they move to the farm Venstøp in the parish of Gjerpen, just east of Skien.

1843 Travels to the coastal town of Grimstad, about 110 km south of Skien, where he is made apprentice in an apothecary's shop.

1846 Hans Jacob Hendrichsen is born to Else Sophie Jensdatter, the apothecary's maid, on 9 October. Ibsen accepts patrimony and is required to pay maintenance for the next fourteen years.

1849 Writes *Catilina*, his first play, as well as poetry, during the winter. Has his first poem, 'I høsten' ('In Autumn'), published in a newspaper at the end of September.

1850 Leaves Grimstad on 12 April, the publication date of *Catilina*. The play is published under the pseudonym Brynjulf Bjarme. Visits his family in Skien for the last time.

Goes to the capital, Christiania, where he sits the national high school exam in the autumn, but fails in arithmetic and Greek.

His first play to be performed, *Kjempehøien* (*The Burial Mound*), is staged at the Christiania Theater on 26 September.

1851 Starts the journal *Manden*, later *Andhrimner*, with friends.

The famous violinist Ole Bull hires Ibsen for Det norske

Theater (the Norwegian Theatre), his new venture in Bergen. Ibsen begins as an apprentice, then becomes director and resident playwright. He agrees to write and produce one new play for the theatre every year.

1852 Spends over three months in Copenhagen and Dresden studying Danish and German theatre.

1853 *Sancthansnatten* (*St John's Night*) opens on 2 January, the founding date of Det norske Theater.

1855 *Fru Inger til Østeraad* (*Lady Inger of Ostrat*) performed at Det norske Theater on 2 January.

1856 First real success with *Gildet paa Solhoug* (*The Feast at Solhoug*) at Det norske Theater; the play is subsequently performed at the Christiania Theater and published as a book.

Becomes engaged to Suzannah Daae Thoresen.

1857 *Olaf Liljekrans* premieres at Det norske Theater to a disappointing reception.

Moves to Christiania during the summer and takes up the position of artistic director at the Kristiania Norske Theater (Kristiania Norwegian Theatre) from early September.

First performance outside of Norway when *The Feast at Solhoug* is staged at the Kungliga Dramatiska Theatern (Royal Dramatic Theatre) in Stockholm in November.

1858 Marries Suzannah Thoresen in Bergen on 18 June.

Hærmendene paa Helgeland (*The Vikings at Helgeland*) has its first night at the Kristiania Norske Theater on 24 November and is met with a resoundingly positive response.

1859 A son, Sigurd Ibsen, is born to Suzannah and Henrik Ibsen on 23 December.

Writes the long poem 'Paa Vidderne' ('On the Moors') as a 'New Year's Gift' to the readers of the journal *Illustreret Nyhedsblad*.

1860–61 Ibsen accumulates private debt, owes taxes and is taken to court by creditors. He drinks heavily during this period, and the family has to move a number of times. He is criticized for his choice of repertory at the Kristiania Norske Theater.

His epic poem 'Terje Vigen' appears in *Illustreret Nyhedsblad*.

1862 The theatre goes bankrupt, and Ibsen is without regular employment.

Ethnographic expedition to the West of Norway in summer, collecting fairy tales and stories.

Publishes *Kjærlighedens Komedie* (*Love's Comedy*) in *Illustreret Nyhedsblad*.

1863 Employed as 'artistic consultant' at the Christiania Theater from 1 January and made able to pay off most of his debts. The first, short Ibsen biography published by his friend Paul Botten-Hansen in *Illustreret Nyhedsblad*. Applies for a state stipend in March, but is instead awarded a travel grant of 400 *spesidaler* (in 1870 a male teacher would earn around 250 *spesidaler* a year) for a journey abroad.

Kongs-Emnerne (*The Pretenders*) published in 1,250 copies in October.

1864 *The Pretenders* performed at the Christiania Theater on 17 January. A great success.

Ibsen leaves Norway on 1 April and settles in Rome.

1865 Writes *Brand* in Ariccia.

1866 The verse drama *Brand* is published in 1,250 copies by Ibsen's new publisher Gyldendal in Copenhagen on 15 March, with three more print runs before the end of the year. The play is Ibsen's real breakthrough, helping to secure financial stability.

Given an annual stipend of 400 *spesidaler* by the Norwegian government, plus a new travel grant.

1867 Writes the verse drama *Peer Gynt* on Ischia and in Sorrento. Published in 1,250 copies on 14 November, with a second, larger print run appearing just two weeks later.

1868 At the beginning of October moves to Dresden in Germany, where he lives for the next seven years.

1869 Travels to Stockholm for a Nordic meeting for establishing a common Scandinavian orthography. Publishes *De unges Forbund* (*The League of Youth*) in 2,000 copies on 30 September; the play is performed at the Christiania Theater on 18 October.

Travels from Marseilles to Egypt in October and participates as official guest in the festivities at the opening of the Suez Canal.

1871 *Digte* (*Poems*), his first and only collection of poetry, is published in 4,000 copies on 3 May.

The Danish critic Georg Brandes, the propagator of the so-called 'Modern Breakthrough', comes to Dresden and meets Ibsen for the first time.

1872 Edmund Gosse's article 'Ibsen's New Poems' appears in *The Spectator* in March.

1873 Gosse's 'Henrik Ibsen, the Norwegian Satirist' appears in *The Fortnightly Review* in January.

Travels to Vienna in June, as a member of the jury for fine art at the World Exhibition.

Kejser og Galilæer (*Emperor and Galilean*) published in 4,000 copies on 16 October; there is a new print run of 2,000 copies in December.

Love's Comedy performed at the Christiania Theater on 24 November.

1874 Ibsen and his family in Christiania from July to the end of September, his first visit since leaving Norway in 1864.

1875 *Catilina* published in revised edition to celebrate Ibsen's twenty-fifth anniversary as a writer.

The family moves from Dresden to Munich on 13 April.

1876 *Peer Gynt* receives its first performance at the Christiania Theater, with music composed by Edvard Grieg.

Emperor and Galilean translated by Catherine Ray, Ibsen's first translation into English.

The Vikings at Helgeland premieres at Munich's Hoftheater (Court Theatre) on 10 April, making it the first Ibsen production outside of Scandinavia.

1877 Is made honorary doctor at the University of Uppsala in Sweden in September.

Samfundets støtter (*Pillars of the Community*) is published in 7,000 copies on 11 October and performed at the Danish Odense Teater on 14 November.

1878 Moves to Rome in September.

1879 Travels to Amalfi with his family in July and writes most of his new play, *Et Dukkehjem* (*A Doll's House*), there. Goes on to Sorrento and then Rome in September and moves back to Munich in October.

Edmund Gosse publishes *Studies in the Literature of Northern Europe*, devoting much space to Ibsen.

A Doll's House is published in 8,000 copies on 4 December and receives its premiere at Det Kongelige Theater (the Royal Theatre) in Copenhagen on 21 December.

1880 Ibsen returns to Rome in November.

Quicksands, an adaptation by William Archer of *Pillars of the Community*, at London's Gaiety Theatre, 15 December.

1881 Goes to Sorrento in June and writes most of *Gengangere* (*Ghosts*) there; the play is published in 10,000 copies on 13 December and is met with much harsh criticism, affecting subsequent book sales.

1882 First performance of *Ghosts* takes place in Chicago on 20 May.

Miss Frances Lord translates *A Doll's House* as *Nora*.

En folkefiende (*An Enemy of the People*) published in 10,000 copies on 28 November.

1883 *An Enemy of the People* first staged at the Christiania Theater on 13 January.

1884 *Breaking a Butterfly*, Henry Arthur Jones and Henry Herman's adaptation of *A Doll's House*, premieres at the Prince's Theatre, London, on 3 March.

Vildanden (*The Wild Duck*) is published in 8,000 copies on 11 November.

1885 First performance of *The Wild Duck* at Den Nationale Scene (the National Stage) in Bergen on 9 January.

First performance of *Brand* at the Nya Teatern (New Theatre) in Stockholm on 24 March.

Henrik and Suzannah Ibsen go to Norway in early June. They travel back via Copenhagen at the end of September, and in October settle in Munich again, where they live for the six following years.

Ghosts, translated by Miss Frances Lord, serialized in Britain in the socialist journal *To-Day*.

1886 *Rosmersholm* published in 8,000 copies on 23 November.

1887 A breakthrough in Germany with the production of *Ghosts* at the Residenz-Theater (Residency Theatre) in Berlin on 9 January.

Rosmersholm staged at Den Nationale Scene in Bergen on 17 January.

1888 Ibsen turns sixty. Celebrations in Scandinavia and Germany. Henrik Jæger publishes the first biography in book form.

Fruen fra havet (*The Lady from the Sea*) published in 10,000 copies on 28 November.

Newcastle-based Walter Scott publishes *Pillars of Society, and Other Plays* (it includes *Ghosts* and *An Enemy of the People*) under the editorship of the theatre critic William Archer and with an introduction by Havelock Ellis.

1889 *The Lady from the Sea* premieres both at the Hoftheater in Weimar and at the Christiania Theater on 12 February.

The production of *A Doll's House*, with Janet Achurch as Nora, at the Novelty Theatre in London on 7 June, marks his breakthrough in Britain. This production goes on a world tour.

Pillars of the Community is produced at London's Opera Comique.

1890 André Antoine produces *Ghosts* at the Théâtre Libre (Free Theatre) in Paris, leading to a breakthrough in France.

The Lady from the Sea translated into English by Karl Marx's youngest daughter, Eleanor.

Hedda Gabler published in 10,000 copies in Copenhagen on 16 December, with translations appearing in near-synchronized editions in Berlin, London and Paris.

1891 *Hedda Gabler* receives its first performance at the Residenz-Theater (Residency Theatre) in Munich on 31 January with Ibsen present. Competing English translations by William Archer and Edmund Gosse soon follow.

Several London productions of Ibsen plays, starting with *Rosmersholm* at the Vaudeville Theatre in February. In order to avoid censorship, *Ghosts* is given a private performance by the new Independent Theatre on 13 March, leading to a big public outcry. *Hedda Gabler* is produced under the joint management of Elizabeth Robins and Marion Lea in April, with Robins in the title role, and *The Lady from the Sea* follows in May.

George Bernard Shaw publishes his *The Quintessence of Ibsenism*, based on his lectures to the Fabian Society in the preceding year.

Henry James publishes 'On the Occasion of *Hedda Gabler*' in *The New Review* in June.

Ibsen returns to Kristiania (as it was now written after the Norwegian spelling review of 1877) on 16 July and settles there for the remainder of his life. This year he befriends the pianist Hildur Andersen, thirty-six years his junior, often considered the model for Hilde Wangel in *The Master Builder*.

1892 *The Vikings at Helgeland* is performed in Moscow on 14 January.

William and Charles Archer translate *Peer Gynt* in a prose version.

Sigurd marries the daughter of Ibsen's colleague and rival Bjørnstjerne Bjørnson.

Bygmester Solness (*The Master Builder*) is published in 10,000 copies on 12 December.

1893 *The Master Builder* is first performed at the Lessing-theater in Berlin on 19 January. It is co-translated by William Archer and Edmund Gosse into English, and premieres at London's Trafalgar Square Theatre on 20 February.

The Opera Comique in London puts on *The Master Builder*, *Hedda Gabler*, *Rosmersholm* and one act from *Brand* between 29 May and 10 June.

An Enemy of the People is produced by Herbert Beerbohm Tree at the Haymarket Theatre on 14 June. Ibsen's first commercial success on the British stage.

F. Anstey (pseudonym for Thomas Anstey Guthrie) writes a series of Ibsen parodies called *Mr Punch's Pocket Ibsen*.

1894 *The Wild Duck* at the Royalty Theatre, London, from 4 May.

Lille Eyolf (*Little Eyolf*) is published in 10,000 copies on 11 December.

Two English verse translations of *Brand*, by C. H. Herford and F. E. Garrett.

1895 *Little Eyolf* is performed at the Deutsches Theater (German Theatre) in Berlin on 12 January.

1896 *Little Eyolf* at the Avenue Theatre in London from 23 November, in a translation by William Archer.

John Gabriel Borkman is published in 12,000 copies on 15 December.

1897 World premiere of *John Gabriel Borkman* at the Svenska Teatern (Swedish Theatre) and the Suomalainen Teaatteri (Finnish Theatre) on 10 January, both in Helsinki.

1898 Gyldendal in Copenhagen publishes a People's Edition of Ibsen's collected works.

Ibsen's seventieth birthday is celebrated in Kristiania, Copenhagen and Stockholm, and he receives greetings from all over Europe and North America.

1899 *Når vi døde vågner* (*When We Dead Awaken*), his last play, is published in 12,000 copies on 22 December.

1900 *When We Dead Awaken* is performed at the Hoftheater in Stuttgart on 26 January.

C. H. Herford translates *Love's Comedy*; William Archer translates *When We Dead Awaken*.

Ibsen suffers a first stroke in March, and his health deteriorates over the next few years.

James Joyce's 'Ibsen's New Drama' appears in *The Fortnightly Review* in April.

1903 Imperial Theatre, London, produces *When We Dead Awaken* on 25 January and *The Vikings at Helgeland* on 15 April.

1906 On 23 May Henrik Ibsen dies in his home in Arbins gate 1 in Kristiania.

The Collected Works of Henrik Ibsen, translated and edited by William Archer, appears in twelve volumes over the next two years.

Introduction

Nordic Frustrations

The series of twelve prose dramas for which Ibsen is generally known outside Norway were all written quite late in his life, from 1877 (*Pillars of the Community*) to 1899 (*When We Dead Awaken*). By 1877 he was forty-nine years old and already had over half of his literary production behind him; his first play, *Catalina*, was published in 1850, and he went on to publish a further fourteen plays as well as a volume of poetry over the following twenty-five years. It was during this period that he acquired the skills of writing for the stage which he was to use with such assurance in his mature works. By the time he published *Brand* and *Peer Gynt*, in 1866 and 1867 respectively, he had written and seen staged several of his own plays.

Henrik Ibsen had an inauspicious beginning as a writer; the son of a bankrupt father, he had left school at fifteen to start work as an apothecary's apprentice. Largely self-taught, he failed his university entrance exams, but persevered in writing plays and managed to attract the attention of the new Norwegian Theatre in Bergen, which had been set up by the world-famous violinist and entrepreneur Ole Bull. Here Ibsen was appointed 'dramatic author' in 1851, a post he held for six years; this was followed by five years at the Norwegian Theatre in Christiania (Oslo). During this time it was his responsibility to write plays for performance at the two theatres, as well as directing plays by other authors. In the tradition of the time, his plays were written largely in verse, and in line with the National Romantic ideals fostered by the growing movement for independence they often took their inspiration from earlier Norwegian history, such as *Lady Inger of Ostrat* (1855), about sixteenth-century Dano-Norwegian dynastic battles, and *The Vikings at Helgeland* (1858), which dramatized the tenth-century conflict between the warriors Sigurd and Gunnar and their ill-matched wives Dagny and Hjørdis. The plays he was directing were often foreign ones imported as light entertainment, largely French comedies by dramatists such as Eugène Scribe or Danish ones by Ludvig Holberg, from which he learned much about the techniques of stagecraft.

His tenure as contracted dramatic author and theatre director was not a happy one, however; his own plays had variable success, and he was not gifted as an entrepreneur or as an administrator. In Christiania things went from bad to worse, as the theatre's finances became precarious. Ibsen was attacked in the press for his bad management and reacted with apathy; his productions failed to arouse any interest, and for a few years he found himself unable to write any more plays. To some extent he was also a scapegoat for the theatre board's extravagance in incurring debts for a programme of rebuilding which far exceeded the theatre's income. The final result was that the theatre went bankrupt in June 1862, and Ibsen was fired. For the next couple of years he had no regular income. He applied to the government for an annual stipend as an author and was refused, although the only other two applicants, his friend and dramatic rival Bjørnstjerne Bjørnson and the poet Aasmund Olavsson Vinje, were awarded grants. Release from the theatrical grind did allow him to write his best two plays so far, *Love's Comedy* (1862) and *The Pretenders* (1863). The former, a comedy of contemporary manners in verse, was due to be performed by the Christiania Theatre, but then withdrawn because of the theatre's financial problems. The latter was a historical play, taking as its subject the fourteenth-century struggle for power between Earl Skule and King Haakon, often interpreted as a dramatization of the power struggle between the self-doubting Ibsen and the supremely confident Bjørnson. It was also Ibsen's first attempt at writing a play in modern colloquial prose. He directed it himself at the Christiania Theatre in January 1864, and this time he had a critical and popular success. But by now Ibsen had already decided to leave Norway.

The mid nineteenth century was a turbulent time politically for the three mainland countries of Scandinavia, and links between Norway, Denmark and Sweden were much closer then than now. Norway had been ruled by Denmark until 1814 and was released from that dependence only to be constrained by European political negotiations to become the junior partner in a union with Sweden, which lasted until 1905. Ties to Denmark were still particularly close during Ibsen's lifetime. Christiania was a small provincial town, and Copenhagen a cultural centre for writers and artists; many moved there, and most leading Norwegian authors came, during the second half of the century, to be published in Denmark. A movement for the promotion of closer political and cultural ties between the countries, called Scandinavianism, had attracted support from academics and politicians since the 1840s, and Ibsen was an ardent supporter. King Karl XV of Sweden-Norway and his ministers had made assurances of mutual self-defence and military aid. Thus when Denmark was threatened by Prussian invasion from the south in 1863–4, Ibsen was in no doubt that Norwegians at least would take up arms for their 'brother in need', as he declared in his poem of that name.[1] The fact that it did not happen was a bitter blow and strengthened his determination to turn his back on what he saw as his pusillanimous native land.

Money, however, was still a problem, as it had been for many years, and Ibsen now had a wife and small son to support. He managed to obtain a travel grant of 400 speciedaler from the government for a study trip to Rome and Paris, two-thirds of what he had asked for, which was then supplemented by a further 700 speciedaler raised by the ever-generous Bjørnson. The latter demonstrated an unfailing readiness to support his less successful colleague both in word and in deed.

At the beginning of April 1864 Ibsen left Christiania for a sojourn abroad which would last for twenty-seven years before he finally returned home to settle in Norway. While he was in

Copenhagen on the way south the news came of the final defeat of the Danes by the Prussians at Dybbøl and the surrender of two-fifths of Danish territory. When he reached Berlin in May he saw the Danish cannon paraded in triumph through the streets, a sight which sharpened his dismay at what he saw as his country's failure. Finally, on 9 May he crossed the Alps into Italy, reaching Rome in the middle of June. Emerging from the tunnel into the sunlight of the south was a revelation which he recalled vividly several decades later:

> Over the high mountains the clouds hung like great dark curtains, and beneath these we drove through the tunnel and suddenly found ourselves at Mira Mara, where the beauty of the South, a marvellously brilliant light shining like white marble, suddenly opened before me and coloured all my later work, even if not all of it was beautiful.[2]

The Light of the South

It may seem at first sight as if the creative floodgates opened when Ibsen reached Rome; after his arrival in June 1864, his two ground-breaking poetic dramas were soon published, *Brand* in 1866 and *Peer Gynt* in 1867. Inspiration did not flow as easily as that, however. Despite his enthusiasm for the newly unified Italy and the sense of creative and personal liberation he experienced on leaving Norway, he struggled to find both a form in which to express his frustration at recent events and a peaceful environment in which to work. It was not until he moved to the countryside in the summer of 1864 that he started to write – and then he began work, not on a drama, but on a long narrative poem, usually referred to as the 'Epic Brand'.[3]

This poem, which exists in differing variants, contains much of the same material as the first two acts of the later play: the meeting between Einar, a fair-haired boy from a productive farm and a happy family, and the darker Brand, who grew up in poverty and strife in a narrow valley to the north; the triangle Einar–Brand–Agnes, in which Agnes feels compelled to abandon the joyful celebration of life with Einar in order to follow the harsh demands of Brand's calling; the contrast between the little church in the valley and the Ice Church in the mountains, to which Brand is enticed by a deranged gypsy girl. It begins with the poem 'To My Fellows in Guilt', which addresses more directly than the later play the ignominious failure of Norway's delusions of greatness and the poet's shame at having fostered the illusion. It is written in iambic pentameters, in eight-line stanzas with regular rhymes – a more rigid form than the freer metre he later adopted.

It soon became apparent to Ibsen that the form he had chosen for his ideas was not working. He struggled with it for a year in increasing frustration, from the summer of 1864 to the summer of 1865, before he finally abandoned it. As he later described it in a letter to Bjørnson, the new shape of the work came to him in a moment of inspiration: 'Then one day I went into St Peter's Basilica – I was in Rome on some business – and there all at once it came to me, a strong and clear form for what I wanted to say.'⁴ Then the floodgates really did open, and Ibsen completed his new play in only four months, finishing it in mid-November. And, after having failed to attract any commercial interest with most of his earlier plays, with this play at last he found a supportive and influential publisher: Frederik V. Hegel, head of the Copenhagen-based firm of Gyldendal, publisher of many of Scandinavia's leading writers. Hegel took the play on the recommendation of the indefatigable Bjørnson, and, after some delay caused by missing letters and misunderstandings, *Brand* was published in March 1866.

The play was an immediate bestseller, appearing in four editions in the first year and accruing royalties which provided Ibsen with financial security for the first time in his life. It was also a critical success across Scandinavia, enthused over by literary arbiters and by other writers – although there were some reservations about its transgression of accepted aesthetic norms. It was not staged, and it was not intended to be staged; it is subtitled 'A dramatic poem' and was read as a work of poetry. The mutually beneficial working relationship with Gyldendal was to continue for the rest of Ibsen's life.

'After *Brand*, *Peer Gynt* followed as it were of its own

accord,' declared Ibsen in a letter from 1870.[5] This is a truth
with modifications. For some time after finishing the earlier
play, Ibsen was not sure what he was going to write next. The
delay in the publication of *Brand* made it difficult to settle to a
new work, and he considered various different projects, including a historical drama about Emperor Julian, to which he was
to return years later and which would eventually become the
ambitious double drama *Emperor and Galilean* (1873). Finally,
in January 1867 Ibsen could inform Hegel that he had started
work on another long dramatic poem 'whose protagonist will
be one of the Norwegian peasantry's half mythical folk-tale
characters from more *recent* times'.[6] He had hoped to have it
ready by the summer, though in the event it took him nine
months to write; the last two acts had ballooned out of all pro-
portion to the first three. He sent it to Hegel piecemeal as the
various sections were ready, finishing with Act Five in October
1867, so that the book could be published – as were all his later
plays – in time for the Christmas market.

This new drama was eagerly awaited after the sensation of
Brand and was snapped up in the bookshops; two editions
were printed in the first month. Critical acclaim was led by
Bjørnson, who welcomed the play as a hard-hitting and
uproariously funny satire of Norwegian self-righteousness –
although he also found it a little self-indulgent. Others had
difficulties with the unconventional form of the drama, particularly the influential Danish critic Clemens Petersen, who
found that neither *Brand* nor *Peer Gynt* could be called 'prop-
erly poetry'.[7] (*Peer Gynt,* like *Brand,* was subtitled 'a dramatic
poem'.) Ibsen, never one to take criticism lying down, retorted
forthwith to Bjørnson that *Peer Gynt was* poetry – 'or if it is
not, then it will become so. The concept of poetry in our country, in Norway, will come to adapt itself to my work.'[8]

Ibsen and his family stayed in Italy for four years, and *Brand*
and *Peer Gynt* in different ways bear traces of that time. Living
outside Norway meant that Ibsen could look back at Norway,
as he was to do in many of his later plays, with a clearer sense
of its challenges and its limitations, and of how his own views
had been coloured by his early environment. In May 1868 he

and his family left Italy, finally settling in Dresden in October, where they were to remain for the next six and a half years.

Brand

This 'cathedral of a play', 'the most powerful drama of ideas in the whole of Scandinavian literature', is dominated by the towering central figure, who is present in nearly every scene.[9] Both charismatic and forbidding, Brand demands absolute and unwavering commitment in those around him as he does in himself and finds it as difficult as anyone else to carry his ideal unscathed through the vicissitudes of life.

It is not hard to find the germ of the character and the ideas in the play in recent international events. One oft-cited model for Brand is the young Norwegian theologian Christopher Bruun, who had taken seriously the ideals of Nordic brother-hood and was one of very few Norwegian and Swedish volunteers who fought beside the Danes at Dybbøl. He spent the winter of 1864–5 in Rome and had frequent conversations with Ibsen. Brand's scorn for fine but empty promises is Bruun's own, and several of the representatives of authority in the play – the mayor, the schoolmaster, the sexton – are targets for the author's indignation at hollow political rhetoric and hypo-critical self-interest. The harshness of Brand's indictments might also owe something to some stirrings of bad conscience on Ibsen's part; after all, he had not volunteered to fight along-side his brothers either. The title of the poem 'To My Fellows in Guilt' ('Til mine medskyldige') means literally 'to those guilty *with* me'.

Religion is central to the play, with its many discussions of what it means to be a Christian. The Dano-Norwegian church was riven by dissent in the mid nineteenth century, with oppos-ing factions asserting different interpretations of God's word. On the one hand was a more optimistic, sunnier kind of belief, stressing the positive sides of living a good life, having faith in God and judging mildly, often referred to as Grundtvigianism after the Danish theologian N. F. S. Grundtvig. This is the school of thought represented by Einar early in the play, by

Agnes throughout and to some extent by the Dean. On the other hand were the pietistic movements which sprang up around the country from early in the century, demanding remorse and repentance in an unending battle against man's sinful nature, seen here in Einar's later incarnation and in some of Brand's more extreme pronouncements. One such pietist, Gustav Adolph Lammers, was the vicar of Ibsen's home town of Skien, and Ibsen acknowledged him as a source of inspiration for the play. And then, of course, there was the prominent Danish philosopher Søren Kierkegaard. Ibsen maintained that he had read little of Kierkegaard and understood even less, but his ideas were current in intellectual debate in the mid nineteenth century. *Brand* explores the conflict between what Kierkegaard refers to as the aesthetic and the ethical modes of living, as represented by the opposing philosophies of Einar, the man whose life is dedicated to the pleasures of sensory experience, and Brand, with his focus on living in a principled way, not for his own profit but for the good of society. The play also mirrors Kierkegaard's criticism of the established church and his insistence on the necessity of absolute commitment to an ideal. [10]

Brand strongly reflects the events of Ibsen's own life – not only his political indignation but his personal odyssey. He may have been writing in the light of the Italian south, but his thoughts were still in Norway, drawn back mentally as Brand is physically to the ice and snow, the deep sunless valleys and what he represented as the petty provincial obstructionism. Norway rarely gets a good press in Ibsen's writings after 1864; he rejected it as he felt it had rejected him. The obsession with heredity, with the inheritance of sin, which weighs so heavily on Brand – the burden of his mother's greed, his parents' hateful marriage and the unintended consequence of the birth of the deranged Gerd – runs like a red thread through many of his later plays, such as *Ghosts* and *Rosmersholm*. Money, the acquiring of it and the losing of it, was an insistent personal issue and is the catalyst for intergenerational conflict here as it is, for example, in *The Wild Duck* and *John Gabriel Borkman*.

In the end, however, it is not the topicality of the play or its reflection of its author's mental state which makes it appeal to audiences and directors today; it is the fascination of the central character's battle with his surroundings and his own demons. What starts out as a crusade against the folly of others – the fecklessness of Einar and Agnes, the dullness of the peasant community, the madness of Gerd – slowly becomes a shutting out, literally, of any light in the darkness of despair. The demands of absolute commitment to his ideal drive Brand into a corner where he must collude in the destruction of all that is dear to him; whenever he wavers, some portent or warning materializes to cut off his retreat. Even the doctor, the voice of reason here as in so many of Ibsen's plays, goads him into inflexibility by commenting that Brand's harsh repudiation of his mother's pleas melts into compromise when his son is ill ('One law for the world, / another for your child'). Brand denies himself and those around him any chance to say 'I have done enough' and climbs further and further into an icy barren region where his only companion at the last is his soul-sister Gerd, his own reflection in a broken mirror. His dream of a new society has grown into a nightmare which cuts him off from all society; in his striving to create a utopia he has become a dictator. As Helge Rønning says in his study of the play, at the end he has become his own victim, and *Brand* is thus a tragedy – the only one, he maintains, that Ibsen wrote.[11]

It is perhaps more difficult in these secular times for an audience to sympathize with a character who feels called upon by God to deny his own humanity. Yet the play is nevertheless compelling in its study of devotion to a calling taken to its ultimate conclusion, a conclusion as devastating for the individual as for his surroundings. 'Brand is myself in my best moments,' Ibsen declared a few years later.[12] Like many other of Ibsen's pronouncements, this one might well be treated with a little scepticism, but it is a corrective to a complete condemnation of the character. So too is the ending of the play. Brand's ultimate anguished questions – have I done enough to be saved? Does all my striving count for nothing? – are answered by the cryptic pronouncement 'He is the God of Love' ('Han er deus caritatis!' in the original). This might be understood as a rebuke

to Brand – you have misunderstood all your life, the harsh God
you have served is your own creation – or as a statement of rec-
onciliation: he is a loving and accepting God, you too will be
forgiven and welcomed. Or perhaps, probably, both.

The verse in which the play is composed is as accomplished
as it is difficult to reproduce in translation.[13] Nearly all of it is
written in four-foot lines which sweep the action along, sometimes in iambic and sometimes in trochaic metre, with frequent
but not always regular rhymes. It is a flexible verse form which
can convey both the rapid interchange of colloquial dialogue
and the more reflective musings of Brand's monologues. The
action often proceeds by a series of repetitions, parallels and
oxymorons which bring the opposing values in the play into
stark contrast and are also a feature of Geoffrey Hill's poetic
rewording ('A middling this, a middling that, / never humble,
never great. / Above the worst, beneath the best, / each virtue
vicious to the rest.') The exception to this verse form is Einar
and Agnes' bridal song in Act One, where the steady rhythm of
Brand's observations is broken by a leap into a traditional ballad form, a springing, dancing celebration – and the only
section of the 'Epic Brand' to survive practically unchanged
into the final drama. Hill's version of *Brand* does not attempt
a direct translation of the original, but it does follow closely
the shifts in mood and tempo of the different scenes and cap-
tures the muscular beat of the central character's relentless
compulsion.

Peer Gynt

Peer Gynt stands for everything Brand despises. Or rather, one
might say, he doesn't *stand* for anything. He runs, he hides, he
evades pursuit and definition. If Brand is placed at one extreme
in his refusal to compromise, Peer must be seen at the other;
rather than confront any challenge or face down any obstacle,
he goes round and about, takes a detour, as he does with the
Boyg. He refuses to make a choice and stick to it; whenever
any commitment is demanded, he backs off. Playing with the
trolls, even marrying one and adopting their lifestyle, is fine;

but when asked to agree to an action which would cut him off irrevocably from the human world, he baulks at it. He needs to be assured, as he tells his business associates in Act Four, that 'one who's crossed a bridge can take / at any time the same bridge back'. That is why he realizes in the Cairo madhouse: 'I am a sheet of paper on which nothing is written'; and why, when he peels the onion of the Gyntian self, he finds no core. He spends his life asserting himself bombastically but does not know who he is. And that is also why, as the Button Moulder explains, he must be melted down; he is a failed project whose components can be reused for something better.

Yet although the conclusion may be a depressing one, both the protagonist and the author have a lot of fun on the way. Peer is a liar, that is established in the first line of the play; but by the same token he is also a poet (a duality which is evident in several of Ibsen's later flawed heroes). Peer's refusal to face unpleasant facts diverts him into realms of fantasy in which he creates and peoples whole worlds; he leads his listeners off on riotous adventures and sees in nearly every situation a chance to invent new kingdoms and new dreams. Indeed, the play as a whole, or the latter part of it, might be seen as a dream, as Peer's dream about himself, in which the other characters represent aspects of himself or embody alternative directions he might follow.[14]

The whole play is also a poem, and Ibsen's most impressive poetic achievement. Unlike *Brand* it uses a wide variety of different verse forms: iambic and trochaic tetrameters, iambic pentameters, three-beat ballad verse and four-beat *knittel* verse, and short two-beat lines. It often gallops along at a furious pace, as if trying to keep up with Peer's imagination. 'It is wild and formless,' Ibsen later declared in a letter to the English critic Edmund Gosse, 'recklessly written in a way that I could only dare to write while far from home.'[15] A new mood or a new speaker is generally the cue for a change in rhythm and pace. *Knittel* was a popular medieval verse form, close to Norwegian everyday speech, with four-beat lines and a varying number of unstressed syllables, often used as the devil's verse form (e.g. by Goethe in *Faust*). It is the most frequently used form in the play, spoken for much of the time by Peer as well as by characters like the Dovre King, the trolls and the Thin Man; with its abundance of syllables it is jaunty and witty. The ballad verse, on the other hand, is a lyrical, more reflective form, used for example by the dying Aase waiting for Peer to return home. Only one scene in the play is written in iambic pentameters, and that is the priest's funeral oration in Act Five about the man who chopped off his finger as a boy to avoid conscription. It underlines the solemnity of the occasion and the importance of the speech about someone who remained true to himself. (This story originated in the 'Epic Brand'; the fact that Ibsen saved it from there and transferred it, much expanded, to this later play, indicates its significance to him.)

As he did with *Brand*, Ibsen drew on a variety of sources for this play. There was a renewed interest in folk belief and the oral tradition in mid-nineteenth-century Norway as part of the National Romantic movement, and folk tales and legends were collected and published by scholars such as P. Chr. Asbjørnsen and Jørgen Moe. One of Asbjørnsen's tales tells of Per Gynt from Gudbrandsdal, a hunter who shot bears and encountered the Boyg of Etnedal, and the story of the ride on the buck's back is taken from another of his tales about a local character, Gudbrand Glesne.[16] Ibsen himself had been on a walking tour of Gudbrandsdal in 1862 to collect folk legends and sayings. Stories of trolls are legion in Norwegian folklore; they are threatening but usually not very bright, and easy to outwit. The perky young adventurer from folk tales Askeladden (the Ash Lad), who starts with nothing and ends up marrying the princess and inheriting half the kingdom, is another obvious model for Peer. Topical references abound; Norwegian self-satisfaction is pilloried, though with more good humour than in the previous play – and the idiosyncrasies of other nationalities are also satirized. National Romanticism itself is not spared, as when the much reduced Dovre King reappears at the end to complain that he is told he only exists in books, and the best way he can survive is to audition for a role in a national drama.

Other literary antecedents can also be traced in the play. It can be seen as a kind of morality play, a story of Everyman in a search for salvation, and has elements of the picaresque and the travel narrative, borrowing especially from Ludvig Holberg's *Niels Klim's Subterranean Journey* (1741), a satirical utopia peopled by fantastic monsters in the vein of *Gulliver's Travels*. There are many – frequently misquoted – biblical allusions, and clear parallels with and references to Goethe's *Faust*, as well as to the writings of Ibsen's friend Paul Botten-Hansen, whose play *The Hulder Wedding* contains a madhouse scene, a troll-king under the mountain and a fast-talking devil similar to the Thin Man. And there are clear autobiographical elements in the story of the rich but improvident father who reduces his family to penury, and the wandering son who continually questions his own motives and his own vocation.

As with *Brand*, the ending of this play raises more questions than it answers. Twice the Button Moulder returns to judge Peer's objections to obliteration inadequate; he has failed to be good enough or evil enough to have realized his potential as an individual, he has just been mediocre. The play ends before the Button Moulder returns for the third time. Will Solveig's intercession be Peer's salvation? It seems unlikely, as his aversion to commitment has been as stark in this relationship as in any. In her final song he returns full-circle to the beginning of his life, to be the child at his mother's knee. His journey of education has taken him nowhere and taught him nothing. Or is Solveig just Peer's wish-image of a woman? Is he dreaming still?

On Stage and Page

Peer Gynt was the first of these two dramatic poems to be transferred to the stage. In January 1874 Ibsen wrote to the Norwegian composer Edvard Grieg and asked him to consider composing a musical score for the play; he also suggested the kind of music which might accompany various scenes and proposed sweeping changes to the text, which involved among other things leaving out almost the whole of Act Four. Grieg accepted the commission, although it was to take him far longer and be much more demanding than he had anticipated. ('I've written something for the Dovre King's Hall,' he complained to a friend, 'which I literally cannot bear to listen to, it simply resounds with cow-pats, Norwegianness and tothyselfsufficientness!')[17] Finally, in September 1875 he had finished the score, and the world premi-ère opened on 24 February 1876 at the Christiania Theatre, directed by the Swede Ludvig Josephson. Expectations had been high, and the reception was enthusiastic, despite the length of the performance (five hours for the première). The play was per-formed twenty-five times in the first season, an unusually high number and a lucrative business for the author.

The first translation of the play was into German, by Ludwig Passarge, who published it in 1881 despite Ibsen's warning about the folly of choosing this particular play: 'I have grave doubts in this respect. Of all my books I regard *Peer Gynt* as the one least constituted to be understood outside the Scandinavian coun-tries.'[18] The first translation into English was by Charles and William Archer in 1892, but the play had to wait until 1922 for its first substantial London production at the Old Vic.

Once *Peer Gynt* had been put on stage, it began to seem less impossible to do the same with *Brand*. Act Four had been sin-gled out as a 'performance piece' and staged several times in the late 1860s, partly due to the desire of the leading actress Laura Gundersen to play Agnes. Ibsen discussed a possible production with Ludvig Josephson in the 1870s, when *Peer Gynt* was staged, but plans were shelved for some time until Josephson finally produced the play (in Swedish translation) at his own New Theatre in Stockholm, on 24 March 1885. Again, once it had reached the stage it was a great success, with six-teen performances in the first season, despite the fact that a performance lasted nearly seven hours. The Norwegian premi-ère came ten years later, in 1895, the same year as Aurélien Lugné-Poë staged the play in Paris.

Germany, the first country of export for much of Scandina-vian literature, also saw the first translations of *Brand*, with four independent versions published in the first six years. Three translations into English were published in the early 1890s, and the first English performance was in 1912, at the Court Theatre in London. As theatrical conventions changed, the staging of troll halls, shipwrecks, snowstorms and avalanches came to seem a less daunting prospect, and the plays became established as a part of international theatrical repertoire.

Notwithstanding Ibsen's remarks about the fact that *Peer Gynt* was the least likely of his plays to be understood outside Scandinavia, it has proved to be one of the most enduring in its appeal to different national audiences. George Bernard Shaw, not otherwise remembered as an advocate of Ibsen's poetic works, declared Peer Gynt to be 'a hero for everybody' alongside the likes of Hamlet and Faust.[19] And Frederick J. and Lise-Lone Marker, in their analysis of the often wildly experimental twentieth-century productions of the play, conclude: 'Far more open and associational in its structure and hence less confined to a specific theatrical mode, [*Peer Gynt*] has . . . seemed to grow more modern, rather than less so.' [20]

Peer Gynt was to be the last of Ibsen's poetic dramas. After these two expansive and idiosyncratic creations, the rest of his plays were written in a prose which more and more closely approached the rhythms of contemporary colloquial speech. And with the major exception of *Emperor and Galilean* – a work as ambitious in its scope, if not as impressive in its achievement, as the two dramatic poems – they remained largely within the domestic sphere. Ibsen's investigations into the clash between aspirations and human fallibility were to move to a more intimate canvas.

Janet Garton, 2016

NOTES

1. 'En broder i nød!' (1863), published in *Digte* (1871). *Henrik Ibsens Skrifter* [*HIS*], vol. 11, pp. 514–16. *HIS* is available at http://www.ibsen.uio.no/forside.xhtml.
2. From a speech at a gala dinner in Copenhagen, 1 April 1898. *HIS*, vol. 16, p. 513.
3. James McFarlane's prose translation of the 'Epic Brand' is printed in *The Oxford Ibsen*, vol. 3, ed. J. W. McFarlane

(London: Oxford University Press, 1972), pp. 37–71. The work was considered lost for much of Ibsen's lifetime and not published until after his death.

4. Letter to Bjørnson, 12 September 1865. *HIS*, vol.12, p. 181.

5. Letter to Peter Hansen, 28 October 1870. *HIS*, vol. 12, p. 428.

6. Letter to Frederik Hegel, 5 January 1867. *HIS*, vol. 12, p. 260.

7. Bjørnson's review was printed in *Norsk Folkeblad*, 23 November 1867, Petersen's in *Fædrelandet*, 13 November 1867. Translated excerpts from reviews of the play are printed in *The Oxford Ibsen*, vol. 3, pp. 494–6.

8. Letter to Bjørnson, 9 December 1867. *HIS*, vol. 12, p. 283.

9. See Michael Meyer, *Henrik Ibsen* (London: Cardinal, 1971), p. 259, and John Northam: 'Dramatic and Non-dramatic Poetry', in *The Cambridge Companion to Ibsen*, ed. J. W. McFarlane (Cambridge: Cambridge University Press, 1994), p. 28.

10. For a fuller exploration of echoes of Kierkegaard in both *Brand* and *Peer Gynt*, see David Thomas, *Henrik Ibsen* (London: Macmillan, 1983), pp. 41–3.

11. Helge Rønning, *Den umulige friheten. Henrik Ibsen og moderniteten* (Oslo: Gyldendal, 2006), pp. 161–3.

12. Letter to Peter Hansen, 28 October 1870. *HIS*, vol. 12, p. 428.

13. See Åse Hjorth Lervik's study of the poetry of the play, *Ibsens verskunst i Brand* (Oslo: Universitetsforlaget, 1969), and John Northam's elucidation of the varieties of rhythm and rhyme in 'Dramatic and Non-dramatic Poetry'.

14. This interpretation is suggested by Helge Rønning, *Den umulige friheten. Henrik Ibsen og moderniteten*, pp. 163–6.

15. Letter to Edmund Gosse, 30 April 1872, *HIS*, vol. 13, p. 69.

16. See P. Chr. Asbjørnsen, *Norske Huldre-Eventyr og Folkesagn* (Christiania: P. T. Steensballe, 1870). Digitized text available at: https://archive.org/details/norskehuldreeveo1asbjgoog.

17. Letter to Frants Beyer, 27 August 1874. Quoted in *HIS*, vol. 5, p. 587.

18. Letter to Ludwig Passarge, 19 May 1880. Quoted in *The Oxford Ibsen*, vol. 3, p. 492.

19. See Tore Rem: '"The Provincial of Provincials": Ibsen's Strangeness and the Process of Canonisation', *Ibsen Studies* 4, no. 2 (2004), pp. 205–26.

20. Frederick J. Marker and Lise-Lone Marker, *Ibsen's Lively Art: A Performance Study of the Major Plays* (Cambridge: Cambridge University Press, 1989), p. 43.

Further Reading

Book Studies and Articles in English

Aarseth, Asbjørn, *Peer Gynt and Ghosts* (Basingstoke: Macmillan, 1989).

Anderman, Gunilla, *Europe on Stage: Translation and Theatre* (London: Oberon, 2005).

Binding, Paul, *With Vine-Leaves in His Hair: The Role of the Artist in Ibsen's Plays* (Norwich: Norvik Press, 2006).

Bloom, Harold, ed., *Henrik Ibsen*, Modern Critical Views (Philadelphia: Chelsea House, 1999).

Bryan, George B., *An Ibsen Companion* (Westport, Conn.: Greenwood Press, 1984).

Durbach, Errol, ed., *Ibsen and the Theatre* (London: Macmillan, 1980).

—— *'Ibsen the Romantic': Analogues of Paradise in the Later Plays* (London: Macmillan, 1982).

Egan, Michael, ed., *Henrik Ibsen: The Critical Heritage* (London: Routledge, 1997 [1972]).

Ewbank, Inga-Stina et al., eds., *Anglo-Scandinavian Cross-Currents* (Norwich: Norvik Press, 1999).

Fischer-Lichte, Erika et al., eds., *Global Ibsen: Performing Multiple Modernities* (London: Routledge, 2011).

Fulsås, Narve, 'Ibsen Misrepresented: Canonization, Oblivion, and the Need for History', *Ibsen Studies* 11, no. 1 (2011).

Goldman, Michael, *Ibsen: The Dramaturgy of Fear* (New York: Columbia University Press, 1999).

Helland, Frode, 'Empire and Culture in Ibsen: Some Notes on the Dangers and Ambiguities of Interculturalism', *Ibsen Studies* 9, no. 2 (2009).

Holledge, Julie, 'Addressing the Global Phenomenon of *A Doll's House*: An Intercultural Intervention', *Ibsen Studies* 8, no. 1 (2008).

Innes, Christopher, ed., *Henrik Ibsen's Hedda Gabler: A Sourcebook* (London: Routledge, 2003).

Johnston, Brian, *The Ibsen Cycle* (University Park, Pa.: Pennsylvania University Press, 1992).

Kittang, Atle, 'Ibsen, Heroism, and the Uncanny', *Modern Drama* 49, no. 3 (2006).

Ledger, Sally, *Henrik Ibsen*, Writers and Their Work (Tavistock: Northcote House, 2008 [1999]).

Lyons, Charles R., ed., *Critical Essays on Henrik Ibsen* (Boston, Mass.: G. K. Hall, 1987).

— *Henrik Ibsen: The Divided Consciousness* (Carbondale, Ill.: Southern Illinois University Press, 1972).

McFarlane, James, ed., *The Cambridge Companion to Ibsen* (Cambridge: Cambridge University Press, 1994).

— *Ibsen and Meaning: Studies, Essays and Prefaces 1953–87* (Norwich: Norvik Press, 1989).

Malone, Irina Ruppo, *Ibsen and the Irish Revival* (Basingstoke: Palgrave, 2010).

Meyer, Michael, *Henrik Ibsen* (abridged edition) (London: Cardinal, 1992 [1971]).

Moi, Toril, *Henrik Ibsen and the Birth of Modernism: Art, Theater, Philosophy* (Oxford: Oxford University Press, 2006).

Moretti, Franco, *The Bourgeois: Between History and Literature* (London: Verso, 2013).

Northam, John, *Ibsen's Dramatic Method: A Study of the Prose Dramas* (Oslo: Universitetsforlaget, 1971 [1953]).

Puchner, Martin, 'Goethe, Marx, Ibsen and the Creation of a World Literature', *Ibsen Studies* 13, no. 1 (2013).

Rem, Tore, ' "The Provincial of Provincials": Ibsen's Strangeness and the Process of Canonisation', *Ibsen Studies* 4, no. 2 (2004).

Sandberg, Mark B., *Ibsen's Houses: Architectural Metaphor and the Modern Uncanny* (Cambridge: Cambridge University Press, 2015).

Shepherd-Barr, Kirsten, *Ibsen and Early Modernist Theatre, 1890–1900* (Westport, Conn.: Greenwood Press, 1997).

Templeton, Joan, *Ibsen's Women* (Cambridge: Cambridge University Press, 1997).

Törnqvist, Egil, *Ibsen: A Doll's House* (Cambridge: Cambridge University Press, 1995).

Williams, Raymond, *Drama from Ibsen to Brecht* (Harmondsworth: Penguin, 1974).

Digital and Other Resources

Ibsen.nb.no is a website with much useful information on Ibsen and on Ibsen productions worldwide: http://ibsen.nb.no/id/83.0.

Henrik Ibsens Skrifter is the new critical edition of Ibsen's complete works. So far only available in Norwegian: http://www.ibsen.uio.no/forside.xhtml.

Ibsen Studies is the leading Ibsen journal.

A Note on the Text

This Penguin edition of *Peer Gynt* is the first English-language edition based on the new historical-critical edition of Henrik Ibsen's work, *Henrik Ibsens Skrifter* (2005–10) (*HIS*). The digital edition (*HISe*) is available at http://www.ibsen.uio.no/forside.xhtml. The texts of *HIS* are based on Ibsen's first editions.

BRAND

*A version for the stage by Geoffrey Hill based on
a literal translation by Inga-Stina Ewbank*

CHARACTERS

BRAND[1]
PEASANT
PEASANT'S SON
EINAR
AGNES
GERD
STARVING MAN
MAYOR
SCRIVENER
NILS SNEMYR
WOMEN OF THE VILLAGE
MEN OF THE VILLAGE
DISTRESSED WOMAN
BOAT OWNER
PEASANTS' SPOKESMAN
BRAND'S MOTHER
DOCTOR
MESSENGER
SECOND MESSENGER
MAN WHO BRINGS WARNING
GYPSY WOMAN
SCHOOLMASTER
SEXTON
DEAN
OFFICIAL
CLERIC
CHORUS OF SPIRITS
SPECTRE OF AGNES
A VOICE

ACT ONE

SCENE 1

In the snow, high up in the mountains. The mist lies thick; rain and semi-darkness. BRAND, *dressed in black, with a staff and a pack, is slowly making his way westwards. A* PEASANT *and his half-grown* SON, *who have joined him, are a little way behind.*

PEASANT [*calling after* BRAND]:
  Hey, stranger, not so fast!
  Where are you?
BRAND: Here.
PEASANT: We're lost;
  it's never been so thick.
BRAND: We've lost sight of the track.
SON: Hey, look, look, a great split
  in the ice.
PEASANT: Stay clear of it
  for God's sake!
BRAND: I can hear
  a cataract. That roar,
  where is it?
PEASANT: That's the beck
  brasting through ice and rock;
  the devil knows how deep.
  You will, with one more step.
BRAND: I am a priest; I said
  no faltering.
PEASANT: Ay, so you did.

And I say it's beyond
all mortal strength. The ground –
hollow – d'you feel it quake?
Don't tempt your luck. Turn back!
BRAND: This is my destined road.
PEASANT: Ay, and who said so?
BRAND: God
said so; the God I serve.
PEASANT: Man-of-God, you've got nerve.
But just heed what I say!
Though you're bishop or dean,
or some such holy man,
you'll be dead before day.
I can't see past my nose!
It's miles[2] to the next house,
I know that for a fact.
Don't be so stiff-necked.
You've only got the one
life, and when that's gone . . .
BRAND: If we can't see the way
we'll not be led astray
by marsh light or false track.
PEASANT: There's ice tarns, worse than t'beck;
they'll be the death of us.
BRAND: Not so! We'll walk across.
PEASANT: Walk on the water?
BRAND: He
walked on Lake Galilee.
PEASANT: A good few years ago
that was. It's harder now.
Try if you must, go on;
but you'll sink like a stone!
BRAND: I owe God life and death.
He's welcome to them both.
PEASANT: You're worse than lost, you're mad!
BRAND [*stopping; approaching the pair*]:
But lately, man-of-earth,
you thought this journey worth

the risk. 'Come ice, come snow,'
you said; and told me how
your lass, down at the fjord,
lies at death's door.

PEASANT: Afeard,
'less she bids me farewell,
Old Nick will grab her soul.

BRAND: You must get there today;
you said so.

PEASANT: I did, ay!

BRAND: What would you sacrifice
that she might die in peace?

PEASANT: To keep her soul from harm
I'd barter house and home;
I'd give all that I have.

BRAND: 'All', you say. Would you give
your life?

PEASANT [*scratching his ear*]:
                Life? Now wait,
now that's asking a lot,
Christ it is! There's my wife,
[*Points to* SON.]
and him.

BRAND: Christ gave His life.
Christ's mother gave her son.

PEASANT: Maybe. Those days are gone,
and so are miracles.
It's different nowawhiles.

BRAND: Go! You know not the Lord,
nor He you!

PEASANT: Agh, you're hard!

SON [*tugging at him*]:
Come home, let's be gone!

PEASANT: We will that! And you, man-
of-God!

BRAND: If I refuse?

PEASANT: Stranger, think on! Suppose
we go and leave you here;

suppose you disappear
in a snow drift or get drowned,
suppose word gets around.
I'd soon be up in court
accused of God knows what.
BRAND: A martyr in His cause.
PEASANT: And that's not worth a curse –
   I'm done with God and you!
SON [*screaming, as a hollow rumbling is heard in the
      distance*]:
   An ice-fall!
BRAND [*to the* PEASANT, *who has seized his collar*]:
                 You! Let go!
PEASANT [*wrestling with* BRAND]:
   Not I!
BRAND: Let go, you fool!
      BRAND *tears himself free and throws the* PEASANT *down
      in the snow.*
PEASANT: Go to the devil!
BRAND: You'll
   go to him. That's your fate,
   you can be sure of that!
      He walks off.
PEASANT [*sitting rubbing his arm*]:
   That's doing the Lord's work,
   is it? He nearly broke
   my arm.
   [*Shouts after* BRAND *as he gets up.*]
             Hey, man-of-faith,
   help us to find the path!
BRAND: No need. You've found your road:
   the way that is called broad.
PEASANT: I pray he's right this time –
   God bring us safely home.
      He and his SON *walk off in an easterly direction.*
BRAND [*appears higher up, looking in the direction that the
      PEASANT *took*]:
   Crawl off, then, you poor slave!

Drudge where you fear to strive.
When our weak flesh alone
fails us, we struggle on
and on with bleeding feet.
Sheer willpower bears the weight.
Strange how the lifeless cling
to life with 'Life's the thing!'
Small men, who set great store
by life, dread all the more
its vision and its pain.
How can you save such men,
who talk of 'sacrifice'
yet barter truth for peace?
[*Smiles as if remembering something.*]
When I was a boy
daydreaming at school,
I thought, 'Suppose an owl
were frightened of the dark.'
I laughed behind my book.
Many and many a day
the teacher had me out.
'And there's a fish,' I thought,
'somewhere, that hates the sea.'
As the taws cracked, I grinned;
those two thoughts gripped my mind.
I gazed across a gulf
dividing those who dare
from those who fear to be.
Too many souls are still
like that fish, or that owl:
with their true life to make
in the depths of the dark,
if they could but endure;
who flee from their dark star,
each from his own true self;
perish in this world's air.
[*Stops for a moment, notices something and listens.*]
Yet, for a moment, there is song

in the air; and laughter among
the singing; and the sound of cheers.
The sun rises and the mist is thin
already; and the plains begin
to glitter. I see travellers
clearly outlined along the crest
of the near ridge; signs of farewell,
handclasps and kisses, a lifted veil,
two youngsters parting from the rest.
They race towards me hand in hand
across the moorland, like brother
and sister, through vivid heather.
Light as a feather she skims the ground;
and he is lithe, like a young birch.
They play a childish game of catch
and all of life becomes a game.
Their laughter's like a morning hymn.

> EINAR *and* AGNES, *clad in light travelling clothes, both of them warm and glowing, come across the plateau, as if in the midst of a game. The mist is gone; it is a clear summer morning in the mountains.*

EINAR: Butterfly, butterfly,
  Where are you flying?
AGNES: Far far away
  From your cruel sighing.
EINAR: Butterfly, butterfly,
  Rest from your dance.
  You're all of a flutter.
AGNES: Why
  All this pretence?
EINAR: Butterfly, butterfly,
  Lie in my hand.
AGNES: If I do I shall die.
  Let me go on the wind.

> *Without noticing, they have come to a precipice; they are now on the edge of it.*

BRAND [*crying out to them from above*]:
  Stop! Stop, you foolish pair!

EINAR: Who's that?
AGNES [*pointing upwards*]:
                          Look! Up there!
BRAND: That cliff – it's undermined! –
  beneath you – can't you understand? –
  You are both dancing on thin air!
EINAR [*putting his arm around* AGNES *and laughing as he
    looks towards* BRAND]:
  Agnes and I don't have a care.
AGNES: Old age is time enough for fears.
EINAR: Our youth shall last a hundred years.
BRAND: I see. A summer of sweet mirth,
  young butterflies. Then back to earth.
AGNES [*swinging her veil*]:
  No, not to earth. My love and I
  are wandering children of the sky.
EINAR: A hundred years, in this bright world,
  of never really growing old.
  Time on our side, all time a game . . .
BRAND: And then?
EINAR: Restored to heaven and home!
BRAND: You seem so very sure.
EINAR: Oh yes,
  heaven's our permanent address!
AGNES: Einar, Einar! He knows we came
  over the ridge. Stop teasing him!
EINAR: We've said our fond farewell to friends,
  kissed and embraced and shaken hands
  and made all sorts of promises.
  Don't stand there like a troll of ice!
  Come down, and let me thaw you out
  with wonders that will melt your heart.
  Be moved, man, by the power of joy;
  don't cast a gloom across our day.
  My tale begins. As you perceive,
  I am an artist. I can give
  wings to my thoughts, and charm all life
  to radiance: a flower, a wife.

I take creation in my stride,
as I chose Agnes for my bride
that day I strode up from the south . . .
AGNES: The spirit of eternal youth!
His confidence was like a king's
and he could sing a thousand songs.
EINAR: A thousand? Yes! Some inner voice
kept whispering, 'Your masterpiece
awaits you. Seek her where she dwells
beside the streams, on the high fells!'
And so I sought, up through the woods
of conifers and where the clouds
fly swiftly under Heaven's vault,
that creature without flaw or fault.
Suddenly, suddenly, she was there:
beauty enough for my desire!
AGNES: Poor simple Agnes neatly caught,
a butterfly in passion's net.
EINAR: Oh, nothing ventured, nothing won!
Formalities must wait their turn.
But their turn came; and the guests came;
and there was feasting at the farm,
where blessings sought and blessings given
made the old rafters ring to heaven.
Three days and nights of feast and song!
And, when we left, that loving throng
followed and cheered us on our way
and were true celebrants of joy.
We drank the wine of fellowship
together from a silver cup.
AGNES: All through the summer night . . .
EINAR: The mist
parted before us, where we passed.
BRAND: And now you go . . . ?
EINAR: On to the town,
our wedding and our honeymoon.
We'll sail away, two swans in flight,
far to the south!

BRAND: And after that?
EINAR: A legend! An unbroken dream
   made safe from sorrow, as from time.
   There, on the height, without a priest
   in sight to bless us, we were blest.
BRAND: Oh, indeed. Who blessed you then?
EINAR: Our friends, with love; as you'll have seen,
   this very morning on the ridge.
   In parting, we received their pledge
   that every dark word, every dark
   thought, that could raise a storm or lurk
   in the bright foliage of a bower,
   is banished from love's book-of-prayer.
   Even such words as bear a shade
   of darker meaning, they forbade.
   They named us the true heirs of joy.
BRAND: So be it then.
   He prepares to leave.
EINAR [*taken aback and looking more closely at* BRAND]:
              I say . . .
   I remember that face!
   Surely I recognize . . .
BRAND [*coldly*]:
   A man you never met . . .
EINAR: Impossible to forget . . .
BRAND: I was your childhood friend
   but we are men now.
EINAR: Brand,
   it's you! So I was right!
BRAND: As soon as I caught sight
   of you, I knew you.
EINAR: Still
   the same old Brand! At school,
   even, you seemed remote,
   secure in your own thought.
BRAND: And with good cause. Your calm
   South-land was never home
   to me. And I felt cold,

shut in that easy world.
EINAR: Is this where you belong?
BRAND: Not now. When I was young
   I did. Now I obey
   the call, and cannot stay.
EINAR: So you're a man-of-God.
BRAND [*smiling*]:
   I have been so described.
   I bear the Word, now here
   now there. The mountain hare
   is more settled than I.
   But this is the true way.
EINAR: Where will it end, this true
   journey?
BRAND: What's that to you?
EINAR: Brand!
BRAND [*changing his tone*]:
                        Well, never mind . . .
   I'll soon be outward bound
   like you . . . on the same boat.
EINAR: Agnes, do you hear that?
   Brand's journey is the same
   as ours!
BRAND: Fondle your dream,
   Einar. The place I seek,
   if you came near, could turn
   your wedding to a wake,
   your dancers into stone.
   I seek the death of God,
   that dying God of yours
   dying these thousand years.
   I'll see him in his shroud.
AGNES: Einar, we should go.
EINAR: Wait,
   Agnes, wait a while.
   [*To* BRAND]
                        What
   madness! You must be ill!

BRAND: Sanity's what you call
  sickness, I suppose.
  A generation whose
  pastimes are its care
  has sunk almost past cure.
  You flirt and play the fool
  and leave the bitter toil
  to that poor Holy One
  sweating blood to atone,
  your dear Christ hurt with thorns,
  the saviour of your dance.
  Dance on, dance to the end,
  dance yourselves deaf and blind!
EINAR: You're good at breathing fire,
  a real hot-gospeller;
  that fear-and-trembling school
  has taught you very well!
BRAND: Einar, I leave the new
  fashions in faith to you.
  I've not come here to preach
  for any sect or church.
  Not as a formal Christian
  even, but as my own man,
  I tell you this: I know
  the nature of the flaw
  that has so thinned and drained
  the spirit of our land.
EINAR [smiling]:
  We're not the kind to drink
  deep of life's cup, you think?
BRAND: No. If only you would,
  high-stepping meek-and-mild!
  Sin if you dare, but have the grace,
  at least, to be fulfilled in vice.
  At least live up to what you claim;
  don't water your good wine with shame!
  Among our people I observe
  such littleness and loss of nerve.

A little show of holiness
strictly reserved for Sunday use;
little charity, but much talk
of simple, plain, God-fearing folk.
A middling this, a middling that,
never humble, never great.
Above the worst, beneath the best,
each virtue vicious to the rest.

EINAR: Bravo, Brand! Have your say,
just as you will. I'll play
'Amen' in the right place:
I'm quite ready to please.
I'm wholly unperturbed;
my God is still my God.

BRAND: Indeed He's yours! You've even
been favoured by heaven
with that vision of Him –
it brought you some small fame –
the picture that you did
of your old, pampered God:
white-haired, moist-eyed with age,
his comic turns of rage
send children off to bed
giggling and half-afraid.

EINAR [*angry*]:
This is . . .

BRAND: 'No joke', you'd say?
Do you want sympathy?
You trim off life from faith,
haver from birth to death,
self-seekers who refuse
man's true way-of-the-Cross,
which is: wholly to be
the all-enduring 'I'.
My God is the great god of storm,
absolute arbiter of doom,
imperious in His love!
He is the voice that Moses heard,

He is the pillar of the cloud,
He is the hand that stayed the sun
for Joshua in Gibeon.
Your God can hardly move;
he's weak of mind and heart,
easy to push about.
But mine is young: a Hercules,[3]
not fourscore of infirmities.
Though you may smile and preen,
Einar; though you bow down
to your own brazenness,
I shall heal this disease
that withers heart and brain,
and make you all new men!

EINAR: [*shakes his head*]:
You'll blow the old lamps out
before new lamps are lit;
abandon the known word
for speech as yet unheard.

BRAND: Why must you misconstrue
so much? I seek for nothing new.
I know my mission: to uphold
truths long forgotten by the world;
eternal truths. I have not come
to preach dogmatics or proclaim
the right of some exclusive sect
to rule through pain of interdict.
For every church and creed
is something that this world has made;
and everything that's made must end.
I speak of what endures,
of what is lost and found
eternally. Faith did not climb
slowly from the primeval slime,
nor burst from the volcanic fires.
It is incarnate through recourse
of spirit to our spirit's source.
Though hucksters in and out of church

   make tawdry everything they touch,
   hawking the relics of their trade,
   their bits of dogma, parts
   of broken creeds and hearts,
   that spirit shines amid the void,
   amid the travesties
   of things that are, the truth that is.
   And truth-begotten, God's true heir,
   the new Adam . . .
EINAR: We should part here,
   I think. It's for the best.
BRAND: Here are two paths: the west
   for you; for me the north.
   Different ways, yet both
   end at the fjord. Farewell,
   butterflies!
   [*Turning as he starts the descent*]
          Learn to tell
   true from false. Don't forget
   life's the real work of art!
EINAR: [*waving him away*]:
   Though you may shake my world
   my God stands firm!
BRAND: He's old,
   Einar; don't worry Him.
   Leave me to bury Him!
   He goes down the path. EINAR *walks silently across and*
   looks down after BRAND. AGNES *stands for a moment as if*
   lost in thought; then she starts, looks about her uneasily.
AGNES: It's all so gloomy. Where's the sun?
EINAR: Behind that cloud, there. Things will soon
   look bright again.
AGNES: And there's a fierce
   wind out of nowhere. It's like ice.
EINAR: Some freak gust hurtling through the pass,
   I'd say. It's much too cold for us
   to linger here. Come on!
AGNES: How black

   and forbidding that great south peak
   seems now. It wasn't always so,
   surely?
EINAR: You've let Brand frighten you
   with his dour face and talk of doom.
   Look here, I'll race you! You'll get warm!
AGNES: I can't. I'm tired.
EINAR: To tell the truth,
   love, so am I. This downhill path
   is tricky too. But we'll be safe
   on terra firma soon enough.
   And, Agnes, now the sun's come back
   the world no longer looks so bleak.
   What a picture! Such harmony
   of sky with sea and sea with sky;
   deep azure lit by silver streaks,
   suffused with golden lights and darks,
   out to the far horizon's edge,
   the boundless main! And, look, that smudge
   of smoke – the steamer coming in,
   the very ship we go to join.
   By early evening we shall be
   clear of this place, well out to sea.
   We'll dance on deck and sing; our games
   will make Brand giddy if he comes.
AGNES: [*without looking at him and in a hushed voice*]:
   Tell me, are we awake,
   Einar? When that man spoke
   he burned! It seemed each feature
   changed! He grew in stature!
     She goes down the path. EINAR *follows.*

SCENE 2

A path along the mountain wall with a wild valley on the right-hand side. Above and behind the mountain one can see glimpses of great heights with peaks and snow. BRAND *appears high up on the path, starts to descend, stops midway on a rock which juts out, and looks down into the valley.*

BRAND: Now I see where I am:
   strangely close to home.
   Everything I recall
   from childhood here still
   but smaller now and much
   shabbier; and the church
   looks in need of repair.
   The cliffs loom; the glacier
   juts and hangs: it is an
   ice wall concealing the sun.
   And for all their rough gleam
   the fjord waters look grim
   and menacing. A small
   boat pitches in a squall.
   Down there's the timber wharf
   and nearby – iron-red roof,
   red-flaking walls – the house
   to which I would refuse
   the name 'home' if I could;
   the place where I endured
   harsh kinship, an alien
   life that was called mine.
   Solitude and desire
   magnified what was there.
   As though in recompense
   to my own soul, a sense
   of greatness visited me,
   made even a poverty-
   stricken smallholding shine,

a visionary demesne.
All that has faded. Now
there is nothing to show
what my child-soul once made
out of such solitude.
Returning, I am shorn
of all strength: Samson
in the harlot's lap.[4]
[*Looks again down into the abyss.*]
It seems they have woken up.
Men, women, children come
from the cottages, climb
slowly among the outcrops
of rock, the lowest slopes;
now lost from sight and now
seen again, on the brow
by the church. Slaves to both
day labour and the sloth
of their own souls; their need
crawls and is not heard
in the courts of heaven;
and their prayers are craven:
'Give us bread! give us bread!'
So they still eat their God.
Nothing else matters
to them: tossed on storm waters
of the age, the merest flotsam,
or rotting in a foul calm.

BRAND *is about to go; a stone is thrown from above and
rolls down the slope just missing him.* GERD, *a fifteen-year-
old girl, runs along the ridge with stones in her apron.*

GERD: Hey! Now he's really wild!
BRAND: Who's there? Ah – stupid child!
GERD: Look, he's not a bit hurt,
    though I'm sure he was hit.
    [*Throws more stones and cries out.*]
    Oh . . . he's back . . . swooping down . . .
    his claws . . . I'm all torn!

BRAND: Tell me, in God's name, what . . .
GERD: Stay there and keep quiet
  if you want to be safe.
  It's all right, he's flown off.
BRAND: Who has flown off?
GERD: You
  didn't see the hawk?
BRAND: No.
GERD: Not that great ugly thing
  with some sort of red ring
  round his eye?
BRAND: I did not.
GERD: And with his crest all flat
  against his head?
BRAND: No. Which
  way are you going?
GERD: To church.
BRAND: But the church is down there.
GERD: [*looking at him with a scornful smile and pointing
    downwards*]:
  Not that one. That's a poor
  tumbledown little place.
BRAND: You know a better?
GERD: Yes,
  yes, yes! Follow me up
  these mountains, to the top.
  That's where my own church is,
  in the heart of the ice.
BRAND: Ah, now I understand.
  I'd forgotten that legend
  of the Ice Church: a great cleft
  in the rock, where the drift-
  ing snow and ice have built
  the roof of a huge vault.
  The church floor is a lake
  frozen as hard as rock,
  so all the stories say.
GERD: Well, they're true!

BRAND: Stay away
   from there. It's sure to fall.
   A gust of wind, a call,
   or a gunshot, could bring
   the end of everything.
GERD [*not listening*]:
   I'll show you where a herd
   of dead reindeer appeared
   out of the glacier last
   spring, when it thawed.
BRAND: You must
   never go there. I've told
   you why.
GERD [*pointing downwards*]:
             That musty old
   church of yours! Stay away
   from it. I've told *you* why.
BRAND: God bless you. Go in peace.
GERD: Oh, do come! Hear the ice
   sing mass, and the wind make
   sermons over the rock.
   Oh, how you'll burn and freeze!
   It's safe from the hawk's eyes.
   He settles on Black Peak
   just like a weathercock.
BRAND [*aside*]:
   Her spirit struggles to be heard;
   flawed music from a broken reed.
   God in His judgement sometimes draws
   evil to good. Not from *these* thraws.
GERD: O the hawk, O the whirr
   of his wings! Help me, sir!
   I must hide. In my church
   it's safe. Hey! hey! can't catch
   me! O but he's angry. Now
   what shall I do? I'll throw
   things. Ugh! keep off me, keep
   off me with those great sharp

claws! Strike me, I'll strike you!
　　She runs off up the mountain.
BRAND: So that's churchgoing too;
　　those howls are hymns of praise.
　　But is she worse than those
　　who seek God in the valley?
　　And is her church less holy?
　　Who sees? And who is blind?
　　Who wanders? Who is found?
　　Feckless, with his garlands on,
　　dances till he plunges down
　　into the terrible abyss.
　　Dullness mutters 'thus and thus',
　　his catechism's sleepy rote,
　　and treads the old, deep-trodden rut.
　　Madness wanders from itself,
　　half shadowing the other half;
　　immortal longings gone astray,
　　confusing darkness with the day.
　　My way is clear, now. Heaven calls.
　　I know my task. When those three trolls
　　are dead, mankind shall breathe again,
　　freed from old pestilence and pain.
　　Arm, arm, my soul! Take up your sword!
　　Fight now for every child of God!
　　　He descends into the populated valley.

ACT TWO

SCENE 1

Down by the fjord with sheer mountains rising on three sides. The old dilapidated church stands on a small knoll nearby. A storm is gathering. The PEASANTS, *men, women and children, are gathered in groups, some on the shore, some on the slopes. The* MAYOR *is sitting in the midst of them on a stone; a* SCRIVENER *is helping him; grain and other provisions are being distributed.* EINAR *and* AGNES *are standing surrounded by a group of people, farther towards the background. A few boats are lying off the shore.* BRAND *appears on the slope by the church without being noticed by the crowd.*

A MAN [*bursting through the crowd*]:
    Let me past! Let me past!
A WOMAN: Hey you, we was first!
MAN [*pushing her aside*]:
    Get out of the way, or . . .
    See to me first, mayor!
MAYOR: Give me time, give me time . . .
MAN: I must have my share;
    I've bairns back at home,
    starving, all four, five . . .
MAYOR: [*jokingly*]:
    You don't sound too sure.
MAN: One was barely alive
    when I left.

MAYOR: Here, hold on,
  have I got your name down?
  [*Leafs through his papers.*]
  H'm . . . h'm . . . you're in luck.
  Twenty-nine . . . in the sack.
  [*To the* SCRIVENER]
  Whoa there, whoa there,
  that's enough, that's his lot.
  Nils Snemyr?
SNEMYR: I'm here.
MAYOR: Your ration's been cut.
  Well, you've one less to feed.
SNEMYR: My wife, ay, she's dead;
  passed on yesterday.
MAYOR: It's an ill wind they say . . .
  she'll need no more porridge.
  [*To* SNEMYR, *who is leaving*]
  Forget about marriage;
  just give it a rest.
SCRIVENER: Hee, hee!
MAYOR: What's the joke?
SCRIVENER: Just hearing you talk,
  Mr Mayor, it's a treat.
MAYOR: Hold your jaw shut!
  I don't find this funny.
  But 'laugh or you'll cry',
  it's the only way.
EINAR [*coming out of the crowd with* AGNES]:
  They've had my last crust,
  and all my money.
  Never mind, I can pawn
  my watch, or my stick
  and my haversack.
  I'll rake up the fare
  for the boat, never fear!
MAYOR: My word, you arrived
  not a moment too soon.
  These folk are half-starved.

And they're plump and thriving
compared to the starving!
[*Catches sight of* BRAND *and points upwards.*]
Bravo! Welcome, friend!
You've heard, too, no doubt,
of our deluge and drought.
We'll be glad to receive
any gift you can give,
in cash or in kind.
I tell you this parish is
chewing on air.
'We need miracles, mayor!'
A fat lot of help,
five loaves and three fishes!⁵
They'd go at one gulp!
BRAND: Feed the five thousand in the name
of Mammon and you'd famish them.
MAYOR: Spare us your homilies.
Fine words fill no bellies.
EINAR: Brand, Brand, use your eyes!
Look, famine and disease
all around us. They're
dying by the score.
BRAND: Yes, I can recognize
all the dread signs.
I know the lord who reigns
here, and his tyrannies.
[*Steps down among the crowd and says emphatically.*]
If life were set in its old course,
the old routine of Adam's curse,
spiritless labour, soulless greed,
I might throw you some hunks of bread.
If all a man does is crawl home
each night, dog-tired, let him become
the thing he seems – an animal.
A stifling weariness of days
entombs us in the blank belief
that God has torn our destinies,

our very names, out of the Book of Life.
And yet He is merciful.
ONE OF THE CROWD: Argh! Kick us when we're down!
MAYOR: Who does he mean, *Mammon*?
BRAND: If I could heal you with my blood
  I'd willingly see it poured
  out of every vein.
  But that would be a sin
  against God, and His gift
  of suffering. His desire
  is to show mercy, to lift
  you out of your own mire.
  Rejoice in what He gives.
  A people that so strives,
  though all else has gone,
  will be restored to its own.
  But when that spirit's dead
  it is death indeed.
A WOMAN: A storm, a storm! The fjord's
  lashing out at his words!
ANOTHER WOMAN: Don't heed what he says!
  He utters blasphemies.
BRAND: What wonders can *your* God perform?
A THIRD WOMAN: A storm, look, a storm!
ONE OF THE CROWD: Stone him! Grr, drive him out!
ANOTHER: Yes. Yes! Grab his coat!
    The PEASANTS *swarm threateningly round* BRAND. *The*
    MAYOR *intervenes. A* WOMAN, *wild and dishevelled, comes*
    running down the slope.
DISTRESSED WOMAN: Help me, for the love of Christ!
MAYOR: I'll do what I can, ma'am,
  provided that your name
  is on our parish list.
  Let me take a look.
DISTRESSED WOMAN: No, no! For pity's sake . . .
  hunger's nothing now . . .
  I've seen a horror worse
  than you can know!

MAYOR: What d'you mean? Speak up!
DISTRESSED WOMAN: I can't
  tell *you*. It's a priest I want.
MAYOR: There isn't a priest
  in these parts.
DISTRESSED WOMAN: Then I'm lost,
  utterly alone.
BRAND [*approaching*]:
  A priest, you say? There may be one . . .
DISTRESSED WOMAN: Tell him to hurry. Please . . .
BRAND: I must know what's the matter.
  I assure you, the priest will come.
DISTRESSED WOMAN: Across all that wild water?
BRAND: Yes.
DISTRESSED WOMAN: Back there . . . at home . . .
  my husband . . . bairns as well . . .
  Say he won't go to hell!
BRAND: First you must tell me why
  you've come.
DISTRESSED WOMAN: My breasts were dry,
  and the babe went unfed.
  Folk wouldn't heed, nor God.
  My man couldn't bear it.
  It broke his spirit,
  and he just upped and killed
  it, like that, the child . . .
BRAND: He killed . . .
ONE OF THE CROWD [*with dread*]:
                        His child.
DISTRESSED WOMAN: The moment
  it was done, his torment
  was dreadful to see,
  and he wanted to die.
  He turned the knife on himself, and screamed Satan's name.
  He'll not live, but he's afraid
  to go. He lies with the child dead
  and frozen in his arms,

and cries and blasphemes.
Come with me, sir. At least
he'll not go unconfessed.
MAYOR: What's your name?
[*Points to his papers.*]

                  Is it here?
BRAND [*sharply, to the* PEASANTS]:
Take me across the fjord.
A MAN: In this? We wouldn't dare!
BRAND: A soul facing its doom
can't linger till it's calm.
ANOTHER MAN: The madman's tempting God!
MAYOR: Go the long way round.
DISTRESSED WOMAN: There'd still be the river
to cross; and the bridge is down.
Just after I'd crossed over . . .
it went . . . I might have drowned.
BRAND [*stepping down into a boat and loosening the sail*]:
You! Will you risk your boat?
OWNER: No . . . yes . . .
BRAND: Good, that's a start!
Now, who'll chance his life?
FIRST MAN: I'm staying where it's safe.
DISTRESSED WOMAN: Oh, my man, sir, my man,
he'll die all unshriven,
and shut out of Heaven!
BRAND [*calling from the boat*]:
I need someone to bale
and to trim the sail –
one! No more!
You there, so keen to give
just now! Give all you have!
A MAN [*threatening*]:
Get back on t'shore.
BRAND [*holding on with the boat hook and shouting*]:
None of you man enough?
Very well, then, a woman . . .
[*To the* DISTRESSED WOMAN]

You there! Come on, come on!
DISTRESSED WOMAN: Oh, I can't . . . it's so rough . . .
  my poor bairns, orphan'd
  they'll be if I'm taken . . .
  oh . . . oh . . .
BRAND [*laughing*]:
        You built on sand,[6]
  poor soul, and your house is shaken
  to pieces.
AGNES: [*turning, with flaming cheeks, quickly to* EINAR, *and
    putting her hand on his arm*]:
      You heard? Everything?
EINAR: Yes! Admirable! So strong
  in his calling!
AGNES: Follow that call!
  God bless you, farewell!
  [*Calls out to* BRAND.]
  Here's one worthy man:
  take *him*!
BRAND: Quickly then!
  Here take the rope!
EINAR [*pale*]:
  Which one do you mean,
  Agnes? Not *me*, surely?
AGNES: I was blind. I see clearly
  now. Go, I offer you up.
EINAR: Believe me, I would
  have gone; I would! I'd have sailed
  joyfully into that storm,
  once upon a time.
AGNES [*trembling*]:
  But now . . . ?
EINAR: Life is so very sweet,
  Agnes; I daren't do it.
AGNES [*shrinking away from him*]:
  Einar, what do you mean?
EINAR: I mean . . . I'm afraid.
AGNES: Then you have made

an impassable ocean
rage between us for ever.
[*To* BRAND]
I'll come with you. Wait!
BRAND: Now or too late!
DISTRESSED WOMAN [*terrified as* AGNES *leaps on board*]:
   Mercy, sweet Saviour!
EINAR: Stay, Agnes, for my sake!
BRAND [*to the* DISTRESSED WOMAN]:
   Woman, where do you live?
DISTRESSED WOMAN: Over there. There, d'you see?
   Behind the black rock.
      The boat moves off from the shore.
EINAR [*shouting after them*]:
   Don't throw your life away,
   my dearest! Save yourself, save
   yourself. Think of your family!
AGNES: I'm as safe as can be,
   Einar. Don't be afraid.
   We journey with God.
      The boat sails off. The PEASANTS *throng the slopes and
      gaze after it in tense excitement.*
A MAN: There they are, clear of the Point
   already!
ANOTHER MAN: No they ain't.
FIRST MAN: They are, they are, you fool.
   It's astern and to leeward
   I tell you!
A THIRD MAN: See that squall!
   Ugh . . . they'll not weather that.
MAYOR: Whoo-oo! There goes his hat!
A WOMAN: Look, his hair, all raven-black,
   Look how it's blown back.
FIRST MAN: The sea's hissing and boiling
   up, like a fountain.
EINAR: What was that? That scream?
   I heard it through the storm.
ANOTHER WOMAN: From high on the mountain.

A THIRD WOMAN [*pointing upwards*]:
  Would you believe . . . ? See, Gerd,
  Gerd, laughing and howling,
  Driving the boat on!
FIRST WOMAN: Blowing a ram's horn,
  And calling up the fiends
  to ride on the winds.
SECOND WOMAN: She's hooting through her hands
  now. Drearsome it sounds.
FIRST MAN: Hoot away, you vile troll,
  choke on your own spell,
  you'll not do them harm.
  True faith, that's their shield!
SECOND MAN: With that man at the helm,
  I'd go as his crew
  through a sea twice as wild.
FIRST MAN [*to* EINAR]:
  Who is he, d'you know?
EINAR: Some kind of – priest.
THIRD MAN: Well, one thing's plain.
  Priest or not, he's a man.
FIRST MAN: There's our pastor, I say –
  our new pastor.
ONE OF THE CROWD: Ay!
      They disperse over the hill slopes.
MAYOR: God help us, why such fuss?
  The woman's not from here;
  and he's not one of us.
  Why should he interfere,
  rushing off, risking his neck,
  and for nothing, so to speak?
  Well, I go by the book
  in my own bailiwick!
      Exit.

SCENE 2

*Outside the cottage on the headland. It is late in the day. The
fjord lies smooth and still.* AGNES *is sitting by the shore. Pres-
ently* BRAND *comes out of the cottage.*

BRAND: So now it's finished. Death's quiet hand
   has smoothed away his grin of dread
   and wiped the terror from his mind.
   It seems so peaceful to be dead.
   He knew as much of his own crime
   as his tongue fumbled at to name,
   as his stained hands could bear to touch,
   as his poor brain could grope to reach.
   He knew the half of what he'd done,
   mumbling, 'I killed the little one.'
   What of the ones he didn't kill
   but murdered just the same? Two boys,
   staring from the dark ingle-nook,
   constrained to look, and look, and look,
   with more than terror in their eyes,
   not understanding what they saw.
   Who can redeem *their* souls from hell?
   What purifying flame shall burn
   to ash their memories' carrion?
   Condemned to burgeon in the glare
   of that one awful, endless sight
   like leaves in darkness, sickly-white,
   growing more sickly as they grow,
   they in their turn shall generate
   offspring of their own despair,
   scions of wretchedness and hate,
   and all the streams of life shall run
   from the one ever-spreading stain.
   Where did it all begin, and why,
   eternal culpability?

What answer blares from the abyss?
'Remember who the father was.'
When the Day of Judgement comes
every soul shall stand accused,
shall be condemned as it condemns,
shall curse, knowing itself accursed.
There'll be no mercy for the plea
'Forgive us our heredity'!
Absurd riddle, making all
capacities incapable!
Not one soul in a thousand sees
the mountain of offences rise
from the base origins of life,
the two bare, basic words *to live*.

    A few PEASANTS *come from behind the cottage and approach*
    BRAND.

SPOKESMAN: So then, we meet again.
BRAND: Why are you here? The man
  is dead now; he's no need
  of anything you could give.
SPOKESMAN: Not for himself, maybe.
  He's with the Lord above.
  But what about the three
  poor souls he left behind,
  and left without a crumb?
  We're here because of them . . .
  brought them some scraps of food . . .
  what bits we could find.
BRAND: Until you hazard all,
  the gift's of no avail.
SPOKESMAN: I'll tell you how it is.
  If that stranger who lies
  in there, all stiff and stark,
  had been mid-fjord,
  clinging to a rock
  or an upturned boat,
  I'd have gone to his aid

and hauled him out.
I'd not see him drown.
BRAND: Yet you've little concern
  for the death of the soul.
SPOKESMAN: It's scholar's talk, is that.
  We're simple folk. We toil
  morn to night with our hands,
  all the hours that God sends.
BRAND: Then turn your backs on the dawn light.
  Gaze at nothing but the ground,
  stoop your shoulders to the yoke,
  bend your backs until they break.
SPOKESMAN: I expected you'd say,
  'Look up, look up, my friend,
  look up and be free!'
BRAND: Then be free, if you can.
SPOKESMAN: Ay, sir. But teach us how.
  You must lead us.
BRAND: Why?
SPOKESMAN: Many times we've been shown
  the road we should take
  to find our destiny.
  With you it's more than show.
  It is, and that's a fact!
  The truth is, one brave act
  is better than fine talk.
  You're just the man we need
  in this neighbourhood.
BRAND [*uneasy*]:
  What do you need me for?
SPOKESMAN: To be our pastor, sir.
BRAND: Your pastor? I, remain
  here? Impossible, man!
SPOKESMAN: It wasn't always
  like this! In the old days,
  when the harvests were good
  and the cattle well fed,
  and nobody was clemmed

with hunger, nor numbed
with cold and despair,
we had our own priest
and a church full of prayer.
But that's in the past.
These days the sheep starve
twice over, you might say.
BRAND: Don't ask me to stay.
Ask anything but that!
God has called me to serve
a hungry multitude
in the world outside.
What could I do here, shut
in by mountain and fjord?
How would I be heard?
SPOKESMAN: Speak out bold and clear
and all the mountains hear
and add their voice to yours,
and then the world hears.
BRAND [*preparing to leave*]:
It's time I set sail.
SPOKESMAN [*barring his way*]:
No, wait! This call, this call
to serve, that you go on
about: it means a lot to you, then?
BRAND: I have no other life.
SPOKESMAN: Then stay. Remember: 'If
you hazard less than all,
the gift's of no avail'!
BRAND: No man can give away
his inmost spirit,
that's his for ever,
or hold back, or divert,
the relentless river
of his destiny.
SPOKESMAN: Why, sir, if you drown
destiny in a tarn,
it's not lost, you know!

Come what may,
it'll reach the sea
as rain, or dew.
BRAND [*staring at him*]:
How do you know that?
SPOKESMAN: You taught us it,
when the sea raged,
and the wind surged,
and you went out
and defied death,
put all your faith
in a small boat,
risked life and all
for that poor soul
in there, you shook
our souls awake,
by God you did!
I'd swear we heard
a voice that rang
out clear and strong,
bells on the wind.
You understand . . .
[*Lowers his voice.*]
tomorrow's too late,
tomorrow we'll forget,
tomorrow we'll haul down
the brave flag that's flown
over our heads today.
We'll not glance at the sky.
BRAND [*sternly*]:
If you flinch from the call,
and if you won't fight
to be as you ought,
then be honest; remain
earth-bound, grovelling men,
dumb creatures of toil.
SPOKESMAN [*looking at him for a few moments*]:
You've quenched the flame you lit.

God forgive you for that,
and pity us who saw
a great light that's gone now.
  He leaves and the others follow silently.
BRAND [*gazing after them*]:
One by one, see, one by one,
homeward in a straggling line,
head bowed and shoulders stooped,
half-expecting to be whipped,
as Adam must have looked, when told
to turn his back on Paradise
and go and wander through the world.
Like Adam with his stricken face
staring at nothing, each of them
bears this knowledge for his shame:
blind creatures formed from my desire
to make man new and whole and pure.
Formed and deformed – whose the default?
My masterstroke? *This* thing of guilt?
I seek what's worth the being-won,
some end well worthy its renown!
[*He is about to leave, but stops as he sees* AGNES *on the shore.*]
Has she sat there all this while?
What is it she can hear?
Is it singing in the air?
In the storm, as we drove
on through the wild sea-wave,
she sat, so rapt and still,
wholly without fear,
with the spindrift glistening
upon her brow and hair,
gazing and listening,
yes, listening with her eyes
to secret harmonies!
[*Approaches her.*]
Tell me, what do you stare
at, so intently there?

The fjord winding its way
down to the great sea?
AGNES [*without turning round*]:
Not the fjord; not this earth
even; for both
are veiled from my sight.
Something more great
I glimpse, a world
beautiful to behold,
outlined against the sun.
How all things shine!
Rivers and seas, white peaks,
a glittering wilderness,
with great palm-trees
that sway in the wind,
shadows on bright sand.
It is a world that wakes
yet waits for life. A voice
cries through the emptiness:
'Creator and creature
of your own nature,
Adam, come forth
to life or death!'
BRAND [*rapturously*]:
Tell me . . . tell me . . . do you see more?
AGNES [*putting her hand on her breast*]:
I feel within me, here
in my heart and my soul,
the things that I foretell;
all births, all destinies.
Everything that is
awaits its hour,
and the time is near.
Already, from above,
He gazes down
with infinite love;
and already the crown
of infinite sorrow

pierces His brow.
And a voice cries
through the dawn-wilderness:
'Creator and creature
of your own nature,
Adam, come forth
to life or death!'
BRAND: The new Adam, yes!
We in him, he in us.
Truth at the heart's core,
our rightful sphere,
our destiny, the abode
of our selfhood-in-God.
There the old vulture
of self-will shall be no more.
I'll let this world
go, self-enthralled,
let it go its way . . .
But if the enemy
strikes at my work,
then I strike back!
I pledge myself to that
truth of the inmost word,
everyman's right
rightly understood,
to be what in truth I am.
[*Thinks in silence a while.*]
But how should that be?
The curse of heredity,
hereditary guilt,
the aboriginal fault,
stakes its own claim.
[*Stops and looks into the distance.*]
Who is this who comes
so slowly; who climbs
with such anguish; who bends,
so, her head; who stands
gasping for breath; who drags

her body in its rags
as if it were a hoard
of precious, secret greed;
who looks like a crow or
hawk nailed to a barn door?
Why is it I feel,
suddenly, a chill
of childish fear,
insidious like hoar frost
here in my breast
as she comes near?
Dear God . . .

> BRAND's MOTHER *comes up the slope, stops half visible against the hill, shades her eyes with her hand and looks around.*

BRAND's MOTHER: They said I'd find
   him hereabouts. Brand,
   son Brand, you there,
   then? Ugh, this glare
   burns out your eyes.
   That you, son?
BRAND: Yes.
MOTHER: Let's see. Can't hardly tell
   priest from carl
   I'm that mazed. Ay, it's you.
BRAND: Mother, at your house
   I never saw sunrise
   from summer's end till the return
   of the first cuckoo.
MOTHER [*laughing quietly*]:
   Ay, you grow a thick skin
   there: like an icicle-man
   over the waterfall.
   Do what you like,
   skin gets that thick,
   'twill guard your soul.
BRAND: Mother, I can't stay
   any longer.

MOTHER: Ay, ay,
  like when you were a lad,
  always up and about,
  I'll grant you that.
  And you made off
  soon enough!
BRAND: You made sure that I did.
MOTHER: Always had it in mind
  to see you book-learn'd,
  fit for a parson.
  It stood to reason;
  still does.
  [*Looks more closely at him.*]
        H'm, but you've grown
  some sinew and brawn
  on you, no mistake.
  You mind you take care,
  son. Don't risk your neck!
BRAND: Is that all you can say?
MOTHER: Say more if you know more,
  all nice and scholarly.
  That madness on the fjord,
  d'you think I've not heard?
  It's all they talk about
  back there, you and that boat.
  What happens if you drown,
  eh? I'm robbed by my own
  son, that's what. Ay a thief,
  that's what you'd be! My life
  you're fooling with. I gave
  you it, didn't I? I've
  got first claim on what's mine.
  You're not just flesh and blood.
  You're roof-beam, corner-post,
  the nails, the wood,
  every plank, every joist
  I've spliced into a house
  for nobody but us.

You're the last of our line.
Stick fast, then; don't give
half-an-inch while you live,
not half-an-inch, d'you hear?
I've named you my heir,
I have that. Never fret,
you'll inherit the lot.
BRAND: So that's what makes you crawl
bent double. All that coin,
it's weighing you down.
MOTHER [*shrinking away from him*]:
Eh, what? What? Keep away!
Help! Daylight robbery!
[*Calmer*]
Stay there. I've half a mind
to tan your hide, you brat!
I've said, you'll get it all.
Every day, bit by bit,
I crawl nearer the grave.
And then it's yours. Believe
me, everything I've earned.
You'll never need to beg.
But carry it on me?
I'm not mad! It's at home,
all snug in wad and bag.
Keep off, you varmint,
do as you're bidden,
wait till I'm gone!
As God's my judge I shan't
bury it in the midden
or under the hearth-stone
or under the floor;
shan't cram it in crevices
or such-like places.
It's yours, that I swear!
BRAND: On condition, no doubt.
You'd better spell it out!
MOTHER: Get wed; get your own brood,

   lad; that's the sole task
   I set you now; I ask
   no other reward.
   Keep my treasure safe,
   eh? Guard it with your life.
   Don't give nor divide.
   Save everything; hide
   everything you save,
   like in the troll-king's cave.
BRAND [*after a short pause*]:
   Ever since I was a boy
   I've had to defy
   you. I was never your child.
MOTHER: Agh, then be obstinate,
   be sure you don't thaw!
   It's little enough I care
   For your love, or your hate.
   I'm used to the cold,
   can live without fire,
   just so long as I know
   that you'll breed and hoard.
   Give me your word.
BRAND [*moving a step closer*]:
   But what if I've a mind
   to scatter it on the wind,
   all that treasure of yours?
MOTHER [*reeling back in horror*]:
   No, curse you! All those years
   raking it together
   while I grew old and my flesh
   withered to ash.
BRAND: Ash on the wind, Mother.
MOTHER: You'd scatter my soul
   on the wind!
BRAND: Shall
   I scatter it, all the same?
   Supposing I come
   and stand by your bed

   the first night that you're dead
   and lying cold and quiet
   with the psalm-book pressed
   against your stone-cold heart;
   suppose that I'm there,
   not 'mourning the deceased',
   but rummaging for treasure,
   ferreting around
   for what bits I can find . . .
MOTHER [*approaching, tense*]:
   Where d'you get such ideas?
BRAND: You truly wish to know?
MOTHER: Yes.
BRAND: Then I'll tell you a story.
   It's here in my memory,
   burned deep, the scar
   of an early fear.
   It was one autumn;
   it was one evening; a room
   candle-lit, shadowy.
   There my father lay.
   I'd sneaked in; I stayed,
   bewildered, afraid,
   like a little owl,
   crouched there, very still,
   wondering why he slept
   on and on, why he gripped
   his old psalm-book,
   why his hands were claw-like
   and yet so paper-thin.
   And then . . . and then . . .
   Mother, I can still hear
   those footsteps at the door;
   and again the door hinge
   creaks open and that strange-
   faced woman creeps in.
   I mustn't be seen!
   Into the shadows, hide!

She goes to the bedside.
Now she begins to feel
between the bed and the wall,
pushing aside his head.
Something's there. Yes, tied;
flat oilcloth bound with twine.
It won't come undone.
She tears at it with her nails, bites
and gnaws through the tough knots,
stares, throws it down, gropes again.
A pocket-book and some coin.
She mutters between her teeth,
'How much was it all worth,
then? How much? How much?'
Like stripping the corpse, the search
proceeds. Her shadow swoops; it looks
like a swooping hawk's.
She tears open a purse
as a hawk rips a mouse.
When there's no place left
she's a woman bereft,
whispering in disbelief,
'Was that all, was that all?';
flees like a hunted thief.
So ends my tale.

MOTHER: It was what I was owed.
God knows I'd paid.

BRAND: You paid twice over then.
It cost you your son.

MOTHER: You pay for what you get,
with brain and heart
if need be. I did,
a lot more than most.
Something was sacrificed,
something; I can't recall
what it was I had,
but it was good. I believe
people called it love.

Such things aren't practical.
But it was hard at first
to turn from my own choice,
to heed my father's voice:
'Forget that pauper-lad,
take the old man instead,
he'll feather your nest!'
So I did as he said;
and, for all that, I was cheated.
Oh but I've sweated
and I've made my pile.
With pain and with graft
I've made well-nigh double
what that old fool left.
But it's been bitter-hard.
BRAND: Hard indeed, Mother. Harder still
for your poor pawned soul.
MOTHER: I've taken care of that.
You'll get the estate,
I'll get the last rites.
I call that fair profits
for honest dealing.
My worldly goods
in exchange for priest's words
of comfort and healing.
I made you a priest.
I claim my interest.
BRAND: In the world's looking-glass
you don't see what is,
you see some other sight.
And there are many more
in these parts who stare
into that same mirror
of vanity and error.
Sparing their child a thought
now and then, they think,
'That child has me to thank

for his place in the world',
casting upon the child
the shoddy, second-hand
sentiments of their kind.
And they put all their faith
in a kind of living death.
Not knowing how to live,
they stupidly believe
eternity's the sum
of endless earthly time.
MOTHER: Can't you leave folk alone?
  I'll swear you've never known
  the half I've suffered!
  Take what you're offered.
BRAND: That won't cancel the debt.
MOTHER: What are you on about?
  There's no debt.
BRAND: So you say.
  But supposing there were,
  would not justice require
  that each claim should be met
  in full, and by me?
MOTHER: Is that what the law says?
BRAND: Your pen-and-parchment laws!
  Mother, the Holy Spirit
  utters its own decrees,
  summons us to atone
  for what others have done.
  How blindly you have sinned!
  Open your eyes;
  begin to understand.
  [*His* MOTHER *appears confused.*]
  Don't be afraid.
  Your great debt shall be paid.
  God's image, that you've marred,
  shall shine again, purified;
  resurrected by my will;

transfigured in my soul.
Go to your grave in peace.
I shall pay the price.
MOTHER: Let's see now; does that mean
every last little sin?
BRAND: The debt. Only the debt.
I can rid you of that.
I am able to erase
the effect, but not the cause.
I cannot annul
that sin which engendered all;
I cannot assuage or share
that guilt by which you *are*.
That bears a penalty
which you alone must pay.
MOTHER [*uneasy*]:
You're making my head spin,
just like too much sun.
Bad thoughts sprout in my head
like henbane or bindweed.
I've had enough. I'm going
back where I belong.
Under the glacier,
there I'll feel easier.
BRAND: Then go, Mother, go back;
hobble into the dark.
I'll stay here, close at hand.
If you long for me, send
for me; I shall come.
MOTHER: You'll come. Ay, to condemn!
BRAND: As your son, as your priest,
I'll shield you from the blast
of judgement and dread,
melt the ice from your blood.
I'll sing you to sleep
with hymns of sure hope.
MOTHER: You'd swear that on the Good
Book, and all?

BRAND: When I'm sent
  word that you repent,
  I shall come, as I said.
  Like you, Mother, I make
  one condition: give back
  all that you have gained. Go
  naked to the grave.
MOTHER: Oh no,
  son, no! Tell me to starve
  and thirst. Tell me I must,
  I will. Don't make me give
  away what I love the most.
BRAND: Everything you're worth,
  or abide His wrath!
MOTHER: Everything? I can't, son, I
  can't! Not every penny!
BRAND: I see you'll not atone
  till, like Job, all alone,
  covered in earth and ash,
  you cry, 'Let the day perish
  wherein this carcass came
  forth out of the womb!'
MOTHER [*wringing her hands*]:
  I can't bear it; I'm
  going, while I still can; home
  to cradle my sweet gold
  as if it was my child
  and weep for it, like
  a mother will
  for her bairn that's sick.
  Why does God leave a soul
  stuck like this in the flesh
  where your heart's dearest wish
  makes your soul die?
  Stay by me, pastor,
  in my last hour
  and help me out.
  But until then

   let me hold on
   to the things I've got.
     Exit.
BRAND [*gazing after her*]:
   Yes, your pastor will stay.
   And you will send for him.
   And he shall come to warm
   your withered hand in his,
   and let you die in peace.
   [*Goes down the slope towards* AGNES.]
   My life was like this sun at dawn.
   But now the sun is going down.
   At daybreak I could hear the song
   of battle; and my heart was strong.
AGNES [*turning round and looking up at him with shining eyes*]:
   The dawn was pale compared to this
   full radiance. It was fantasies
   and games and pretty lies and art
   and everything that truth is not.
   The dawn was a false paradise.
   Truth must rejoice at such a loss.
BRAND: But how I dreamed! Such dreams I had,
   like flocks of wild swans overhead
   that swooped and bore me up, their wings
   the murmur of the multitudes.
   What vistas of imaginings
   I saw outspread; and what clear roads
   and distances to lead me on,
   God's warrior of world renown!
   What hymns and incense and what gold
   banners brilliantly unfurled,
   my triumph splendid and austere!
   In spirit I was taken up
   to a high place, was tempted there
   with visions of exalted hope
   that faded even as they shone
   and turned to darkness and to stone.
   Now, shadowed by these walls

of rock, where the light fades
hours before night falls,
and the fjord waters hem
me in, once more I stand
in the place I must call home.
There will be no more rides
on cloud-pawing Pegasus.
Unsaddled is that wing'd horse.
And no trumpets sound.
But let us not . . . let us not
falter, nor stoop to regret
triumphs that might have been.
I have received the sign.
I see, now, the true goal
to strive for: humble toil
ennobled by belief,
the sacrificial life.

AGNES: But what of that false god
who was to be destroyed,
you said? Will he not fall,
then? Ever?

BRAND: Fall he shall!
But not in the wild gaze
of crowds, not to their vast applause.
I was wrong, I was wrong.
In vain we stir the soil
round the roots of the soul
unless that soul is strong.
It is not raucous fame
that redeems the time.
It is the will alone
that can purge and refine,
that alone has the power
to make or mar
what we do, whether the work
be famed or not.
[*He turns towards the village, where the evening shadows
are beginning to gather.*]

                              You who walk
with slow and sullen step
in the narrow and steep
places of this land,
I shall teach you to praise,
with heart and mind and hand
in true communion
one with another; to rouse
from mortal sleep the young lion
of the immortal will.
Let us do all things well,
let the pickaxe, the spade,
shine like the battle blade.
Then shall the hand of God
inscribe His holy word
upon the human heart
as though on Sinai slate.
Let nobleness appear,
let those who faint and fear
find strength. Righteousness shall destroy
falsehood utterly.
   He begins to leave. EINAR *meets him.*

EINAR: You there! Yes, you, sir! Give me back
  that which you took!

BRAND: That which . . . ? Ah! Speak to her.
  Speak, but will she hear?

EINAR: Agnes, I beg you, stay;
  stay on the sunlit heights,
  not where dark sorrow waits.

AGNES: I have no choice to make.
  I have one road to take.
  This is the only way.

EINAR: How can you? How can you leave
  your mother, your sisters?

AGNES: Give
  them my love, I shall send
  a letter when I have found

words to express
what my soul clearly sees.

EINAR: Out there, where the great waters gleam,
The white-sailed vessels scud and skim,
Dipping their prows in pearly foam,
Bright emanations of a dream,
Seeking the fabled shore, the calm
Landfall and their longed-for home.

AGNES: Sail with them, then, go east or
west; but think of me as dead.

EINAR: Come, come with me; my sister
if not my bride!

AGNES: Einar, Einar, I have told
you. There is an ocean
of silence. It lies between
us, wider than the world.

EINAR: Go home, then. Go, be safe!

AGNES [*softly*]:
I am drawn by this man towards a new life.

BRAND: Young woman, beware.
And when you choose, be sure.
For, choosing, you are chosen.
In the shadow of these frozen
peaks, I shall remain
a forgotten man.
And life with me will seem
an endless winter gloom.

AGNES: Starshine pierces the cloud.
I am not afraid.

BRAND: All or nothing. That
is my demand. The task
is very great. And the risk,
also, is very great.
There'll be no mercy shown.
There's no provision made
for weakness or dread.
Falter, and you go down

into the depths of the sea.
Mere lifelong sacrifice
itself may not suffice.
Would you die willingly?

EINAR: This is no seaside game.
It is a dark and cruel
commandment that can kill.

BRAND [*to* AGNES]:
You stand where the roads cross.
Once and for all, then! Choose!
     Exit.

EINAR: Choose between storm and calm.
Choose between 'go' and 'stay'.
Choose between joy and grief.
Choose between night and day.
Choose between death and life.

AGNES: Beyond darkness and death
light dawns upon the earth.
     She follows BRAND. EINAR *looks for some time, as if
     lost, in the direction in which she has gone; then he bows
     his head and goes out towards the fjord again.*

ACT THREE

Three years later. A small garden at the pastor's house. A high mountain face above it, a stone wall around it. The fjord, narrow and shut in, in the background. The door of the house leads into the garden. Afternoon. BRAND *stands on the steps outside the house.* AGNES *sits on the step below him.*

AGNES: My dear, why do you gaze
    endlessly over the fjord,
    and with such anxious eyes,
    unwilling to rest?
BRAND: These three years past
    I've waited for some word
    from my mother. Now I hear
    she lies at death's door;
    yet I've received no sign
    that she's dead to her sin.
    Therefore I wait.
AGNES [*softly and lovingly*]:
    Why do you hesitate
    to go now? Go to her,
    go to her!
BRAND [*shaking his head*]:
           Let her repent,
    then; let her sacrifice
    everything that she has.
    No solace, no sacrament,
    until that's done.
AGNES: But your
    own mother, Brand . . .

BRAND: Own? Own?
  Would you have me bow down
  to every household god
  of clay and blood?
AGNES: So harsh . . .
BRAND: To you?
AGNES: Ah, no.
BRAND: I saw
  what must be; foresaw and foretold
  struggle and bitter cold.
AGNES [*smiling*]:
  O my dearest, Brand's law
  sometimes is fallible,
  it seems. Look, I can smile.
BRAND: Life withers; and your cheeks
  grow pale now; mind and soul
  burn in the icy chill.
  The glacier looms; the black rocks
  threaten our house.
AGNES: Look how they shelter us.
  Even under the glacier's rim
  we're safe; and when, in spring, the stream
  leaps from the cliff, we live
  quiet, unharmed,
  behind the waterfall
  in our ferny cave.
BRAND: In a deep cave, unwarmed
  by any shred of sun.
AGNES: Isn't the sunlight lovely to look at when
  it shines on the high fell!
BRAND: Shines, Agnes? When? For a few weeks
  perhaps, a brief glimmer
  at midsummer.
AGNES [*looking firmly at him and getting up*]:
  There's something here that makes
  even you afraid.
BRAND: Surely it is *your* heart

that's thrilled by some secret
dread, some abyss of dread.
It's as though you stand
staring into that abyss.
AGNES: Sometimes, I confess,
  sometimes, yes, I've trembled ...
BRAND: Trembled?
AGNES: For our child,
  for Alf.
BRAND: For Alf!
AGNES: Ah, you see, Brand,
  you tremble too!
BRAND: Agnes, at times
  I fear for our little son.
  But he'll get well;
  God is just; not cruel ...
  not cruel ... Where is Alf now?
AGNES: Asleep.
BRAND [*looking in through the door*]:
                  So he is! No dreams
  of sickness or pain
  haunt his pillow
  with their gaunt phantom shapes.
AGNES: But he's so pale.
BRAND: It will pass,
  it will pass.
AGNES: How sweetly he sleeps.
BRAND [*closing the door*]:
  Sleep and grow strong. God bless
  you, my own child! God bless you both
  for the gifts that you bring with
  such an instinct of grace. Labour
  and grief, now, are easy to bear.
  Day after day I am filled
  with new strength as the child
  plays, as I watch him at play.
  God summoned me to stay.
  I made the sacrifice.

It seemed a martyrdom
that I embraced. How altered
now: here, in the wilderness,
manna for one who starved.
AGNES: For one who toiled, and served,
and never faltered.
I know what tears you've shed
in secret, tears of blood.
You have earned your fame.
BRAND: Love touched me; now each thing
I do is blest. Spring awakening
in heart and in mind,
that is what I have found
with you, and with none other.
Neither father nor mother
had kindled the least spark
of love. I do believe all
the tenderness of my soul
that was clamped into the dark
is here released to shine
on what is truly mine.
AGNES: And upon all who come
to your hearth and home:
the poor and the downtrodden,
the fatherless child, bidden
to enter, each one a guest
at your heart's truth's feast.
BRAND: What I am, what I do, I owe
to Alf and to you: two
souls who crossed the gulf
into my inmost self.
I was too long alone.
Spirit had become stone.
AGNES: Where you caress, you strike.
Those whom you bless, you break.
BRAND: Not you, Agnes?
AGNES: No, Brand.
But that which you demand,

'all or nothing', has driven
souls out of Heaven.
BRAND: That which the world calls 'love'
I do not wish to have.
God's love is hard to bear,
I know that. Those who fear
have cause enough to dread
the summons. When Christ prayed,
'Lord, take away this cup,'
shivering in his sweat,
what answer did he get?
None, Christ had to drain
the terror and the pain
and taste the dregs.
AGNES: What hope
is there for us poor souls
weighed on such judgement scales?
BRAND: Who's doomed by God's just law?
Oh do not seek to know!
Enough that you understand
'Be faithful and endure'
written by His own hand
in letters of fire.
To those who, striving, fall,
God will be merciful.
Those who refuse to strive
He will not forgive.
Agnes, in my book
the first commandment says,
'You shall not compromise'.
Half-done, ill-done work
thwarting the soul's power,
dooms the ill-doer.
Yes, Agnes, it is so.
AGNES [*throwing her arms around his neck*]:
Where you go, I shall go.
BRAND: Where love goes, no road
is too steep or hard.

The DOCTOR *has come down the road and stops outside
the garden wall.*

DOCTOR: And what are you doing?
  Ah, billing and cooing
  among these sylvan groves,
  pretty turtle-doves!
AGNES [*running to open the garden gate*]:
  Doctor, come in! Do, please!
DOCTOR: Now you know very well
  that I won't. I'm so cross.
  Really, why must you stay
  in this place? Call it 'home'?
  It's a troll-cave of gloom,
  all glacier, no sky.
  Brr . . . it shrivels your soul!
BRAND: Not my soul.
DOCTOR: Tch, man!
  You know what I mean.
  With you, 'a promise made
  is a promise kept' indeed.
AGNES: Where love is, there's no need of sun
  to bring the whole of summer in.
DOCTOR: H'm. I've a call to make.
BRAND: My mother?
DOCTOR: Very sick.
  A few more hours, and then . . .
  But you know that of course.
  You'll have been to her house.
  Just back, are you?
BRAND: I've not been.
DOCTOR: Well, now I've heard it all!
  I've trudged mile after mile
  across whinstone and bog,
  tight-fisted old hag
  though she is, just for her!
BRAND: God bless you for that –
  all your skill and care.
DOCTOR: God bless my soft heart.

Perhaps you'd rather
that we went there together . . .
BRAND: Doctor, unless I hear
that she's ready to pay
the full penalty,
not one inch will I stir.
DOCTOR [*to* AGNES]:
His heart's as hard as rock.
You poor defenceless lamb,
I'm sorry for your sake.
AGNES: Don't be. What's more, he'd give
all his heart's blood to save
that woman's soul.
BRAND: I am her son.
Am I not pledged to atone,
to honour every claim?
I tell you, every debt
shall be wiped out!
DOCTOR: By one who's a pauper
himself? Most improper.
BRAND: I have made my choice
freely. Let that suffice.
DOCTOR [*looking hard at him*]:
Pastor, your ledger's full
of 'God's law' and 'man's will'.
But the column marked 'love',
that's still blank, I believe.
     Exit.
BRAND [*gazing after him for a while*]:
Nothing is so much soiled
by the commerce of the world
as the word 'love': this veil
hiding the deformed soul.
Man's pathway's dark and steep:
here's 'love' to guide his step.
He wallows in his sin:
'love' hauls him out again.
He cringes from the fight:

with 'love' there's no defeat.

AGNES: I know such things are false.
  Love is something else.

BRAND: Agnes, if souls are athirst
  for truth and righteousness,
  let us assuage that longing first;
  then speak of love.
  Merely to perish on the cross,
  or to writhe in the flame,
  daily to be buried alive,
  this is not martyrdom.
  But to make a burned offering
  out of the suffering,
  to ordain the anguish
  of our spirit and our flesh,
  that is salvation, there we seize
  hold of martyrdom's prize!

AGNES [*clinging tightly to him*]:
  Brand, when I weaken,
  when I flinch from the task,
  speak then as you have spoken
  now. That much I do ask.

BRAND: Man's will must blaze the way
  for God's victory,
  so that love can alight,
  the white dove with the olive-leaf
  of mercy and new life.
  But – until then – hate!
  [*In terror*]
  Hatred, the one redeeming word!
  Hatred, the angel of the Lord!
    He hurries into the house.

AGNES [*looking in through the open door*]:
  Now he's with Alf, kneeling by his bed.
  I think he's crying; he rocks
  to and fro, to and fro. He seeks
  comfort; that great-hearted man
  seeks comfort from a child

innocent of the world.
But he's . . . is the child ill? What is it?
[*Cries out in fear.*]
Brand, what is it? What have you seen
that makes you so afraid?

    BRAND *comes out on to the steps.*

BRAND: Was that . . . ? I heard the gate,
  I thought. No messenger?
AGNES: None.
BRAND [*looking back into the house*]:
         His pulse is much too fast
  and his skin's like fire.
  Agnes, be strong.
AGNES: I tremble
  when you say that.
BRAND: Be strong.
  [*Looking along the road*]
             At last!
A MESSENGER [*coming through the garden gate*]:
  She'll not live long . . .
BRAND: What message do you bring?
MESSENGER: A right old jumble.
  She sat up and screeched,
  'I want the priest fetched;
  my son, mind! Tell him, "half".'
BRAND [*shrinking back*]:
  Half? No!
MESSENGER: Half, I swear,
  as true as I stand here.
BRAND: You misheard. She said, 'all'.
MESSENGER: Look, man, I'm not deaf.
  I know what I heard.
  'Half' is what she said.
BRAND: You'd swear that, at the Day
  of Judgement?

    He clutches the MESSENGER's *arm.*

MESSENGER: On my soul.
BRAND [*firmly*]:

Then take her my reply:
'No bread, no wine,
no comfort, none.'
MESSENGER [*looking uncertainly at him*]:
Perhaps *your* hearing's bad.
She's dying, your own mother . . .
BRAND: I don't make different laws,
one for my own kin, the other
for strangers. My mother knows
that 'all or nothing'
is absolute. One piece
struck from the Golden Calf
is an idol, no less
than the beast itself.
MESSENGER: Well, if she's still breathing
by the time I get back,
I'll tell her, 'Your son
sends his best wishes –
fifty lashes!'
I shan't relish the work,
I tell you plain.
How can you treat her so?
God Himself is less hard.
That's a comfort anyhow!
  Exit.
BRAND: This stinking comfort blown
from their own carrion;
the stench of deathly fear
tainting the world's air!
Even their so-called faith
they keep to bargain with,
to bribe their senile judge,
a sop to soothe his rage.
  Out in the road, the MESSENGER *has met a* SECOND
  MESSENGER; *both return.*
BRAND: Another message?
FIRST MESSENGER: Yes.
BRAND: What does she say?

SECOND MESSENGER: She says,
  'Nine-tenths.'
BRAND: She's not said 'all'?
SECOND MESSENGER: She's not.
BRAND: Go back, then; tell
  her, 'No wine, no bread,
  no comfort.'
SECOND MESSENGER: Hasn't she paid
  enough? More than enough?
FIRST MESSENGER: That woman gave you life.
BRAND [*clenching his hands*]:
  What would you have me do?
  Deal kindly with what's mine
  and deal harshly with you?
SECOND MESSENGER: Her need, her dread, are terrible
  to see. Give her some sign.
BRAND [*to the* FIRST MESSENGER]:
  No sacraments can be brought
  to an unclean table:
  tell her what I have said.
    The MESSENGERS *leave.*
AGNES [*clinging to him*]:
  Brand, sometimes you seem
  like some grim scourge of God,
  like God's own sword of flame.
  I flinch from the sight.
BRAND [*sorrowfully*]:
  But, Agnes, the world's sword
  has already drawn blood
  from me; many times it has cut
  me to the heart.
AGNES: Your own demands go deep;
  they're not easy to bear.
  How many measure up
  to such morality?
  Pitifully few, I fear.
BRAND: This entire age is devoid
  of grace or merit;

it's ruled by creeping pride,
dull frivolity,
meanness of spirit.
Say to the 'man-of-the-hour',
whether of peace or war,
'Enough; be satisfied
with the true victory,
with the triumph of good;
let your own name go down
to dust; let silence reign.'
Would he agree?
Or tell some eager poet
with his sweet cage-birds of song,
tell *him* to live unsung.
He'd fly at your throat.
Rich men who set such store
by largesse to the poor
bargain on gratitude
posthumously accrued.
But selfless charity,
now there's a rarity!
The mighty and the meek,
the strong man and the sick,
are all alike in this
loathing of sacrifice,
this craving to possess,
this thraldom to the world.
In dread of the abyss
they struggle to keep hold,
clinging to root and branch
until the avalanche.

AGNES: Yet still you thunder 'all
or nothing' as they fall.

BRAND: Lose all if you would gain
all. Out of the depths men
scale even the precipice
of their own fall from grace.
[*Silent for a moment*]

Everything that I speak
is spoken in agony.
I'm like a castaway
crying in vain among
the spars of a great wreck.
I could bite out my tongue
that must rage and chastise
and with its prophecies
strike terror where I crave
the touch of human love.
Watch over our child,
Agnes. In a radiant dream
his spirit lies so calm,
like water that is stilled,
like a mountain tarn
silent under the sun.
Sometimes his mother's face
hovers over that hushed place,
is received, is given back,
as beautifully as a bird
hovers, and hovering, is mirror'd
in the depths of the lake.

AGNES [*pale*]:
No matter where you aim
your thoughts, they fly to him.

BRAND: O Agnes, guard him well,
in quietness.

AGNES: I will.
Only . . . a few more
words . . .

BRAND: Words to inspire!

AGNES: All the strength you can give.

BRAND [*embracing her*]:
The innocent shall live.

AGNES [*looking up radiantly*]:
The innocent! You see, even
God dare not destroy
such a gift from Heaven!

She goes into the house.

BRAND [*gazing silently; then*]:
   Does she think God has qualms? –
   the God who chose Abraham's
   beloved child, the boy
   Isaac, as the altar stone
   of his father's faith!⁷
   [*Shakes off his thoughts.*]
   No! I've made my sacrifice.
   The great cause is forgone,
   and I've stifled the voice
   that could rouse the whole earth
   to His redeeming wrath:
   'You sleepers, wake!' I've come
   down from that high dream.
   [*Looks down the road.*]
   This torment of delay!
   Why no repentance, why?
   Why is she not prepared,
   even in this last pain,
   to be rid of her sin,
   to tear its claggy root
   out of her heart?
      The MAYOR *appears on the road, walking in the direction*
      of the pastor's house.

BRAND: A message! Yes, the word
   at last! Ugh, no. The mayor,
   look at him, tasting the air,
   strutting and jolly,
   his hands in his pockets,
   his arms like brackets
   around his belly.

MAYOR [*through the garden gate*]:
   Good day, reverend!
   How are you, friend?
   I fear I've come
   at a difficult time.
   Your mother, I believe,

not much longer to live?
Very distressing!
Death comes to us all.
As I was passing
I thought, 'Why not call?
Very much better
to tackle the matter
head-on.' It's well known
you're at daggers drawn.
BRAND: At daggers drawn?
MAYOR: That's what they say.
  Her treasure's under lock and key.
BRAND: The reckoning's overdue;
  that at least is true.
MAYOR: As soon as the old girl
  (God rest her soul)
  lies in Mother Earth,
  just think what you'll be worth!
  From now on, pastor,
  the world's your oyster.
  Believe me, I know.
BRAND: That means 'Be off with you!'
MAYOR: Best thing for all concerned.
  I'm sure you understand.
  We're happy as we are,
  we liege-folk of the shore.
  Your spiritual fire,
  utterly wasted here!
BRAND: A man's own native soil
  sustains him; he best thrives
  where he first plants his foot.
  If he's cast out, his soul
  withers; nothing he strives
  for blossoms or bears fruit.
MAYOR: A man must do what's best
  in the national interest.
BRAND: How can you ever truly
  know what our nation needs,

    if you bury your heads
    deep in this darkling valley?
    Go, purify your sight
    in the clear air of the height!
MAYOR: That sounds like city talk,
    pastor. We're humble folk.
BRAND: These boundaries you draw
    between 'high' and 'low'!
    This never-ending wail,
    'We are small, we are small, we are small!'
MAYOR: For everything there is a time
    and a due season, says the psalm.
    This lowly parish, sir, has cast
    its mite into the treasure-chest
    of weighty cause and doughty deed,
    a tribute to our Viking blood!
    Those sagas, those heroic lays
    of good King Bele's[8] golden days
    and those great brothers, Ulf and Thor,[9]
    and many a hundred heroes more!
    Some say it's not polite to boast,
    some say, 'Forget what's dead and past';
    but I, for one, am very proud
    of what our great forefathers did.
    Few have done better, I'll be bound,
    to aid the progress of mankind!
BRAND: But you even betray
    your own battle-cry,
    your 'patriots' pledge',
    your '*noblesse oblige*'!
    What do you care
    for that 'goodly fere',
    King Bele's men?
    You've ploughed them in!
MAYOR: But you're wrong, you're wrong!
    Why don't you come along
    to our next 'wassail'
    in the parish hall?

The schoolmaster, magistrate,
myself, all the elite
of the neighbourhood,
pounding the festal board
and drinking hot toddy!
King Bele lives, laddy!
At such times I feel stirred
by the power of the word,
by heroic verse.
I'm partial to a bit
of rhyming; and that goes,
I'd say, for most of us
round here. Enough's enough,
though. Art isn't life,
as I hope you'll agree. But,
say, between seven and ten
of an evening, when work's
over and folk can relax,
we dally with the muse,
and pipe a lyric strain,
we play at hunt-the-rhyme,
and bathe in the sublime.
Now, just between ourselves,
pastor, there's something odd
in your whole attitude.
You don't do things by halves.
We do. You want to fight,
turn every wrong to right
at one fell swoop, it seems.
These, I think, are your aims?
Correct me, if they're not.
BRAND: Something of the sort.
MAYOR: Keep your lofty ideals
for your intellectuals
in the big city.
We're tillers of the soil,
we're toilers of the sea.
BRAND: Then justify that toil!

Into the ocean cast
each vainglorious boast;
and deep in the earth hide
every platitude.
MAYOR: Surely great nations thrive
  on memories!
BRAND: If you have
  nothing but memories
  you keep vigil in vain
  at an empty cairn.
MAYOR: It's plain you're much too good
  for this neighbourhood.
  Look, leave it to me –
  I'll soon restore morale
  among our 'sons of toil'.
  That I can guarantee.
  It's not too much to claim
  that my mayoral term
  has won deserved applause
  for grit and enterprise.
  The birth-rate has increased
  thanks to my zeal and zest.
  What wonders men perform,
  under their own steam!
  A new road or a bridge,
  real marvels of the age!
BRAND: Between the life of earth
  and the living faith
  you've built nothing at all.
MAYOR: My road up to the fell!
BRAND: Between vision and deed
  I see no new road;
  but I have seen God's hand
  writing His words of flame:
  'The place where you are come
  is your abiding place.'
  Here I take my stand.
MAYOR: Well, stay if you must.

But stick to your last;
castigate crime and vice,
God knows, there's need enough,
wickedness is rife.
But we don't want fuss.
And please remember this:
six whole days a week
are devoted to work.
One day for sober thought
is more than adequate.
And don't expect the Lord
God to walk on the fjord,
either!

BRAND: To make use
of such practical advice
I would have to change
souls, or my soul's range
of vision. Souls are called
by God, not by the world.
And I shall set free
by my soul's victory
the people whom you led,
lulled and betrayed,
starved, and constrained
in your poverty of mind.

MAYOR: So we're to fight it out?
You'll be the first to fall.
Mark my words, you will!

BRAND: Victorious in defeat.
You'll never understand . . .

MAYOR: And can you wonder? Friend,
don't turn your back on life!
Don't hazard every good
that this world has bestowed
with such generous hands –
your mother's gold, her bonds,
your child and your good wife.

BRAND: And if I must renounce

such an inheritance?
And if I must, what then?

MAYOR: It doesn't make sense!
You haven't a chance!
Think on, think on!

BRAND: Here's where I stake my claim;
here, in my own home;
and if I shrink from the call
I lose my own soul.

MAYOR: But a man on his own
can't hope to win.

BRAND: The best are on my side.

MAYOR [*smiling*]:
I've thousands on parade!
    Exit.

BRAND [*gazing after him*]:
There goes a stalwart democrat,
filled with the democratic urge,
the civic sentiments at heart;
but what a scourge!
No avalanche or hurricane
has done the damage he has done
with a good conscience all these years.
How many smiles he's turned to tears!
What gifts, what ardours, have recoiled
to darkness, all their music stilled.
What impulses of joy or wrath
he cheerfully deprives of breath.
How many hearts has he destroyed,
without the slightest trace of blood!
[*The* DOCTOR *appears at the garden gate.* BRAND *suddenly
notices him and cries out in anguish.*]
Doctor! Is there some word?

DOCTOR: We must leave her to God . . .
I'm sorry, my boy . . .

BRAND: But surely, before she died,
surely she must have said . . .

DOCTOR: 'I repent, I repent!'

Is that what you want?
She gave nothing away.
BRAND [*gazing in silence before he speaks*]:
Then she's lost for ever?
DOCTOR: God may be less severe.
She whispered, at the end,
'He is kinder than Brand.'
BRAND [*sinking down, as if in pain, on the bench*]:
In the final agony
of guilt, on the brink of death
itself, the same old lie.
   He hides his face in his hands.
DOCTOR [*coming nearer, looking at him and shaking his head*]:
You live by the old law,
do you not? Here and now,
'An eye for an eye, a tooth
for a tooth'.[10] But I believe
that each generation
has its own life to live
in its own fashion.
Ours has the wit to laugh
at every 'old wife'
with her rag-bag of ghouls,
changelings, damned souls,
and dead bodies that rise.
Our first commandment is:
'Be humane, be humane!'
BRAND: Words foolish and vain!
Try to make 'all or nothing'
fit your 'humane' clothing.
Was God 'humane' to Jesus Christ?
Was He a bloodless altruist?
Your God of liberal discernment
would doubtless manage the atonement
with a brisk noncommittal note
like any cautious diplomat.
   He hides his head and sits in mute grief.
DOCTOR [*softly*]:

Rage, rage, you soul in a storm,
till you have spent your force.
Better if you could weep . . .
    AGNES *has come out on to the steps; she is pale and terri-*
    fied and whispers to the DOCTOR.
AGNES: Doctor, please; please come;
  come to the child!
DOCTOR   Of course,
  my dear, of course! And stop
  trembling; you'll make *me* afraid!
AGNES [*pulling him along with her*]:
  Hurry, please! Merciful God!
    They go into the house. BRAND *does not notice them.*
BRAND: She died as she had lived,
  past hope of being saved.
  Therefore God's writ thrusts home
  the justice of the claim:
  her son must bear the cost
  or be himself accurst.
  So be it. I am sworn
  from this moment on
  never to turn aside
  from my great crusade,
  this travail towards the will's harsh
  triumph over the flesh.
  God is my strength. The word
  of His mouth is like a sword
  for me to wield. His wrath
  kindles my very breath.
  I am possessed of His will.
  I shall make mountains fall.
    The DOCTOR, *followed by* AGNES, *comes hurriedly out*
    on to the steps.
DOCTOR: Get ready at once, and leave.
BRAND: If I felt the whole earth
  shudder, I would not move.
DOCTOR: Then your child will die;
  you have condemned him to death.

BRAND [*bewildered; making to go into the house*]:
  Alf? What troll-tale is this?
DOCTOR: Stay
  a moment. Tell me, when
  did you last see the sun?
  Must I tell you how fierce
  the gusts are; how the fog
  is like the breath of the ice?
  Your house is an iceberg.
  One more winter spent
  here, and your tender plant
  will perish. Go! Go soon!
  Tomorrow if you can.
BRAND: This very evening.
  Agnes, we'll lift him up
  gently in his sleep.
  No more shall the ravening
  ice-winds from the shore
  scorch him with their cold fire.
  Never again shall he feel
  the glacier's deathly chill.
  We must find a new home
  far away where it's warm,
  where he can thrive and grow.
  Hurry! Hurry now!
  His death's a web that's spun
  closer each minute!
AGNES: I've known
  a secret dread. In my heart
  I foresaw this threat;
  I feared for his life.
  But not enough.
BRAND [*to the* DOCTOR]:
  If we make our escape
  now, there truly is hope
  that his health will improve?
  I have your word?
DOCTOR: You have.

BRAND: Doctor, you've saved my son.
Agnes, be sure to fold
round him the warm eiderdown.
The evening air strikes cold.

> AGNES *goes into the house. The* DOCTOR *gazes silently at* BRAND, *who stands motionless looking in through the door; then he goes up to him, putting his hand on his shoulder.*

DOCTOR: For a man without remorse
you're quick to compromise
when the lamb to be slain
is yours, your own first-born.
One law for the world,
another for your child,
a double standard,
is that it? You thundered
'all or nothing' in the ears
of those poor villagers
in their terror and want.
You refused to forgive
your mother unless she went
naked to the grave.
But now it's your turn
to be the shipwrecked man
clinging to the keel
in the howling gale.
What good are they now,
those tables of the law?
Your sermons on hell-fire,
what a burden they are!
Jettison them!
Now it's sink or swim;
and it's 'God keep him safe,
my own darling boy!'
You'd best be on your way.
Take your child and your wife
and go. And don't glance back
at your forsaken flock.

And don't spare a thought
for the hapless plight
of your mother's soul.
Renounce the call.
Farewell, then, priest!
'*Consummatum est!*'[11]

> BRAND *clutches his head in bewilderment as if to collect his thoughts.*

BRAND: Have I been struck blind?
Or was I blind before?

DOCTOR: Please don't misunderstand.
I entirely applaud
this change in your mood.
I very much prefer
the new family man
to the old man-of-iron.
Believe me, I've spoken out
for your own good. I've put
a mirror in your hand.
Look hard at what you find.

> *Exit.*

BRAND [*gazing for a while in front of him; then suddenly exclaiming*]:
As I am now . . . as I was then . . .
where does truth end, error begin . . . ?
Blind man or seer, which man am I?

> AGNES *comes out of the house with a cloak over her shoulders and the child in her arms.* BRAND *does not see them. She is about to speak but stops as if struck by terror when she sees the expression on his face. At the same moment a* MAN *comes hurriedly through the garden gate. The sun sets.*

MAN: A word in your ear.
Watch out for the mayor.
You've roused an enemy.

BRAND [*pressing his hand against his breast*]:
An enemy indeed!

MAN: He's after your blood.
The good seed you'd sown,

thriving it was;
ay, really thriving.
Then up he slinks and says,
'The pastor's leaving.
I told you he would;
I said he'd be gone
at the first glint of gold.'
Well, that was that:
mildew and blight!
BRAND: If what he said was true . . . ?
MAN: Nay, pastor, not you!
  We all know the reason
  he's spreading poison.
  You always speak your mind;
  and you won't break or bend.
  That's what he can't abide.
BRAND: But suppose he's not lied . . .
MAN: Then you've betrayed us all;
  and yourself as well.
  Again and again you've said
  how you've been summoned by God,
  how your heart's home is here,
  how you're fighting this war
  right through to the end,
  here on your home ground;
  how brave men, once they're called,
  can't quit the fight, nor yield.
  It's been like a great song
  you've sung us. Ay, and strong
  and steady is the flame
  you've lit in many hearts.
BRAND: A rabble of deaf-mutes,
  and sleepers who won't wake.
  This battle's not for them.
MAN: Pastor, it is; as you
  well know! Things gleam and glow
  as never before, like the sunrise in Heaven!

BRAND: One in ten
  thousand turns to the light.
  The rest crouch in the dark.
MAN: You are a torch in the night!
  I'm not booklearned, sir.
  I live by inward prayer.
  It's you that's lugged me out
  from the depths of the pit.
  If you let go, I'm lost.
  You can't! I hold you fast!
  Bless you, sir! Praise the Lord!
  You'll not play false to Him;
  nor leave us to our doom.
    Exit.
AGNES [*timidly*]:
  Your cheeks are deathly white;
  your lips are bloodless; it
  seems that your very heart
  is crying out its hurt.
BRAND: Every resounding word
  is my accuser now.
  My own prophetic voice
  echoes with mocking force
  from that blank face of snow.
AGNES [*taking a step forward*]:
  I am prepared.
BRAND: Prepared? Prepared for what?
AGNES [*forcefully*]:
  For all that I must meet.
    GERD *runs past on the road outside and stops at the garden*
    gate.
GERD [*clapping her hands and shouting with a wild joy*]:
  Hey! Have you heard?
  The priest's flown away.
  And now the throngs
  of dwarfs and trolls,
  all swart and spry,
  swarm on the hills.

The spiteful things,
they scratched my eyes,
look! with their claws.
And half my soul
they tweaked and stole;
left me with half
a soul for life.

BRAND: Curb your tongue, girl.
Don't prance and shrill
so! I've not gone,
you simpleton,
I'm here!

GERD: O sir,
I can see *you* are.
But you're not him.
You're not the priest,
you're not. My hawk,
it swooped and hissed,
an angry gleam
through mist and murk.
With that one swoop
it snatched him up.
Away he rode,
the priest, astride,
as though with saddle,
whip, spur, and bridle!
His church stands cold and bare,
and its poor day is done.
But mine, now! Look at mine!
It soars so close to Heaven!
A true priest worships there.
His cope is woven
from strands of ice and fire.
And when he chants and sings,
the whole earth rings.

BRAND: You witch, why do you try
to lead my soul astray
with your wild riddles

of heathen idols?
    GERD *comes inside the garden gate.*
GERD: Idol? What does that mean?
    Ah . . . I know what it is.
    Sometimes it's like a man,
    but a giant in size.
    Sometimes it's very small,
    like a little doll.
    Always it's of gold.
    Sometimes it's like a child,
    a child fast asleep.
    [*Points.*]
    Is that your idol? Hey,
    don't snatch it away;
    let me take a peep!
    Let me touch, let me feel
    under that pretty shawl!
AGNES [*to* BRAND]:
    Have you any tears
    left? Have you any prayers?
    My sorrow's all been burned
    away, by dread . . .
BRAND: O Agnes, this poor
    mad creature – she has been sent
    by some all-seeing power . . .
GERD: Listen! Listen! That sound
    echoing round the fells!
    Look! Look! Look how they march
    and jostle to my church,
    trolls that the priest had drowned,
    all risen from the reefs,
    all summoned by the bells!
    Look there! A thousand dwarfs.
    The old priest locked them in,
    buried them in the screes,
    sealed with his holy sign,
    sealed with the Christians' cross.
    Look how they rise and swarm,

troll-children, the undead,
thronging the mountainside.
How they chatter and scream,
how they whimper and cry,
'Mother! Mother!' The womenfolk
gaze on them with joy
and fondle them; and some
give them their breasts to suck.
O look, they're in a dream!
All those good pious souls
walking with the trolls
as though among their own
dear children!

BRAND: Now be gone,
will you! Out of my sight!

GERD: Look! Do you see him sit,
do you, there where the road
starts to climb to the fell?
He's writing in his book
the names of his great flock.
Soon he will have them all.
How he's laughing! He's glad
the little church stands bare,
shut with bolt and bar;
glad the old priest has flown
far away through the murk
on the great hawk's back.
Hey! Catch me if you can!

   *She springs over the garden wall and disappears among
   the rocks. Silence.*

AGNES [*approaching, and speaking very quietly*]:
   And now we too must go.

BRAND [*staring at her*]:
   But where, though,
   out or in?

   *He points first to the garden gate, then to the door of the
   house.*

AGNES [*shrinking back in terror*]:

Brand! What do you mean?
Your child . . .
BRAND [*following her*]:
                    Answer me!
What am I first –
his father, or their priest?
AGNES [*shrinking back even further*]:
If a voice through a cloud
spoke in thunder, 'Reply!',
what could I find to say?
Not a word, not a word.
BRAND: You have a mother's right
to choose. This way, or that?
AGNES: Ask what you dare to ask,
I am your wife. My task
is simply to obey.
BRAND [*as if about to seize her arm*]:
Then I implore you: take
this cup of agony.
Drink of it, for my sake.
AGNES [*drawing back*]:
But if I did, I would not
have a mother's heart.
BRAND: So the judgement is given . . .
AGNES: What choice do you have . . . ?
BRAND: Is given and upheld.
AGNES: Do you truly believe
that you are called?
BRAND [*grasping her hand tightly*]:
Yes. Is it life, or death?
AGNES: Follow your true path.
BRAND: Then let us go.
AGNES [*tonelessly*]:
                    The road,
Brand; where does it lead?
[BRAND *is silent.* AGNES *points to the garden gate.*]
Is this the way?
BRAND [*pointing to the door of the house*]:

No, this.

AGNES [*lifting the child high in her arms*]:

That which you have dared

to ask of me, O Lord,

I dare to give to Heaven.

Accept my sacrifice.

Now lead me through your night.

She goes into the house. BRAND *stares blindly for a
moment; bursts into tears; clasps his hands over his head
and throws himself down on the steps.*

BRAND [*crying out*]:

Lord, grant me light!

ACT FOUR

Christmas Eve in the pastor's house. It is dark in the room. On the back wall, a door leading out; a window on one side of the stage, a door on the other. AGNES *stands dressed in mourning at the window and stares out into the darkness.*

AGNES: Another night. And still he's not
  returned. I've waited, my heart
  heavy with cry upon cry.
  And heavily, silently,
  the snow falls. Thick and soft,
  already it has roofed
  and robed the old church in white.
  Ah, what was that? The gate!
  Footsteps, now, at the door!
  Hurry, oh hurry!
  [*Goes to the door and opens it.* BRAND *enters, covered with snow, in travelling clothes, which he throws off during the following lines.*]
            My dear,
  dear love, how long you've been!
  O Brand, don't ever leave me again!
  I'm lonely; I can't endure
  this shadow-house when you're
  not with me. I'm so cold.
  Comfort me!
     BRAND *lights a candle; it glimmers faintly in the room.*
BRAND: My poor child,
  how pale you look, so very pale
  in the candlelight. Are you ill?

AGNES: No, no, not ill; but tired
   and faint with watching. I feared
   so much for you. Look, I've twined
   the few evergreens I could find
   as garlands for our tree.[12] They seem
   more like wreaths, though, for him . . .
   for our son . . .
      She begins to cry.
BRAND: He's dead and buried,
   Agnes. So let your tears be dried.
AGNES: Be patient with me. The hurt
   I had was deep. It will smart
   for a while. But pain
   withers. I shall be quiet soon.
BRAND: Agnes! Agnes! Is this how
   you keep Christmas – with sorrow?
AGNES: I beg you: bear with my grief.
   My little son . . . he was all life . . .
   and now . . . now . . .
BRAND: In his grave.
AGNES: Don't taunt me, for the love
   of God!
BRAND: It must be said.
   The more you are afraid
   the more you must hear
   his knell, as waves toll on the shore.
AGNES: You suffer. Will you not admit
   you suffer? Even now, the sweat
   glistens on your forehead.
BRAND: It's only spray from the fjord.
AGNES: That moisture on your cheek,
   what will you say that is? A flake
   of snow, melting? No, no, it
   flows from your anguished heart.
BRAND: Agnes, my own, my wife, let us both
   be steadfast, even unto death.
   Out there I was a chosen man
   indeed. I was God's champion.

While, in mid-fjord, the boat
laboured, sea-drenched I fought.
The tiller strained in my hand
yet steadied as it strained.
Eight souls froze at the oars
like corpses on their biers.
The mast groaned, cordage clashed, flung
loose on the wind. Our seams were sprung.
The canvas blew to shreds,
whipped to leeward. The seabirds'
cries were drowned. Through darkness I saw
cliff-falls, cataracts of snow,
crash down upon the rocks.
And all this while, He who makes
storm and calm held me to His will.
Through sea-howl I heard Him call.

AGNES: How easy it is to wage war
on the elements, and to dare
all. How hard it seems to wait
as I must, so very quiet,
while life ticks by; and be at home
to all the visitings of time;
and hear the ceaseless sparrow-
flutterings of sorrow
in the eaves of the heart's house.
I long to be of use
in the great world. I dare not
remember, cannot forget.
Know me for what I am.

BRAND: Agnes, for shame, for shame!
How can you think to scorn
your life's work, its true crown:
my helpmate and my wife?
Listen, and I'll reveal
strange mercies wrought from grief.
Sometimes, Agnes, my eyes fill
with tears of gratitude.
I think that I see God,

so close. As never before
I greet Him face to face,
feel His fatherly care.
Then I desire to cast
myself on His breast,
weeping in His embrace.

AGNES: And may He always appear
so to you, Brand. Fathers forgive.
It is tyrants who rave.

BRAND: O Agnes, you must ever fear
to question Him. Never presume
to turn your face away from Him.
I am the servant of the Lord.
I am the warrior with the sword
of righteousness. Your gentle hands
shall soothe and heal my wounds.
Agnes, embrace your task!

AGNES: Everything that you ask
of me seems too heavy to bear.
I'm so weary I can scarcely hear
what you say. Thoughts ravel my mind
without beginning or end.
I gaze at my own life
almost with disbelief.
My dearest, let me grieve
and I may learn to live
and serve you, purged of sorrow
at last . . . I don't know.
Brand, while you were away,
I saw my little boy
again, I saw him! He came
smiling into my room.
He looked, as once he did,
bright-eyed and rosy-cheeked.
He came towards my bed
as though to be cradled and rocked
in my arms. It made my blood run cold.

BRAND: Agnes!

AGNES: I knew that he'd turned
  to ice, out there in the icy ground.
BRAND: Believe me, Agnes, our child
  has been gathered to God,
  he is in Paradise.
  It is a corpse that lies
  out there under the snow.
AGNES [*shrinking away from him*]:
  Why do you tear and prod
  at the wound, make the blood flow?
  The body and the soul
  go down into the soil
  together. Together they rise up
  out of our mortal sleep.
  I cannot discriminate
  like you; I cannot tell them apart.
  To me they are as one,
  soul, body . . . my son.
BRAND: Many an old wound shall
  bleed to make you well.
AGNES: Stay by me in my need,
  Brand; for I'll not be led
  against my will. Please try
  to be gentle; speak gently.
  Your voice is like a storm
  when you drive a soul to choose
  its own poor martyrdom.
  Is there no gentler voice
  that says to pain, 'Be still,'
  no song that greets the light,
  no gentleness at all?
  Your God, I see Him sit
  just like some grim seigneur
  in His stronghold. I fear
  to irritate His gaze
  with my weak woman's cries.
BRAND: It seems, then, you'd prefer
  the God you knew before.

AGNES: Einar's mild God? Never!
  Yet I feel as if I were drawn
  by a longing for clear, pure air
  where it's drawing towards dawn.
  Your visions, your new realms,
  your calling, your iron will,
  everything looms, overwhelms,
  threatens me, like the cliff
  that would bury us if it fell
  or the fjord that cuts us off
  from the world. Brand! Brand! Such
  pain! And for what? Your little church
  that crouches under the rock
  like a mouse from a hawk?
BRAND [*struck*]:
  Again, again, that thought,
  like a tremor of air. What
  makes you speak so? Why do you say
  the church is too small?
AGNES [*shaking her head sorrowfully*]:
                        How can I
  give reasons? How do I know?
  How do the winds blow,
  how does a scent travel
  on the air? Must I unravel
  everything that goes through my mind?
  It is enough that I understand.
  Call it instinct, if you will.
  Brand, your church is too small.
BRAND: 'The young shall see visions and the old
  dream dreams.'[13] What mysteries unfold,
  my Agnes! Even she I met
  wandering on the mountain height
  in madness froze me with that call:
  'The church is hideous and small, small.'
  Whether she knew of what she spoke
  I cannot tell; but the womenfolk
  echo her, murmuring all the time,

as though possessed of the same dream,
visionary things, things yet unknown,
strange intimations of new Zion.[14]
Dear angel of my destiny,
you bless and guide me on my way.
The church is small, I see it now.
It shall be built anew,
and the Lord God shall enter in
to His own temple once again.

AGNES: From this time forward, let it seem
as if a wide deserted sea
lay blank between my grief and me.
I shall decide upon a tomb
and bury the dead hopes of life;
and make each mirrored citadel
vanish as in a fairy tale.
I'll be your consecrated wife.

BRAND: Agnes, the road leads on.

AGNES: You sound so cold and stern,
even now.

BRAND: It is God
who speaks, not I.

AGNES: You've said
that He is merciful
to those who faint and fall,
if they'll but persevere.
  She turns to leave.

BRAND: Agnes, must you go?

AGNES [*smiling*]:
It's Christmas Eve, my dear,
and I have things to do.
Last Christmas you chided me
a little for my extravagance:
a lit candle in every sconce,
and shining glass and greenery,
the room alive with laughter's song
and all the gifts that love could bring.
The candles shall be lit again;

we'll deck the tree; do what we can
to keep our Christmas, and rejoice
inwardly in the silent house.
If God should stare into this room
tonight, Brand, I need feel no shame.
I've watched and prayed, wiped every trace
of grief, each tear smudge, from my face,
you see; all gone now! I would meet
Him with a truly chastened heart.
    BRAND *pulls her towards him in an embrace; then abruptly
    lets her go.*
BRAND: Go, light the candles. There, hush!
AGNES [*smiling sorrowfully*]:
    And let the church be built all new
    and bright by the spring thaw.
    Let us make that our Christmas wish!
        Exit.
BRAND [*gazing after her*]:
    Help me, O help me, God,
    to spare her more agony.
    It's like watching her die
    in martyrdom's slow flame.
    What else must I perform
    that Your law may be satisfied,
    lex talionis,[15] Your hawk
    that will swoop down and take
    the heart out of her?
    Let me be the martyr,
    not her. Dear God! Haven't I faith
    and strength, and will, enough for both?
    Let her devoted love suffice.
    Remit, O Lord, remit the sacrifice.
    There is a knock at the door. The MAYOR *enters.*
MAYOR: Well, here I am, d'you see,
    come to eat humble pie!
    Sir, I'm a beaten man,
    beaten and trampled on!
BRAND: You, mayor?

MAYOR: I'm not joking.
  I tried to send you packing.
  I admit, I said at the time,
  I said, there isn't room
  for both of us. I was right,
  no shadow of a doubt,
  no doubt at all. Yet here
  I am with my white flag.
  My friend, I come to beg.
  There's a new spirit abroad
  in the region, praise God;
  suddenly it's everywhere,
  but not mine: *yours*,
  pastor. The war's
  over. Stop the fight.
  Now, let's shake hands on that!
BRAND: Between the two of us
  the strife can never cease;
  for spiritual war
  is endless, must be waged
  however bruised and scourged
  and desolate we are.
MAYOR: Don't try to win a fight
  if it pays you to lose:
  I call that compromise.
BRAND: Though you deride God's law,
  nothing can make black white!
MAYOR: My dear man, you can holler,
  'White as the driven snow,'
  till you're blue in the face.
  If our wise populace
  prefers snow to be black,
  then black it is. Hard luck!
BRAND: And what's your favourite colour?
MAYOR: Mine's a nice in-between
  delicate shade of grey.
  I've told you, I'm humane.
  I meet people halfway.

I don't gallop head-on
against opinion.
I let the crowd decide,
run with the multitude.
You're the crowd's candidate,
it seems; so here's *my* vote.
I've had to shelve my plans
for new ditches and drains,
for new jetties and roads,
and Lord knows what besides.
Still, if that's the game,
I'll play it. 'Bide your time,'
I tell myself, 'and smile.
Hang on to fortune's wheel
like the grim death. Your turn
always comes round again.'

BRAND: There speaks the 'public spirit'
in essence, mayor. It
seems, then, that greed, if shrewd,
can pass as zeal-for-good.

MAYOR: That's not how it is at all!
I've lived a life of real
self-sacrificing labour,
a man who's served his neighbour
more than he's served himself.
I spit on this world's pelf.
But surely, surely, it's fair,
isn't it, minister,
that honesty and good sense
should gain some recompense?
When all's been said you can't
let your own kith and kin
go hungry. I've got daughters.
I must think of their futures.
You know what that can mean.
Chewing on the ideal
won't get you a square meal
and it won't pay the rent.

    He who says otherwise
    doesn't know what life is!
BRAND: What will you do now?
MAYOR: Build.
BRAND: Did you say build?
MAYOR: I did.
    I'll serve the nation's need
    as I served it of old.
    I'll dazzle people's eyes
    with some great enterprise.
    I'll be cock of the roost,
    I'll strut upon my post.
    By God, you'll hear me crow
    pro bono publico![16]
    My new election cry
    is 'Banish poverty!'
BRAND: And how will you do that?
MAYOR: I've given it some thought.
    Well, come on, use your wits!
    What am I planning? It's
    my 'hygienic edifice',
    and cheap at the price!
    A workhouse and a gaol
    under the same roof;
    perfectly clean and safe
    and economical.
    Then, having made a start,
    I'll add an extra wing
    built to accommodate
    wassail, that sort of thing,
    banquets and lantern-slide
    lectures, what you will:
    the Patriots' Pledge hall.
BRAND: There may be some need
    for the things you name –
    but there is one thing more,
    with a far higher claim.
MAYOR: A madhouse, to be sure!

But who would foot the bill?

BRAND: Well, if you need to house
  your madmen, why not use
  the Patriots' Pledge hall?
  It would be suitable.

MAYOR [*delighted*]:
  The Patriots' Pledge hall
  a madhouse all the time –
  O pastor, what a scheme!
  How could it ever fail?
  We'll soon have crime and sin
  and madness all crammed in;
  then we'll cram in the poor
  and lock and bolt the door.

BRAND: You've come begging, you said.

MAYOR: I think that puts the case
  fairly enough. Indeed,
  cash for a worthy cause
  seems very hard to find.
  A well-placed word or two
  from 't'People's' Pastor Brand
  would turn the tide. You know
  I shan't forget a friend.

BRAND: I know I'm being bribed.

MAYOR: Couldn't it be described
  as the best way of healing
  old wounds, and that sad breach
  between us, from which each
  of us, I know, has suffered,
  since we're both men of feeling.

BRAND: *Suffered*, did you say?

MAYOR: Of course, of course, the boy . . .
  I trust that you'll accept
  condolences as offered.
  You seemed, though, so imbued
  with Christian fortitude
  I took it that the worst
  excess of grief had passed.

I came because I'd hoped . . .
BRAND: You've hoped and schemed in vain.
　I also plan to build.
MAYOR: To steal my master plan –
　well, I must say, that's bold!
BRAND: You say so? Look out there –
　[*Points out of the window.*]
　no, there; what do you see?
MAYOR: Not much, if you ask me!
　That old barn on the tilt?
　Look, I don't understand . . .
BRAND: The *church*. Mayor, I intend
　the *church* shall be rebuilt
　on a grander scale.
MAYOR: I'm master builder here.
　Just leave things as they are,
　I'll make it worth your while.
　Why pull the old place down?
BRAND: I have said: it is small.
MAYOR: Small? But I've never seen
　it more than half-full.
BRAND: There's no space, no air,
　for the spirit to soar!
MAYOR [*aside*]:
　If he goes on like this,
　he'll need the services
　of the madhouse himself.
　[*Aloud*]
　Pastor, take my advice,
　leave the church to the mice,
　I beg you, on behalf
　of the whole neighbourhood.
　I rise to the defence
　of our inheritance.
　An architectural gem
　destroyed for a mere whim?
　No, it can't be allowed!
BRAND: I'll build God's house with my

    own substance; dedicate
    every last farthing-bit
    out of my legacy.
MAYOR: Well! I'm thunderstruck!
    I can't believe our luck,
    I can't, truly, I can't!
    Riches without stint,
    a great gold, glittering stream –
    tell me it's not a dream!
BRAND: I made up my mind,
    long ago, to renounce
    that cursed inheritance.
MAYOR: I'm with you heart and soul,
    I'm filled with purest zeal.
    How's that for a surprise?
    Onward then! Hand in hand!
    Together, to the end.
    Here's to our enterprise!
    I dare to think that fate
    has brought me here tonight.
    I even dare to think
    that you have me to thank
    and that your miracle
    is mine after all.
BRAND: Destroy that 'hallowed fane'
    out there? Why, it's a shrine!
MAYOR: H'm, that's as may be.
    I must say, viewed from here
    now that the moon's so bright,
    it's exceedingly shabby.
    The weathercock and the spire,
    they're in a dreadful state!
    And the roof and the walls,
    ugly beyond belief,
    a mere hotchpotch of styles.
    Is that *moss* on the roof?
BRAND: And if the populace
    cried out, as with one voice,

'Leave the old church alone!',
what would you do then?
MAYOR: I'll show you what I'd do.
I know a trick or two
for rousing the nation.
I'll canvass, agitate,
start a petition.
If that doesn't succeed
in whipping up the crowd,
I'll tear the place apart
myself; and I'll be brisk
about it, even if
I have to set my wife
and daughters to the task
of demolition.
BRAND: Well, mayor, you've changed your
    tune,
slightly, since we began!
MAYOR: A liberal education
rids one of prejudice.
Good heavens, how time flies!
I must be on my way,
I must indeed. Goodbye,
Pastor, goodbye.
[*Takes his hat.*]
                     I'm
hot in pursuit of crime.
BRAND: What crime?
MAYOR: Early today
right on the parish bounds,
a gypsy tribe – such fiends
they are! I took the lot.
What do you think of that?
They're all snugly tied up
and under lock and key.
Well, not all. Two or three
managed to escape.
BRAND: And this is the season

of peace and goodwill!
MAYOR: All the more reason
  to clap them in gaol;
  they bring trouble and strife.
  And yet, they've cause enough.
  In an odd sort of way
  they belong to the parish;
  to you, even; though 'Perish
  the thought,' I hear you say.
  Look here, do you like
  riddles? Here's a joke.
  Decipher this rune:
  Not of your kith nor kin
  but of your origin.
  Why were we born?
BRAND: Where is the answer?
MAYOR: Not too hard,
  surely? You must have heard
  many and many a time,
  about that lad who came
  from yonder, from the West;
  as clever as a priest
  or four priests put together.
  This lad loved your mother.
  She'd property of her own,
  a few acres of stone,
  wouldn't be wooed nor wed,
  not she. Showed him the door,
  she did. And that put paid
  to *his* hopes. He went half
  out of his mind with grief,
  half out of his mind.
  But there it is. In the end
  he took another lass,
  a gypsy she was,
  and fathered a whole brood
  out of her gypsy blood.
  Those imps of sin and shame,

they're his, some of them.
Oh yes, we pay the fine
for his fine goings-on.
Why, one of his brats
even gets clothed and fed
out of the parish rates!
BRAND: Of course . . .
MAYOR: That troll-wench, Gerd.
BRAND: Now I begin to see . . .
MAYOR: A right riddle-me-ree.
    Who'd believe it? A lad
    goes silly in the head
    because of your mother,
    how many years ago?
    Now here you are. And I've
    to waste all Christmas Eve
    chasing his sons and daughters
    for miles across the snow
    in this foul weather.
BRAND: But whips and fetters . . . !
MAYOR: Pastor, don't waste your time.
    They're sunk in sin and crime.
    Shove them behind bars.
    Let charity go shares
    with Satan in this world.
    Keep Old Nick from the cold.
BRAND: Surely you had a plan
    to house the destitute?
MAYOR: My plan has been withdrawn
    in favour of your own.
BRAND: *If* you had my support . . .
MAYOR [*smiling*]:
    Well, you *have* changed your tune!
    [*Pats his shoulder.*]
    What's done can't be undone.
    Life has its rewards.
    And now I must be off.
    Merry Christmas. Regards

   to your good lady wife!
      Exit.
BRAND [*a brooding silence; then*]:
   Atonement without end,
   guilt with guilt intertwined,
   deadly contagion
   of sin breeding with sin;
   deed issuing from deed
   hideously inbred.
   Right ceasing to be right
   even as one stares at it!
   [*Goes to the window and looks out for a long while.*]
   The innocent must atone.
   Therefore God took my son.
   And the hurt soul of Gerd
   pays for my mother's greed.
   And it was Gerd's voice
   that drove me to my choice.
   Each generation
   of us hunted down
   by that just God, who is
   terrible to praise.
   The sacrificial will
   is what redeems man's soul!
   Even in those darkest days
   when grief and dread possessed
   me; and I saw that our child slept
   too deeply ever to be kissed
   awake; even then my prayers
   never ceased. Even then,
   amid all that pain,
   I was held, still and rapt,
   as though by some serene
   music, steadily drawing near,
   carried upon the air.
   But was I then restored?
   Did I speak with God?

Did He, then, turn His gaze
on this grief-stricken house?
The 'efficacy of prayer' –
what does that mean:
that prayer is a talisman
fingered by rich and poor,
a superstitious fear
that goes justly unheard,
an indiscriminate
battering at the gate
of the silent Word?
O Agnes, it's so dark!

> AGNES *opens the door and enters with the lighted candles*
> *in festive holders; a clear radiance suffuses the room.*

AGNES: The Christmas candles, look!

BRAND: Ah! How the candles gleam!

AGNES: Have I been long?

BRAND: No, no.

AGNES: It's like ice in this room.
   You must be frozen, too.

BRAND: No.

AGNES: Why are you too proud
   to show me that you need
   comfort? Why, my dear?

> *She puts wood in the stove.*

BRAND: Too proud?

> *He walks up and down.*

AGNES [*softly to herself as she decorates the room*]:
                       The candles here,
   so. He sat in his chair
   and laughed, and tried to touch,
   and said it was the sun.
   The sun! He was such
   a happy little boy.
   [*Moves a candlestick slightly.*]
   And a whole year has gone;
   and the candle shines clear

over the place where he lies.
And he can see us
if he chooses to come
and gaze in, quietly,
at the still candle-flame.
But now the window blurs
with breath-mist, like tears.
   She wipes the window.
BRAND [*slowly, following her with his eyes*]:
  When will the sea of grief
  subside and let her rest?
AGNES [*to herself*]:
  How clear it is; as if
  this room had opened out;
  as if the earth were not
  iron-hard and icy cold
  but soft, warm as a nest
  where our sleeping child
  can lie snug and secure.
BRAND: What are you doing there?
AGNES: Why, a dream; it was
  a dream.
BRAND: Snares are laid
  cruelly, in dreams, Agnes.
  Close the shutters.
AGNES: Brand,
  I beg you, don't be hard.
BRAND: Close them.
AGNES: There. It's done.
  [*Pulls the shutters to.*]
  My dreams will never offend
  God, of that I'm sure.
  He'll not grudge me a mere
  blessing in desolation.
BRAND: Grudge? Of course He'll not grudge!
  He's a lenient judge
  if you bow down to Him
  and if you grease His palm,

practise idolatry
a little, on the sly.
AGNES [*bursting into tears*]:
How much . . . oh how much more
will you make me endure?
BRAND: I have said: if you give
less than everything,
you may as well fling
your gift into the sea.
AGNES: All that I had, I gave.
There's nothing left of me.
BRAND: I have said: there's no end
to what God can demand
of us.
AGNES: I'm destitute,
so I've nothing to fear.
BRAND: Every sinful desire,
each longing, each regret . . .
AGNES: You've forgotten my heart's root!
Sacrifice that as well!
Rip *that* out! Rip it out!
BRAND: And if you grieve at all,
if you begrudge your loss,
then God will refuse
everything you have given.
AGNES [*shuddering*]:
Is this your way to heaven?
It's hard and desolate.
BRAND: Steep, narrow and straight;
and the will is able!
AGNES: But Mercy's path . . . ?
BRAND: Is hewn
from sacrificial stone.
AGNES [*staring in front of her, shaken*]:
Now I know what the Bible
means; now I can fathom,
as never before, those grim
words.

BRAND: Which words?

AGNES: 'He who sees
  Jehovah's face, dies.'

BRAND [*throwing his arms around her and pressing her close*]:
  Hide your eyes!

AGNES: Hide me!

BRAND [*letting her go*]:
                                No.

AGNES: You are in torment too.

BRAND: I love you.

AGNES: Your love is hard.

BRAND: Too hard?

AGNES: Don't ask me that.
  I follow where you lead.

BRAND: You think I drew you out
  of Einar's trivial dance
  unthinkingly, or by chance?
  Or that for nothing
  I broke every plaything?
  Or that for less than all
  I bound you to obey
  the unconditional
  demand for sacrifice?
  Woe befall us, I say,
  if ever that were so!
  Agnes, you were called
  by God to be my wife.
  And I dare to demand
  your *all*, even your life.

AGNES: I am yours; I am bound.
  Ask of me what you will,
  but don't, don't go away.

BRAND: My dear one, I must.
  I must find rest and peace.
  And soon I shall build
  my great church.

AGNES: My little
  church crumbled to dust.

BRAND: The heart's idolatry
  must be so destroyed!
  [*Embraces her as if in agony.*]
  Peace be with you, for then
  peace is with me and mine.
AGNES: May I move the shutter aside,
  just a little? Let me, Brand, let me.
BRAND [*in the doorway*]:

                       No.

   He goes into his room.
AGNES: Shut out, everything shut
  away. Where is my hope of Heaven?
  I cannot seek oblivion;
  or touch his hand and weep;
  or rend my body to escape
  from breathing this fierce air.
  There's no release from fear,
  the solitude that we call God.
  [*Listens at* BRAND*'s door.*]
  His voice moves on; so loud
  he cannot hear, and never will.
  High above grief the lords of Yule
  bring tidings to another world
  than mine. Even the Holy Child
  has turned away. He smiles on those
  with the most cause to sing His praise,
  fortune's good children, who enjoy
  His love like any longed-for toy.
  [*Approaches the window cautiously.*]
  But if I disobeyed
  Brand, if I opened wide
  the shutters, all this light,
  flooding the darkness, might
  comfort my little son
  out there under the stone.
  No, no, he's not dead.
  Tonight the child is freed,
  for this is the Child's feast.

But what if Brand knows best?
What if I now do wrong?
O little one, take wing!
This house of ours is sealed
against you, my own child.
Your father turned the lock
against you. Love, go back,
go back to Heaven and play.
I dare not disobey
Brand. Say that you saw
your father's sorrow –
how can you understand,
my darling? Let's pretend
it was his grief that made
this wreath out of leaves,
so pretty! Tell them, 'He grieves.'
[*Listens, considers and shakes her head.*]
No! You are locked outside,
my dear, by stronger powers
than doors or shutter bars.
Fierce spiritual flame
is needed to consume
their strength, make the vaults crack
open, the barriers break,
and the great prison door
swing loose upon the air.
I must purge the whole world
with my own sacrifice, child,
before I see you again.
And I shall become stone
myself, struggling to fill
the bottomless pit
of Brand's Absolute.
There's still a little time,
though; time for festival;
and though it's far removed
from Christmas as it was,
I'll be glad of what is,

give thanks for what I have –
the treasures that I saved
from the wreck of my life's good,
all of them, all of them!

> *She kneels down by the chest of drawers, opens a drawer
> and takes out various things. At the same moment* BRAND
> *opens the door and is about to speak to her but when he
> sees what she is doing he stops and remains standing
> there.* AGNES *does not see him.*

BRAND [*softly*]:
This hovering over the grave,
this playing in the garden of the dead!

AGNES: Here are the robe and shawl
he wore to his christening;
and here's a bundle full
of baby things. Dear heaven,
every pretty thing
he was ever given!
Oh, and I dressed him
in these mittens and scarf,
and this little coat,
to keep him warm and safe
when he went out
in spring for the first time.
And the things I prepared
all ready for the road,
that journey of his life
which was never begun.
And when I took them off
him, and put them away,
I felt so utterly
weary and full of pain.

BRAND [*clenching his hands in pain*]:
O God, spare me this!
How can I condemn
these last idolatries
of hers? She clings to them.

AGNES: Tear stains, here and here . . .

like pearls on a holy
relic. I see the halo
of inescapable choice
shine now, terribly clear.
This robe of sacrifice
was his and is mine.
I am a rich woman.

> *There is a sharp knock on the house door.* AGNES *turns*
> *round with a cry and, in doing so, sees* BRAND. *The door*
> *is flung open, and a* GYPSY WOMAN, *in ragged clothes,*
> *comes in with a child in her arms.*

GYPSY WOMAN: Share them with me, you rich lady!
AGNES: But you are richer than I.
GYPSY WOMAN: Mouthfuls of pretty words.
  Rich folk, you're all the same.
  Show us some good deeds!
BRAND: Tell me, why have you come?
GYPSY WOMAN: Tell you? Not I! Talk to a pastor?
  I'd as lief walk the storm again
  as hear your ranting about sin,
  and how us curs'd folk have no rest here.
  I'd as lief run until I die
  or leave my bones out on the skerry
  as look you in the eye, you black
  priest full of hell-fire talk!
BRAND [*softly*]:
  That voice, that face . . . the woman
  stands there like an omen,
  like a visitor from the dead.
AGNES: Rest, rest. If you are cold,
  come to the fire. If the child
  is hungry, he shall be fed.
GYPSY WOMAN: Can't stay, lady; can't rest.
  House and home, they're for the likes
  of you, not for us gypsies' sakes.
  Folk long since turned us out-o'-door
  for a bit lodging on the moor
  or in the woods, as best we can,

bedded on rock and the rough whin.
We come and go, and we go fast,
wi' lawyer-men, just like dogs,
howling and snapping at our legs.
Won't let us rest, yon lawyer-men,
clinking up close wi' whip and chain.
BRAND: Be quiet, woman. Here, you're safe.
GYPSY WOMAN: Safe? Here? Crammed in wi' walls and roof?
Nay, master, nay; we're better far
to wander through the bitter air.
But gi'e us something for the brat.
His own brother stole the clout
o' rags that he was swaddled in.
Look, lady, look, his naked skin
all white wi' frost and blue wi' cold!
BRAND: Woman, I beg you, set this child
free from the path of death-in-life.
He shall be cherished; every stain
of blood and guilt shall be washed off.
GYPSY WOMAN: Why, it was you folk cast him out,
it was, and now I curse you for it.
Where do you think, then, he was born?
Not in a bed! His mother took
bad at the bottom of a syke.
Christened he was, wi' a dab o' slush
and a charcoal stick out of the ash;
a swig o' gin his comforter.
And when we lugged him out of her,
who cursed him and his puny whine?
His fathers – ay, he'd more than one?
BRAND: Agnes?
AGNES: Yes.
BRAND: What must you do?
AGNES: Give them to *her*? O Brand! No!
GYPSY WOMAN: Oh yes, rich lady, all you have!
Ragged sark or silken weave,
nowt's too rotten or too good
if I can wrap it round his hide.

Like as not he'll soon be dead.
At least he'll die wi' his limbs thawed.
BRAND: The choice, Agnes! Hear the call,
   harsh and inescapable!
GYPSY WOMAN: You've plenty. You could dress your bairn
   ten times over. Look at mine!
   Spare us a shroud, for pity's sake!
BRAND: The demand, Agnes! Hear it speak,
   absolute and imperative!
GYPSY WOMAN: Gi'e us that, lady, gi'e us that!
AGNES: Don't you dare, gypsy! Desecrate,
   would you, my babe, my love,
   and all these pretty things?
BRAND: Hush, child.
   He's dead. I say: he died in vain
   if you lose faith. Then the road leads
   nowhere but to the threshold
   of the grave.
AGNES [brokenly]:
                           Thy will be done.
   With my last strength I'll tear out
   my heart, trample it underfoot.
   Share, then! Put my 'superfluous
   riches' to some better use.
GYPSY WOMAN: Give it here! Give it here!
BRAND: Agnes, did you say 'share'?
AGNES: Yes. I beg you, let me be killed
   now, and not be made to yield
   any more. Give her what she needs,
   half, even. Let me keep the rest.
BRAND: Then half would have sufficed,
   would it not, for your own son?
AGNES: Here, gypsy, take the christening-
   robe, and the scarf, and the silken
   bonnet; take everything
   that will keep out the cold.
GYPSY WOMAN: Gi'e us, then.

BRAND: Agnes, are you sure
  that's all?
AGNES: Here's the shirt he wore
  on the day he died. I called
  it his robe of martyrdom.
GYPSY WOMAN: It'll do. Is that the lot,
  lady? Right, then; I'll flit –
  after I've seen to him.
    Exit.
AGNES: Demand on top of demand –
  is it reasonable, Brand?
BRAND: Did you give with heart and soul,
  without bitterness at all?
AGNES: No!
BRAND: No? Then you have flung away
  your gifts, and you are still not free.
    He prepares to leave.
AGNES: Brand!
BRAND: Yes?
AGNES: Oh, Brand, I lied!
  Forgive me, for I hid
  the last, my very last
  relic. Hadn't you guessed?
BRAND: Well?
AGNES [*taking a folded child's cap from her bosom*]:
               Look, one thing remains.
BRAND: His cap?
AGNES: Marked with the stains
  of my tears, and his cold fever sweat;
  and kept close-hidden at my heart!
BRAND: Worship your idols, then.
    He prepares to leave.
AGNES: No, wait!
BRAND: For what?
AGNES: You know for what.
    She holds out the cap.
BRAND [*coming towards her without taking it*]:

Without regret?

AGNES: Without regret!

BRAND: Very well, then. His cap,
　give it to me. The woman
　is still there, sitting on the step.
　　Exit.

AGNES: Everything's gone now, everything's lost.

　　　[AGNES *stands for some moments completely still; grad-*
　　　ually the expression on her face is transformed into pure
　　　radiant joy. BRAND *returns; she goes exultantly to meet*
　　　him, throws her arms around his neck and cries out.]

　O Brand, O Brand, at last I'm free
　of everything that drew me to the dust!

BRAND: Agnes!

AGNES: The darkness has gone,
　and the ghosts, and the nightmares,
　the leaden fears that weighed me down.
　And I know that victory
　is certain, if the will endures.
　The mists have all dispersed
　and all the clouds have passed
　away; and at the end of night
　I see the first faint rosy light
　of dawn. And I'll not be afraid,
　or hurt, or weep to hear the word
　'death', or the sound of my child's name.
　I know that heaven is his home.
　I have overcome grief,
　and even the grave itself
　yields, and our little Alf
　shines in his immortality,
　his face radiant with joy
　just as it was in life.
　If my strength were a thousandfold,
　if my voice were like that
　of a great choir, if I could
　be heard in Heaven, I'd not
　plead, now, for his return.

How wondrous is our God,
how infinite His resource
in making His ways known
to men. Through the sacrifice
of my child, through the command
'Atone, and again, atone!',
my soul has been restored.
God gives, takes back, His own.
I was purged by ordeal,
You guided my hand,
you battled for my soul,
though your grim silent heart
cried out even as you fought.
Now it is you who stand
in the valley of the choice,
you who must bear the cross,
the terrible birthing
of all or nothing.

BRAND: You speak in riddles, Agnes. It
is finished, all that agony.

AGNES: Beloved, you forget:
'Whoever looks on God shall die.'[17]

BRAND [*shrinking back*]:
Dearest! What terrors wake
in my heart when you speak
like that! Be strong!
I could let all things go,
every earthly good; everything,
everything but you!

AGNES: Choose. You stand where the roads cross.
Quench this light new-lit in me,
choke the springs of divine grace,
allow me my idolatry.
The gypsy woman, call her back,
give me back the things she took.
Let me clutch them, weak and craven,
blindly ignorant of heaven.
Clip the wing-feathers of my soul,

fetter me at wrist and heel
with the constraints of each bleak day,
and then I'll be as I once was,
a prisoner of mortality.
Choose. You stand where the roads cross.
BRAND: All would be lost if I
    weakened, if I chose the way
    you point to . . . but . . . far from this place,
    beyond the memories
    of all this bitter grief,
    my Agnes, we shall find that life
    and light are one.
AGNES: But you are bound,
    by your own choice and His demand.
    You must remain; must be the guide
    of many souls in their great need.
    Choose. You stand where the roads cross.
BRAND: No choice . . . I have no choice.
AGNES [*throwing her arms round his neck*]:
    I give you thanks for all I have,
    and for your own dear love
    to me, poor, weary, stumbling one.
    My eyes are heavy, and the mist
    gathers, and I must rest.
BRAND: Beloved, sleep. Your work is done.
AGNES: Yes, the day labour, the soul's fight,
    are finished. Now the night-
    candle shall burn with steady flame
    as my thoughts rest on Him
    from whom we came.
        Exit.
BRAND [*clenching his hands against his breast*]:
    Be steadfast, O my soul,
    For in the loss of all
    This world's good lies our gain.
    We, at the end, are blest
    And all that we have lost
    Is ours for evermore. Amen.

ACT FIVE

SCENE 1

A year and a half later.[18] *The new church stands ready and decorated for the consecration ceremony. The river is close by. It is early misty morning. The church organ can be heard playing softly. A crowd is murmuring in the distance. The* SEXTON *is hanging up garlands outside the church. After a few moments, enter* SCHOOLMASTER.

SCHOOLMASTER: Sexton? Up with the lark!
SEXTON: I'm never one to shirk;
   not like some, schoolmaster.
   Pass me that bunting.
SCHOOLMASTER: They're
   making a dreadful din
   round at the pastor's house.
   Whatever's going on?
SEXTON: They're putting up a plaque,
   gold-plated if you please!
SCHOOLMASTER: Well, Brand's drawing the crowds,
   no doubt of that! The fjord's
   already white with sails.
   They're flocking in from miles . . .
SEXTON: He's chivvied folk awake,
   has Brand. But for what?
   In the old pastor's time
   everything was calm,

year in, year out.
Now it's all rage and strife.
SCHOOLMASTER: That's life, sexton, that's life!
  That's what it takes to build
  'the brave new world'!
SEXTON: Maybe. But I feel lost.
  This can't be for the best.
  Are you and I asleep?
  Are we both out of step?
SCHOOLMASTER: Others slept. We had work
  to do. And then they woke
  and said we'd had our day,
  just like they always say.
SEXTON: But you've just sung the praise
  of this newfangledness!
SCHOOLMASTER: 'When in Rome', sexton, 'when
  in Rome'! You've heard the dean.
  It's not for us to march
  contrary to the Church,
  the spiritual elite.
  We're servants of the state.
  But, sexton, man to man,
  I'm all for discipline.
  We live in troubled times.
  Why should we fan the flames?
  There's no reason to feed
  every faction and feud.
SEXTON: Brand, now; he's in the thick
  of things . . .
SCHOOLMASTER: Up to his neck!
  But then, of course, he's shrewd
  and very hard to catch.
  He knows the common herd,
  he's got the common touch.
  If he says, 'I've got plans,'
  no one asks him, 'For what?' –
  far-sighted citizens
  all clutching at his coat

and tagging at his heels
up hill, down dale, blind fools!
SEXTON: You've been in politics,
  you're wise to all such tricks;
  you know the public mind.
SCHOOLMASTER: This is the promised land,
  but who's it promised to?
  Will someone tell me that?
  I'd really like to know.
SEXTON: Listen!
SCHOOLMASTER: What's that?
SEXTON: That sound!
SCHOOLMASTER: Strange . . . the organ . . .
SEXTON: That's Brand
  for sure! Only Brand plays
  like that; sometimes whole days
  and nights.
SCHOOLMASTER: He's early.
SEXTON: Late,
  more like. I'll wager he's not
  slept at all. Since he became
  a widower, his soul's been gnawed.
  Sometimes, I think, he grows half-mad
  with grieving for his wife and son.
  And then he plays some endless tune
  as though, in every note you hear,
  they cry and he's their comforter,
  or he weeps and they comfort him.
SCHOOLMASTER: Ah, if only one dared
  let one's soul be stirred . . .
SEXTON: And if one weren't constrained
  by rules of every kind . . . !
SCHOOLMASTER: Right-thinking men must take
  a stronger stand. 'Lord, make
  me worthy to be mayor'
  is no ignoble prayer.
  That fire at the mayor's house,
  remember? The flames rose

and danced above the roof
and roared like Satan's laugh.
And the mayor's wife! Such screams,
as though she'd seen hell's flames
and seen Old Nick and all
agog for the mayor's soul!
'Stay clear! Let it all go!'
she begged. He wouldn't, though.
That good and faithful man,
he had the strength of ten,
saved every last receipt,
the archives, all complete!
The mayor – he's my ideal
official: heart and soul
a mayor; inside and out
and tooth and nail, the lot!
SEXTON: Brave deeds and words may seem
old-fashioned, but, like you,
I find that they ring true;
worthy of all esteem!
Folk ought to show respect
for standards, that's a fact.
SCHOOLMASTER: 'The old order must die,'
there's a fine rallying cry.
'Feed history to the fire,'
you hear that everywhere.
When they saw fit to pull
down the old church and all
that went with it, the custom
of our lives, their trim and form . . .
SEXTON: I was there, schoolmaster!
A great groan rent the air.
Folk were terrified!
Some had a look of shame;
some knew the fear of God,
I'd say, for the first time.
SCHOOLMASTER: For a while they felt bound
to the old in a thousand

ways. Then they took stock
of the new building work.
Dazzled by what they saw,
with a good deal of awe-
struck relish, one might say,
they awaited the great day.
Then, even as the spire climbed
higher, they grew alarmed.
Well, the great day has come.
SEXTON [*pointing to one side*]:
   Lord bless us, what a swarm
   of people! And that murmuring sound . . .
   the sea under a rising wind . . .
SCHOOLMASTER: The spirit of the age! It stirs
   the hearts of men with strange new fears,
   with the deep tremors of the time;
   as though a voice had summoned them.
SEXTON: I think . . . no, it's absurd . . .
SCHOOLMASTER: What is? . . .
SEXTON: That we've been stirred
   more than we dare admit.
SCHOOLMASTER: What nonsense! Do be quiet,
   sexton! We're both grown men,
   not silly maids at school.
   Discipline! Discipline!
      Exit to one side.
SEXTON [*to himself*]:
   Pah! Sexton, you're a fool;
   you'll blether yourself sick.
   'I think that we've been stirred . . .'
   Suppose the dean had heard!
   What *was* it that I saw . . . ?
   Agh, I don't want to know!
   Idle hands, idle talk . . .
      *Exit on the other side. The organ is suddenly heard
      very loudly, and the playing ends with a shattering discord.
      Shortly afterwards* BRAND *comes out of the church.*
BRAND: What have I made? Not music, not

music! Cries wrung from music's throat!
Splayed chords of discord, a groan
rising in the place of praise, the organ
stormed, faltered; as if the Lord sat
in the empty choir, raging and quiet,
rebuking with His presence the voice
of thanksgiving and sacrifice.
'Come, let us rebuild the Lord's house,'
how splendid that sounded! Promise
like fulfilment, a temple hall
sacred to the immortal will.
High-arching over the world's woes,
my great church: what a vision it was!
O Agnes, if you hadn't died,
things would be different indeed.
Heaven and home were near your heart.
You were the laurel of true life.
[*Notices the preparations for the festival.*]
Those garlands, flags on every roof,
the people swarming to my house,
I'm scorched and frozen by this praise!
God grant me light, or cast me out
to the oblivion of the pit!

    The MAYOR *enters in full regalia and greets* BRAND
    effusively.

MAYOR: So the great day is here!
  May I be first to cheer?
  I'm privileged to greet
  a personage so great,
  so honoured, so well loved,
  I truly feel quite moved.
  What a red-letter day!
  And how do you feel, eh?
BRAND: As though my heart would burst –
  into ashes, or dust.
MAYOR: Come, come, dear sir, come, come!
  I'll not permit such gloom.
  We want your very best

performance, the true zest,
thunder and lightning, all
the trimmings; yes, the full
range of your repertoire.
Everyone will be here.
The acoustics are first-class
too, so the dean says.
The dean is most impressed!
I also know he praised
the style of the architecture
and the size of the structure.
BRAND: Ah, so he's noticed that.
MAYOR: Beg pardon? Noticed what?
BRAND: It seems so very . . . big.
MAYOR: Seems? Is!
An awe-inspiring size!
BRAND: The things for which I've striven
are turned to parodies.
The new paradise?
A master-builder's heaven.
MAYOR: Folk here are well content,
so what more could you want?
All right, they're a bit dim.
So let's not worry them
with talk of 'truth' and 'light'.
Truth isn't worth the fright.
Just give them something big
and they're happy: church, dog-
house, it doesn't matter;
the bigger the better.
BRAND: A finger on the scales
and damn all principles!
MAYOR: For all our sakes, do try
to keep such thoughts at bay.
You've won the silver cup
for good citizenship.
I'll make a stirring speech,
we'll sing the 'Patriots' Song'.

And all's well in the Church.
Today let truth go hang!
BRAND: And at your liars' feast
who gives the loyal toast?
MAYOR: There's no call for abuse.
Just let me put the case.
Right now, my lad, you sit
as fortune's favourite.
The final accolade,
that's yours too. You'll be made
a knight, by royal grace,
Knight of the Cross (Third Class).
BRAND: I have my cross right here.
Deprive me if you dare.
You've never understood
my words – not a single word!
You take a metre rule
to measure the sublime
measureless universe,
God's grandeur over all;
visions of fire and ice,
those blazingly supreme
powers that radiate –
the focus, man's own heart!
I can't . . . I can't go on . . .
You speak to them! Explain . . .
    He goes up to the church.
MAYOR [*to himself*]:
'Grandeur' indeed! I think
he's mad. Or is he drunk?
    Exit.
BRAND [*coming down across the open space*]:
Never – not even on
the dark heights – so alone
as here and now, amid
this bleating multitude!
[*Looks in the direction which the* MAYOR *has taken.*]
He struts back to his lies

and safe hypocrisies.
O Agnes, O my dear,
unable to endure
the things that I've endured,
I'm lonely and I'm tired.
Here there's no gain, no loss.
Mere total emptiness.

DEAN [*arriving*]:
My dear flock! You poor sheep!
Poor sheep? Tch! A slip
of the tongue. Pastor! I'll
join you! A rehearsal –
my sermon, you understand –
must keep the text in mind.
Our thanks, sir, for the way
you've fought so manfully,
overcome doubt, abuse,
re-edified God's house.

BRAND: I dreamed a Church reborn;
a people cleansed, within.

DEAN: Oh, they'll be clean all right.
You'll find they wipe their feet.
A fine church! Resonant!
It echoes every tone –
two for the price of one;
a one-hundred-per-cent
profit. May I repeat
on behalf of the state
and of the diocese
our gratitude, our praise?
You'll hear many a wing'd word
sung at the festal board
in the mead hall! The luncheon
today. They did mention . . . ?
They did? Good! Colleagues of mine,
young up-and-coming men,
most eager to meet you. But
you're white as a sheet!

BRAND: I've spent my strength; I've failed;
  now I'm to be wassailed
  by such as you.
DEAN: Overwrought!
  Hardly surprising . . . fought
  the good fight, alone.
  But now that battle's won.
  Be cheered by such a day.
  Rest in your victory,
  revel in your reward.
  Just think of it: a crowd
  of thousands from the far-
  flung regions drawn to hear
  you speak, such is your fame!
  My colleagues, all of them,
  proud to sit at your feet.
  And then – the banquet!
  Talk of the fatted calf!
  The chef's excelled himself.
  Lord, what a spread! Tables
  groaning with comestibles!
  Look, I welcome this chance
  to speak in confidence . . .
BRAND: That's right, dean, turn the rack!
DEAN: Now, now, pastor, tck, tck! . . .
  in confidence, as I've said,
  and amity, let me add,
  concerning some slight
  details to be set right
  in your *unique* approach
  to matters of the Church.
  Put first things first: maintain
  custom and precedent.
  It saves embarrassment,
  or worse, in the long run.
BRAND: I don't think I quite heard . . .
DEAN: The Church fulfils a need.
  It's a repository

for the nation's soul,
for praise and glory
and patriot zeal.
It's a bulwark, a base
for true morality,
every good quality.
I'd have said 'treasure-house'
but these are straitened times.
Today, 'good Christian' chimes
best with 'good citizen',
if you see what I mean.
As the state keeps its eyes
fixed on an earthly prize,
so the state Church prefers
conformity as the theme
for its own officers.
BRAND: Your words touch the sublime.
DEAN: Let reason lead the way.
Reason can satisfy
two masters at one time
without rebuke or shame.
But don't ask every oaf
you meet, 'Is your *soul* safe?'
The modern state, young man,
thrives on republican
sentiments: equal rights
and so on; though it hates
real freedom like the plague.
Égalité?[19] Mere blague!
But you, with your quaint views,
discover avenues,
nooks, crannies, that reveal
we're not equal at all.
The state deals in numbers.
You speak of 'true members
one with another'.
You've caused us some bother.
BRAND: The eagle is brought down;

the goose soars to the sun.
DEAN: Thanks be to God, we're men,
   not fowls of the air.
   Still, if you must begin
   to quote, quote holy writ.
   You'll not improve on that.
   Genesis to Revelation,
   a wealth of quotation
   most instructive to hear.
   The Tower of Babel,[20]
   now there's a parable
   to conjure with. It seems
   written for our own times:
   everybody talking at once,
   nobody making sense.
   It's obvious you can't
   thrive without government.
   We all need rules. The odd
   man out, defying God,
   perishes by God's law.
   Solitude on the brain
   can drive a man insane!
BRAND: That vision Jacob saw[21]
   rising from earth to heaven:
   it is for that I have striven!
DEAN: Personal piety!
   That's different! When we die,
   of course we go to Him.
   (In confidence, ahem!)
   You talk of Jacob's ladder –
   a most uplifting text.
   Faith's one thing, life's another.
   Try not to get them mixed.
   Six days a week we toil,
   'our duties to fulfil';
   the seventh day, we rest;
   piety soothes the breast.
   Religion's like high art,

much better kept apart
for those who can commune.
Be sparing with the Word.
Don't scatter it like seed,
or pearls in front of swine.
I know how you must feel,
in love with the ideal,
seeking for some crusade;
but let me be your guide.
Things are done differently
in the harsh light of day.
There must be discipline.
Some things are just not done.
We must know where we stand.
I've spoken like a friend.
BRAND: You'll find I don't fit in
to your contrivance, dean.
DEAN: Tut, tut! tut, tut! You must!
You'll find that we insist:
'Good servant, come up higher . . .'
BRAND: By plunging in the mire!
DEAN: 'The meek shall be exalted'[22] –
now how can that be faulted?
BRAND: Dean, I'm ill-qualified
to serve. Bring out your dead.
DEAN: God help us all, you can't
believe that I would ever . . .
BRAND: Conscript a cadaver?
You would! The man you want,
that focus of your hopes,
is a convenient corpse
down at the mortuary,
a bag of bones bled dry.
DEAN: Bled dry? God bless my soul,
young man, I'm not a ghoul!
I speak with fair intent.
For your own betterment,
for your future career,

you must knock on the right door.
BRAND: Dean, when the cock crowed thrice
    it sounded like your voice.
    Do you suppose that I'll
    deny . . . ?
DEAN: Who said 'denial'?
    Eschew every risk –
    that's not much to ask.
BRAND: 'The fear of strife, the greed for gain,
    Upon thy brow the mark of Cain,
    Emblazoned there when thou did smite
    Innocent Abel in thy heart.'[23]
DEAN [aside]:
    Far too familiar!
    Why can't he call me 'sir'?
    [Aloud]
    I fear that we must cut
    short our little debate.
    To sum up what's been said:
    you can't hope to succeed
    unless you come to terms
    with the mood of the times.
    It's just as the mayor says –
    this nation's changed its ways,
    and soft and soothing words
    prevail, and blunted swords.
    Why, even our poets
    take care now to carol
    their praise of the moral,
    the civil, pursuits.
    'More mediocrity',
    that's now the nation's cry.
    'It's better to be led,
    citizens, than to lead!'
BRAND: God, to be gone from here!
DEAN: One finds one's proper sphere,
    all in good time. Be calm,
    acquire a uniform

in keeping with the age. A
drill-sergeant or drum-major
drumming up church parades,
the Eucharistic squads,
a pastor marching his
recruits to Paradise.
A man can do things blind-
fold, my young friend,
if he's a believer.
Well, well, think it over.
There's a lot to be done.
I really must rehearse
my forthcoming address.
I need to strike the *ton*.
By the way, Brand,
by the way, I intend
to take as my main theme
'Spirit versus Flesh' – you know –
Dualism, the tragic flaw,
it's all here. Have I time
for a quick – ah – repast?
  Exit. BRAND *stands for a moment, stricken by his own*
  thoughts.
BRAND: Like Mammon's trumpet-blast
  taunting my sacrifice,
  making the clouds disperse,
  showing me the depraved
  spirits that I served,
  how hideously that creature 'spake'
  the truth, though never for truth's sake.
  This bitter place has drained my blood
  and buried all my earthly good
  and ruined all my great design
  and nothing that was mine is mine
  except the soul that I withhold
  from the smooth demons of the world.
  The holy dove has not descended.
  If I could find once more on earth

faithfulness answering my faith,
and know that solitude had ended . . .
[EINAR, *pale, emaciated, dressed in black, comes along the*
road and stops as he sees BRAND.]
Einar!
EINAR: That is my name.
BRAND: Einar, it's like a dream!
  I prayed I might find one
  person not made of stone.
  Let me embrace you!
EINAR: Please
  refrain. I've reached my haven.
BRAND: You reject my embrace?
  So you've still not forgiven?
EINAR: What was there to forgive?
  Reprobate that you are,
  I know you for a mere
  instrument of God's love
  to me, His child of grace.
BRAND: Harsh words.
EINAR: Pure words of peace
  that we, the blessèd, learn
  when our souls are reborn.
BRAND: Strange – for wild rumour said
  that you'd gone to the bad—
EINAR: But true! I went astray
  lured by the world's display,
  believing its false gauds,
  with pride in my own words,
  my songs as they were called.
  How little they availed!
  But, God be praised, He broke
  my strength to draw me back.
  He thrust me down: I sank
  into His mire; I drank
  brandy and took to cards.
BRAND: You call such tricks the Lord's?
EINAR: He tested my poor worth

with sickness unto death;
and I was stripped of all
I had. In hospital,
in my delirium,
I saw swarm upon swarm
of monstrous bloated flies.
Then, after my release,
I met – and not by chance,
by divine providence –
three sisters, three pure souls
who freed me from the toils
of sin, and from the world.
And I became a child
of grace. God's ways with us
are strange; and various
are the paths we must tread
to our doom or reward.
BRAND: Various indeed! And then?
EINAR: I sought my brother-man,
brought him to God. At first,
as an evangelist,
I plucked many a soul
from fiery alcohol
till I began to dread
the old pull that it had.
So I'm joining a mission
for Bible propagation
among the heathen.
BRAND: Where?
EINAR: Far enough from here –
among the Negroes, so I'm told –
Caudates[24] I think they're called.
BRAND: Look, Einar, won't you stay,
at least for today,
just for the festival?
EINAR: No. I bid you farewell.
BRAND: Has nothing, then, remained;
no glad or grieving thought,

no tenderness of heart,
no warmth of any kind?
EINAR: Ah, the young female who
enticed me, to my woe,
before faith made me pure!
Well, what became of her?
BRAND: Agnes became my wife.
You hadn't heard? Our life
knew grief as well as joy.
EINAR: That doesn't signify.
BRAND: We were blessed with a son,
our only child. He soon
died, though, our little boy.
EINAR: That doesn't signify.
BRAND: And then Agnes died.
Close by my church I laid
them both to rest. Now say,
'That doesn't signify'!
EINAR: Such things mean nothing. Tell
me: what of her state of soul?
BRAND: She fell asleep with utter faith
in new life dawning after death;
by love and gratitude possessed
and strength of will, until the last
breath of her being. Thus she died:
trusting the great things that abide.
EINAR: Vaingloriousness and sham
piety to cover shame!
What assurances did
she have?
BRAND: Firm faith in God;
rock-firm!
EINAR: That won't avail
her now. She's damned.
BRAND [*calmly*]:
                        You fool.
EINAR: Both reprobate; both damned;

you – and she whom you named.

BRAND: You dare say that? You who were
　　sprawled in corruption's mire?

EINAR: But newly risen without stain!
　　I was immersed in the divine
　　wash-tub; pounded by the dolly-
　　stick of His anger! I was wholly
　　cleansed on the scrubbing-board of our
　　redemption, by the soap of prayer!

BRAND: Soap of prayer? Spit it out!

EINAR: I am pure heavenly wheat;
　　and you, chaff for the fire.
　　I can smell sulphur here.
　　I see the devil's horns.
　　　Exit. BRAND *looks after him for a few moments; then
　　　suddenly his eyes light up.*

BRAND [*exclaiming*]:
　　And I have burst the chains
　　you bound me with! I shrug
　　them off. From now on I
　　fight under my own flag
　　whether or not any
　　man chooses to follow.

MAYOR [*entering hurriedly*]:
　　Brand! Be a good fellow
　　and hurry up. It's late
　　and they're shouting, 'Why wait?'
　　and 'Start the procession!',
　　'We want Pastor Brand!',
　　and so on, in a fashion
　　most unseemly. They're
　　getting out of hand.

BRAND: Then let them, Mister Mayor,
　　I'll not chaffer again
　　with you, or any man
　　who jumps at your nod.

MAYOR [*shouting*]:

Keep back, back to the road!
[*More quietly*]
My dear pastor, I urge
you, wield the scourge,
exert your influence
as a man of the cloth!
We'll be trampled to death!
Too late! There goes the fence!
    The CROWD *surges in and breaks in wild disorder through*
    the festive procession towards the church.
ONE OF THE CROWD: Pastor, give us a sign!
ANOTHER: Show us the new Zion!
DEAN [*overrun by the mob*]:
  Use your authority,
  mayor!
MAYOR: They won't heed *me*!
SCHOOLMASTER: Pastor, for pity's sake,
  don't just stand there. Is this
  the truth you promised us?
  Make them see reason. Talk
  to them; turn their minds
  to higher things!
BRAND: Fresh winds,
  fresh winds of change are blowing,
  purging and renewing!
  [*Shouts to the* CROWD.]
  Here's where the roads divide;
  here you must turn aside
  out of the old rut,
  to seek the Absolute,
  God's one true dwelling place!
AN OFFICIAL: He's mad!
A CLERIC: It's a disgrace!
BRAND: I *was* mad. I believed
  that even you still served
  the mighty God of truth.
  I set foot on the path
  that led to compromise.

I played your petty games;
I walked as you walk;
I talked in your terms.
So, my church was too small.
So, I thought I'd amaze
God Himself with the bulk
of His new citadel.
In my pride I forgot
that the words 'all or nothing'
mean what they say. The trumpet
of His judgement has shrilled
above this place. I'm filled
with dread and self-loathing,
as David stood accurst
for an unholy lust.
But this much is certain:
the riches of Satan
are our self-betrayals,
are our perjured souls.

ONE OF THE CROWD [*in mounting excitement*]:
    He's right! We must have been
    blind!
ANOTHER: Cast them out!
ANOTHER: Swine!
BRAND: 'Close behind thee squats the Fiend.
    In his meshes thou art bound.
    By his wiles thou art possessed,
    All thy hardihood laid waste,
    Made a stranger to thyself,
    Drowned in desolation's gulf.'
    You who go to church to stuff
    your souls with solemn fustian,
    tell me: was that spiced enough?
    Or did it seem un-Christian?
    You love the organ and the bells,
    love to hear a well-rehearsed
    sermon full of little thrills,
    trills of dogma nicely phrased,

sacred torrents in full spate,
cascades of the speaker's art.
MAYOR [*aside*]:
  He's hit the dean off, loud and clear.
DEAN [*aside*]:
  Surely he must mean the mayor.
BRAND: The candles in the holy place,
  the vestments and the carapace
  of piety, that's all you ask:
  pantomimes to send you home
  deafened, surfeited, and dumb,
  fitted for the daily task,
  glad to put your souls away
  in camphor with your Sunday best,
  ready for the next day of rest,
  unready for the Judgement Day.
DEAN: Citizens, eschew that man!
  He's not a Christian. Well, I mean,
  he spurns our faith!
BRAND: You speak of faith?
  That's long since vanished from the earth.
  It vanished when man lost his soul.
  It doesn't answer when you call.
  Show me the man who has not cast
  spiritual treasure in the dust
  and ashes of a wasted life.
  Jigging to the scrawny fife,
  clown and cripple show their legs,
  dance themselves into the muck
  of blasphemy before the Ark,[25]
  all drained and bitter as the dregs.
  It's reckoning time: 'Repent! repent!'
  Time for amendment and for cant.
  Hey presto, penitence and prayer!
  Hey presto, 'Save us from despair!'
  What a sick parade of wretches
  lurching towards heaven on crutches,
  maimed in body and in soul,

besieging mercy's citadel!
Yet listen to the voice of God:
'Give me now thy precious blood,
give to me of thy pure spirit.
Thou art chosen to inherit.
Be then as a little child:
· be the child within the man;
flesh and spirit undefiled,
enter into thy domain.'
MAYOR: Unlock the church, then.
ONE OF THE CROWD [*crying out as if in anguish*]:
No! No!

Pastor, tell us what to do!
BRAND: Jerusalem's temple, seek it out,
that altar blazing on the height.
It is the earth on which we stand,
the world of Adam reordained.
Let faith be life; your daily work
like David's dance before the Ark.
Then truth and dogma shall be one,
and body shall belong to soul,
and soul embody the divine,
and majesty shall be the small
child's wonder at the Christmas game;
shall be the starlight through the storm.
There is movement, as of a storm, among the CROWD;
some shrink back; most gather closely around BRAND.
ONE OF THE CROWD: He brings us light! Drives out the dark!
DEAN: Scoundrel! Seducer of Christ's flock!
Desist at once, d'you hear?
Have him arrested, mayor!
MAYOR: Not I! I'd be a fool
to fight with a mad bull.
Let him bellow and snort.
Let him tire himself out.
BRAND: Far from this hideous place,
from Pilate, from Caiaphas,[26]
still shines the promised land

and the unfinished quest.
Here I'm no longer priest.
Snatch this key from my hand
if you dare.
[*Throws it into the river.*]
          I revoke
my covenant. I take
back from you each gift
I ever gave. What's left
is all yours, child-of-dirt,
feeble-thought, faint-heart!
MAYOR [*aside*]:
  There goes his Knight's Grand Cross.
DEAN [*aside*]:
  There goes his diocese.
BRAND: You who are still young,
  with strength to stay the course,
  awake from the dead sleep
  of shame and compromise
  and dust and squalor.
  Listen to the air sing
  over summit and steep.
  Arise, arise, and learn
  what it is to be men
  possessed of true valour
  in a holy war!
ONE OF THE CROWD: Lead on, pastor, we'll
  follow you anywhere!
BRAND: Follow, then, those who will!
  March away across the frozen
  crests, across that sea of snow,
  to valleys waiting for the thaw.
  'Rouse the captives in their prison,
  Topple Dagon[27] at his feast;
  By your strength and your example
  Be the builders of the temple,
  Make of every man a priest!'

The CROWD, *which includes the* SEXTON *and the* SCHOOL-
MASTER, *surges around him.* BRAND *is raised aloft on the
men's shoulders.*

ONE OF THE CROWD: Such visions!
ANOTHER: Ah, such prophecies!
  Like the sun to our eyes!
DEAN [*as they begin to leave*]:
  Visions? Visions? You're blind!
  Led astray by the Fiend!
MAYOR: You hear what the dean says!
  Stay put in the parish;
  enjoy the good life;
  avoid stormy seas,
  good people, or perish.
  You fools, are you deaf?
ONE OF THE CROWD: Our lives are now the Lord's!
MAYOR: You wait! You'll eat your words!
ANOTHER: The Israelites were given
  manna from heaven![28]
MAYOR [*shaking his fist at* BRAND]:
  Disgraceful! But you'll pay
  for this, come reckoning day!
DEAN: The scoundrel! O my sheep,
  my stipend! I could weep.
MAYOR: They haven't gone far yet.
  They'll soon start to bleat.
    He follows them.
DEAN: Hey! Where are you going?
  What on earth's the mayor doing?
  Is he out of his mind?
  This stirs up my old blood!
  I'll follow them; by God,
  I'll not be left behind.
    Exit.

SCENE 2

At the highest pasture of the village. The landscape rises in the background and turns into vast, desolate mountain heights. It is raining. BRAND, *followed by the crowd – men, women, and children – comes over the slopes.*

BRAND: Look up, look far and high!
  Fare forward to your spirits' home,
  you men-of-God! Your dead selves lie
  behind you in the valley gloom.
A MAN: My old dad, he's worn out.
ANOTHER MAN: Gi'e us summat to eat.
A WOMAN: And we're that parched wi' thirst.
BRAND: On, on to the crest!
SCHOOLMASTER: But which way?
BRAND: Any road
  that gets us there is good.
SEXTON: The Ice Church is up there.
ANOTHER WOMAN: Eh, but my feet are sore.
BRAND: The steep way's the shortest.
  Fight! When you've fought, rest.
SCHOOLMASTER: Give them strength; their courage fails!
ONE OF THE CROWD: Miracles, we want miracles!
BRAND: You want! You want! The mark
  of slavery's deep in you yet!
  You want profit without sweat.
  Press forward; or fall, back-
  sliding into the grave.
SCHOOLMASTER: He's right . . . we must be brave.
  We shall have our reward.
BRAND: As surely as the Lord
  turns on us His just gaze!
ONE OF THE CROWD: Hear him! He prophesies!
ANOTHER: Pastor, will the fight be hot
  and bloody?

ANOTHER: Oh, I hope it's not.
ANOTHER: What's my share when we've won?
ANOTHER: Don't take my only son.
SEXTON: Will the victory be ours
  by Tuesday, d'you suppose?
BRAND [*looking around the crowd, bewildered*]:
  What is it? What do you want?
SEXTON: We want the full account.
  First: how long will it last?
  Second: what will it cost?
  Third: what's the profit for us?
BRAND: So that's the question!
SCHOOLMASTER: Yes,
  pastor. We want the truth,
  'straight from the horse's mouth'.
BRAND: How long will the strife last?
  Till you have sacrificed
  all your earthly good,
  every last farthing;
  till you have understood
  what the words 'all or nothing'
  truly mean; till you control
  your own strength, your own soul.
  What will your losses be?
  Ancient idolatry,
  and servitude that shines
  weighed down with golden chains
  and deep pillows of sloth,
  your thraldom to earth.
  What will the victor's wreath
  be? It will be faith
  raised up; it will be joy
  in sacrifice; integrity
  of the soul; everyman's
  triumph, his crown of thorns!
ONE OF THE CROWD [*furiously*]:
  Judas! We've been betrayed!

BRAND: I have kept my word!

ANOTHER: You promised victories –
  but talk of sacrifice,
  and ask us to lay down
  our lives for those unborn.

BRAND: To get to Canaan we must pass
  like Moses through the wilderness.
  All who keep faith shall walk this road
  as victors chosen of the Lord.

SEXTON: Here's a fine to-do.
  We'll never dare to show
  our heads.

SCHOOLMASTER: We can't go home,
  Sexton, think of the shame.

SEXTON: We can't go on. We're stuck,
  for certain-sure.

ONE OF THE CROWD: Turn back!

ANOTHER: Hey! Stone him, lads!

ANOTHER: Curse
  him!

SCHOOLMASTER: 'Thou shalt not murder.'²⁹
  And our plight would be far worse
  without a leader.

A WOMAN [*pointing back down the path*]:
  Lordy – the dean – it's *him*!

SCHOOLMASTER: Please try to stay calm!
    The DEAN *arrives, followed by a few of those who had
    stayed behind.*

DEAN: O my flock,
  hear your old shepherd speak!

SCHOOLMASTER [*to the* CROWD]:
  Too late, too late. We'd best
  follow the pastor now.

DEAN: You plunge knives in my breast,
  you set thorns on my brow!

BRAND: Dean, dean, you've tortured souls
  year in, year out.

DEAN: O heed

him not, my friends. He's fed
you dreams and wicked tales.
ONE OF THE CROWD: Ay, that he has!
DEAN: The Church
is ready to forgive
those who show true remorse.
Look deep in your own hearts
and surely you'll perceive
the black and hellish arts
you're caught with.
ONE OF THE CROWD: Why, of course!
We were deceived!
ANOTHER: The wretch!
DEAN: What weapons can the humble wield
upon the heroes' battlefield?
And how, I wonder, would you fare
helpless between the wolf and bear,
between the eagle and the hawk?
The strong prey on the weak,
and you are weak, my lambs.
Go back to your homes.
ONE OF THE CROWD: True! Everything he says!
SEXTON: We locked the village doors
and threw away our keys.
There's nothing left that's ours.
SCHOOLMASTER: For my part, I'm prepared
to put in a good word
or two for the priest.
We slept in the past.
He opened our eyes
to a world of old lies;
brought life where there was none.
I say we've been reborn!
DEAN: Such feelings will soon pass.
You'll fold to the old crease,
you'll plod down the old rut,
I can promise you that.
BRAND: Choose – all of you!

ONE OF THE CROWD: We want –
  we want to go back!
ANOTHER: We can't!
  Move forward!
ANOTHER: To the crest!
MAYOR [*arrives, running*]:
  What luck! Found you at last!
  Must catch my breath . . .
A WOMAN: Sir, please
  don't take it out on us,
  we never meant no harm.
MAYOR: Be quiet . . . What a climb!
  Listen to me, you'll all
  be rich by nightfall!
ONE OF THE CROWD: Rich by nightfall, he says!
MAYOR: A mighty shoal of fish
  out there in the fjord –
  millions – all yours to take –
  you'll find they jump aboard –
  I've never seen the like
  in all my born days!
  It's new life for the parish.
  Come home with me, good folk!
  This is no time for talk!
BRAND: Choose between God and Mammon!
MAYOR: Don't heed him. Use your common
  sense!
DEAN: It's an oracle
  from heaven; a miracle
  beyond your wildest dreams,
  eh, children, eh, my lambs?
BRAND: If you yield now, you're lost.
ONE OF THE CROWD: Fish in the fjord – the most
  there's ever been!
MAYOR: Billions!
DEAN: Bread for your little ones,
  gold coins in your pockets.

MAYOR: Don't question luck; it's
   high time for you to learn
   what things to leave alone
   and where to stake a claim.
   Fare forth, my friends, bring home
   the bounty of the deep.
   No need for blood and sweat,
   no need at all. Let's keep
   sacrifice out of it.
BRAND: Sacrifice is written in words
   of fire, blazing high in the clouds!
DEAN: It depends how you feel,
   of course. Any fine Sunday I'll
   be happy to extol
   sacrifice to one and all.
MAYOR: Yes, *some* fine day, eh, dean?
SEXTON [*to* DEAN]:
   Look, sir . . . you'll keep me on?
SCHOOLMASTER [*to* DEAN]:
   You'll not have me dismissed
   (heaven forbid) from my post?
DEAN [*quietly*]:
   Well, again, that depends –
   a quiet word with your friends . . .
   Make the crowd walk *our* way,
   then, no doubt, leniency . . .
   you understand? h'm? h'm?
MAYOR: Come on, we're wasting time!
SEXTON: I'm off to find my boat.
ONE OF THE CROWD: The pastor . . . what about?
SEXTON: Argh! Let him rot, the fool . . .
SCHOOLMASTER: 'Tis the Lord's will, the Lord's will.
MAYOR: Act as God's law requires
   with all such thieves and liars.
ONE OF THE CROWD: He lied to us!
ANOTHER: He lied
   to us!

DEAN: Nothing but lies.
  If you ask me, he's
  not even qualified!
ONE OF THE CROWD: The nerve!
ANOTHER: What *has* he got?
MAYOR: The Order of the Boot!
SEXTON: That fellow's a wrong
  'un; I've said so all along!
DEAN: He cursed his dear mother
  as she lay at death's door,
  refused her communion.
MAYOR: He killed his own son.
SEXTON: He broke his poor wife's heart.
A WOMAN: Men like that should be shot.
DEAN: Cruel father, cruel spouse!
  What, I ask, could be worse?
ONE OF THE CROWD: He tore the old church down.
ANOTHER: Locked us out of the new 'un.
MAYOR: The scoundrel stole my plan,
  my gift to the insane.
BRAND: That gift? It's yours, mayor,
  all yours: madness, despair!
ONE OF THE CROWD: Flay him!
ANOTHER: Throttle him!
ANOTHER: Shut
  his mouth!
ANOTHER: Out! Out!
CROWD [*bellowing*]:
                      Out! Out! Out! Out!
    BRAND *is driven and stoned across the wastelands. Then,*
    gradually, his pursuers return.
DEAN: My children, O my lambs,
  return to your homes!
  Gaze with repentant eyes
  on God, all-good, all-wise.
  He'll not eat you. He'll
  not pack you off to hell.
  You'll find the government

extremely tolerant;
the justices of the peace
will fold you in their embrace
while I, in my own right,
exude sweetness and light.
MAYOR: We're ready to appoint –
(by 'we', of course, I mean
myself and the dean) –
a regional committee
to deal with each complaint
in peace and charity.
A clergyman or two,
the schoolmaster, he'll do;
the sexton; plus a couple
more, two sturdy sons of toil
picked out from the people
to sit with their betters.
We'll give you all you want,
progress, enlightenment,
self-help? free thought? We'll
knock off your fetters!
DEAN: Why, yes. We'll ease your load,
just as you've lightened mine
(I can rest easy again!)
so rejoice and be glad.
And now, get back to work.
Good fishing, and good luck!
SEXTON: True Christians both, as fine
as ever I've seen!
ONE OF THE CROWD: Oh yes! They know what's right.
SEXTON: They don't tell you to 'fight,
fight till you drop'!
SCHOOLMASTER: You feel those two can cope
with more than mere pieties.
They know what life is.
   The CROWD *begins to move down the slopes.*
DEAN [*to* MAYOR]:
Well, that's improved the tone,

all the harm's been undone
and reaction's restored,
praise be to the Lord!

MAYOR: And who, may I inquire,
came and put out the fire?
Who else but yours truly!

DEAN: Tch, mayor, that's a wholly
uncalled-for remark!
'Twas the Lord's handiwork.

MAYOR: You think so?

DEAN: Yes, that shoal
in the fjord . . .

MAYOR: That wasn't *real*.

DEAN: You uttered an untruth?

MAYOR: I just opened my mouth –
hey Bingo – out it came!
Don't tell me that's a crime.

DEAN: Such sleights may be allowed,
my son, in time of need.

MAYOR: In dire emergencies
what are a few white lies?

DEAN: I'm neither prig nor prude.
   [*Looks across the barren wastes.*]
Good heavens above! Look there –
isn't that our friend
limping over the ground?

MAYOR: Like a lost warrior
seeking his lost crusade.

DEAN: And trudging close behind –

MAYOR: Poor Gerd, I do declare!
Well, they're two of a kind.

DEAN [*jestingly*]:
He'll need an epitaph.
How's this for a laugh?
'Here lies a pure young pastor.
He was a pure disaster.
He's left, of all he had,
one convert, and she's mad.'

MAYOR [*with his finger on his nose*]:
    But, come to think of it,
    his treatment's not been quite –
    how can I put it – *fair.*
DEAN [*shrugging*]:
    Vox populi, vox Dei,[30] mayor!
        Exeunt.

SCENE 3

Out on the great open heights. The storm is gathering strength and driving the clouds, low and heavy, over the snowy wastes; black pinnacles and peaks now and then appear and are again blurred by the mist. BRAND *comes, bruised and bleeding, across the heights.*

BRAND [*stopping and looking back*]:
    A thousand followers. And not one
    followed me here. Where have they gone,
    then, the struggle and all the great
    yearning to reach the farthest height?
    Their pitiful vainglorious dream
    of sacrifice! Have they no shame;
    or do they think Christ Crucified
    made all sins decent when he died?
    We battle for our souls. I knew
    fear in my time; watched it; it grew;
    it moved as I moved, as I tried
    to find my heart a place to hide:
    'The trolls are dead; and it is not
    night; and the sun grows round and hot
    above the fjord in its round dance,
    in pure midsummer radiance.'
    How fearful, then, when I awoke
    from vividness into the shock
    of dark where men moved shadowy
    like ghosts beside the frozen sea;

sad mockeries of that old king
of Norway,[31] his weird suffering,
locked in his grief for his dead queen,
her heartbeats locked inside his brain.
You cannot bury death in dreams
of life; and nothing else redeems
death from itself but life-in-death,
the live seed buried in the earth.
But now this hideous age ordains
blood and iron (for as few pains
as possible). Some flinch. And some
go in good faith to fight the storm.
The best go. The worst wring their hands,
groaning, 'The age, the age demands!'
Worse times, worse visions, they are here
already: locust swarms of fear,
war clouds and clouds of industry –
rich England's shame, stormclouded rack,
shedding her bale of fiery smoke –
drawing their filth across the sky.
Deep down, the soulless dwarfs who made
an empire quarrying men's greed
set free the stony-fettered ore
the better to constrain its power.
They labour so, grow old and die
enslaved by their own mastery;
the clicking water of the mine
cold requiem when they are gone!
Truth is not seen or else is seen
too late, ruins where storms have been.
A nation smug amid the gloom
savours its penitential psalm:
'Not for us His cup was drained,
not for us the kiss that burned,
not for us the thorny crown
rooted in His blood that ran.
Not for us, O not for us
to seek salvation at His Cross.

For us only the whip that rakes
fresh scars across our spineless backs!'
[*He throws himself down in the snow and covers his face
with his hands. After some moments he looks up.*]
Am I now waking from a sleep
of sickness, from some demon's grip?
Did I hear once, through the world's din,
the song of the soul's origin?
CHORUS OF SPIRITS: God is God and man can never
Be like Him. You thing of dust,
Defy him; be His abject lover;
Either way your soul is lost!
BRAND: I have been dispossessed by God.
God has withdrawn from His own Word;
His clouds of wrath blot out the sun,
accursèd is the altar-stone.
CHORUS: God is God and *is* for ever.[32]
You shall live your life of death,
Self-inspiring self-deceiver,
Cheated by your dying breath.
BRAND: I sacrificed my wife, my child,
and all my comfort in this world,
and yet the serpent was not slain!
And was my sacrifice my sin?
CHORUS: God is God. He grants no favour,
No return for life that's past.
All your sacrificial savour
Smells like any carnal feast.
BRAND [*beginning to weep quietly*]:
Agnes, my wife; and oh, my son,
my son, Alf – what have I done,
and why? And do you – poor ghosts –
cling together in these weeping mists?
> BRAND *looks up; an area of growing light opens and
spreads itself in the mist; the spectral form of a woman
stands there, dressed in light colours, with a cloak over
her shoulders. It is* AGNES.
SPECTRE OF AGNES: Look at me, Brand.

BRAND: Love! Is it you?

SPECTRE: Yes, I am Agnes.

BRAND: The child, too,
  is he . . . ?

SPECTRE: He is safe and sound.
  He misses you. No, Brand!
  Stay where you are. The stream
  divides us now.

BRAND: A dream!

SPECTRE: No dream.
  I stay as long as you desire.

BRAND: For ever, then!

SPECTRE: Brand, all my care
  has been for you. When you were filled
  with frantic rage against the world
  I tried to calm you. I was beside
  you, even though you dreamed I died.

BRAND: You are alive!

SPECTRE: And you shall live
  once more in what you have.
  I've said, the child is well;
  he's with your mother. Oh how tall
  he's grown! The village church still stands
  or falls at your will. Your friends
  are watching for the day
  of your return. Love, come away!
  Surely the good days wait for us!

BRAND: It *is* a dream.

SPECTRE: Refuse
  these gifts of life? Be lost
  for ever in a mist?
  Love, love, come and be healed.

BRAND: I still
  know, despite all, that my own will
  is my salvation, my true peace.
  You plead for a false sacrifice.

SPECTRE: Brand, *I* am your salvation now!
  Our friend, the old doctor, saw

deep, deep into your soul
where you hid from us all,
enraptured by your cruel visions.
He called you a man of dark passions.
'Most passionate for each extreme.
He must will himself to be calm,'
he said, 'teach his heart a new tune.
"All or nothing" is good for no one.'
BRAND [*turning away*]:
   Is this true?
SPECTRE: As true as I live;
   true as your way of death. O love,
   all that I did was for your good!
BRAND: *That* you have never understood!
   You condemn me. Your care betrays
   me, and insinuates old ways.
   You have betrayed us both. A sword
   gleams between us, and always would!
SPECTRE: Be gentle, Brand. In my embrace
   the anguish and the fearful price
   can be forgotten. No more pain . . .
BRAND: Old wounds won't bleed again.
   Anguish of dreams is dead.
   Life's horror comes instead.
   Follow me, Agnes.
SPECTRE: But the child,
   Brand!
BRAND: Leave him!
SPECTRE: No! No wild
   nightmares of riding at your back
   like a dead woman wide awake!
BRAND: All or nothing. Truth, not lies.
   My vision, not your fantasies!
SPECTRE: The seraph with the sword of flame,
   remember, Brand? And Adam's doom,
   remember? And the dread abyss
   before the gate? You shall not pass
   into your self-willed paradise!

BRAND: God left one last approach for us:
   the way of longing!

   SPECTRE OF AGNES *disappears as in a thunderclap; the*
   mist rolls in over the place where she stood; there is a
   sharp and penetrating cry, as from one fleeing.

SPECTRE: Die, Brand, die!
   All life disowns your destiny!

BRAND [*standing for a few moments as if stunned*]:
   It vanished so suddenly.
   Cheated of what it came to seek –
   my soul's blood on its claws and beak –
   it screamed for its lost prey.
   Was *that* the ghost of compromise?

GERD [*enters, carrying a rifle*]:
   The hawk! Did you see him?

BRAND: This time,
   yes, there was a hawk.
   It came so very close.

GERD: Which way has he flown? Quick,
   tell me! I'll follow him.

BRAND: Shape-shifter that it is, sometimes
   it vanishes. Sometimes it looms
   large and terrible. We imagine
   it is dead; then, at the margin
   of vision, watch it reappear,
   playing catch-who-can with the wild air.

GERD: See what I have!

BRAND: A bullet?

GERD: Made of pure silver. I stole it
   from a huntsman. They say it works
   wonders against demons.

BRAND: And hawks?
   Real phantom-hawks?

GERD: Who knows?

BRAND: Well, aim
   to kill.

      He starts to leave.

GERD: Hey, preacher-man, you're lame!
  Why are you lame?
BRAND: My own
  people – the people – scourged and stoned
  me; hunted me down.
GERD: Blood's pouring from your face;
  and your clothes are stained.
BRAND: Everything and everyone –
GERD: Your voice,
  it's rasping like dead leaves . . .
BRAND: Betrayed –
  I have been betrayed!
GERD [*looking at him, wide-eyed*]:
                  I know
  who you are; I know you now!
  You're not the preacher, not a bit
  like him. He makes me spit.
  You're some great man!
BRAND: I dreamed so indeed.
  Was I mad?
GERD: Show me your hands.
  It's true, it's true! . . . those wounds!
  Oh, and your lovely head,
  all snagged and smeary from the thorn!
  Dear saviour-man, why aren't you dead,
  like in the stories I was told?
  Long, long ago, and far away,
  a little gypsy-boy was born;
  and he was king of all the world,
  and so they killed him on a cross.
  It was my father told me this.
  Why did he tell me such a lie?
  O Saviour, let me kiss your feet!
BRAND: Out of my sight!
GERD: Your blood can save us all!
BRAND: Not even my own soul.
GERD: I'm canny; I can shoot;

you told me, 'Aim to kill.'
I can! I can do it!

BRAND [*shaking his head*]:

Child, let them be: weak, struggling men.
Let them strive and stumble on
until they fall.

GERD: You'll never fall.

For on your head's the thorny crown;
and in your hands the prints of nails
bear witness that you're God's dear Son.

BRAND: I am the meanest thing that crawls.

GERD [*looking upward; the clouds are breaking*]:

Do you see where we are?

BRAND: I see the mountain and the stair
clear through the mist; the pure ascent,
the void that is the firmament.
It is the Ice Church!

GERD [*uttering a wild cry*]:

                    Yes! *Now* you come!

BRAND [*starting to weep*]:

Redeemer, when I called Your name,
prayed for the comfort of Your arm,
You passed close by and never heard.
Dear name, the ghost of an old word ...
Redeemer, look, I try to touch
Your white robe, but I cannot reach.
Sinners whose tears have stained its hem
put all my agony to shame.

GERD [*pale*]:

Oh now the priest-of-ice
is melting; rags and tatters drop
from his glacier cope;
the tears pour down his face.
The ice in my own brain
melts to a gentle rain
and all that freezing fire
is gone. You would not weep before.
Why? Why?

BRAND [*radiant and as if reborn*]:
                Narrow was my path,
  straitened between wrath and wrath.
  My own heart was the Sinai slate
  on which the hand of God could write.
  Before this hour, until this place,
  I knew no other power, no grace,
  beyond my own unyielding will.
  But now the sunshine and the thaw.
  And life shall be my song. Here, now,
  I am released, and kneel!
GERD [*looking upward and speaking slowly and fearfully*]:
  Silver to silver, steel to flesh
  of ice where those great feathers thresh:
  look how he beats against the rock.
  Now, silver bullet, flash and strike!
    She puts the rifle to her shoulder and fires. A hollow
    booming, as of a roll of thunder, sounds from high up the
    mountain face.
BRAND: What have you done?
GERD: That strange white bird,
  he screamed; he screamed as I fired!
  Silver-white ice-dove, do you cry
  with terror now? Ah, the beauty!
  He's plunging down, he's scattering
  whirlwinds of feathers from each wing;
  a mountain whirling like a swarm
  of feathery snow. And now that scream,
  nearer, nearer . . . Oh the noise, the noise!
    She throws herself down in the snow.
BRAND [*shrinking under the approaching avalanche and*
    crying out]:

                         Tell

  me, O God, even as Your heavens fall
  on me: what makes retribution
  flesh of our flesh? Why is salvation
  rooted so blindly in Your Cross?
  Why is man's own proud will his curse?

Answer! What do we die to prove?
Answer!
   The avalanche buries him. The whole valley is filled.
A VOICE [*calling through the noise of thunder*]:
            He is the God of Love.[33]

PEER GYNT

A version by Geoffrey Hill based on a literal
translation by Janet Garton and
edited by Kenneth Haynes

CHARACTERS

AASE, *widow of a farmer*
PEER GYNT,[1] *her son*
TWO PEASANT WOMEN *with sacks of grain*
ASLAK, *a blacksmith*
WEDDING GUESTS, MASTER OF CEREMONIES,
FIDDLER, *etc.*
AN INCOMER *and his* WIFE
SOLVEIG and HELGA, *their daughters*
THE HÆGGSTAD FARMER
INGRID, *his daughter*
MADS MOEN, *the bridegroom, and his* PARENTS
THREE GIRLS *from the seter*[2]
A WOMAN IN GREEN
THE TROLL KING[3]
TROLL COURTIER *and others like him*
TROLL MAIDENS *and* TROLL CHILDREN
TWO WITCHES
AN UGLY CHILD
BOYG[4]
BIRD VOICES
KARI, *a crofter's wife*
MR COTTON, M. BALLON, HERR V. EBERKOPF,
HERR TRUMPETERSTRAALE, *travelling gentlemen*
A THIEF *and* A FENCE
ANITRA, *daughter of a Bedouin chieftain*
ARABS, FEMALE SLAVES *and* ATTENDANTS *at a
Moroccan camp*
THE STATUE OF MEMNON *(singing)*
THE SPHINX AT GIZA *(silent)*
BEGRIFFENFELDT, *Professor, Ph.D., director of the
Cairo madhouse*

HUHU, *an advocate of language reform from the Malabar coast*
A FELLAH *carrying a royal mummy*
HUSSEIN, *a Near Eastern cabinet minister*
SEVERAL INMATES OF THE MADHOUSE *together with their* GUARDS
A NORWEGIAN SHIP'S CAPTAIN *and his* CREW
A STRANGE PASSENGER
A PRIEST
A FUNERAL PROCESSION
A SHERIFF
A BUTTON MOULDER
A THIN MAN

ACT ONE

SCENE 1

A hillside with deciduous trees near AASE's *farm. A rushing river. An old mill on the opposite bank. A hot summer's day.* PEER GYNT, *a strongly built twenty-year-old boy, comes down the path.* AASE, *his mother, small and slight, follows him. She is angry and scolding.*

AASE: Lies, Peer, lies!
PEER [*without stopping*]:
  Plain truth it is!
AASE: Swear then!
PEER: Why?
AASE: Affeared to? Fie!
  Such stuff and all; such rigmarole!
PEER [*stopping*]:
  'Strewth, Ma!
AASE [*in front of him*]:
              You're shameless! First you took
  off up the fells, left *me* the work –
  spent though I am – sloped off to stalk
  reindeer (you said) among the crags.
  Return in rags, without your gun –
  months you were gone – and meatless too.
  D'you think I'll eat your lies, lad? So:
  where was that buck you almost took?
PEER: West, by Lake Gjendin.[5]

AASE [*laughs scornfully*]:
                              More tall tales!
PEER: Bitter it was, mind, a dread wind,
   and he behind an alder-tump the whiles.
   Moss he was after.
AASE [*as before*]:
   Take me for daft, Peer?
PEER: Heard his hoof scraping. Saw his tines.
   Didn't dare breathe, hugging the stones,
   on my belly, there in the gully,
   chanced a quick look – oh, Ma! – that buck
   all plump and gleaming! You've
   seen never the like!
AASE: Believe
   that, who feels free to!
PEER: Crack-o! Whack!
   Down goes the buck! I'm on his back,
   grab his left ear, see here, rear-skull,
   straight to the spot, my hunting-steel
   to make the kill. The brute is up!
   A single leap, a beastly cry,
   and we're away!
   Knife lost, torn from my fist,
   my calves, my thighs, gripped fast
   by some contortionist
   it seemed; I mean, his horns
   gripped me like pincers: for, some twist
   of nature there possessed that creature.
   We rode at the charge
   along Gjendin Ridge![6]
AASE [*involuntarily*]:
   Bless, us, sweet Saviour!
PEER: Have you ever
   been up along that razor-back?
   Two miles of track; and sheer
   its drop. Look! scree, glacier,
   voiding themselves to either side.
   Two thousand feet you'd fall, not slide.

So: there we were, riding air,
me and my steed at such a speed,
racing those suns – ay, they were many –
whirling about us, small and shiny.
We could look down
on eagles high above the tarn,
a snatched look as we overtook.
Seen but unheard the ice-floes broke
against the shore. Those earth-sky-folk –
Vættir – you know – surrounded us,
shrilling wild songs, and hounded us.

AASE [*dizzy*]:
  Lord 'a' mercy!

PEER: In that very
  place – now hear me! – quite the worst –
  a ptarmigan, of all things, burst
  out of hiding, flap and shriek,
  just where the buck and I were striding.
  Upon the instant, we had swung
  out from the ridge and hung
  over a gulf.

  [AASE *staggers and takes hold of a tree trunk.* PEER
  continues.]

                Behind us, sheer,
  the cliff-side, black; beneath us, ne'er
  a glimpse of ground. Mists we cleft, broke
  through many a wailing flock
  of seagulls. Down and down we came
  until, deep in the tarn's womb,
  a thing began to glimmer palely,
  whiteish, like a reindeer's belly.

AASE [*gasping for breath*]:
  Peer, lad, you mean . . . ?

PEER: Lordy, yes! It was our own
  image that rose as we plunged down,
  pace for pace; the tarn's face
  broke like a mirror. Their horns lock –
  buck from the air with phantom buck,

all in a fleeting! Spray's far-flung,
rainbows we dip our toes among!
At length the buck begins to swim
in earnest; I hold fast to him;
we reach the north shore; I head home—
AASE: But where's the buck?
PEER: Maybe still there;
   [*Clicks his fingers, turns on his heels and adds*:]
   first come first served, and none to spare!
AASE: Lad, let me take it in! Your neck
   not broken! Both your legs and back,
   right as a trivet: God be praised
   for keeping safe the boy I raised!
   The seat's out of his trousers, h'm;
   today, nary a word of blame
   shall pass my lips. Even to think
   how close he came . . .
   [*Suddenly stops, looks at him with open mouth and wide
   eyes, is speechless for a long time, finally bursts out.*]
                          Damned mountebank!
   God help us, what a liar,
   what a liar you are!
   That fable you've just spun:
   Gudbrand Glesne[7] 'twas that took
   the famous ride astride a buck.
   A wench of twenty, I first heard
   that tale; it's here, still in my head!
PEER: Ain't I just like him? 'Gudbrand rides again!'
   Folk can repeat the same feat.
AASE [*furious*]:
   Well, yes, a lie can (truth to tell)
   strut in fine clothes to work us ill.
   Like a death's head 'twould be, if known.
   Such is your ill work, my son:
   nothing decent and home-spun,
   crazy high talk of eagles, bucks,
   rides through the clouds on phantoms' backs,
   such dreadful lies – small things and great

made falsehood to give folk a fright.
And, what's to me most terrible,
your own soul stuck 'twixt truth and fable!
PEER: If anyone else than you
said that to me, I'd beat 'em black and blue!
AASE [*weeping*]:
Wish to God I were dead,
that deep in black earth I was laid;
prayers and tears of no avail
to keep him from hell.
PEER: Dear little sweet Mother,
it's true, all you say,
but best not to bother,
live life for the day.
AASE: I, who have borne
such a pig of a son?
Be happy – how can I,
without friends or money,
but rich in shame,
poor widow that I am?
[*Renewed weeping*]
Where have they gone,
those coffers of coin?
Grandad, old Rasmus Gynt,
got them, enjoyed their glint.
Your father gave them leave
to wander off, or scattered them like sand:
speculations in land!
A gilt coach he must have!
Then – the great winter feast
when he urged every guest
to break bottle and glass – all! –
in spendthrift wassail,
broken against the wall!
PEER: 'Where are the snows of yesteryear?'
AASE: Be silent, Peer!
Look around: the farm, the house –
'most every window robbed of glass

and crammed with rags. Hedges stripped,
fences down; cattle stark-ribbed,
swept by the rain-soaked wind.
None left but us to scrape the ground.
Each month the bailiffs take yet more.
PEER: Old woman, what a Norn you are!
Fortune may fail; it soon gets well.
AASE: Soil that fed ours is strewn with salt,
and you're a big man but in talk;
fancy yourself cock-o'-th'-walk.
Your witty tongue ne'er known to halt:
like when the pastor came to call –
a Copenhagen man[8] and all –
to ask for your baptismal name.
He heard you, was quite overcome,
swore that such talents would go far –
Denmark itself had no such star –
which pleased your father, so that he
went off with horse and sled for fee.
Ah yes, mainfool, then all was well:
deacon, archdeacon, and the rest,
swigged, gorged, until they almost burst.
What's that they say – 'fair times, fair friends'?
When hardship strikes false friendship ends.
All went, the hour that 'Gilded Jack'
took to the roads with peddler's pack.
[Dries her eyes with her apron.]
I'm frail, now. Bide
here, as you're bid.
Be my strength and stay.
Work the farm. Save
the little we have –
that's what I pray,
[weeping yet again]
for all the good it does.
You lurk around the house
and fossick with the hearth.
When you swagger about

the village, you lout,
I'm shamed nigh to death.
You terrify the girls,
fight the worst men in miles.
PEER [*moving away from her*]:
   Agh! – leave me be!
AASE [*following*]:
   Deny,
   if you dare,
   it was you there
   heading the pack that time
   at Lunde Farm.
   They fought like dogs, the rogues.
   It was you that broke
   his arm – Aslak
   the smith's – or put
   his finger-joint out.
PEER: Who's been telling tales?
AASE [*agitated*]:
   The crofter's wife heard the yells.
PEER [*rubbing his elbow*]:
   My yells, though; he's tough.
AASE: Who's tough?
PEER: Aslak. He thrashed me.
AASE: Aslak? Ugh!
   I could spit for shame.
   Beaten by him,
   that guzzling tosspot? All my days
   I've suffered, but this takes the bays!
   No matter what his strength
   you should have made him measure his length.
PEER: Whether I thrash or am thrashed
   your joy seems dashed.
   [*Laughs.*]
   Cheer up!
AASE: You've lied again!
   You weren't beaten, you mean?
PEER: A couple more lies, yes.

Come, dry your eyes.
[*Clenches his left fist.*]
Look, in these iron tongs I gripped
and beat him. When he's nicely hooped
my right fist here's a sledgehammer—
AASE: You bully! I shall die of shame, Peer.
PEER: You deserve better than that,
twenty thousand times better,
without a doubt.
Little, angry, lovely Mother,
I pledge you my word.
You shall be honour'd
by folk near and far;
the whole village for sure.
Wait till I bring about
something truly great!
AASE [*snorts*]:
You? Great?
PEER: Who knows what I might meet?
AASE: I wish you had sufficient wit
that – just once! – you might mend
the rip in your own nether end.
PEER [*becoming excited*]:
I shall be emperor! A king!
AASE: Dear God, his fancy's taken wing.
PEER: Don't prate. Just wait.
AASE: 'Bide time enough thou'lt come at t'crown,'
that saying's well known.
PEER: Hold hard,
Mother!
AASE: No, I'll be heard!
Your brain's hexed. Though
it's true enough
something splendid might have occurred
if only, day after day,
you'd not wasted, on daft play,
make-believe, downright lies,
the substance you had.

That lass from Hæggstad
had tenderness in her eyes.
There was your future, Peer,
but you didn't care.
PEER: You think not?
AASE: The old man
is a feeble creature
despite his stubborn nature;
wherever Ingrid leads he totters
after; his self-will's his daughter's,
that much is plain.
[*Weeping*]
Oh, my dear lad, oh such a prize:
Hæggstad's endowments in her gift;
yours for the taking, once, with ease;
her fancied bridegroom, if you please.
Look at you now – in rags, bereft!
PEER [*abruptly*]:
I'll get her to say 'yes'
right now. When I propose!
AASE: Now? Where?
PEER: At Hæggstad!
AASE: My poor boy,
That path is closed; you'll have no joy.
PEER: Why so?
AASE [*sobbing*]:
                    My dear son, let me weep.
Your luck is lost, your time is up.
[*Sobbing*]
While you were on your western jaunt
riding your fancy to the hunt,
Mads Moen . . .
PEER: That weed?
AASE: . . . went and proposed
and was accepted.
PEER: All's not lost!
Wait! I'll make ready mare and cart.
    Begins to leave.

AASE: Spare the effort.
  Tomorrow's the great day.
PEER: That right? –
  No matter: I'll be there tonight.
AASE: Shame on you. Will you add the weight
  of folks' contempt: more shame and slight?
PEER: Be of good cheer, all shall be well!
  [*Shouting and laughing*]
  The cart would be too slow. I'll . . .
    Lifts her up.
AASE: Put me down! Put me down!
PEER: No fear!
  I'll carry you in my arms as far
  as Hæggstad. Then we'll see who's wed.
    Wades out into the river.
AASE: More likely we'll both drown.
PEER: For something better I was born,
  a nobler death!
AASE: Yes, to be sure,
  you'll end by dancing on the air.
  'None shall drown going gallows-ward,'
  that's what they say. You brute!
PEER: It's hard to keep our foot-
  ing here, 's all weeds and mud.
AASE: You donkey!
PEER: Spit and swear.
  There's nothing that we can't repair.
  It's getting shallower.
  One, two, we're almost through!
  Let's play! Let's play 'Peer and the Buck'!
  I'll be the Buck and you be Peer.
AASE: Where are we, lad? Lad! where's the track?
PEER [*wading ashore*]:
  Here. Right here. Now that we're clear
  across, give Buck a kiss,
  say 'thanks for the ride'.
AASE [*boxing his ears*]:
  'Thanks for the ride', then!

PEER: Ouch!
  Wish you'd kept that in your pouch!
AASE: Let be!
PEER: When we reach the farm
  I need *you* to speak to *him*,
  act go-between; your wits
  are sharper than his. It's
  your job to run *him* down –
  I mean Mads Moen –
  and sing *my* praises.
AASE: You can bet I will!
  A testimonial
  you *shall* have – of curses.
  I'll rake you end to end,
  you imp of the fiend –
  for the world to admire.
PEER: Oh, Ma!
AASE [*kicking him*]:
              My tongue won't tire;
  I'll make that old man set the dog
  on you, as if you'd come to beg.
PEER: H'm. Think I'd best leave you here.
AASE: I'll not stay behind.
PEER: You've
  not the strength, my dove!
AASE: Haven't I just!
  I've so much rage that I could brast
  rocks wi' bare hands; I could munch flint.
  Leave go of me.
PEER: Promise me, then.
AASE: I'll promise nothing; and I mean –
  when they discover you're Peer Gynt –
  to tell my tale.
PEER: No; here you stay.
AASE: Think I'm not fit for company?
PEER: You're not invited, that's for sure.
AASE: What are you doing?
PEER: You'll be safe

enough here, on the millhouse roof.
  Puts her up there. AASE *screams.*
AASE: Get me down, you churl!
PEER: I would this minute if – stay still,
  don't lie full length or kick your legs,
  don't try your strength with hapless tugs;
  otherwise things may not go well;
  to put it plainly, you could fall.
AASE: You beast!
PEER: Don't struggle.
AASE: Why can't you go
  back where you came from, as changelings do?
PEER: Shame on you, mother.
AASE: Pah!
PEER: I'd rather
  go with your blessing than your blather.
AASE: You, mother's pride! I'll tan your hide;
  no matter what, you hulking brat!
PEER: Farewell for now, fair goodly dame.
  [*Begins to leave, but turns around and lifts a finger in warning.*]
  Back soon. Be patient. Do stay calm.
    Exit.
AASE: Peer! God help me, he's galloped off
  across the fields. And will he heed?
  No, of course not. Oh my head,
  I'm dizzy! Help!
    TWO WOMEN *carrying sacks on their backs walk down towards the mill.*
FIRST WOMAN: Who's kicking up
  that din, I wonder, raising the roof?
AASE: Here!
SECOND WOMAN: Aase? Well, you've surely come
  up in the world for real this time!
AASE: Lord, heaven's gate is my last hope.
  When I get there . . .
FIRST WOMAN: God bless you, neighbour,

upwards and onwards as you labour.

AASE: Bah! Fetch a ladder; I'll get down.
It's my confounded son.

SECOND WOMAN: Your son?

AASE: My son. Now everyone can say
they've seen him at his work and play.

FIRST WOMAN: Well, count on us.

AASE: Lend me your aid
to get to Hæggstad.

SECOND WOMAN: Is he there?

FIRST WOMAN: He'll have come-uppance, that's for sure.
Aslak the smith will be a guest.

AASE: My lad! My lad! They'll strike him dead!

FIRST WOMAN: It's been arranged and much discussed.
He'll meet with his predestined end.

SECOND WOMAN: Poor old soul's out of her mind!
[*Shouts up the hill.*]
Eivind! Anders! Need you here!

A MAN'S VOICE: What's happening?

SECOND WOMAN: It's Peer
Gynt's mother on the millhouse roof –
he's put her there, the oaf!

SCENE 2

A low hill with bushes and heather. The country road runs behind it, with a fence separating them. PEER *comes along a path, walks quickly up to the fence, stops and looks across to where the view opens out.*

PEER: There's the farm. I've made good time.
[*Begins to climb over fence; then stops to consider.*]
                                    I wonder if Ingrid
will be on her own there?
[*Shades his eyes and looks into the distance.*]
                        No; friends and kindred

are swarming all over the old place already.
Should I turn around? Go back over the ground? Well,
    should I?
[*Swings his leg back over the fence.*]
Backbiters – hordes! – will be there: they always are.
Down on your luck, they attack; it goes through you like fire.
[*Takes a few steps from the fence and tears off some leaves,
lost in thought.*]
If only I'd brought strong spirits to drink, or could pass in a
    wink,
unseen by all. If my name were unknown. Yes, something
    strong!
Gone at a gulp! Despair's best help. So their laughter can't
    sting.
    *Suddenly looks around him as if frightened; then he hides
    among the bushes. Some people with provisions walk
    past on their way to Hæggstad.*
A MAN [*in conversation*]:
's old man was a tosspot, his mother's a wretched creature.
A WOMAN: No wonder, then, that the lad has a skewed
    nature.
    The people walk past. After a while PEER *emerges; his
    face is red with shame. He looks after them.*
PEER [*quietly*]:
Was it me that they spoke of? Well, let the slander go round,
[*Makes a theatrical gesture with one arm.*]
they'll not steal what is mine, nor unbind what is bound.
[*Throws himself down on the heather-covered slope and
lies for a long time with his hands behind his head, gazing
into space.*]
What an odd cloud that cloud is! It looks like a horse
with a man on its back, and the proper tack, set on its course.
Behind, an old woman comes riding upon a new broom.
[*Laughs quietly to himself.*]
Good Lord! It's my mother! My mother. From whence has
    she come?
Wailing and scolding, 'You beast O you beast!' and 'Oh, Peer!'
[*His eyes begin to close.*]

My eyes I will close for a while. Ah, she melts in her fear.
Peer Gynt rides at the head of his troop; many follow
  his lead.
 Gold shoes for his charger, a fine silver band for its head.
He's wearing new gloves, and a sabre he has, and a sheath,
his cloak is of fine weave, lined with white silk underneath.
It is splendid, his meinie, yet none sits so tall on his mount
as this fellow does. Sun glitters, the harness bells chant!
Plain folk in dull weeds are crowding behind a low wall;
the men doff their hats, their wives and daughters turn pale,
make me low curtseys. Everyone, everyone, knows
who this emperor is – *Peer Gynt* – and these fine fellows
his liegemen, a thousand all told. He casts wide abroad
gold coins by the bushel: a peasant's soon rich as a lord!
Peer Gynt, who but he?, rides over the sun-kindled sea;
the Prince of England waits at his nation's gates
in homage. Prim English maidens cry 'welcome' to him.
Grand English aldermen rise from their high teas,
England's emperor happily bows both knees,
and says . . .

ASLAK THE SMITH [*as he and others pass by on the other
   side of the fence*]:
             Well, look'ee here, Peer Gynt, the sot!
PEER [*half-rising*]:
  My dear Emperor! . . .
ASLAK [*leans on the fence, smirking*]:
              Hey, up you get!
PEER: Aslak the smith. I might have known.
ASLAK [*to the others*]:
  Thinks he's still at Lunde.[9] Clown!
PEER [*leaps up*]:
  I don't want a fight!
ASLAK: All right. But – fecks! –
  where have you been these past six weeks?
  Were you bewitched, or what?
PEER: Strange deeds
  have I done.
ASLAK [*winking at the others*]:

Right, Peer, speak on!

PEER: None of your business.

ASLAK [*after a pause*]:

                                    Lass that weds
today at Hæggstad, she was one
that fancied you, the folk here say.

PEER: Don't croak at me, vile bird of prey.

ASLAK [*backing off slightly*]:
Easy, now! There's tastings more
left in that pot, you can be sure.
You're Jon Gynt's son! Come to the farm;
plenty of mutton dressed as lamb.

PEER: You go to hell!

ASLAK: I'll kiss the bride
for you. You'll make some old maid glad!
    They leave, laughing and whispering.

PEER [*stares after them for a short time, shrugs, half turns
    around*]:
The Hæggstad girl, for all I care,
can wed with every fellow there.
[*Looks down at his clothes.*]
Look at yourself – your filthy rags –
I wish you had some decent togs.
[*Stamps his foot.*]
Curse them! I'd like to rip
their scorn from them with my iron butcher's grip!
[*Looks round, startled.*]
What's that? Who's there? Snigger away!
I'll break! Is no one here but me?
I must get home
to Mother.
[*Begins to walk away; stops again, listening.*]
            Dancing at the farm!
[*Gazes and listens intently; moves forward with cautious
steps; his eyes shine.*]
The fiddler's striking up. They're doing
the halling![10] The halling –
dancing it in the yard.

A bevy of girls
watches each lad as he whirls:
that can't be bad!
I must join in
though Mother's squatting like a djinn
on the millhouse yet.
Ah, that Guttorm is great
with his fiddle in spate,
it sings and it leaps,
plunges into the deeps!
And the girls there, so pretty!
I will join the party!
  Leaps over the fence at a bound and goes down the road.

SCENE 3

*The farm enclosure at Hæggstad; the farmhouse furthest back.
Many guests. There is lively dancing on a grassy slope. The*
FIDDLER *sits on a table. The* MASTER OF CEREMONIES
stands in the doorway. SERVING WOMEN *walk to and fro
between the buildings;* OLDER PEOPLE *are sitting and chat-
ting here and there.*

A WOMAN [*joins a group of people sitting on some logs*]:
  The bride? Yes, she's sniffling a little, of course;
  but I say, ignore that; it's often a ruse.
MASTER OF CEREMONIES [*in another group*]:
  Now, come up, good people, and help drain the keg!
A MAN: Thanks for such bounty! There's almost too much
    here to swig!
A BOY [*to the* FIDDLER, *as he flies past with a* GIRL *clinging
    to him*]:
  Hey-up there, Guttorm! Don't spare the new fiddle strings!
A GIRL: Ply your bow so that now high over the meadows it
    sings!
SECOND GIRL [*in a circle around a dancing* BOY]:
  That was a fine leap!

THIRD GIRL: Legs are they? Hey! they're springs!
BOY [*dancing*]:
   'Here it's high to the roof and it's wide to the walls!'
     THE BRIDEGROOM *(who is* MADS MOEN*) approaches his*
     FATHER, *who is chatting, and tugs at his jacket. He is*
     nearly in tears.
BRIDEGROOM: Dad, she won't let me; it's proud that she is!
FATHER: Won't let you do what?
BRIDEGROOM: Door's locked, and she won't heed my calls.
   Don't know where the key is . . .
FATHER: Well, find it, you ninny!
   Brains – haven't you any?
     He turns back and resumes his conversation. The BRIDE-
     GROOM *wanders across the yard.*
A BOY [*coming from behind the house*]:
   Things will be getting warm –
   Peer Gynt's at the farm!
ASLAK [*joining in*]:
   Well, who invited him?
MASTER OF CEREMONIES:
   No one I know of.
     Goes towards the house.
ASLAK [*to the* GIRLS]: If he comes up, and speaks . . .
A GIRL [*to the others*]:
   Ignore him, or, better, give him unfriendly looks.
PEER [*enters, flushed, in high spirits, stops in front of the*
     group and claps his hands]:
   Who 'trips the light fantastic' best?
A GIRL [*to whom he turns*]:
   Not me.
SECOND GIRL [*likewise*]:
     Nor me.
THIRD GIRL: Nor me neither.
PEER [*to a fourth* GIRL]:
   You, then, before I choose another!
FOURTH GIRL [*turning away from him*]:
   I don't have time.

PEER [*to a fifth*]:
  You, then!
FIFTH GIRL [*leaving*]:
          I'm going home.
PEER: The night is young! *Madame*, you jest!
ASLAK [*after a pause, sotto voce*]:
  Look, Peer, see there! See, there she goes,
  dancing around an old man's toes!
PEER [*quickly addressing an older* MAN]:
  Are there any still in need
  of partners?
A MAN: Find them yourself, my lad.
    Turns away. PEER *has suddenly become quiet. He glances
    surreptitiously and timidly towards the group that re-
    jected him. Everyone stares, but no one speaks. He tries
    approaching other groups. Whenever he comes close they
    fall silent. As soon as he moves off they smile and follow
    him with their eyes.*
PEER [*hushed*]:
  Knife-sharp their ill-will, each hateful smile;
  all grates like saw-blade scraped with file.
    Humiliated, he makes his way along the fence. SOLVEIG,
    holding little HELGA *by the hand, enters the enclosure,
    together with her* PARENTS.
FIRST MAN [*to another standing not far from* PEER]:
  There's those new incomers.
SECOND MAN: Out o' the west?
FIRST MAN: Ay, from Hedalen.[11]
SECOND MAN: That so?
PEER [*steps into the path of the newcomers, points to*
    SOLVEIG *and asks the* MAN *walking with her*]:
                        May I dance
  with your daughter, sir?
MAN [*quietly*]:
                    That you may. First, we must
  go to the house – that's good manners! – announce
  our arrival.

MASTER OF CEREMONIES [*to* PEER *as he offers him a drink*]:
                    Some beer?
PEER [*is immobile, gazing after* SOLVEIG *and her* FAMILY]:
                              Not that much of a thirst,
  but thanks. There's dancing calls to be done!
  [*The* MASTER OF CEREMONIES *moves away.* PEER *gazes at
  the house; smiles.*]
  There! So fair! So modest! Her eyes cast down
  to the tips of her shoes, to the hem of her gown;
  the fresh white apron – how it gleams –
  I see she carries a book of psalms
  wrapped in trim cloth; her other hand
  clasping her mother's skirt. Beauty new-found,
  [*Begins to enter the room.*]
  I must see you again!
A BOY [*comes out with several others*]:
                              Why are you leaving
  so early?
PEER: I'm not!
BOY: But you're oddly behaving –
  that's quite the wrong way!
       Takes PEER *by the shoulder, attempting to turn him
       around.*
PEER: Here, let me through!
BOY: You're scared of Aslak, aren't you, though!
PEER: Me? Frit?
BOY: Like at Lunde!
       The crowd laughs, jeers; goes across to the dancing area.
SOLVEIG [*in the doorway*]:
                              You're the one
  that's keen to dance?
PEER: I am indeed!
  Don't say you'd forgotten!
SOLVEIG: But not too far, so Mother said.
PEER: *She* said! *She* said! Are you still
  wet behind the ears, fair chiel?
  How old are you?

SOLVEIG: I was confirmed
  last spring.
PEER: And have you yet been named?
SOLVEIG: They call me Solveig. Pray, what's yours
  to be remembered by your heirs?
PEER: Peer Gynt.
SOLVEIG [*pulling her hand from his*]:
  Law' sakes!
PEER: What now, you goose?
SOLVEIG: Ah, let me be! My garter's loose.
    Exit.
BRIDEGROOM: Mother, she won't!
MOTHER: Won't what? Won't what?
BRIDEGROOM: Unbolt the door; she's in a state!
FATHER [*quietly furious*]:
  You should be tethered to a mule!
MOTHER: Don't 'rate him so, poor lad; he'll thole.
A BOY [*accompanied by a large group comes across from the
    dancing*]:
  Some brandy, Peer?
PEER: No.
FIRST BOY: Wet your lips?
PEER: You have some on you?
FIRST BOY: Well, perhaps . . .
  [*Pulls out a pocket flask and drinks.*]
  It burns so sweetly.
PEER: Let me taste.
SECOND BOY: Have some of mine; 'twill slake your thirst.
PEER: I'll not take more.
SECOND BOY: Ah, don't be frit.
PEER: Then just the smallest taste of it.
    Drinks again.
A GIRL [*in a low voice*]:
  We'd best be off.
PEER: So you're afeard
  as well, my lass. The things you've heard?
THIRD BOY: Ay, tales she's heard of Lunde Farm!

FOURTH BOY: We know what skills *you* can perform!
PEER: I can do more if I've a mind.
FIRST BOY [*whispering*]:
   He's warming to it!
      A group forms around PEER.
ONE OF THE GROUP: Come, show your hand!
PEER: Tomorrow, then.
ONE OF THE GROUP: No, no, right here!
PEER: Well, I can make Old Nick appear!
A MAN: My gran did that, in years gone by.
PEER: Fool! I can do what she could not.
   I conjured him into a nut.
   There was this little wormhole. He
   cursed and promised things, and wept . . .
ONE OF THE GROUP [*laughing*]:
   And then? And then?
ANOTHER: Then in he crept!
PEER: I sealed the hole up with a pin;
   he buzzed and made a merry din
   just like a drunken bumble bee.
A GIRL: Well, fancy that!
   D'you still keep him in the nut?
PEER: Moved with the times to kinder climes.
   It's *his* fault that the smith and I
   no longer quite see eye to eye!
   I went to Aslak's forge to ask
   him to perform a simple task,
   to crack the nutshell. He agreed,
   and placed it on the anvil's head.
   But he's a heavy-handed churl;
   the sledgehammer's his favourite tool!
ONE OF THE GROUP: He struck?
PEER: Ay, like a man inspired!
   That crafty devil, though, self-fired,
   rushed in a flame, out through the roof,
   vanished with an almighty whoof!
ONE OF THE GROUP: Aslak?
PEER: Just stood there with scorched hands.

And since that day we've not been friends.
   General laughter.
ONE OF THE GROUP: That's a right good 'un!
ANOTHER: Well-nigh his best!
PEER: I didn't invent it!
A MAN: That's true; for most
   came from my grandad.
PEER: Plain truth, I swear!
MAN: Like all you tell us.
PEER [*with a swagger*]:
                I take rides
   high in the sky on airy steeds.
   I can work other wonders.
    Uproarious laughter again.
ONE OF THE GROUP: Peer,
   ride through the skies!
MANY: Ride! Ride the air!
PEER: No need to beg; no need to bawl –
   I'll ride the storm! I'll blast you all!
   The parish at my feet shall fall!
AN OLDER MAN: He's raving mad.
SECOND MAN: Or a mere fool.
THIRD MAN: Loudmouth I'd call him.
FOURTH MAN: Hopeless liar.
A MAN [*half-drunk*]:
   Just wait; you'll get your reckoning, Peer!
ONE OF THE GROUP: With a good dusting, too! Your back
   beaten and aching; both eyes black.
    The crowd disperses; the older ones angry, the younger
    ones laughing.
BRIDEGROOM [*moving close to* PEER]:
   Peer, say it's true. You truly can
   work wonders? Ride on air, I mean?
PEER [*somewhat curtly*]:
   You heard me, Mads.
BRIDEGROOM: That means you wear
   the cloak that makes folk disappear?
PEER: *Hat*, Mads, *hat*! I do; I shall.

He turns away. SOLVEIG *walks across the enclosure,*
holding HELGA's *hand.*

PEER [*goes over to them; he appears somewhat more*
    cheerful]:

Solveig, welcome! My cup is full!

[*Holds her by the wrist.*]

Ah, let me swing you high! And higher!

SOLVEIG: No, let me be!

PEER: But why, my fair?

SOLVEIG: You're crazy-wild.

PEER: The tined reindeer

is crazy-wild when summer's near.

Come, dance, dear girl, don't look so stricken.

SOLVEIG [*freeing her arm*]:

I daren't.

PEER: But why?

SOLVEIG [*solemn*]:

                        You have drink taken.

    Walks off, with HELGA.

PEER: I could murder them all;

my knife through each loath'd caul

ere I unstuck the blade . . .

BRIDEGROOM [*elbowing him*]:

My bride, eh, my bride?

PEER [*as if absent-mindedly*]:

Your bride? She's where . . . ?

BRIDEGROOM: Oh, Peer! She's shut

in the girls' summer sleeping-hut.

So work your will to fetch her out,

I beg you, Peer!

PEER: Fetch her yourself.

I'll not cast spells on your behalf.

[*A sudden thought strikes him; he says, quietly but*
urgently.]

To the girls' summer-hut she went . . .

[*Approaches* SOLVEIG *and speaks.*]

You've changed your mind?

[SOLVEIG *tries to leave, he stands in her way.*]

                                        Seeing me here,
   you grieve that I'm this man-of-mire?
SOLVEIG [*quickly*]:
   Don't speak as if God's truth were spent.
PEER: Too true, alas! I'm drunk for spite
   of cruel things you've said: a spate!
   Come, girl!
SOLVEIG: But even if I so desired,
   even if, mark you! I'm too scared . . .
PEER: Of *him*?
SOLVEIG: Yes, Father.
PEER: A Quietist,
   a Seeker, some such pious sect,
   is he not? Who bows his head
   each day above his bitter bread?
   A Bible-thumper? And the rest!
   Who binds you with God's interdict?
   Well? Answer me!
SOLVEIG: No; let me go in peace.
PEER: Never!
   [*In a low-pitched voice, but vehement, terrifying*]
                   I'll turn myself into a troll!
   Midnight tonight I shall pass through your bedroom wall.
   So be well warned. Hear someone, some thing, hiss and spit;
   it's not, you know, the household cat.
   It'll be me: and your poor heart must pay the price.
   I'll drain your blood into a cup, and I'll eat up
   your little sister. A werewolf I become each night.
   Your back, even your thighs, shall feel my bite . . .
   [*Suddenly his tone changes; he begs, as if terrified*]
   Dance, dance with me, Solveig!
SOLVEIG [*looking appalled*]:
                                    That was vile!
   She goes into the house.
BRIDEGROOM [*wanders in, looking even more helpless than
      before*]:
   I'll give you an ox if you'll help me; so help me, I will!
PEER: Quickly then!

Both men go behind the house. At the same moment a large
crowd leaves the dancing area; most of them are drunk.
Tumult. SOLVEIG, HELGA *and their* PARENTS *come to the*
door, accompanied by a number of the older folk.

MASTER OF CEREMONIES [*to* ASLAK, *who heads the rabble*]:
                              Order! Keep the peace!
ASLAK [*pulling off his shirt*]:
   Not likely! Let's see justice done.
   Peer Gynt and me fight one to one!
A MAN: Ay, let 'em scrap, 'tis sound advice.
SECOND MAN: A disputation – that's my motion!
THIRD MAN: I second that!
ASLAK: Nah, fists 'n' blood!
   Fists it shall be; words ain't no good!
SOLVEIG'S FATHER: Restrain yourself!
HELGA: Mama, will he get hurt?
A BOY: Let's rub his pack o' lies in the dirt!
SECOND BOY: Boot him back where he came from!
THIRD BOY: Spit in his eyes!
FOURTH BOY [*to* ASLAK]:
   You're not chucking it in?
ASLAK [*throwing down his shirt*]:
                          'The jade
   to the knacker's yard', that's what is said.
SOLVEIG'S MOTHER [*to* SOLVEIG]:
   That fool's awarded his well-earned prize.
AASE [*enters, carrying a stick*]:
   My son, where is he? I'll whack his bones,
   ay, good and proper! I'll tame him for once!
ASLAK [*rolling up his sleeves*]:
   That puny switch won't make its mark
   on Peer Gynt's hide!
FIRST BOY: Let the smith set to work!
SECOND BOY: Thrash him!
THIRD BOY: Tear him!
ASLAK [*spitting on his hands and nodding to* AASE]:
                          Hang and be sure!
AASE: Eh? Hang my Peer?

Let's see if you dare!
Old Aase and me – you see? you see! –
still have our tooth and claw.
Where's the lad now?
[*Calls across the enclosure.*]
Peer? Peer!
BRIDEGROOM [*running frantically in*]:
             Mam! Dad! Oh, oh!
I need you so!
HIS FATHER: What's wrong, lad?
BRIDEGROOM: That Peer Gynt . . .
AASE [*screaming*]:
You've killed him! Woe!
BRIDEGROOM: I can't
believe he's done it. Look, my wife
and him!
AASE [*lowering her stick*]:
        Come down, come down, you thief!
BRIDEGROOM: My wife with Gynt . . .
ASLAK [*standing as if thunderstruck*]:
                  There! On the cliff,
nearing the crest sure-footed. It's
like watching a pair of goats.
BRIDEGROOM [*weeping*]:
More as a man might heft a pig!
AASE [*calls up to PEER, threateningly*]:
I hope you fall!
[*Screams in terror.*]
        Don't fall, I beg!
BRIDE'S FATHER [*rushes in, bareheaded, white with rage*]:
I'll murder him! He's got the bride!
AASE: If I let you, then let God strike me dead!

ACT TWO

SCENE 1

A narrow mountain path up in the heights. It is early morning. PEER, *in an ill temper, walks quickly along the path.* INGRID, *wearing vestiges of her wedding finery, tries to delay him.*

PEER: Keep your distance.
INGRID [*weeping*]:
                              After this
  what's left for us?
  And where?
PEER: As far as you can fare.
  We part here.
INGRID [*wringing her hands*]:
  Oh, I feel so betrayed.
PEER: Well, there's no need
  to quarrel.
INGRID: We are tied
  by what we did.
  Our crime is our bond.
PEER: The devil take
  you; and all womankind,
  save for her alone.
INGRID: Who is that one?
PEER: Never you mind.
INGRID: Tell me.
PEER: No. Go back

to your father; quick-
foot it to Hæggstad.

INGRID: My sweeting!

PEER: No bleating!

INGRID: I can't believe you mean
   what you say.

PEER: *I* can,
   I *do*!

INGRID: Spoil and reject,
   is that it?

PEER: Cash the bond!

INGRID: Hæggstad, and all I can expect
   when my old dad's in the ground.

PEER: But do you have a psalm book bound in cloth?
   Have you long golden hair that stays unbound?
   No, on my oath!
   Do you glance down so modestly? Is your hand
   still holding fast to your mother's kirtle band?
   How could you answer?

INGRID: I . . .

PEER: Were you confirmed
   last spring? Have you . . .

INGRID: Oh, Peer . . .

PEER: . . . made me ashamed?
   Could you, as she has, so disdain my thirst
   for things ill-famed? No, nor the rest!
   When I see you, does that day always peal
   with a perpetual sabbath?

INGRID: Well . . .

PEER: Of course not. So what's there to mourn?

INGRID: You do yourself an ill turn.
   If you betray me, it's no game,
   it's a hanging crime.

PEER: So I've heard say.
   That's no cause to stay.

INGRID: You could be a rich
   man, after we wed.

PEER: Your bride-price is too much.

INGRID: But you misled me.
PEER: You were hungry to bed me.
INGRID: I was heartbroken.
PEER: And I was drunken.
INGRID [*threateningly*]:
  This will cost you dear.
PEER: As you have made clear.
INGRID: You are set on
  this ending?
PEER: As stone.
INGRID: And we fight?
PEER: Right!
    INGRID *walks away down the hill.*
PEER [*stands quietly watching for a while. Abruptly he*
    cries out]:
  To the devil with all
  such memories, and to hell
  with all women!
INGRID [*turns and shouts up to him, scornfully*]:
                    All save one?
PEER: All – but for her alone!
    They go their separate ways.

SCENE 2

By a mountain pool; around it, marshy ground. A storm
gathers. AASE, *frantic, is shouting, first staring in one direction,*
then in another. SOLVEIG *has trouble in keeping up with her.*
Her FATHER, MOTHER *and sister* HELGA *follow closely behind.*

AASE [*waving her arms wildly; tearing her hair*]:
  Everything pitched against me and against him –
  earth, sky, the mountains that stand so grim.
  Cold fog's on the boil, closes about his way;
  moor-tarns lurking and luring where he will stray;
  the mountains stride after him with their dour trek,
  with rock-fall and snow-slide, forever at his back;

and now and forever the rage of our own folk;
they will murder him for the evil thing he has done.
No, they shall not kill him, my own dear changeling son,
not while I live, though Satan himself has led him on.
[*Turns to* SOLVEIG.]
What cannot be thought of has to be thought of now.
He who did nought by the honest sweat of his brow;
whose only strength is the strength of his fabling jaw –
lies and inventions he works with, you wouldn't believe,
in sorrow and want he was nourished, in want we must live,
my husband a drunkard, a teller of tall tales,
braggart and broken, forever a-swim in his ales,
our peace and our joy dead with him – my own and my chiel's.
What could we do, young Peer and me, but endure
and forget the old life? He was nursed by a small fire.
I could both laugh and weep, making a mock of despair,
as others must do. So hard to look fate in the eyes
without flinching. Some take to brandy. Young Peer took
     to lies,
not that we called them that: legends both mine and his,
stories of princes and trolls, the strangest of tales,
of brides who were stolen, still in their wedding-veils,
not to be seen again in this world of ills.
D'you see why I let fancies – d'you see how hard it has been –
take root in his child-mind, and flourish, and become sin?
Why I cannot speak truthfully with my son?
[*Her terror returns.*]
Hear that? Hear that? Some water-demon, or orc,
or dragon-man – Peer! Peer! He *is* there, look!
[*Runs up a low hill and stares out across the tarn.*]
     SOLVEIG'S FAMILY *arrives.*

AASE: Not a sign. Not a sign.
SOLVEIG'S FATHER: And all the worse for him.
AASE: My poor lost lamb.
FATHER [*with a mild expression*]:
     Lost indeed, ma'am.
AASE: Don't dare speak of him so,
     he's a bright lad with his own way to go.

FATHER: You deceive yourself.

AASE: Not when
I speak of my fine young son.

FATHER [*still speaking in mild tones and gazing on her benignly*]:
But his mind is hardened. He is a lost soul.

AASE: The Lord will hearken readily when we call.

FATHER: But can your son repent of his sins, I mean?

AASE [*eagerly and as if with new hope*]:
With luck he will ride up to heaven astride a buck!

SOLVEIG'S MOTHER: Poor lady, her wits are struck.

FATHER: Do you comprehend quite what you intend, good dame?

AASE: I say that no deed is too strange or too high for him –
as he will show the wide world if he lives.

FATHER: Better to watch him hang among the thieves.

AASE: Jesu save him! And me!

FATHER: Bound with the law's thongs
he may repent sincerely ere he swings.
He may indeed repent,
Widow Gynt!

AASE: I am dazed with your talk.
We must find the lad quick.

FATHER: Indeed we must, for the sake
of his soul.

AASE: And his body and all!
If in the slough we must hard-haul him; or,
if trolls are his masters, then church bells must clamour.

FATHER: There's a track just here that cattle have made in the sward.

AASE: May the good Lord grant to you a fair reward.

FATHER: It is our Christian duty, no more, no less,
to labour beside all those in like distress.

AASE: Then what of those heathen from Hæggstad, eh?
Not one of them! Not one step of the way!

FATHER: They know your son too well, ma'am, and his fame.

AASE: Too well? Why, he's ever too clever for them!
[*Wringing her hands*]

And now! To think his life hangs by a thread.

FATHER: The mark of a foot, see, here, it's a man's tread.

AASE: A sign! A sign!

FATHER: We'll go to the summer pasture. Follow on.

He and his WIFE *set off.*

SOLVEIG [*to* AASE]:
Tell me, tell me much more.

AASE [*drying her eyes*]:
Much more? Much more? My poor son d'you mean?

SOLVEIG: All that you think, and know, and care
to speak of; and to have me hear.

AASE [*lifting her head and looking somewhat more cheerful*]:
Well then, young lady, then you will be tired.

SOLVEIG: You with the telling maybe. I, never, for all I have
heard.

Exeunt.

SCENE 3

Low, treeless hills near the mountain plateau; peaks in the distance. There are long shadows; it is late in the day.

PEER [*enters, running, and halts on the side of the hill*]:
The parish has joined in the hunt, Peer!
Popguns and rattles – I can hear
that Old Man Hæggstad's in good voice:
'Peer Gynt's away, halloo-hallay!'
Better than scrapping with Aslak any day.
I've the brawn of a bear, grip hard as a vice;
I'll wrestle the fell, grapple the waterfall.
Here goes a firtree, up by its roots!
This is the way to live! Oh, how it puts
thews in your zest for life. To hell
with piety, its watery gruel!

THREE SETER GIRLS [*come running along the slope, shrieking and singing*]:
Trond! Baard! Kaare! Trolls of the fells!

Listen to us, you need to lie in our arms.

PEER: Who is it you serenade so?

GIRLS: Our trolls!

Trolls! You deaf?

FIRST GIRL: Oh, Trond, be gentle with our charms!

SECOND GIRL: Don't listen to her, Baard; knock us about!

THIRD GIRL: The beds stand empty in the seter hut!

FIRST GIRL: In love, gentle and rough are the same thing.

SECOND GIRL: In love, rough and gentle are the game-thing.

THIRD GIRL: No boys to hug, of course we play with trolls!

PEER: Where are the boys?

ALL THREE [*shrieking with laughter*]:

Found themselves other joys!

FIRST GIRL: Mine was my kinsman and my lover, both.

He's married a widow pretty long in the tooth.

SECOND GIRL: Mine met a gipsy girl, up in the north parts.

Now both are beggars begging crusts and clouts.

THIRD GIRL: Mine murdered our bastard child. They struck

his head off. Now it grins at me from a stake.

ALL THREE: Trond! Baard! Kaare! Trolls from the fells,

come down and bed with us this very hour.

PEER [*takes a leap so that he stands among them*]:

I'm a troll with three heads and a lad for three girls!

FIRST GIRL: It's busy you are!

PEER: Judgement comes later.

FIRST GIRL: So it's off to the seter!

SECOND GIRL: There's mead to drink.

PEER: We'll all get drunk.

THIRD GIRL: There'll be three beds put to use

tonight in the seter house.

SECOND GIRL [*kissing* PEER]:

He's fizzing like white-hot iron, my bonny spark!

THIRD GIRL: Dead baby's eyes from the black tarn, his look.

PEER [*now part of the dancing group*]:

Heavy the heart; randy the other part.

Bright the eyes; grief clogs the throat.

GIRLS [*thumbing their noses towards the hilltops, screeching
their song*]:

Trond, Baard, Kaare, poor pack of trolls,
gone your last hope to lie with us lusty girls!
  Exeunt.

SCENE 4

In the Rondane mountains.[12] *Sunset. Gleaming, snow-covered*
peaks.

PEER [*enters dizzy and bewildered*]:
  Tower upon tower they rise
  and there's a shining portal.
  Are you deceived, my eyes?
  The scene fades; what does this foretell?
  The cock on the weathervane
  makes ready for departure –
  all passes into the blue inane,
  the mountain resumes its locked nature.
  What kind of life-form is that
  in a cleave of near-distance?
  Ah, giants with herons' feet!
  All's vacuous here, without substance.
  Rainbow patterns disturb
  my mind through my sight now.
  Whatever is a remote discord
  shifts to dull weights on my brow.
  And also on my brow is set
  a red-hot circlet, a crowning
  of some kind; but I forget
  who pressed upon me the damn thing.
  [*Sinks down.*]
  High over Gjendin – poetry
  and damned lies. Over
  the hill the bride and me.
  Drunk as ever,
  hunted by hawks and such,
  menaced by trolls, more lies,

damned Poetry (again!) lech-
ery with three houris.
[*Stares upward for a considerable time.*]
Paired eagles ride – see them! see there!
Wild geese head south, while
I, knee-deep in mire,
trudge to my toil.
[*Leaps up.*]
I so desire to soar – higher! –
to bathe in keenest winds, plunge
to redemption, to become pure,
naked in keeping with my heart's pledge.
Seter meadows shall not
detain me. I need to ride
until I'm clean of heart,
rushing far over the salt tide.
On I press, gaze down a moment
at England's prince. You may well stare,
English lasses, ignorant
as to why I journey here.
Can't stop! Well, perhaps briefly.
Say again? Those paired eagles?
Old Nick knows where they fly.
In Shadowland, now, I see gables
rise, becoming clearer all the time;
and there, in welcome, the open door.
This – why, this! – is grandad's new farm!
The old and tattered vestige is no more,
the fence no longer about to fall,
every window a-shine again.
And there's a feast in the great hall.
I hear the pastor amid the din
rapping with knife on glass.
There the captain hurled that bottle,
and over there the mirror went smash,
all to smithereens, that grand fettle,
but no matter, Mother, all is for the best,
don't you see? Rich Jon Gynt

presides, the master at his own feast.
His, and our, clan roars triumphant –
what a grand hubbub it all is!
The captain, stentorian,
is heard again, amid the noise,
calling the pastor to wassail the son.
Enter, Peer, thy judgement here!
To thine own worth stand witness.
Great, O Gynt, is thy descent,
secure, thy further greatness!

Runs forward but crashes into the rock face, falls to the ground where he remains stunned.

SCENE 5

A grassy slope with tall soughing deciduous trees. Stars twinkle through the leaves; birds sing in the tree tops. A WOMAN DRESSED IN GREEN *is walking in the meadow.* PEER *follows her, his gestures betraying that he is in love.*

WOMAN IN GREEN [*stops and turns around*]:
  Is this true that you say?
PEER [*runs his finger across his throat*]:
  As true, I swear, as that my name is Peer,
  as true as your beauty, as the words with which I woo you here.
  Will you accept me? Shall I go on? You'll see how I proceed.
  You'll have no call to work the loom, to spin there'll be no need.
  You shall eat your fill at my table, more even than you're able.
  I will never pull your hair.
WOMAN IN GREEN: Nor beat me, I trust.
PEER: Beat you? No fear!
  We who are the sons of kings don't do such things.
WOMAN IN GREEN: So you're a king's son?
PEER: Yes.
WOMAN IN GREEN: And I a princess,

the Dovre King's daughter.

PEER: Well, isn't that splendid!

WOMAN IN GREEN: Deep within Mount Ronden,[13] far
    underground,
  my father's castle is to be found.

PEER: Then my mother's castle is larger, rightly comprehended.

WOMAN IN GREEN: Do you know my father? King Brose is
    his name.

PEER: Have you met my mother? Queen Aase as she is known
    to fame.

WOMAN IN GREEN: When my father shakes his fist
  the mountains quake and burst.

PEER: When my mother's less than jolly
  rockslides fill the valley.

WOMAN IN GREEN: My father can kick sky-high in the
    halling.

PEER: My mother can do things even more thrilling.

WOMAN IN GREEN: And do you always go about in rags?

PEER: I have several more opulent rigs.

WOMAN IN GREEN: Every day I am attired in gold and silks.

PEER: Is that what they are? I thought they were old hemp
    stalks.

WOMAN IN GREEN: That is because – do, please, remember
    this,
  for it is one of our folk mysteries –
  all our possessions are twofold in nature,
  exist in different dimensions, as it were.
  When you reach my father's domain it
  may more resemble – in your eyes – an old stone-pit.

PEER: I'm bound to say it's likely that you will find
  the same out here among us human kind.
  Our gold to you may appear mere straw and trash,
  and every window pane that we see flash
  you may see as a bare frame stuffed with things
  I won't describe.

WOMAN IN GREEN: So black will appear
  white, the ugly will seem fair.

PEER: So greatness seems shrunken, the vile appears pure.

WOMAN IN GREEN [*clasping him around his neck*]:
    So each of us to the other best belongs!
PEER: As leg to pants' leg, or as hair to the comb.
WOMAN IN GREEN [*calling across the meadow*]:
    Bridal horse, bridal horse, bridal horse, come!
        An enormous pig comes running with a rope's end as a
        bridle and an old sack as a saddle. PEER *swings himself*
        up and lifts the WOMAN IN GREEN *to sit in front of him.*
PEER: We shall gallop through Rondane's doors at topmost
    speed!
    Giddy-up, giddy-up, giddy-up, then, noble steed!
WOMAN IN GREEN [*tenderly*]:
    But lately I was feeling so very forlorn –
    you can never tell how things will move on.
PEER [*whipping the pig and trotting along*]:
    The greatness of a great person appears
    in what he wears!
        Exeunt.

SCENE 6

The great hall of the DOVRE KING. *A large gathering of* COURT
TROLLS, GNOMES *and* SUBTERRANEAN SPRITES. *The* DOVRE
KING *enthroned, with crown and sceptre. His* CHILDREN *and*
other CLOSEST KIN *are on either side of the throne.* PEER
stands before him. General commotion.

A COURT TROLL: To the butcher's bench with him! The son
    of a mortal thing –
    a Christian too – has led astray the fairest daughter of our
    king!
A TROLL CHILD: Please, may I gash his finger?
SECOND CHILD: I want to hack his hair!
TROLL MAIDEN: I'd love to bite him in the thigh, right here,
    or just there . . .
A TROLL WITCH [*with a ladle*]:
    Make soup from him!

SECOND TROLL WITCH [*with an executioner's knife*]:
                              Best roast the monster. Turn the spit.
  Or bring him slowly to the boil, why not?
DOVRE KING: Temper your hungry relish, I command!
  [*Summons his trusted* COUNSELLORS *to approach the throne.*]
  Let us not deceive ourselves. Of late
  our troubles have increased. Whether we'll stand
  or fall in days to come is our debate.
  Whatever help we can get, from wherever it comes,
  even from mortal kind, is welcome in these times.
  This lad's a perfect beauty, very nearly,
  and strong with it also. You can all see, surely?
  His having only one head may count against him
  with some of you. But my daughter is the same
  I'll have you remember! Trolls with three heads,
  two heads, even, are rarely met with now;
  and even the heads they have are only make-do.
  [*Addresses* PEER.]
  We're to haggle over my daughter, is that the case?
PEER: Your whole kingdom now; not just half of it: yes!
DOVRE KING: Half of it now, with her; half after I am gone
  as one day I shall be, my not-quite-yet son.
PEER: I'll shake on that.
DOVRE KING: Hold hard! This treaty needs
  your pledges also, here, now, before it is sealed,
  and which, if reneged on, means all is annulled,
  means, for you, instant death. First, you must swear
  never to stray more beyond my kingdom so fair,
  to shun the light of day, and every action
  fit to be seen by daylight: such is my instruction.
PEER: If, to become king, this is all it takes,
  show me the treaty, I'll sign it in two shakes.
DOVRE KING: Not so fast! Let us first put to the test
  your mental faculties – in fine fettle, I trust!
THE OLDEST COURT TROLL [*to* PEER]:
  Let's see if you have a wisdom tooth in your skull
  that can break the Dovre King's puzzle-nut from its shell.

DOVRE KING: What sets our troll-kind apart from your
    humankind?
PEER: Nothing at all, so far as I now find.
  Big trolls want to fry, small trolls need to scratch,
  just as we do, but dare they?
DOVRE KING: Ay, there we make a match.
  But day remains day, night continues to be night,
  and differences remain between us, despite
  all that we share. Let me therefore explain
  the rift that abides between trolls and the tribe of men.
  Out there – remember? – under the sky's high-gleaming vault,
  'be thyself, be thyself, even to thy most inward fault'
  is the great injunction. Down here, with the race of trolls,
  'be to thyself sufficient' is the motto that appeals.
A COURT TROLL [to PEER]:
  Can you find the profundity there?
PEER: Well, I can't say for sure.
DOVRE KING: 'Sufficient', sufficient unto thyself, O Peer,
  'sufficient' drives its wedge betwixt serf and sire,
  set it on thy scutcheon . . .
PEER: But . . .
DOVRE KING: . . . if you mean to be master here!
PEER: Oh well, what the hell, if it means nothing worse than
    that!
DOVRE KING: And you must also be taught to appreciate
  our folksy ways; things you would do well to heed.
  [He beckons; TWO TROLLS with pigs' heads, white night-
  caps, etc., bring food and drink.]
  Here are tasty cow-pancakes, and from the ox fresh mead.
  Sweet or sour you must drink it for it is home-brewed:
  Home-grown, home-made, home-is-best—
PEER [pushing away the food and drink]:
  and home-pissed!
  To the devil with your tasty domestic fare;
  I'll never be at home with what is here.
DOVRE KING: The golden bowl will be yours when you are
    my heir.

My daughter's favours attend such heirlooms.

PEER: It is well put
by one who knows: 'Govern first thine own self. That is what,
before all else, will turn sour to sweet.'
So, 'skol!'

DOVRE KING: That was indeed a wise observation.
You're spluttering!

PEER: I'll grow accustomed to my portion,
given time, no doubt.

DOVRE KING: Further, you must divest
yourself: that heavy Christian habit must be cast
aside. You must be fettled like us. It is our pride
to wear nothing that is not mountain-made
apart from the silken bows on the ends of our tails.

PEER: *We* have no need of such prehensiles.

DOVRE KING: Here you do. Court Troll!
Stick *my* Sunday tail, firmly, on his rump.

PEER: Hey! Hey! Hands off! I'll look a right fool!

DOVRE KING: Do not dare to approach my child with a
              bare *cul*.

PEER: You cannot stamp
men into beastly patterns.

DOVRE KING: That is your error, my son.
I'm making you fit for the role.
You shall have a brimstone yellow bow for your tail,
one of the highest honours that can be won,
so we reckon.

PEER [*pauses to thinks*]:
It is taught that no man is more than dust.
What argues, then, against placing one's trust
in local belief and practice? Tie it on!

DOVRE KING: Dear fellow, you're too kind.

A COURT TROLL: Twitch your behind,
you'll soon be told how fetchingly it moves.

PEER [*irritated*]:
What else do you want of me while we're at shoves?
How about faith, my Christian
birthright, my heritage as a man?

DOVRE KING: Birthright-belief – you can maintain that
  in peace and quiet.
  Belief is free, untaxed; it's the crust and cut
  that reveal the troll.
  Just so long as we're identical
  in manner and style
  of undress, speech is free.
  By all means call faith what we call monstrosity.
PEER: Despite the prohibitions and conditions, you've now
    appeared
  as a more decent cove than I had feared.
DOVRE KING: We trolls are indeed better than our reputation
  paints us; that's what distinguishes trolls from men.
  I see that we are now done with nutrition,
  let's treat our ears and eyes. Music girl, come, tune!
  Let the great Dovre harp sing us its finest refrain.
  Come, dancing girl, make throb the roof of our hall!
    Harp playing and dancing begin.
A COURT TROLL: How do you like it?
PEER: *Like* it? H'm . . .
DOVRE KING: Speak without fear of reproof.
PEER: A belled cow striking a gut-stringed instrument with
    her hoof,
  a sow in trunk-hose mincing to the beat . . . !
SECOND COURT TROLL: He is condemned to be eaten. Let
    us eat!
DOVRE KING: Remember his human senses and sensibilities.
TROLL MAIDEN: Aarrgh! Tear out his ears and eyes!
WOMAN IN GREEN [*sobbing*]:
  Boo-hoo! Such things my sweet sister and I
  are forced to endure whenever we dance and play.
PEER: Ahem! Was it you? Merely a party game?
  I do assure you that I meant no harm.
WOMAN IN GREEN: I put you on oath!
PEER: The dancing and harping, both,
  were really pretty. Katten flay me if I speak untruth.
DOVRE KING: That's the odd thing about human nature:
  it's so remarkably persistent a feature.

If, during clashes with us, its blood is drawn,
the gash, though not imaginary, mends amazingly soon.
My son-in-law obeys me almost too well;
his Christian unmentionables quickly fell,
he tossed back his draught of mead, as you all
witnessed; he even submitted to wearing a yellow tail.
I was reassured, even, that he had been ex-Adam'd
finally, and felt suitably ashamed
of what he once was. But, look, in a split second,
we find that once more he has the upper hand.
Ah, well, my son, it seems you must take the cure
against these lingering signs of your human nature.
PEER: Hey! What are you doing to me?
DOVRE KING: In your left eye
   I'll make a little scratch, so that you'll see askew
   ever after; all will appear to be splendidly new.
   Next I'll excise the right-hand quizzing-pane . . .
PEER: You're drunk!
DOVRE KING [*placing some sharp instruments on the table*]:
                        Here are my glazier's tools. And then
   we'll fix to your skull what is fixed to the skull
   of a vicious ox to stop it breaking its stall
   and attacking people. Then you will understand
   that your bride is the loveliest lady underground,
   and never again will your sight be distorted –
   belled cows and mincing sows as you reported . . .
PEER: That's crazy talk!
THE OLDEST COURT TROLL: Nay! Our great king's best
      style of address.
   You are the crazy talker, he the wise.
DOVRE KING: Consider how much torment
   you will be spared, moment by moment,
   and over the years to come.
   It is a human distortion of the eyes
   that brings about men's tears with their bitter lyes.
   Their vision is their doom.
PEER: I have to agree with that.
   'If your eye offends you, pluck it out'

it says in the old book of sermons.
But – hey – tell me: when
you have scratched my eye, will it ever again
be healed, be my old human sight, if you see what I mean?
DOVRE KING: Never! Forever this, your troll-vision, remains.
PEER: In that case, 'no thanks, and goodbye!'
DOVRE KING: What do you need out there?
PEER: I need to be on my way.
DOVRE KING: Hold hard! The Dovre King's gate will not open
    inwards to outwards; it just doesn't happen.
PEER: You would keep me by force here?
DOVRE KING: Be sensible, Prince Peer!
    You have a gift for the ways and arts of us trolls.
    Does he not, my people, already have some of our skills?
    Your highest ambition
    is to join our nation?
PEER: It is indeed, by God; I would give an arm
    and a leg for my bride and my promised kingdom.
    But that's the limit. I let them pin on that tail,
    it's true, that prestidigitation by a Court Troll,
    but things done can be undone, things undone be restored.
    I can once more, surely, be decently trousered.
    And doubtless, also, I can cast myself off
    from this Dovrean way of life.
    I don't mind swearing a cow is a girl for a day –
    an oath is something you can always unsay –
    but to be stuck forever
    in the world of the trolls – that makes me shiver.
    To know you can never be free,
    that you can't even die
    decently among your kind
    that's what shakes the mind!
    To lose all hope of at last returning to God –
    that makes me feel really bad.
    I'll not accept that bargain.
DOVRE KING: As true as I am upright-upside-down,
    I am not to be insulted by you, vile man,
    pining-for-daylight starveling! Do you still not know

who I am, or what the fury of our law?
First you seduce my daughter . . .
PEER: That's a lie for a start!
DOVRE KING: . . . and now you must marry her.
PEER: I'll not be forced into that!
DOVRE KING: You mean to deny
    casting upon her your lascivious eye?
PEER [*huffing*]:
    Lascivious eye? Oh, is that all? A quibble –
    'Whoever looketh . . .' as it says in the Bible –
    nobody cares about that these days.
DOVRE KING: Your humankind is truly set in its ways.
    You chew spiritual cud,
    your jaws chomping, hands grasping at your true good,
    the riches of the world and all that it conveys.
    So, you discount lust
    of the eyes, do you? We'll put that to the test.
PEER: You'll not trap me with legal niceties!
WOMAN IN GREEN: Is that what you think it is?
    I tell you, before the year's turn
    your child shall be born.
PEER: Please – let me pass . . .
DOVRE KING: Sewn into a goat-skin.
    You'll see it turn up
    on your doorstep.
PEER [*wiping sweat from his face*]:
    When shall I awaken?
DOVRE KING: Where would you have us convey the child?
    To your palace threshold?
PEER: The little bastard
    had better be fostered!
DOVRE KING: Very well, Prince Peer, the choice is yours.
    But remember this: over the years
    what's done is done. Your child will grow,
    as mixed-blood creatures do,
    so rapidly it will astonish all!
PEER: Young lady, please be reasonable.
    Old fellow, stubborn as an ox,

I beg you, relax,
accept a settlement.
I'm not rich; nor do I have a prince's entitlement.
You may wish to weigh me in the scales
with diamonds or gold, or what best pleases trolls,
but you'll find how quickly I kick the beam.

> *The* WOMAN IN GREEN *goes into labour and is carried out by the* TROLL MAIDENS.

DOVRE KING [*glances briefly at* PEER *with utter contempt and raps out*]:
   Break him, my children! Against the mountain wall! Break him!

A TROLL CHILD: Papa, may we first play 'Owl and Eagle'?
SECOND TROLL CHILD: No, no, the 'Wolf Game'!
THIRD TROLL CHILD: No, no, 'The Mouse and the Cat with Ember Eyes'!
DOVRE KING: My children, I am weary and out of sorts.
   Be brief, then. And not too high-pitched the sports.

> *Exit.*

PEER [*chased by* TROLL CHILDREN]:
   Let me go, devil's spawn!

> *Tries to escape up the chimney.*

TROLL CHILDREN: Goblins and Pixies! Goblins and Pixies!
FIRST TROLL CHILD: Bite his arse!
PEER: Yarrooo-oo!

> *Tries to escape through the trapdoor into the cellar.*

SECOND TROLL CHILD: Seal all the cracks!
A COURT TROLL: The little innocents! What japes, what jokes!
PEER [*struggling with a small* TROLL CHILD *which has fastened upon his ear with its teeth*]:
   Let go, you little shite!
A COURT TROLL [*rapping his knuckles*]:
   That's to requite,
   base serf, your taking hold
   of a royal child!
PEER: A rathole!

> *Makes a dash for it.*

FIRST TROLL CHILD: Stop him! That's right!

PEER: The old man was monstrous but his spawn's much worse!
SECOND TROLL CHILD: Shred him! Shred him!
PEER: How I wish I were a mouse!
    Runs frantically from one spot to another.
THIRD TROLL CHILD [*as they swarm around and over him*]:
    Shut the gate! Shut the gate! He's not to get away!
PEER [*weeping with terror*]:
    How I wish I were a flea!
FIRST TROLL CHILD: And now each eye!
PEER [*half-buried under a mound of* TROLL CHILDREN]:
    Help, Ma! I'm dying! I'm meat for trolls!
    Church bells heard distantly ringing.
TROLL CHILDREN: Bells in the mountain! Bells in the
    mountain! The black priest's cattle-bells!
    The TROLLS *flee, screaming, among enormous seismic
    rumblings and quakings. The great hall falls in ruins.
    Everything vanishes.*

SCENE 7

Pitch darkness.

PEER [*can be heard lashing out at things around him. From
    the sound it could be with a tree-branch*]:
    Who are *you*? Answer!
VOICE IN THE DARKNESS: I am what I am.
PEER: Well, thing with no name,
    make way for me.
VOICE: Take a detour, Peer;
    there's space for us both
    on this broad heath.
PEER [*heard trying to break through in another place; it
    sounds as though he is blocked by something*]:
    Who *are* you?
VOICE: I am what I am.
    Can *you* say the same?

PEER: I can say all I need
  with my sword's bright gleed!
  On guard! Ha! Ja! Peer Gynt has slain a horde!
  King Saul blundered:
  he slew barely a hundred.
  [*Heard once more hacking wildly.*]
  Again – who *are* you?
VOICE: I am what I am.
PEER: Well, let's forget
  how slow you are. Let me change the question a bit.
  What are you?
VOICE: The Boyg. I am the great Boyg.
PEER: Not yet there.
  The mystery was total.
  Now it's a kind of a mottle.
  Shift yourself, Boyg!
VOICE: Best not try here, Peer!
PEER: Through, though, coming through!
  [*Strikes, lashes out as before.*]
                          Hit something! Heard it fall.
  [*Tries to move forward; collides with something.*]
  Ha! What the –! Are more here?
VOICE: Just the Boyg, Peer. All is one and one is all:
  the Boyg still unharmed, the Boyg that is hurt sore;
  the Boyg that is dead; the Boyg that for aye shall endure.
PEER [*hurling his branch to the ground*]:
  This sword's under a spell
  but my fists he shall feel!
    *Lashes out, struggling to break through the unseen
    opposition.*
VOICE: Ay, trust to the fists, brute strength of body.
  Hee-hee, Peer Gynt, then you'll be top-noddy!
PEER [*staggering back*]:
  Forwards, backwards, out and in,
  in and out too blurred to scry
  yet tight as in a needle's eye
  there he is, there he's just been,

I struggle out, I'm in the midst of the ring.
Your name again! Let me see who you are. Or what kind of
    thing.
VOICE: The Boyg. I am the Boyg.
PEER [*stumbling and fumbling around*]:
    Neither dead nor alive; a sort of slimy fog.
    Formless, then. I feel I've been struggling for years
    in a pit of snarling but still sleepy bears.
    [*Yells.*]
    Strike, damn you, strike! Why won't you strike me?
VOICE: Boyg's not mad and you can't make me.
PEER: Hit me! Go on! Biff! Bash!
VOICE: The Boyg is – I am – never so rash.
PEER: Look here! I've given you my ultimatum!
VOICE: The great Boyg has his way with mortals though he
    doesn't fight 'em.
PEER: Is there no one here, no pixie, no infant troll,
    that I could scrap with, you know, back-to-the-wall?
    Nothing, no one, no one but him,
    and now he's snoring. Boyg!
VOICE: What, you again?
PEER: Boyg, it's your call!
VOICE: The great Boyg hazards nothing and wins all.
PEER [*biting his own hands and arms*]:
    Grrr! Grrr! Now I feel 'em, tearing claws and teeth
    in my own flesh. Feels great, like a rebirth!
    A sound like the wingbeats of great birds.
FIRST BIRD VOICE: Dear sisters from afar,
    all must gather here.
PEER: Lass, if you mean
    to save me, do it soon;
    don't cast your eyes down
    with such a modest demean-
    our, fixed upon the ground.
    That book in your hand,
    the one with the clasps, yes,
    hurl it straight at his eyes!

SECOND BIRD VOICE: He's rambling.
VOICE: He's ours.
FIRST BIRD VOICE: Sisters, sisters, hasten!
PEER: Too much – to buy your life
  with an hour's play
  come to grief,
  deep-laden with such exhaustion.
    He sinks to the ground.
SECOND BIRD VOICE: Boyg, there he fell. Now carry him away.
    The sound of church bells and hymn singing can be heard
    in the distance.
BOYG [*shrinks to nothing and just manages to say, between*
    gasps]:
  He was too strong for us. The prayers of good women were
  keeping him safe.

SCENE 8

Sunrise. On the mountain-slope outside AASE'*s seter hut. The*
door is shut. All is quiet, the area appears to be deserted. PEER
lies asleep outside, sheltered by the seter wall.

PEER [*wakes, looks about him morosely and spits*]:
  A bit of sharp salted herring would go down a treat.
  [*Spits again. Catches sight of* HELGA, *who approaches*
  bearing a basket of food.]
  Hey, young 'un, you here! Well, what cheer?
HELGA: It's Solveig.
PEER [*leaping up*]:
           Solveig? Where?
HELGA: Back of the wall there.
SOLVEIG [*staying out of sight*]:
  If you come near I'll run.
PEER [*pausing*]:
  Afraid of a man's hand? Mine?
SOLVEIG: Shame on you!

PEER: Know where I was last night?
  The Dovre King's daughter clung like a leech, that tight!
  She's still after me.
SOLVEIG: So it's as well
  that they rung the church bell.
PEER: Peer Gynt's not a lad any more,
  taking the lure.
  What's that you say?
HELGA [*crying*]:
  She's running away!
  [*Starts to run after her.*]
  Wait, oh wait!
PEER [*seizing* HELGA *by the arm*]:
  Look what's in my pocket –
  a silver bullet, young 'un, and it's yours
  just as long as you keep me in that head of hers.
HELGA: Let go; let me go!
PEER: But here, look!
HELGA: And now the basket's broke.
PEER: God help you if you don't . . .
HELGA: Don't what, you bully!
PEER [*meekly, releasing her*]:
  No – no – I simply meant –
  beg her not to forget me wholly.
      HELGA *runs off.*

ACT THREE

SCENE 1

Deep inside a forest of conifers. Gloomy autumn weather.
Snow is falling. PEER *is in shirt sleeves, felling trees in order to*
have wood for building.

PEER [*chopping at a big pine tree with gnarled branches*]:
Yes, you're a tough 'un, old fellow, but there's no help for it,
down you must fall, despite that strong coat of chain-mail
    you wear. It
will be riven by me, you'll see, no matter how strong it's become.
Yes, yes, and despite your shaking at me that crooked arm.
Indeed I can quite understand why you're so angry, old
    friend.
And yet, as you know, you'll be brought to your knees at
    the end.
[*Breaks off abruptly.*]
What lies I am weaving, what lies! It's no corseleted veteran,
it's a tree long past its best, a pine with cracked bark that I
    mourn.
Because of hard labour, felling these giants for timber,
I find I invent fables for fables I can't remember.
It's the very devil when you both hack and dream.
I must find a way through this soul-fog, fantasist that I am.
You've been outlawed, my lad, driven from the parish;
you must learn to fend for yourself or else perish.
[*Works energetically for a time.*]
Outlawed, yes. And you don't have a mother at call,

spreading the tablecloth, readying your next meal.
Need to eat, my lad, off you must toddle to find,
secreted in forest and watercourse, things that will fend
off hunger a while, though raw, though they have to be skinned.
So then you chop small the resinous wood for kindling
and get a blaze going nicely with self-taught handling.
If you wish to be warmly clad you must hunt reindeer;
if your desire is a stone house, dressed stone does not simply
    appear.
For a house of wood you fell trees then chop trees into logs,
carry the logs on your back; you soon learn how weight drags,
stack the logs in the yard, and then – oh my word! –
[*His axe-arm sinks to his side; he stares straight ahead.*]
what a building that building will be: many-towered,
each tower with a weather-vane; a well-sealed ridge to the roof.
At the gable-end a splendid mermaid I'll carve,
a mermaid formed like a fish from the navel down.
Brass there shall be on doorlock and weathervane.
And glass, yes glass – I must somehow obtain that –
glass a-plenty for passing strangers to marvel at:
'Whose is that fine house afar-off shining on the hill?'
[*Laughs angrily at himself.*]
Lies, lies, straight out of hell! My mind is a-whirl.
You're an outlaw, Peer lad, for that I'm ready to vouch.
[*Hacks away violently at the tree.*]
It's a cabin you need, roofed with tight shingles of birch,
that will keep out rainstorms and the soundless bite of frost.
[*Looks up through the branches of the tree.*]
Well, he's standing and swaying, just about ready at last.
A kick should do the trick. And over he goes!
A shudder passes through the forest's tribe of young trees.
[*Begins to strip the branches. He stops abruptly and listens,
his axe raised.*]
Somebody's coming! So here comes an enemy –
Old Man Hæggstad, still on my trail. Has he seen me?
[*Ducks down behind the tree and peers around.*]
Well, that's not old Hæggstad; it's nobody but a lad;
he's looking here, there, everywhere, and he seems afraid.

What's that he's carrying, hidden under his short coat?
It looks like a pruning knife; he stops now, still looks around,
spreads out his right hand on a fence-post. Great heavens,
   he's cut
off a finger, the whole finger! Blood's gushing from the wound
like when you castrate a bull-calf. He's wrapped his fist in a
   cloth
and now he staggers away, he's gone. What a thing to do!
A queer kind of pluck, that; to maim yourself so.
Nobody forced him to do it. Now I remember though!
Conscription – that's it! The army wanted to claim him;
he didn't want – and I can't say that I blame him.
But to maim yourself like that! It fairly took my breath
just to see him do it, and that's the truth.
   Shakes his head, then resumes work.

SCENE 2

A room down at AASE's *farm. Everything is in disarray. Chests
are standing open; clothes are lying scattered around. There is
a cat on the bed.* AASE *and* KARI, *a crofter's wife, are busily at
work, packing things up and sorting things out.*

AASE [*running to one side of the room*]:
   Listen, Kari!
KARI: Listen to what?
AASE [*running to the room's other side*]:
                        Listen! Oh, where
   did I put it? – where is it? – what am I looking for?
   I think I'm going mad – where's the key to the chest?
KARI: In the lock of the chest.
AASE: What's that rumbling?
KARI: The last
   load on its way to Hæggstad.
AASE [*weeping*]:
                        I'd be happier if 'twere me
   driven off in a black coffin for all to see.

Oh, what I've had to suffer, had to endure,
the good Lord only knows! And now, my house stripped bare.
What old Hæggstad didn't want, the bailiff made off with,
even the clothes from my back he's been paid off with.
Shame on all, I say, who have put me through it!
[*Sits on the edge of the bed.*]
The farmhouse and the land are both forfeit.
Old Man Hæggstad was brutal but the courts were more so,
there was no help whatever and there was no mercy;
Peer nowhere to be found, no neighbours gathered round . . .

KARI: Well, you can stay on here until you die.

AASE: The cat and me living off charity – ay.

KARI: God keep you, good lady! He did you a bad turn,
he surely did, did your good-for-nothing son.

AASE: Nay, woman, you're wrong there. Why blame Peer?
Ingrid got back safely to Hæggstad, I hear.
They should have made an outlaw of Old Nick: he'd
more to do with those goings-on than my son had.

KARI: Perhaps, good Mother Gynt, we should send for the
pastor.
Things are, I believe, past your poor strength to restore.

AASE: The pastor? Why, yes, I think that perhaps we should.
[*Getting abruptly to her feet*]
But, dear God, I can't; I'm the lad's closest kin.
I'm plighted to give him aid when all have let him down.
They've thrown him this old jacket and I must darn it.
And here's a sheepskin; do I dare to purloin it?
Where are the trousers?

KARI: There, with the rest
of the castaway remnants.

AASE [*rooting around in the rags and other junk*]:
                                    Well I'm blest!
Look what's here, Kari; it's that old casting-ladle
my husband had; that he taught Peer how to handle.
He – young Peer, that is – pretended he was a button-
moulder: melting, then shaping, then stamping the pattern.
One day, in the thick of a feast, the lad comes in
and asks his dad for some pewter to melt down.

'Not pewter,' says Jon, 'but silver, King Christian's coin!'
God forgive him, my Jon, but it all melted away –
pewter, and silver, and gold, in his drunken sway.
Here are the trousers – agh – there's less cloth than air;
they must be patched, Kari.
KARI: Ay, they could stand repair.
AASE: And when that's done I must repair to my bed.
   I'm all done in and as weak as a kitten.
   [*Cries out in joyful excitement.*]
   Two woollen shirts, Kari, that they've forgotten!
   Kind fortune be thanked! Put one to one side;
   no, hear me, Kari: best both of 'em are hid.
KARI: God save us, Mother Aase, theft is a mortal sin!
AASE: So I've heard tell; but you know the pastor preaches
   forgiveness for worse sins than stealing shirts and breeches.

SCENE 3

*Outside a newly built cabin in the forest. Reindeer horns over
the door. High-piled snow. Dusk.* PEER *standing at the door,
nailing a large wooden latch into place.*

PEER [*breaks into laughter but stops abruptly*]:
   Locks there must be; locks that can withstand
   battering by troll-fiends or the odd brutal human kind.
   Locks there must be, locks that withstand the creatures
   of darkness, in darkness, aggressive weird natures.
   They sidle like shadows; they stand and they batter:
   'Let us in, Peer Gynt, we have come for a merry natter.
   Under your bed we rustle. With fear you shall awaken.
   We disturb the ashes; in the stove-pipe act the fire-draken.
   Hee-hee, Peer Gynt, do you yet trust nails and planking
   to keep out of your thoughts thoughts that the trolls are
      thinking?'
      SOLVEIG *is seen approaching, on skis, across the heath.
      She has a large shawl wrapped around her head and car-
      ries a bundle in her hand.*

SOLVEIG: God's blessing upon your labour. You must not
  turn me away.
  You sent for me to come; I have come through the short day.
PEER: Solveig? It can't be . . . ? Yes, it is you! You're not still
  afraid
  of my nearness?
SOLVEIG: She told me – Helga – what you had said;
  and there were other messages – from wind and silence,
  from your mother chatterboxing her cares for the nonce;
  words half-caught on the wing as dreams drifted past;
  nights heavy, days empty, and then your summons at last.
  Back there in the village it seemed that life was suspended;
  I could not laugh or cry as if I minded;
  I, minding only your moods, knowing the moods that had
  been;
  sure only of one purpose. I now have no kin.
  I have been set at variance, as that gospel tells,
  with father and mother; am alone in the world's toils.
PEER: Solveig, my fair, my fair one, you have come away
  to find me, to be mine alone: is that what you say?
SOLVEIG: To be alone with you and to be yours alone,
  my friend, my comforter; other friends have I none.
  [Weeping]
  To leave my little sister, that was the worst part;
  no, to wound my father was the worst thrust; and the last,
  surely, was to leave her at whose heart
  I had long since been carried. The supreme woe
  was the grief on all three faces as I turned to go.
PEER: Have you heard the court's sentence that was passed
  this spring?
  It strips me of farm, inheritance, everything.
SOLVEIG: Do you think it was for property and inheritance
  that I cut myself off from the life I had loved once?
PEER: And do you know the village? Once out of this forest
  I am liable to citizen's arrest
  by anyone whom I may see, but who sees me first.
SOLVEIG: I have journeyed on skis, I have asked, I have lost,
  my way.

When questioned I replied 'I am going home today.'
PEER: So, off with the nailed boards!
No reason to dread more those elvish lords.
Since you dare enter the cave of the hunter
great blessings will be bestowed on him and his.
Solveig! Ah, let me look at you – not too close! –
simply behold: how fair and delicate you are.
Let me lift you: how slight and how light you are.
And if I carry you, Solveig, I shall never grow weary;
I'll not sully you with my folly; with outstretched arms
shall part you from my baseness, as from all harms.
Beneficent lovely creature – every feature –
oh, who would have thought that I could so have brought,
even with the magnetic force of my longing,
night and day, for what you are now bringing,
your divine grace to this place so meanly wrought!
This hut of logs, my love, it is ugly and poor.
I shall raze and rebuild it worthy of your . . .
SOLVEIG: Poor it may be; it is everything I desire.
The wind that roars in the trees is a free air.
Back in the village everything was constrained;
I had to be free of that, free in my own mind –
it is partly that which has brought me – the tall trees
soughing by day and night – what song, what stillnesses!
Here is my true home.
PEER: Art thou so sure,
my lass? For the length of thy days?
SOLVEIG: This path I have made to your door
can never be unmade.
PEER: And so I have you! Enter!
I will set you by my hearth; I will fetch resinous wood
for the burning; I will make all good.
Snug you shall be. And mine. And all will shine.
You shall take your ease and never shall you freeze.
[*He opens the door;* SOLVEIG *enters. He waits a moment;
then, laughing, gleeful, he leaps and shouts.*]
My king's daughter! Now at last I have caught her!
My palace fit for a king – rebuilt, it will be a grand thing!

He takes up the axe and begins to leave; at the same
moment an ELDERLY WOMAN *wearing a ragged green*
skirt emerges from the copse. An UGLY CHILD *carrying a*
wooden ale bowl limps after her, clutching at her skirt.

WOMAN: Evening, my lightfoot lad!

PEER: Who's there? What's up?

WOMAN: We're friends, Peer,
old friends, you could say; we're neighbours. My hut is very
near.

PEER: That's news to me.

WOMAN: While your hut was a-building mine
was a-building too.

PEER [*restless*]:   I'm in haste to be gone.

WOMAN: You always were, you always are, in a great hurry,
my lad.

I'll trudge along after you; meet you at the end of the road.

PEER: You're in error, old dame.

WOMAN: I was greatly mistaken before:
that time you promised me wonders by the score.

PEER: I promised you? You? What are you on about,
you old witch?

WOMAN: You've forgotten, then, the evening that
you drank with my father? How could you possibly forget?

PEER: How can you remind me of what was never in
my mind?

Thou'rt out of thine, granny! So, when did we meet last?

WOMAN: We met last when we met first.

Offer your father a drink, child; I'm sure he has a thirst.

PEER: 'Your father'?

WOMAN: Yes. You can surely tell a pig by its hide.
You've eyes, haven't you? Can't you see he has crippled
shanks

as you have a crippled mind?

PEER: You tell me that warped kid
is some brat of mine?

WOMAN: He has grown quickly.

PEER: Vile snout of oinks,
you dare blame me for him?

WOMAN: Why not, you get, you goat?
　　You suit well.
　　[*Weeping*]
　　　　　　　　　Is it my fault I'm not the girl you met
　　among the meadows and hills, when I was virgin yet,
　　and made your victim? When I gave birth last fall
　　old Katten rubbed my back; small wonder I am foul.
　　If you desire me fair, fair as I was before,
　　it's time you showed that wench in there the door.
　　Put her out of mind as you remove her from sight.
　　Do it, my dear love, and my face will look right!
PEER: Get thee far hence, thou troll-witch!
WOMAN: See me do it.
PEER: I'll split thy skull to shivers!
WOMAN: Do that, you'll rue it.
　　Ho-ho, Peer Gynt, I'm proof against any dunt
　　of blows you might rain down. Each single day
　　I'll nudge your door and leer at your content:
　　you in your tender dalliance and play,
　　playful tenderness mounting to full desire.
　　I'll lie between you and demand my share;
　　or she and I will share; you'll lie between us.
　　Briefly, farewell; tomorrow we shall be wed.
PEER: Out of my sight, thou damned obsceneness!
WOMAN: Wait! I almost forgot: this child is yours to raise,
　　light-footed one! Devil's imp, greet your dad.
CHILD [*spitting at him*]:
　　Pfff! See me set my axe to him instead.
WOMAN [*kissing the child*]:
　　What a wise head there is on that small body.
　　When grown he'll be the spitting image of daddy.
PEER [*stamping his foot in wild vexation*]:
　　I wish – I wish – you were as far . . .
WOMAN: As we now are near?
PEER [*wringing his hands*]:
　　And this . . .
WOMAN: . . . is born of idleness and vanity and lust.
　　I pity you, Peer.

PEER: Better you pity her. Solveig! my best,
   my clearest, purest gold!
WOMAN: Ah, yes, as Old Nick says,
   it is the innocent who are hurt the most.
   His mother beat him for his father's drunken ways.
       The CHILD *throws his ale bowl at* PEER. *Then the*
       WOMAN IN GREEN *takes him abruptly by the hand and*
       walks with him into the copse.
PEER [*after a protracted silence*]:
   Best go round and about, the Boyg said. I need to do that
       here.
   My great house has toppled with an almighty din.
   I had enclosed her – her to whom I simply wished to be
       near,
   suddenly making desire ugly, turning joy into an old pain.
   Go around, make a detour. There is no straight path from
       you to her.
   Straight path? Strait gate? Isn't there something given
   in the great Book concerning seventy times seven,
   something else about the direct route to heaven?
   But what – what does it say? I long ago lost the book,
   have forgotten most of it; nor can I look
   for any counsel here in this bleak yonder.
   Repentance? Doesn't that take too much of your
       precious time
   with all to hazard: a meagre life of self-harm,
   breaking to fragments all those precious things –
   the delicate, the lovely, the calm – to which one clings,
   only to piece together what one has put asunder,
   mostly in vain. It's as fragile as a clock:
   no matter what tinkering the thing won't work.
   In order to let grow the plants you've sown
   be very careful not to tread them down.
   But what lies were expelled via that witch's snout!
   Even though the abomination is no longer about,
   out of sight, alas, does not mean out of mind.
   Ugly thoughts have a way of hanging around:

Ingrid, for one; and the three randy girls
with whom I had a fine time on the hills.
Will they also, with a kind of laughing anger,
claim, like her, that they still belong here,
here, in my embrace, to be lifted as one would lift a child
with arms outstretched, so innocent, so fulfilled?
Ah, Peer, if your arms were the length of a tree's height –
pine, spruce – you would still hold her too close, too tight,
to let her go again without the taint of your lust!
Somehow or other this must be sidled past
without illicit gains but also without shipwreck.
One must push certain things away; contrive they don't creep
    back.
[*Takes a few steps towards the cabin, then stops.*]
Go back to her after all this? So ugly, so utterly ruined?
Go back to her now, with that troll-pack so close behind?
To speak to her yet be silent, still nursing the unconfessed . . .
[*He lets the axe drop.*]
And this the eve of the holy day! Trysting with Christ
in my present state would be a mortal sin.

SOLVEIG [*appearing at the open half-door*]:
    All finished there? Are you coming in?
PEER [*sotto voce*]:
    Say rather, coming around.
SOLVEIG: What's that . . . ?
PEER: I said, stay where you are.
    It's dark; and there's something heavy out here.
SOLVEIG: Then let me help. For that, two are better than one.
PEER: Solveig, stay there. This burden I must bear alone.
SOLVEIG: Then don't stray too far . . .
PEER: Be patient, my own girl;
    far or near you must wait a fair while.
SOLVEIG: I shall.
        PEER *walks away, following the wilderness path.* SOLVEIG
        remains standing at the open half-door.

SCENE 4

AASE's *cabin at evening. A log fire is burning on the hearth, the only light in the room. The cat sits on a chair at the foot of the bed.* AASE *is lying in the bed, her hands moving restlessly on the bedcover.*

AASE: Is he not coming, Lord?
　　For I am tired of waiting.
　　No one to take him word;
　　I with no power of writing.
　　Tell him to hasten, Lord.
　　So suddenly I've been stricken!
　　Ah, was I then too hard
　　when the child wouldn't hearken?
　　　　PEER *enters.*
PEER: Mother!
AASE:　　　　　My son! May God
　　in His great goodness bless you!
　　You've not come by the road?
　　You're dead if some foe sees you!
PEER: My life – who cares about that
　　now we're together
AASE: Well, Kari has words to eat.
　　I must go far, and farther;
　　like Simeon depart in peace.
PEER: Mother, what are you saying?
　　What kind of journey is this?
AASE: Peer, dear son, I am dying.
　　We have but a short time.
PEER [*draws away from her, moves a little distance apart*]:
　　I can bear no one's burden.
　　I thought, why not go home?
　　Guilt will not so bear down.
　　I was wrong. Are your hands cold,
　　and your feet?
AASE:　　　　　All will be over
　　soon. When my eyes grow dulled

close them gently for ever.
My coffin also, see to my
coffin; and let all be splendid.
What am I saying?
PEER: There'll be time
to reconsider.
AASE: Look what those men did!
They left me so little.
PEER [*pulling brusquely away yet again*]:
                         My fault –
I've no need of reminders!
AASE: Son, let us lay the guilt:
'twas drink, wherein all founders.
Yes, you were drunk, way back,
and not in right possession
of your senses. You rode that buck
in your brain. It stands to reason.
PEER: Just as you say. We'll forget –
as you say – the whole sorry story.
Such heaviness we'll set
aside for another day.
[*He sits down on the edge of the bed.*]
Just about homely things
let us talk together;
forgetful of past wrongs,
a son with his mother.
And, see here, the old cat
is alive still and thriving.
AASE: It yowls something dreadful at night.
'Tis a sign of . . .
PEER [*quickly changing the subject*]:
                         Village behaving,
I take it?
AASE [*smiles faintly*]:
                 They say there's a lass –
no names – who pines for the mountain.
PEER [*hastily*]:
Mads Moen, how is he these days? .
He's no wife to maintain.

AASE: And she turns a deaf ear
  to her old folks, they tell me.
  Perhaps you should visit her;
  it might cure her melancholy.
PEER: Aslak the smith: what's become
  of Aslak?
AASE: That dirty no-good!
  I'd rather tell you the name
  of one who should be wooed.
PEER: We've said that we'll forget –
  as you say – the sorry story.
  Such heaviness we'll set
  aside for a later day.
  Are you thirsty? Would you like a drink?
  Lie straight, can you? The bed should be longer.
  Good heavens, well here's a thing!
  This was *my* bed as a youngster!
  So often you sat on the edge here,
  and sang those improvised verses,
  and spread my sheepskin with care –
  and your goodnight kisses . . .
AASE: So you remember, dear lad!
  And how we played at sledding.
  We journeyed far on this bed,
  vast distances, riding and riding . . .
PEER: Always when he was away,
  my father, such wonderful stories.
  And the pinnacle of our play,
  Mother, those wondrous horses!
AASE: As if I could ever forget them.
  Kari's cat was our accomplice
  in a contented dream.
PEER: My bedroom, for us, became ice-
  castles west of the moon,
  east of where the sun rises,
  and that castle of enchanted stone
  with its gilded trellises:
BOTH: Soria Moria![14]

PEER: You took
  a stick for a whip-handle.
AASE: And you in your travelling cloak –
  the sheepskin . . .
PEER: Distances dwindle!
  And yet you took such care
  of me then; and as we journeyed,
  your whip-hand and rein-hand so sure,
  'Not cold, Peer?' gently inquired.
  God bless you, then, after all,
  you old fright; you were loving
  when all is said, and loved well.
  In pain? Do you need moving?
AASE: My back, son; it's this hard board.
PEER: Stretch out, I'll support you.
  There, now, is it less hard?
  Does anything still hurt you?
AASE: I have to be on my way,
  son Peer; I long to be taken.
PEER: A foolish thing to say,
  Ma; wrap yourself in the sheepskin.
  I'll stay with you, sit here
  on the bedside. More make-believe
  is what's called for.
AASE: No, Peer,
  it's that sermon book I must have,
  my mind's so troubled yet.
PEER: 'In Soria Moria Castle
  there is a great feast set.'
  In the big sled-rug nestle
  (we're racing over the heath)
  and the velvet cushions.
AASE: But am I invited?
PEER: We both,
  Mother, are important persons.
  [*He hitches a rope to the chair on which the cat is lying, takes
  a stick in his hand and sits at the foot of the bed.*]
  Giddy-up, giddy-up, giddy-up!

Say you're not too cold, Mother.
My word! Grane can skip –
famed steed of the dragon-slayer!
AASE: My son, what is it now
   that I hear ringing?
PEER: 'The harness bells, I trow.'
AASE: It is a more hollow song.
PEER: Why, now we're crossing a fjord . . .
AASE: It roars, and I'm still frightened.
PEER: 'Spruce trees chanting, for hard
   blows the wind over the heathland.'
   Lie still.
AASE: That welcome light,
   from where does it shine so bravely?
PEER: 'From that fine castle upon the height.'
   Music and dancing. Are they not lovely?
AASE: They are indeed.
PEER: St Peter
   stands outside that portal.
   He says, 'I must soon meet her,
   that fine lady of whom I hear tell.'
AASE: So he greets us kindly?
PEER: He does, and with great honour.
   The best wine to be found he
   sets aside for your dinner.
AASE: D'you think they have cakes too?
PEER: Cakes? Why, cakes a-plenty.
   The archdeacon's wife says so:
   high tea awaiting your entry.
AASE: What? You and me both
   to be welcomed there together
   by that fine lady of worth?
PEER: Indeed we are, Mother.
AASE: Well, well, such a joyful throng,
   such a joyous welcome,
   and for me, such a poor thing.
PEER [cracks the whip]:
   Giddy-up, Grane, we'll soon be home!

AASE: Is it the right road we are on?
PEER [*once more cracking the whip*]:
   Yes, and it is famed widely,
   'The Broad Highway', as it is known.
AASE: Must you drive quite so speedily?
   It does things to my poor head.
PEER: But see, the castle's nearer;
   it's almost over, our ride.
AASE: I'll close my eyes for a while, dear.
   I'm in good hands, I know.
PEER: Come on Grane, move your haunches!
   Towards the castle the great throngs go,
   like reversed avalanches.
   Hey! You who block our way,
   Gynt and Co. seek entry!
   Herr St Peter, what do you say?
   Mother's a relict of the old gentry;
   and honest as they come. I won't
   sing you my own praises.
   I won't be staying; content
   as I am to have been of service.
   Pour me a drink, I'll gulp it.
   If not, not. I hand lies down
   like Old Nick from the pulpit,
   jovially, in his black gown.
   I called my mother an old hen
   – such brooding and pecking.
   Now I need you to take her in
   with nice etiquetting.
   There's none better en route
   from the old neighbourhood,
   I can tell you that strong and hot.
   Bravo! Here's kind old Father God.
   He'll tell you what's what, St Peter:
   [*Adopting a deep and solemn voice*]
   'That's quite enough of that' – you'll see! –
   'I'm telling you straight, Herr Janitor,
   Mother Aase's to be let in free!'

[*Laughs uproariously and turns to speak to his* MOTHER.]
Isn't that what I prophesied –
a progressive suggestion?
[*Suddenly afraid.*]
Why are your eyes so dead,
Mother? Answer my question . . .
[*Goes to the head of the bed.*]
Speak, Mother: it's Peer, your son!
Don't just lie there staring.
[*Gently lays his hand on her forehead; places the rope back
on the chair; says, in a hushed voice.*]
Well, Grane, you can return
to your ancient careering.
[*He leans over and closes* AASE's *eyes.*]
My thanks, then, for those long games,
the thrashings, the lullabies.
You're to thank me betimes
for the nice ride.
[*Presses his cheek against her mouth.*]
                                        That will suffice.

KARI [*enters*]:
   Peer? You here? You keep well
   your heavy vigil. Sorrow and need
   become our kind. But I can't tell
   whether she sleeps . . .
PEER: She sleeps. Aase is dead.

   KARI *begins to weep over* AASE's *body.* PEER *walks to
   and fro in the room for some considerable time. He stops
   beside the bed.*

PEER: I'll try my luck, slip away.
   Please give my mother decent burial.
KARI: Shall you travel far?
PEER: First to the sea.
KARI: That far?
PEER: And from there further still.
   He leaves.

ACT FOUR

SCENE 1

On the southwest coast of Morocco. A grove of palm trees. A table laid for dinner; there are hammocks. Offshore lies a steam yacht flying both Norwegian and American flags. A dinghy is drawn up on the beach. The sun is sinking. PEER, *a distinguished-looking middle-aged gentleman clad in an elegant travelling-suit with a gold pince-nez dangling on his breast, is presiding at table.* MR COTTON, MONSIEUR BALLON, HERR VON EBERKOPF *and* HERR TRUMPETERSTRAALE *are his guests. The meal is drawing to a close.*

PEER: More wine, my friends, more wine? Since man
   is made for pleasure it's a sin
   not to enjoy; once gone 'tis gone.
   Come now, some brandy? Or stay with wine?
TRUMPETERSTRAALE: Your table is unmatched, Bror Gynt!
PEER: My cook and butler have some claim,
   then, to your thanks; as does my mint
   of money.
MR COTTON: Well, a toast to them
   as well as you!
M. BALLON: In France we have
   refined expressions to extol
   such qualities. So few who live
   en garçon can retain them all.
V. EBERKOPF: A nuance of free spirit we
   detect, combined with, here and there,

the true vein of world-citizenry,
a *Weltanschauung, echt und wahr*;[15]
a vision through the storm-clouds breaking,
all unconfined by prejudice;
the *Ur-natur*, divine self-seeking,
Erhebung of the triune *Kreis*
united at the *Krise*[16]-joint.
I think, monsieur, that's what you meant.

M. BALLON: Quite possibly. It did not seem
so eloquent in French.

V. EBERKOPF: That's so.
French cannot summarize a theme
succinctly as we Germans do.
The base of the phenomenon
is . . .

PEER: My dear sir, summed in a phrase:
that I have lived my life alone.
'I am what I am' sounds my success:
the man himself and what he has.
Such the legitimate extent
of his concerns. Securities:
how can he have these if he's bent
with burdens of another's being?

V. EBERKOPF: And yet, I'd swear, this epic stance
has cost you dearly more than once!

PEER: Indeed, yes; but I left each field
still carrying both sword and shield.
Once only I, in this regard,
came close to fatal self-betraying.
I was a smart, good-looking lad;
and she for whom my young heart bled
came of some royal lineage . . .

M. BALLON: *Royal*, monsieur?

PEER [*dismissively*]:

                              Well, so to speak,
the kind so common in this age.

TRUMPETERSTRAALE [*thumping the table*]:
Ennobled trolls, as I'm a Swede!

PEER [*shrugging his shoulders*]:
   Decayed aristocrats, who make
   sure to erase plebeian blood
   from their escutcheon.
MR COTTON: So the lass
   was lost to you?
M. BALLON: Her next of kin
   forbade the match?
PEER: Quite the reverse!
   [*Speaks with deliberation.*]
   To be as plain
   as delicacy permits, there were
   circumstances – ahem, monsieur! –
   that argued for an early splicing.
   I found the prospect unenticing.
   In some things I'm fastidious.
   I'd rather stand on my own feet.
   So, when my pa-in-law-to-be
   dropped hints that seemed more like abuse –
   that I should change my name and buy
   a patent of nobility –
   from him, mark you – together with
   suggestions that I won't repeat,
   well, I withdrew forthwith, with all
   the pride of rank that I could pull,
   renounced my bride and bounty both.
   [*Assumes a look of piety and drums on the table.*]
   Ah yes, there is a ruling fate;
   on that we mortals can rely;
   a comfort in our hard estate . . .
M. BALLON: And there the matter ended, eh?
PEER: Ah, no; indeed, the opposite;
   for those with no call to intrude
   did so, and raised a hue and cry.
   Worst were the youngest of that brood.
   Seven duels with seven sons I fought.
   It was a time I'll not forget.
   I emerged victor; and though it cost

blood, yet my self-worth increased;
rose in the world's eyes too. Things point
conclusively to my grand creed:
the hand of fate's benevolent!

V. EBERKOPF: You are entitled, worthy sir,
to rank among us as world-seer.
While others merely commentate
on that and this and this and that
and fumble when they half-descry,
you bring all into unity;
and by that norm you measure each
and everything that others touch;
and every nut and bolt you tighten
till every detail of research
is something that your gifts enlighten.
You have no letters to your name?

PEER: I am, as I have said before,
an autodidact pure and simple.
To scholarship I make no claim,
but I have pondered here and there
and found such means of working ample,
know a fair bit about most things.
I started late to cogitate,
by which time ploughing through a book
is heavy labour, shifting rock,
rough with the smooth. The rights and wrongs
of history I've sampled piecemeal,
no time to put it all together.
And since, in hard times, one especially needs faith's consolations,
I took that in the same way rather,
bits here and there, no turgid notions.
It's easier to swallow thus,
and to regurgitate for use.

MR COTTON: Business pragmatics at its best!

PEER [lighting a cigar]:
Consider also, if you will,
my life's course: emigrating west –

in steerage – labouring to live
the moment that I first arrive,
all swallowed as a purgative.
But life is precious, even then,
and death most bitter. Luck was on
my side and fate proved flexible,
as I did too – unhexable!
Within ten years all turned to gold.
In Charleston, Carolina, I
was Croesus as I bought and sold
at ease with that fraternity.
My shipping line was thriving.

MR COTTON: What
  did you carry?

PEER: Chiefly I shipped
  Negroes to Charleston; and to China
  Buddhas made in Carolina.

M. BALLON: Shame on you, sir!

TRUMPETERSTRAALE: Croesus crapped!

PEER: It seems you find my business ethics
  too much for your own moral toothpicks.
  I too have felt a like revulsion,
  believe me! And yet, once you start,
  business becomes its own compulsion.
  Thousands depend on you, the cogs
  keep turning at a faster rate.
  Of 'give it up', 'let it all go',
  'finally retire', you know,
  it's 'finally' that I most hate.
  I, on the other hand, admit
  to having always known what's meant
  by 'consequences' and 'black dogs'.
  Yes, I concede, 'crossing the line'
  is an old phobia of mine.
  Besides, I'd started to find hints
  of threatening age – you know, hair tints,
  full head of hair but touched with grey?
  Although my health was excellent

I sensed that lurking jeopardy
and flinched from it. Who knows how soon
the hour will strike, the jury-foreman
pronounce the verdict: sheep? or goats?
Dread of that judgement's only human.
Yet how to stop, I tell you, that's
the big brain-teaser. My China-trade
ground on, unstoppable. Well, then!
New trinkets on the old machine.
Each spring I still shipped little Buddhas;
each fall, persons in holy orders
(the mission field was thriving), kitted
them out with things well suited:
socks, bibles, rum and rice.

MR COTTON: You made
    a decent profit, I presume.
PEER: Goes without saying. The whole time
    they laboured, with both zeal and zest;
    for every god we shipped out east
    they had a coolie deep-baptized,
    ensuring equilibrium.
    The mission field was never left
    fallow; the little gods they sold
    from door to door they later reft
    back, for John Chinaman's a child.
MR COTTON: Do tell us, now, your other trade?
PEER: There also ethics won the day.
    As I declined towards old age –
    no man can know when he'll conclude
    his journey on this pilgrimage,
    on top of which there was the rage
    of crazed philanthropists at large,
    the perils, too, of reef and rock,
    revenue cutters and the like –
    these things together clinched the deal.
    'Time, Peer', I mused, 'to shorten sail,
    put well behind you your past errors.'
    I bought land at a bargain price

in the Deep South, and took a lien,
bankrupt stock from a cattle-man –
its quality was indeed first class.
Beasts, once I'd put them out to graze,
grew plump and sleek where they'd been thin.
It raised our spirits, theirs and mine.
It's fair to say I cherished them.
My profit margins soared like steam.
And, on the proceeds, I built schools,
that moral virtue's stocks and shares
would never fall below a level
controlled by my thermometers.
But now I've done with trade-affairs,
have set the ranch under the gavel,
made a fiesta of farewells,
dispensed free grog to men and women;
widows got snuff into the bargain.
The fact is, so I've understood,
who does no evil has done good.
If that is not an empty phrase
the errors of my earlier days
are now forgotten; so that I,
more than most others, perhaps may
against fresh virtues weigh past sins
and find myself in credit still.

V. EBERKOPF [*clinking glasses with him*]:
How grand it is that you're at pains
to endow life with principle,
with active principle, no less,
purged of malign obscurities,
dark night of *Theorie*; deliver
from what hypothesis soever . . .

PEER [*who has been drinking heavily from various bottles
      during the previous orations*]:
We of the north best understand
how things get quickly out of hand
and how to bring strife to an end.
The secret is to keep tight-shut

　　your lugholes so that creepy crawlies
　　are something that they don't admit.
MR COTTON: What do you chiefly have in mind?
PEER: A little mean seductive fiend
　　within the holiest of holies,
　　[*Drinks yet more.*]
　　when what's in question is the art
　　of finding how to even start
　　and how to keep free will of choice
　　while facing some malign device,
　　to feel assured that not all days
　　of battle end in forfeit ways;
　　that one who's crossed a bridge can take
　　at any time the same bridge back.
　　That adage has for long sustained me,
　　tinctured my theories of conduct.
　　The childhood home I left behind me
　　gave me those standards, still intact.
M. BALLON: *Norvégien?*
PEER:　　　　　　　　　I was Norway's child
　　but hers no longer. Let me be styled
　　'Peer Gynt, first citizen of the world'!
　　Thus, for my glory and my gain
　　I thank all things American;
　　my well-stocked library reveals
　　the strength of Germany's 'New Schools'.
　　From France my waistcoats I acquire,
　　my poise, my intellectual flair.
　　And in my willingness to drudge
　　for profit, to drive bargains hard,
　　my self-esteem wears England's badge.
　　The Jews have taught me how to bear
　　whate'er befalls. My *dolce far
　　niente*[17] came, once, as a gift
　　from Italy. Caught off my guard
　　on one occasion, I made shift
　　to save myself with Swedish steel.
TRUMPETERSTRAALE: I'll drink to that!

V. EBERKOPF: But to the one
  who wielded it I offer *Heil!*
    They clink glasses and drink with PEER, *who is increas-*
    ingly showing the effects of alcohol.
MR COTTON: All this of course sounds very well
  but I, sir, wish to hear you talk
  of how you'll put your wealth to work.
PEER [*smiling*]:
  H'm? h'm? Do what?
ALL FOUR [*gathering about him*]:
                                    Do carry on!
PEER: Well, first, by voyaging abroad;
  that's why I took you four on board
  when I dropped anchor at Gibraltar.
  You seemed a likely singing-dancing
  troupe of topers to set prancing
  before my golden calf and altar.
V. EBERKOPF: Amusing, no?
MR COTTON: No one would hoist
  sail to be simply all at sea.
  You have – I catch it from your eye –
  a vision of some destined coast.
  That vision is . . . pray tell us, sir.
PEER: My goal? To become emperor.
ALL FOUR: What?
PEER [*nodding*]:
                  Emperor.
ALL FOUR: Of what?
PEER: The world.
M. BALLON: But by what means?
PEER: The power of gold.
  There's nothing new, when all is said;
  it was in everything I did
  while still a child. In dreams I soared
  across deep waters on a cloud.
  With streaming cloak, gold sword-sheath, climbed
  to eminence; woke frosty-limbed.
  But even so, the good remained

firmer than ever in my mind.
It has been writ in scrolls of fire –
I can't recall precisely where –
that if you gain the world entire
but 'lose yourself', all that you've won
is but a withered laurel crown
around a shattered brow. Such words
are not damned poetry's platitudes.

V. EBERKOPF: The Gyntian *Selbst*,[18] mein Herr? Do please
enlighten us.

PEER: *Mein Selbst ist dies*:[19]
the world behind the outward brow
determines that I am the law
unto myself and to no other.
And God is not the devil either.

TRUMPETERSTRAALE: Ah! Now I comprehend the thrust!

M. BALLON: Sublimity of thought indeed!

V. EBERKOPF: Such poetry outsoars the best!

PEER [*with mounting ardour*]:
The Gyntian *self* – that iron brigade
of wishes, passions and desires,
a massive flood that knows no shores,
vortex of impulse, need and claim,
the world that I entirely am.
God grasps our earth that He may be
Emperor of Eternity.
I too have need to grab for gold
to be the emperor of this world.

M. BALLON: But you have wealth!

PEER: Not wealth enough!
Enough perhaps for half a week
if I sat on Lippe-Detmold's[20] throne
and had patience to sit it through.
L'État c'est moi, c'est moi en bloc![21]
The Gynt of Gynts and that alone!
Sir Peter Gynt whose toe-caps shine!

M. BALLON [*enraptured*]:
La belle Hélène, un grand désir![22]

V. EBERKOPF: Johannisberger's[23] greatest year!

TRUMPETERSTRAALE: And swords wrought out of Swedish
    steel
  by Charles the Twelfth's own armourer!

MR COTTON: Nay, all such things are very well,
  but first things first: to look about
  for a transaction swift and sweet.

PEER: Already done! The newspapers
  today are music to my ears.
  It is as if good fortune shows
  favours to one who dares and does.
  Tonight we set sail for the north,

TRUMPETERSTRAALE: Bror Gynt!

M. BALLON   Monsieur!

MR COTTON   Old chap!

V. EBERKOPF   Mein Herr!

ONE OF THE FOUR: We wait with bated breath to hear!

PEER: A late report reads 'Greece in tumult'.

        ALL FOUR *spring up*.

ONE OF THE FOUR: Praise be! And has the Turk been
    humbled?

PEER: The Greeks have risen.

ONE OF THE FOUR: In their wrath!

PEER: The Turks, it adds, are in retreat.
    Empties his glass.

M. BALLON: Fair Greece! Her gates of glory open.
  I shall assist with my French weapon.

V. EBERKOPF: And I with plaudits from the wings.

MR COTTON: While I shall be supplying things.

TRUMPETERSTRAALE: And I shall go to fatal Bender
  King Charles's spurs perchance to find there.

M. BALLON [*embracing* PEER]:
  Forgive me, friend; for a brief while
  I had misjudged you.

V. EBERKOPF [*grasping his hands*]:
                          I too judged ill,
  thought you a scoundrel. I regret
  the slur; I am an idiot.

MR COTTON: That's a bit strong! Maybe a fathead.

TRUMPETERSTRAALE [*attempting to kiss him*]:
  And I thought you a specimen
  of Yankeedom's degraded spawn.
  Forgive me, sir.

V. EBERKOPF: We'd lost our bearings.

PEER: What gabble!

V. EBERKOPF: Now we see united
  all aspects of the 'Gyntian Whole',
  all wishes, passions, all desirings . . .

M. BALLON [*ecstatic with admiration*]:
  . . . in-gathered, waiting on the Call.
  To Monsieur Gynt's apotheosis!

PEER: Will you shut up!

M. BALLON: *Ne comprenez-vous pas?*[24]

PEER: *Niente.*[25]

M. BALLON: We depart tonight
  to fight for Greece, am I not right?

PEER [*with a snort of contempt*]:
  Wrong! My assessment of the foes
  lacks sentiment. I back the Turks.

M. BALLON: *Mon Dieu!*[26]

V. EBERKOPF: Hardly the best of jokes.

PEER [*is silent for a while; then, leaning on a chairback,
    adopts a 'superior' expression*]:
  Gentlemen, it is best we part
  before the remnants flicker out
  of our brief friendship – call it that.
  He who has nothing can risk all.
  When your stake in the nation's but
  the shadow prodded by your boot
  you're done for once they start to shoot.
  But one self-risen from the seter
  as I am, well, his stakes are greater.
  So, it's to Hellas that you sail!
  Free weaponry is yours at call.
  The higher you four fan the flames
  of conflict with heroic games

the stronger I can bend *my* bow.
Freedom and justice! Off you go,
fight in the vanguard, lead the charge
against the khalif's entourage;
and end it all with wriggling dances
stuck on the janissaries' lances.
But, pray excuse me.
[*Slaps his pocket.*]
                              I have 'funds'!
Sir Peter Gynt inspects the grounds.
    He opens his parasol and saunters off into the grove,
    where the hammocks can be faintly discerned.
TRUMPETERSTRAALE: That filthy swine!
M. BALLON: Pah! *Sans honneur!*[27]
MR COTTON: What's honour, though, when all is said?
    But, profit! I too like a winner.
    If I thought Greece was worth a bid . . .
M. BALLON: I saw myself with victor's wounds
    bathed by competing female hands!
TRUMPETERSTRAALE: I saw within my Swedish grip
    those mystic spurs now mine to keep!
V. EBERKOPF: And I saw my great fatherland's
    Kultur endowing foreign strands.
MR COTTON: The worst, for me, is not to salvage
    more of his fortune's bulk and selvage.
    Goddammit, I could weep! I saw
    myself hacking Olympus raw:
    huge veins of copper to be mined!
    Castalia's waters could have churned
    hydro-electric power at
    more than a thousand-horsepower rate.
TRUMPETERSTRAALE: I'll fight – despite! My Swedish sword
    will achieve more than Yankee hoard.
MR COTTON: I doubt it. We'd be cannon fodder,
    just as he said. Pray reconsider
    for there's no profit if we're dead.
M. BALLON: *Coup de tonnerre!*[28] To have so sweet
    a prospect dying at one's feet!

MR COTTON [*shaking his fist at* PEER's *steam yacht*]:
    That devil's casket in its hold
    brews Negro blood and sweat to gold!
V. EBERKOPF: That's it! I have it! So, let's hasten
    his nabob's coffers to unfasten.
    Here is my plan . . .
M. BALLON: Your plan, m'sieur?
V. EBERKOPF: *Machtübernahme*[29] within the hour!
    His crew is ready to be bought.
    That done, I'll commandeer the yacht.
MR COTTON: You'll what?
V. EBERKOPF: I'll grab it willy-nilly!
    He makes his way down to the dinghy.
MR COTTON: Since that's the bid it might be silly
    not to do likewise.
    He follows VON EBERKOPF.
TRUMPETERSTRAALE: Villainy!
M. BALLON: *Et alors?*[30] Though I quite agree.
    He follows the others.
TRUMPETERSTRAALE: And I must join them too, it seems;
    protesting still, and in the strongest terms.
    He also makes his way down to the dinghy.

SCENE 2

*A different part of the coast. Moonlight and scudding clouds.
The yacht can be seen, far out to sea, proceeding full steam
ahead.* PEER, *in a state of extreme agitation, runs along the
beach. One moment he pinches his arm; the next moment he
stares wildly out to sea.*

PEER: This is a nightmare, a nonsense. Soon I must surely
    wake up!
    They have put out to sea without me. They devour the sea-miles.
    Come, Peer, you're drunk still and reeling. Or am I perhaps
    asleep?
    Can I be dying, well, can I? I'll call it a dream.

Yes, a dream let it be; a bad dream for the whiles.
Agh! Dreadful to say, it's the truth and the truth makes me
    weep.
My so-called companions – ah, hear me, Lord God,
You who are wise, who are just – give short shrift to them!
[*Stretches his arms towards the heavens.*]
It's Peer, d'you hear? Oh do pay attention, Milord!
Look after me, Father, for none else will bother.
Command 'Put about!' Why don't they lower the boat?
Make hue and cry, blast all their rigging awry.
I plead, nay demand, that it's *my* woes to which You attend.
The world, as it will, can look after itself pretty well.
Hello? Hello? No change there, for he never listens.
Perhaps He needs some charitable assistance.
[*Gesticulates again at the heavens.*]
Haven't I got rid of my Negro slaves?
To Asia I've sent missionaries in droves.
One good turn deserves another, eh?
Get me back on board without delay.
I'll . . .
    A column of fire shoots upwards from the steam yacht,
    and thick smoke pours out of it; a hollow explosion is
    heard. PEER *shrieks, sinking down upon the sand. Slowly*
    the smoke clears away; the yacht has vanished.
PEER [*quietly, almost sotto voce*]:
That was the sword of wrath if ever I saw it!
Gone, the whole boiling, and before they even knew it!
Eternal praise be to Him, the god of second chances!
[*Deeply moved*]
It was something greater than good luck, even, was it not?
I was destined for salvation; they, destined to go to pot.
Praise be to Thee, then, for Thy grand protecting hand.
In despite of my flaws my great cause, as we see, advances.
[*Exhales.*]
What wondrous security and comfort when you understand
that in some quite unique way you are protected.
Though I am a starving castaway, if I may so describe it,
here too, you may be sure, I am not rejected:

manna, and all that, stuff that Moses' tribe ate.
[*Loudly, ingratiatingly*]
He surely will not allow this especial sparrow to perish.
Be of humble cheer, Peer, and give the Lord some time
to reorder the accounts and make all parade-square-ish.
[*Leaps up in great alarm.*]
Was that a lion roaring? Why doesn't help come?
[*With chattering teeth*]
No, not a lion.
[*Gathering courage*]
                    A lion it was, for certain!
Well, now, he's a thinking creature, your average lion;
has the right instincts, sees what's in front of his eyes;
knows not to attack when he's outnumbered by foes;
won't play tag, say, with elephants. I'd best climb a tree.
Acacias and date-palms abundant, all nicely a-sway.
If I climb one of those I'll be secure from harm.
It might also help were I to recite a psalm.
[*Climbs and settles himself.*]
'The day won't be known until the sun's gone down',
as the Psalmist says; well, that's been much debated.
[*Continuing to make himself comfortable*]
How good it is to find one's spirit so elevated.
To think nobly is to know more than the rich have ever known.
Trust Him as thy sure foundation; He knows to what level
of the Chalice of Privation it is my allotted portion to drink
without cavil.
He is like a father towards this creature He has created.
[*Looks out to where sea meets sky, sighs, murmurs.*]
But economical? Certainly not that, I think!

SCENE 3

Nighttime. A Moroccan camp at the edge of the desert. Campfires; SOLDIERS *taking their ease.*

A SLAVE [*enters, tearing at his hair*]:
  The emperor's best white stallion has disappeared!
SECOND SLAVE [*enters, tearing his garments*]:
  The emperor's sacrèd garments have gone the same road!
ATTENDANT [*enters*]:
  One hundred strokes to the soles of the feet decreed
  for all, unless the thief is apprehended with speed.
    The SOLDIERS *mount their steeds and gallop off in all
    directions.*

SCENE 4

Dawn. Acacias and palm trees. PEER *is sitting in his tree using a wrenched-off branch to defend himself against a group of monkeys.*

PEER: Just my luck; truly, I've passed a most wretched night.
  [*Striking out haphazardly*]
  Have at you, then! Ha! Ja! Now they're pelting me with
    fruit –
  ugh, it's not fruit, the repulsive creatures! It
  is written, is it not, 'Pilgrim, you must watch and fight'?
  But I just can't. Not any more. I am despondent; worn out.
  [*The monkeys renew the assault.*]
  Insult capping insult. I cannot let it continue.
  If I can manage to snatch one of this devil's retinue
  there may be some way to flay him and don his pelt.
  The others might take to me, in a fashion, as a result.
  What, after all, are we humans? Nothing but a speck of dust.
  Local customs are to be respected where they persist,
  as here. Another echelon moving to the attack –

be off! Bah! Boo! It's as if they were berserk!
How I wish, now, that I still had that yellow tail,
anything that might make me more resemble an animal.
Oh, what now?
[*Looks up.*]
                    One of the oldest of their filthy gang
with his paws full . . .
[*Cowers fearfully and keeps still a moment or two. The
monkey makes a move.* PEER *begins to coax it as if it were
a dog.*]
                    Hey, up there, me old mate!
Good lad! Good boy! Hey, who's a friendly fellow?
Who's not going to throw things? Not even think of that?
Ai-ai! I've even got the odd word of theirs to bellow.
My mate here, and me – we're as one in our family tree.
Sugar tomorrow, a treat! Aagh! Two fistfuls of dung,
smack-on! And the stench! Sickening!
Is it dung, though? It might be food, actually.
It tastes like nothing that I would care to devour
but 'spit, and hope that habit makes easier' –
some great thinker said that (his name has slipped my mind).
Here's the entire progeny. How tragic that mankind,
lord of the world, aspirant to the universe,
is reduced to 'on guard!' and 'behind you! behind!'
The old man was monstrous but his spawn is worse.

SCENE 5

*Early morning. A stony area looking out across the desert. To
one side, a mountain; in the mountain a cleft and a cave. A*
THIEF *and a* FENCE *are in the cleft, in possession of the emper-
or's stolen horse and garments. The horse, richly caparisoned,
is tethered to a rock.* HORSEMEN *can be seen in the distance.*

THIEF: The lances' tongues
    lick the light –
    see, it is so.

FENCE: The head springs
  off, blood scattering bright.
  Woe, cry woe.
THIEF [*folding his arms*]:
  The father thieved,
  so must the son.
FENCE: The father received
  goods by theft won.
  So it goes on.
THIEF: Fate must be endured,
  with none else shared.
  I am what I am.
FENCE [*alarmed, listening*]:
  The bushes stir,
  we must flee! Where?
THIEF: This cave is deep. Enter.
  Great is the prophet, blessed be his name.
    *They make their escape, abandoning the emperor's
    possessions. The distant* HORSEMEN *vanish over the
    horizon.*
PEER [*enters, whittling pan pipes from reeds*]:
  How blissful the morning at this early hour.
  The dung beetle rolls his pellet in the gravel;
  the snail's head creeps from the shell in its slow travel.
  Ah, morning truly does have gold in its mouth.
  It is, when you think about it, a remarkable power
  that nature has endowed the daylight with.
  In daylight you feel so secure, feel your courage wax;
  you think, 'If I had to I could take on an ox!'
  And the surrounding silence! The sweet depth of rural joy;
  how could I have so ignored these things previously?
  It's madness to be self-immured in those barrack-towns,
  to leave them only at such times as the mob turns
  violent, when, if you can, you slip away.
  See how that lizard just flickers about and about,
  its pointy little head snippeting without deep thought.
  What innocence there is in the lives of animals,
  compliant with the voice of their Creator when He calls,

each marked with its own intimate nature indelibly;
utterly itself, whether in quarrel or play,
just as it appeared when the Creator uttered His defining Word.
[*Sets his pince-nez on his nose.*]
A toad set in the midst of a block of sandstone.
Everything around it stone, alone with its own head,
just brooding there as if from a glass grandstand,
contemplating the world, sufficient to itself.
[*Stops, as if the thought had snagged on something.*]
Sufficient to itself? Now where did I read or hear that?
I think, in something bulky hauled from a shelf
when I was a boy. That book of sermons? Or, if not,
Solomon's word-book? It distresses me greatly
that, for some years, and much more so lately,
my grasp of past time and place has been, and is, weakening.
[*Sits down in the shade.*]
How restful it is just to sit and to stretch out your feet.
Look, here is a fern that has an edible root.
[*Tastes a little.*]
Well, hardly *haute cuisine*; but then, 'Keep a tight rein
on mortal appetite,' said one or other of our wise men
whose task it is to make a moral reckoning.
'Pride comes before a fall,' read, probably, in the same
     source;
'He that humbles himself shall be exalted'. Of course.
[*Shows signs of unease.*]
'Be exalted.' I have no doubt that this will be granted me.
I find that I cannot think of anything else.
I shall transcend these things with the blessing of destiny.
This catastrophic reversal will go into reverse.
Things will be made clear; I shall relaunch my career.
This has been a martyr's ordeal by fire.
After it comes salvation. I trust my physique
will be up to it; and that faith brings me luck.
[*Shakes off any uneasy thoughts; lights a cigar; stretches;
stares out across the desert.*]
What an immeasurable limitless desert this is.
Over there a solitary ostrich is strutting.

What could you deduce here of God's purposes,
what, in this dead emptiness, is He permitting?
In this blank terrain, inimical to life,
all-consuming, all-consumed, totally burned up and out,
totally unsupportive of humanity's self-belief;
this fragment, or segment, of a world-self that is not;
this corpse which, never since the earth was born,
has given its creator a single word in return.
Why did He do it? Nature's both lavish and deadly.
Over there, eastward, that flat glittering expanse:
is it the ocean, laid there so absurdly?
The ocean lies to westward, where the hills fence
it off from the desert, somewhat like a dam.
[*He has a brainwave.*]
A dam[31] it should be possible to breach
therefore; those hills have low contours.
Breach them, and a flood of new life pours
over the desert its life-creating foam.
That done, this red-hot wilderness that is like Mars
settles itself into a new and fertile calm.
Oases will be renewed as islands that it is joy to reach.
Mount Atlas,[32] to northward, shall grow green, a
     mountainous coast,
tall ships in full sail go where only camels have crossed
in earlier times; life-giving, life-enriching air
create a sweet turbulence, and dew be nightly refreshed.
And soon the builders of cities will arrive here,
hanging gardens a-plenty, as many as might be wished.
Regions to the southward, behind Sahara's barren wall,
enjoying a new status, a true *costa del sol*;[33]
steam power renews the ancient powerhouses of Timbuctoo,
northern Nigeria's reborn, the place of choice to go.
Now through Abyssinia[34] I see expert researchers travel
in specially reserved luxury trains to the Upper Nile.
In the midst of this New Atlantis[35] I propose to settle
Norwegians of the finest mental and physical fettle
(the pure blood of our valleys equals that of royalty,
almost); then to cross-breed them with the best Arab stock.

Also I shall require expert practitioners in realty
since, on a sloping shore that gently enfolds,
on three sides, a bay, imagination unfolds
the plan of my new city, Peeropolis, capital
of Gyntiana, unveiled before the earth's astonished people.
[*Leaping up with intense excitement*]
Capital investment, then, is all that will be needed
and the thing is done: gateway to a grand Mare Nostrum;
vision versus sterility, the powers of death ceded
without a struggle; the miser throws open his sack!
To those who in every land pursue their dream of freedom,
as did the ass in the Ark,
I shall send forth a call, bringing to the benighted
hope of liberation; and, to this lovely littoral,
liberation also from its present sterile thrall.
En avant! From wheresoe'er thou mayst come, O venture-
        capital!
'My kingdom,' let's say half a kingdom, 'for a horse'!
[*The emperor's stolen horse whinnies from the cleft.*]
Great heavens! A charger, and jewels, and a set of robes
an emperor would be proud to wear!
[*Moves closer.*]
It's not possible, surely? I've heard that willpower
will move mountains. But a horse? Yet a horse it is,
ab esse ad posse[36] notwithstanding, philosophical niceties.
[*Puts on the robes over his European clothes and inspects
the result.*]
Let's see how you look, Sir Peter. Quite splendid of course,
befitting the emperor of golden tribes,
with Grane the dragon-slayer to ride upon,
[*Climbs into the saddle.*]
gracing the silver stirrups with my golden shoon.
It is by their appearance that you know the noblest of men!
    He gallops off into the desert.

SCENE 6

The tent of an Arab chieftain standing solitary in an oasis.
PEER, *dressed as an Arab, reclines on long, low cushions. He*
drinks coffee and smokes a long pipe. ANITRA *and a* CHOIR
OF GIRLS *are dancing and singing in his presence.*

CHOIR OF GIRLS: The prophet has come,
   the prophet, the lord, the all-knowing,
   across the barren region once our home,
   like a clean wind over the sands blowing,
   the prophet, the lord, he who is without sin,
   has come to us, and we have welcomed him in.
   Sound! Sound! O you flutes and you drums!
   Cry 'It is the prophet, oh it is the prophet who comes!'
ANITRA: His steed is milk white
   like the river that flows
   through paradise-gate;
   his eyes are the stars:
   they are mild, they are fierce;
   and none of earth's children
   can keep from their gaze.
   We are smitten, beholden,
   to Him with No Name.
   His breast gleams with golden
   adornment close-pearled.
   Where he rode it grew light
   and old darkness refurled.
   Behind, the simoom[37]
   fell back into its dust
   and the ghosts of our thirst.
   Before him, bowed heads
   and bent knees fresh-proclaim
   the joy that has come
   on the palest of steeds.
   And Kaba[38] stands void
   as he said it should.

CHOIR OF GIRLS: Sound! Sound! Oh, you flutes and you
    drums!
  Cry 'It is the prophet, oh, it is the prophet who comes!'
  The GIRLS *dance to a quiet music.*
PEER: The saying is true – I have read it in print even –
  'Save in his own land no man is without honour.'
  Well, this life I now lead appeals to me far more
  than life back in Charleston as a shipowner.
  There was something hollow about my life there,
  alien; one might almost say unproven.
  I was never truly at home in their company;
  never truly paid my professional dues; so why
  did I think to find myself by acting the galley slave,
  feeding on scraps grabbed from the garbage of business?
  When I think about it, it just doesn't seem right;
  dealing with approximations rather than true closeness.
  'It just happened to happen' can't be the final truth of it,
  you tell yourself, finding in the end it is all you have.
  Establishing yourself on a foundation of gold,
  you are shocked when you find it is on sand that you build.
  For a retirement-presentation, gold watches, rings and
    suchlike,
  folk wag their behinds and contrive to abase themselves
    sillier,
  to royal insignia doff their equally silly hats,
  although insignia, gold signets and other memorabilia
  carry no hint of the inward self that does not need suits.
  But speak the word 'prophet': about that there *is* something
    torchlike!
  If people applaud you it is you the people applaud,
  not what you may have in bank-vaults at home and abroad.
  You are what you are, there are no two ways about it;
  you are indebted neither to chance nor luck;
  patents and royalties don't enter the account.
  'Prophet'! Now there's a grand name with which to be stuck!
  Even though in my case the acquiring was inadvertent,
  by chance acquisition of gifts – who would have thought it? –
  because I came riding out of the desert one day,

meeting these children of nature along the way.
The prophet had come; for them the coming was revelation,
and they brought out for me the singers and dancers.
I was not acting to deceive; it just happened.
There is a difference between lies and prophetic answers,
and I can always surrender my stipend,
so to speak, and ease myself from the situation.
The entire business can be regarded as private
arrangements between consenting partners to date;
and when it is dissolved, why, Grane stands ready
to bear me away. No ill feelings from, or to, anybody.

ANITRA [*approaching him from the tent-entrance*]:
  Prophetic majesty!
PEER: What does my slave crave?
ANITRA: She bears supplication from the Sons of the Plain
  for admittance to thy presence –
PEER: Say to such men,
  'Keep your distance, you who do not truly believe.
  We will overhear your pleas distantly. Men are not welcome
    here.'
  Best to add that. All men, Anitra, my child,
  are the weaker vessels; uncaring even when they have to care.
  In your innocence you cannot begin to conceive
  how cruelly womenfolk are eternally beguiled
  by such trickst . . . sinners is the more appropriate term.
  Well, I have spoken. Dance me your dances, come!
  The prophet desires to be disencumbered of shame.
GIRLS [*singing and dancing*]:
  The prophet is a holy man, wholly without sin.
  He is grieved by the evils of the sons of dust.
  The prophet is without wrath; his mildness be praised!
  He opens paradise so that sinners may enter in.
PEER [*watching* ANITRA *as she dances*]:
  Her legs twiddle as fast as drumsticks,
  I've got a taste for her, the little hussy.
  She nicely overfills that dress – I
  really admire the way her bum twerks.
  A bit too ripe, judged by our norms of beauty.

But beauty itself is merely convention,
a coin performing a standard duty.
Overripeness focuses the attention
when you have drained temperance to the dregs.
The hygienic body cheats you of your thrills.
Skin-and-bone or blubber I need my girls,
tempting child-virgin or old maid who begs,
flesh that is supple or the flesh that sags.
With what the norm serves up I've been cold-sated.
Anitra, here, contrives to be smelly-footed
while waving a dirty paw. Yet we are suited.
Her value to me is not reduced by her filth.
I would call it a precondition of sensual wealth.
Listen to me, Anitra!

ANITRA: Master, I hear! I . . .

PEER: You are a seductive child. Your prophet is much
    moved.
    Do you doubt me? I would rather you believed.
    To the keepers of paradise I shall commend you as an houri.

ANITRA: Master, that cannot be!

PEER: My child, I am entirely serious!

ANITRA: But, Master, I do not possess a soul.

PEER: Then get one!

ANITRA: How, Master?

PEER: No problem at all.
    It's true that you're up to the gills in stupidity
    but in this particular that's not deleterious.
    We can squeeze one in. Come, let me measure your skull.
    There's plenty of room; I knew there would be.
    As I've said, things will never go very deep
    where you're concerned; but even so a soul
    you shall have, my child; though one that's small.
    Good enough to get by with I should hope.

ANITRA: The prophet is generous, but . . .

PEER: What, child? Speak up!

ANITRA: Not having a soul . . .

PEER: Yes, yes, go on.

ANITRA: Instead of a soul may I have that precious stone?

She gestures towards a large opal in his turban.
PEER [*delightedly extracts the jewel and hands it to her*]:
    Anitra, to me you are Eve's natural daughter!
    As you are the magnet, so I am the man.
    For, as was written by some distinguished author,
    '*Das Ewig-Weibliche ziehet uns an.*'[39]

SCENE 7

A moonlit night. A grove of palm trees outside ANITRA's *tent.*
PEER, *with an Arab lute, is sitting under a tree. His beard and
his hair are trimmed; he looks considerably younger.*

PEER [*playing and singing*]:
    I turned the lock on paradise
    and bore away the key.
    Towards the south I set my course;
    and lovely women mourned their loss:
    the loss they mourned was me.

    Oh, ever southward did my prow
    divide the ocean stream;
    till, where the stately palm trees grow,
    wreathing a bay in tranquil show,
    I fed it to the flame.

    I rode instead, across the sands,
    a ship that journeyed well,
    obedient to my guiding hands,
    four legs responding, as responds
    to wind and wave a gull.

    Anitra, sweet fermenting juice
    of palm wine, love me, do!
    Angora goat's cheese has its place
    in my desires, but not so choice
    a place, my dear, as you!
    [*Hangs the lute from his shoulder by its strap and approaches
    her.*]

Silence? Does the fair one hear me?
Has she heard my modest warbling?
Who's to say she isn't near me,
veils and suchlike swift-discarding?
Hist! I heard a pop-and-burble,
something fresh out of a bottle?
There again, a little louder;
sighs of love? A murmuration,
whispers like a fizz of soda?
Slow decoction of a potion?
No, it is my sweet girl snoring.
Nightingale, so self-adoring,
you have now a rival near you;
cease your challenge, I can't hear you.
Wait a moment, Peer! 'Tis written
nightingale is truly smitten.
I myself am such a singer
praising all things tweeting-tender.
Nightingale, I am your fellow-
warbler of th'enchanted hollow.
Cool of night is our twin bower,
songs of love our double power,
I am you as you are me,
single in twinned harmony:
thus resolved, my girl's a snorer
grants me licence to adore her.
No higher joy exists in love
than stooping with chaste lips above
the chalice you decline to taste.
But there she is, the dove, at last!
My cup runneth when she appears.

ANITRA [*still within the tent*]:
    Master, you call? Your servant hears!
PEER: Your master calls and has been calling.
    He was awakened by a cat
    making a nocturne of its prowling.
ANITRA: Dear master, it was worse than that.
PEER: Worse?

ANITRA: Spare my blushes at the thought.
PEER [*moving closer*]:
  Was it something like the feeling
  I had when I, soul-revealing,
  to your care gave up my opal?
ANITRA [*scandalized*]:
  Master, it was nothing *like* that!
  Sounds you make are nothing like cat
  on cat makes when they couple,
  sacred being!
PEER: Ah, my clever
  dancer with some limitations,
  never does true love dissever
  cat's cries from our fleshed commotions
  or prophetic comminations.
ANITRA: Master, with how sweet a cadence
  do you chastise me.
PEER: Dearest child,
  like others of your sex you cling
  to outward forms, by them beguiled.
  Inwardly I am rich in humour,
  most at my ease in private chamber,
  with winning grace remove the mask
  of public office, cry good riddance
  to daily round and common task –
  they do not furnish all I ask.
  Prophetic wrath is fresh-applied
  each morning ere I step outside;
  it's such a superficial thing,
  all nonsense! In a tête-à-tête
  I'm simple Peer to you, my sweet.
  You have me to yourself. Tonight
  we keep the prophet waiting, right?
  [*Sits down under a tree and pulls her towards him.*]
  Come, Anitra, let us rest,
  with palm tree fans our brows caressed.
  I shall whisper, you will smile;
  later we'll switch roles a while.

You with your honeyed lips will move
the balmy air to acts of love.
ANITRA [*now reclining at his feet*]:
Your every word is like a song
of which I understand but little.
Might your daughter, ere too long,
learn a soul from such recital?
PEER: A soul, a spirit, knowledge, diction,
you may acquire from my instruction,
as, in the east, first rosy streaks
announce 'It is the sun who speaks';
gold letters, next, in typed display
confirm his hold upon the day:
thus we'll commence your education.
But, in the all-embracing darkness,
wisdom must sleep while passion hearkens.
Pedagogy spurns emotion.
In any case it's not the soul
that I would grant the leading role
in these affairs. It is the heart
that judges wisely, is it not?
ANITRA: Master, when you caress this theme
the opals, that I love so, gleam.
PEER: To be too clever's to be stupid.
And cruelty's the opened bud
of cowardice. I've seen it happen.
And truth, each time that it's pursued
past reason, turns itself around,
goes widdershins and all misshapen.
My child, I cannot tell a lie:
there's folk with over-active souls
who handle their affairs like fools
and cannot see for clarity.
I knew a fellow, once, like that,
the best, I'd say, of the whole band,
who failed his promise and misread his fate.
The teeming sands round this oasis
would be transformed at my command,

the waters of the neighbouring seas
pour in to flash and fertilize.
But I would be an ignoramus
if I did that but to be famous.
Anitra, child, can you conceive
the meaning of the verb 'to live'?
ANITRA: I long to hear!
PEER: It means to glide
along time's river still dryshod;
to be oneself at each extreme
of agency in space and time.
The very core, the I am I,
of selfhood's self, such potency!
With lapse of years the eagle moults
his final moult, the old man halts,
the widow loses her last teeth,
miserdom parts one wizened soul
among the pack of them. Ah, Youth!
It is with you I seek to rule
just like a sultan, hot and whole!
Not on the shores of Gyntiana
with palms and vines and wreathed liana,
but in that virgin wilderness
a woman's heart and mind are, solely.
Now do you see why, with such grace,
I charmed you to possess you wholly?
'Tis in your heart I mean to set
foundations for the caliphate
of my grand Selfhood. So, your passions
become imperial possessions
in which I govern as dictator –
you, mine, alone, we two, alone!
Can you conceive what must be done?
I'll see that you become enthralled
as though with opals or with gold;
and if, at any time, we sever,
life and love – for you – are over.
It is your self that I create here,

every last fibre of your being,
no free will left you, no self-seeing,
utterly subsumed you'll be,
your midnight tresses spread so free,
and everything that you might name
desirable through space and time,
Babylon's gardens[40] at the heart
of human longing, I'll convert
into a sultan's place of sport.
So, basically, it's no bad thing
your skull has such a hollow ring.
Soul's an encumbrance, you would find;
self-searching and self-knowledge bind
us to those things that are beyond.
A pretty fetter for your ankle
shall utter its sweet lisp and tinkle.
All that I take, that All you give!
Mine is the soul you'll never have.
[ANITA *snores.*]
Ha! More snoring! Has it smitten
addled dreams, my exhortation?
This but reconfirms my powers.
Thoughts most intimately hers
paddle in streams of my desires.
[*Stands up and begins to heap jewellery in her lap.*]
Here are brooches and more opals.
Sleep, Anitra; dream of Peer
as you'd dream of golden apples.
You have crowned him emperor.
Dream's the feigner, you unfeigning;
Peer as two in one self-reigning.

SCENE 8

A caravan trail. The oasis is seen far behind. PEER *on his white
horse is galloping through the desert. He holds* ANITRA *in
front of him, supported by the pommel.*

ANITRA: Let me loose, I'm a biter!
PEER: Well, aren't we the little spit-fire!
ANITRA: What is it you want?
PEER: What? To play hawk and dove!
  To kidnap you! Play any old kind of crazy game!
ANITRA: And you a prophet! Don't you have any feelings of
    shame?
PEER: Nonsense, the prophet is in his prime, you goose!
  Do these tricks suggest age and overuse,
  my intermittently attractive love?
ANITRA: Agh, leave me be! I want to get off home!
PEER: Stop playing hard to get, you little coquette!
  Home to the in-laws? That would be a fine thing!
  We're two crazy birds let loose and free on the wing.
  Daren't show our faces back there ever again.
  Besides, my sweeting, it's a well-proven fact
  that if you stay too long in the same place
  what you gain in knowledge you lose in respect;
  especially so, if you've been in some kind of disguise,
  acting the prophet, to cite a recent case.
  Best to be ephemeral, like a poem.
  That visit's over, and it was high time!
  They are fickle converts, these children of the plain.
  Neither frankincense nor progress were much in evidence
  by the time we made our farewells. I say good riddance.
ANITRA: Tell truth, now: *are* you a prophet?
PEER: Emperor
  is the choice of title I now prefer.
  [*Attempts a kiss.*]
  Just so, the woodpecker jerks back her natty head!
ANITRA: Give me that ring.
PEER: Take the lot; trash to trash, could be said.
ANITRA: Your words are like sweetest music to my ears.
PEER: One's blest in a love that's as profound as yours.
  Let me dismount and go on foot, as your slave
  leading the horse.
  [*Hands her the whip and dismounts.*]
  There now, my rose,

my splendiferous flower; I will struggle through the sand
till I'm smitten by sunstroke and get my just deserts.
I'm still young, Anitra; I'd have you keep that in mind.
My antics are performed merely to amuse,
not to be judged in scales that are over-precise.
If your mood had not lately become so grave
you would recognize that I'm a bright lad of parts,
my gracious oleander.

ANITRA: So you're young, all right? Got any more rings and
    things?

PEER: Here, take your pick. See, I can leap like a buck!
    If there were vine-leaves I should weave myself a garland
    here.
    For indeed I am young! I am about to break into song.
    [*Dances and sings.*]
    O I am a jolly cockerel!
    Peck me, my biddybaddy hen!
    I will prance while you count to ten!
    O I am a jolly cockerel!

ANITRA: Prophet, you are sweating; I'm afraid you will melt.
    Pass me that heavy weight that's dangling from your belt.

PEER: Sweet solicitude! Henceforth be custodian of my purse.
    Loving hearts delight in each other; gold is a curse.
    [*Dances and sings again.*]
    Young Peer Gynt, oh, he's a madcap.
    He doesn't know which foot is left and which is right.
    Pooh, says Peer, I could still dance all night.
    Peer Gynt's a cockerel in its red cap!

ANITRA: Joy to the world! The prophet joins the dance!

PEER: That old fraud? Let us swap gaud for gaud!
    Get undressed . . .

ANITRA: Your kaftan's
    too long; this cummerbund must have been a fat man's;
    I can't get these stockings on.

PEER: So nothing fits. *Eh bien.*
    [*Kneeling*]
    But grant me, I beg you, an exquisite sorrow.
    That is a sweetness that all true hearts should know,

when we return at long last to my castle . . .
ANITRA: Paradise
you declared it. Is it a long ride?
PEER: Well, yes,
a thousand miles more or less.
ANITRA: Too far for me.
PEER: But listen, when we arrive
you will be granted the soul that I said I would give . . .
ANITRA: Thanks for nothing, then. I shall get by without it.
That sorrow you so desired?
PEER: That sorrow, right,
short but intense, not more than two or three days . . .
ANITRA: The prophet's wish is my command! Farewell!
    She delivers a stinging blow to his fingers and gallops furi-
    ously away, towards the distant oasis.
PEER: Well, I'll . . .

SCENE 9

The same place, an hour later. PEER, *appearing thoughtful
and composed, is taking off his Arab garments piece by piece.
Finally he takes his little travelling hat out of his coat pocket
and puts it on. He is once more clad* à l'européenne.

PEER [*throwing his turban as far as he can*]:
    There lies the Ottoman, and I am still standing!
    This un-Christian way of life is not me at all.
    I'm lucky that it was in the clothes and the smell,
    not gashes in my flesh and not branding.
    What was I doing sweating on that galley?
    I believe one should live the Christian life fully,
    with sober self-judging, not peacocking about,
    but basing your actions on the moral law,
    thinking 'I am what I am'; and, when you've had your lot,
    deserving a final eulogy, a few decent wreaths on show.
    [*Walks a few steps, cogitating.*]
    That little tart, she came as near as dammit

to turning my head. Call me 'troll' if you will,
her hold over me is incomprehensible
now. Staggering-drunk I was with – you name it.
I'm well rid of her. If the joke had been carried
a step farther I'd have had good cause to be worried.
My error was issue of the situation;
it wasn't the essential Peer who succumbed
to temptation;
it's the prophetic career that should be blamed,
lounging around in tents all day and all night,
no wonder one becomes utterly sick of it.
Prophesying – anywhere – is thoroughly unrewarding;
you're in a fog officially and at the fog's bidding.
If you're wide awake, sober, you're not a prophet.
In the ways I knew best I was being true to my role
in slobbering over that chit and playing the fool.
But, even so—
[*Bursts into laughter.*]
                    Oh, but you have to laugh; it
is, after all, priceless: vying to halt time
by prancing and dancing or trying to swim
against the stream,
by monkeying and tail-flunkeying,
harping, throwing the occasional fit,
strutting like a cockerel. Pfui! I was plucked all right!
Good thing I do have a little bit of cash,
lucky I hid it; and back in the States a small stash.
I'm not totally destitute,
the 'golden mean' and all that!
I'm no longer dependent on the vagaries of servants,
grooms, coaches, porters losing your luggage;
in short, as they say, I'm henceforth my own master;
choice is all mine; there are many ways to choose from.
Bad choice, good choice, is what divides fools from savants.
My business life is buried in its vault,
my love-life galloped off with Anitra, the sweet baggage!
The crayfish may walk backwards, in his wisdom,
but I don't have to follow him by default.

Bitter experience is the best loss-adjuster.
'Forwards or backwards the distance is the same,
in or out, whichever way, a tight fit.'
That brilliant text – such a pleasure to recite!
So, pastures new, and a new programme,
a cause well worth the cost of taking up.
Authorship, then? The story of my life,
'full and frank', 'holds nothing back', 'shocking'.
Moral reflections, stages on life's way?
Perhaps not. Or, since my time's my own,
a travelling 'independent scholar' type
might be my métier. Forms of depraved belief
in pagan times? Yes, I'd enjoy working
on that: historiography,
the study of facts, keeping close to the bone.
As a boy I loved the old chronicles,
the facts and figures of historical cycles.
I will swim like a feather on the stream of history,
knowing that the story of greatness is my story;
heroic battling for what is great and good,
though at a safe distance, as an observer merely;
see philosophers perish, martyrs in their own blood,
see kingdoms rise and fall, vast epochs emerge
from small beginnings on time's verge.
It's history's finest cream I'll skim off for myself surely!
I must get hold of an odd volume of Becker,[41]
going back in time as far as I can trek there.
The inner mechanisms of history are elusive,
but – oddsbodkins! – where the point of departure
best evades commonsense plodding, the nature
of things is such that ingeniously persuasive
results are obtained. How energizing it is
to set yourself a goal and to win the prize
against every obstacle that's set in the path
of truth—
[*Appears quietly moved.*]
To break, thoroughly and completely, the bonds
that bind you to home, parents and friends,

to dynamite your worldly goods, scatter them to the sky,
and, if necessary,
to bid farewell to the happiness of love
in order that truth may live –
[*wiping away a tear*]
that is what drives forward all research!
My present joy defies
measure; I have solved the insoluble riddle
of the true nature of my life's vocation.
It surely will be thought excusable
if I stand here overcome by emotion,
knowing myself to be once more in touch
with Gynthood as it truly is,
Gyntism, alias
Imperialism of the New Humanity;
to have repossessed
the key that had been lost,
this is to be the prize that's mine alone.
Of research into the present age there shall be none.
The present age is not worth the sole of my shoe.
Mankind at present is rich only in puny excesses;
it is earthbound yet lacks gravity. I will take no excuses!
[*Shrugs his shoulders.*]
And womankind? Well, womankind is worthless too.
   He leaves.

SCENE 10

A summer's day in the far north. A cabin deep in the forest. An open door with a large wooden latch. Reindeer horns over the door. A flock of goats is grazing alongside the cabin wall. A middle-aged woman, fair-haired and comely, is spinning and singing. The sun is radiant.

SOLVEIG: Perchance there will pass both the winter and
     spring
   and next summer too, what the whole year will bring;

but one day you will come; I know that in my heart;
I shall wait as I promised on that day we drew apart.

May God give you strength in this world that is so strong.
May God give you joy if with Him you belong.
As my thread I have spun, so in prayer I have striven.
We shall meet, O my love, on this earth or in heaven.

SCENE 11

Egypt. Dawn. The statue of Memnon massive amid the sands.
PEER *enters on foot and stands for a while, surveying the scene.*

PEER: Here we might fittingly begin our quest: Peer Gynt
    now in the guise of an Egyptian gent
    who yet manifests the pure Gyntian thesis
    in the land of Isis.
    Afterwards I shall make tracks for Assyria,
    but I'll leave well alone the Creation-era;
    push the Bible story completely to one side;
    it's always available if there's a need.
    And to niggle at it with a fine-tooth comb
    seems to me a recipe for boredom.
    [*Sits on a stone.*]
    I shall rest and, with the patience I can command,
    await Memnon's much-advertised aubade to the sand.
    Breakfast over, I shall ascend the Pyramid;
    if there's time, turn next to examine what's hid-
    den in the bowels of that grand edifice.
    A trip by land to the Red Sea will next take place;
    King Potiphar's grave I might easily discover.
    Assyria then, as noted. Babylon of course;
    the famous hanging gardens and the famous whores,
    with other features of cultural merit.
    Next to Troy which has been famous for ever.
    Thence to Athens by the direct sea route.
    Near Athens is located the world-famous pass
    so expertly defended by Leonidas,[42]

which I will closely examine stone by stone;
as I shall the place where they made Socrates fatally drunk.
But – that's not possible, why didn't I think?
I can't visit Greece at present; there's a war going on.
Hellenism must be postponed.
[*Looks at his watch.*]
                              One waits
far too long for sunrise in Egypt; there are limits
to the free time one has. Where had I got to?
[*Stands up, startled, and listening attentively.*]
What's that peculiar humming I can hear?
    Sunrise.

THE STATUE OF MEMNON [*sings*]:
From the ashes of one not wholly a god arises
the birds' war-chorus.
All-knowing Zeus
created them thus.
O Wisdom's owl,
where shall they all
sleep? Resolve it, or die,
my riddling monody.

PEER: I seriously believe it was the statue!
That sound came from the statue, I do declare.
The rising and falling of a stone voice is what I heard.
I shall submit my notes to a learned society
of proven sobriety.
[*Makes notes in a small pocket book.*]
'The statue distinctly sang. I could not grasp a word
of its song. Doubtless some illusion.
Nothing else today worthy of mention.'
    He walks away.

SCENE 12

Near the settlement of Giza. The great Sphinx. In the far distance Cairo's spires and minarets are just visible. PEER *enters; he examines the Sphinx with increasingly close attention. He*

peers through his pince-nez; he employs the hollow of a hand,
like a viewing-tube.

PEER: Where on earth have I met, before and elsewhere, this
    monstrosity?
  Something, somewhere, half-remembered, half-forgotten . . .
  A human being, was it? And, if so, which one?
  Back in the far north? Or later? The thought now occurs
  that Memnon resembled the old so-called courtiers
  of the Dovre King (such disgusting ferocity!).
  The way he sat there, solid and rigid,
  with his backside
  a fixture on the stumps of broken columns.
  And, now, this thing, this weird half-breed, changeling,
  stuck part way between lion and woman: it's a strange thing
  but this also strikes chords. Folk tales? Old rhymes?
  Something from real life? Something from my past?
  That's it! I met this old fellow first
  when I clouted the Boyg (or did I dream the Boyg
  in my fever sleep?).
  [*Gets closer.*]
             Yes, same eyes,
  same lips, a little more cunning and a bit less slug-
  gish; but, generally speaking, the same otherwise.
  So here we are then, Boyg, old fellow. You resemble a lion
  when met in broad daylight and rear-end-on.
  Are you still doing riddles? Let's try one out.
  If you know the answer just give a shout.
  [*He bellows at the Sphinx.*]
  Hey, Boyg, who are you?
A VOICE FROM BEHIND THE SPHINX: *Ach, Sfinx, wer*
    bist du?[43]
PEER: 'Echo employs the German tongue. A significant fact.'
VOICE: *Wer bist du?*
PEER: And fluently, too.
  I must set my own stamp on this observation:
  [*Enters in his notebook.*]
  'Albeit employing the Berliner dialect.'

BEGRIFFENFELDT [*appears from behind the Sphinx*]:
   What you thought an echo was the man you see.
PEER: H'm. Him? Scholarly record requires modification.
   [*Makes a second notebook entry.*]
   'Further observation suggests a different category.'
BEGRIFFENFELDT [*making various nervous gestures*]:
   I beg you forgive this intrusion, *mein Herr*!
   I have to put to you the following *Lebensfrage*:[44]
   'What precisely is the purpose of your journey here?'
PEER: I've come to visit a friend from long ago.
BEGRIFFENFELDT: How splendid! And after such a night!
   My head's being pounded by a pile-driver!
   You know him? Speak! Answer! Can you name
   was er ist?[45]
PEER: What he is? Yes, I can do that
   easily enough. He is *him-*
   self.
BEGRIFFENFELDT [*with a little skip and jump*]:
       I see the mystery of things quiver,
   flashing before my eyes.
   I have your absolute
   assurance on this?
PEER: That's what he says.
BEGRIFFENFELDT: Himself! The Revolution's now in motion!
   [*Taking off his hat*]
   May I have the honour of knowing your name, *mein Herr*?
PEER: My family name is Gynt. My baptismal name is Peer.
BEGRIFFENFELDT [*in hushed admiration*]:
   Peer Gynt *beginnt*! Which, as I interpret,
   signifies 'the coming one', 'the new man';
   'he whose coming was foretold by the prophet'.
PEER: No, really? And now you are here to get . . . ?
BEGRIFFENFELDT: 'Peer Gynt *beginnt*.' Profound,
       mysterious, searching,
   each word unfathomable yet profound teaching.
   I ask again, who are you?
PEER [*modestly*]:   I have always sought
   to be myself. You may examine my passport.

BEGRIFFENFELDT: Again that prophetic name. It is the Sign!
   [*Taking hold of* PEER*'s wrist*]
   To Cairo we must go. The divine
   revelator is come!
PEER: Who?
BEGRIFFENFELDT: Make haste!
PEER: And am I truly known . . . ?
BEGRIFFENFELDT: *Selbstgrundlage!*[46] The divine self-
   revelator! Him!

SCENE 13

In Cairo. A large courtyard with high walls. Buildings with
barred windows. Metal cages. Three GUARDS *in the court-*
yard. A fourth enters.

FOURTH GUARD: The Herr Direktor, Schafmann? Where has
   he gone?
GUARD: He left this morning, well before dawn.
FOURTH GUARD: Something deeply disturbing must have
   happened, then?
   Last night . . .
GUARD: Be quiet; he's back; he's at the gate.
   BEGRIFFENFELDT *leads* PEER *in, locks the gate and puts*
   the key in his pocket.
PEER [*to himself*]:
   Truly, an extremely gifted mind.
   His words fly above *my* head, at any rate.
   [*Looking around*]
   So this is the Scholars' Club?
BEGRIFFENFELDT: I think you'll find
   they're all alive and able.
   'Septuagint' was the original label
   but numbers have increased to more than double
   in recent weeks.
   [*Calling the guards*]
   Schlingelberg, Fuchs,

Schafmann, Mikkel,
into the cages with you, *schnell*!⁴⁷
GUARDS: Us, Herr Direktor?
BEGRIFFENFELDT: Who else? Off you go!
While the world is spinning we must spin too!
[*Pushes them into a cage.*]
Our most recent arrival is the grand Gynt.
Work it out for yourselves. I shall be silent.
    Locks the cage and throws the key down a well.
PEER: Herr Direktor, Herr Doktor, whichever you prefer . . . ?
BEGRIFFENFELDT: I am not now entitled to such
    nomenclature.
I bore them once. Can you keep secrets, Herr Peer?
I need to make a confession.
PEER [*increasingly uneasy*]:
                        Well, I . . .
BEGRIFFENFELDT: You must promise not to tremble.
PEER: I shall try.
BEGRIFFENFELDT [*drags him into a corner and whispers*]:
I must inform you that I witnessed Absolute Reason
expire last night: eleven o'clock, on the dot.
PEER: Great heavens!
BEGRIFFENFELDT: Indeed. Most deeply I wish he had not.
For a professional
in my position
it is especially painful.
This institution,
heretofore, stood in high repute
as a madhouse.
PEER: A madhouse?
BEGRIFFENFELDT: No longer so, of course.
PEER [*pale and quiet*]:
How well, now, I understand.
This fellow is raving, and the sane are blind.
    Moves away.
BEGRIFFENFELDT [*following him around*]:
By the way, I trust you have understood:
when I say he's dead I am speaking in code.

He's not in his right mind;
he's leaped out of his own skin
as the fox leaps out of its pelt in Münchhausen.[48]
PEER: Excuse me a moment.
BEGRIFFENFELDT [*holding on to him tightly*]:
                              More like an eel
than a fox. With a pin through his eye
he squirmed on the wall.
PEER: I must escape, and soon!
BEGRIFFENFELDT: A snip round the neck and then –
presto! – he was up and away!
PEER: Tragic, obscene . . .
BEGRIFFENFELDT: It's plain to see, it's impossible to conceal.
This 'from-oneself-going' will have as a result
something resembling a geological fault.
Those who previously had been labelled 'mad'
at eleven o'clock last night suddenly became fit to plead,
in conformity with reason in its new phase.
And if you look at the matter correctly, furthermore
it is evident that, from the aforementioned hour,
all so-called sane people have become crazy.
PEER: You spoke of a clock striking. My time is short.
BEGRIFFENFELDT: Your time? You compel me to speak.
    Come forth,
I say, Time's Future is upon us,
reason is dead, Peer Gynt answers the summons.
Good new dawn to you all, well met.
The dawn of the new dispensation is indeed sweet.
Your emperor has this moment arrived.
PEER: Emperor?
I am not worthy of such an honour, I fear.
BEGRIFFENFELDT: Do not let senseless modesty degrade
this moment.
PEER: But I'm stupefied.
BEGRIFFENFELDT: One who has solved that dire conundrum
posed by the Sphinx? Who is selfhood's self? None worthier
than thou to be our grand panjandrum.
PEER: I am indeed myself *in toto*;[49] but therein,

if I correctly read your mind, we snag.
Self here, you say, is absolute Nonself. I must beg
to stand down, to abdicate, to be left alone.
BEGRIFFENFELDT: No one's himself, emperor, don't you see,
but here: each is himself, here, to the nth degree.
Each to himself, impurities excised,
himself at sea with all the canvas raised.
Bunged in the barrel of himself, fermenting,
hermetically sealed-in with self-cementing.
Wood-preservative-selfhood's all the rage;
no tears for others' woes from selfhood's cage;
no tolerance for what's judged alien;
self at the limit of the diving board,
self on display, unchallenged, self-admired:
none but you so perfectly fits that bill.
PEER: God! No!
BEGRIFFENFELDT: Let neither modesty nor dismay
prevent acceptance. We're making a new start
and that can be unsettling. Tell you what!
I'll pick someone at random, put him before your eye.
You'll see how things can stand open-and-shut.
[To a shrouded figure]
Good day to you, Huhu, my lad; are you still
of the mind that modern things go ill?
HUHU: Can I otherwise conclude?
Generations, now, have died
nameless, uninterpreted.
[To PEER]
You're the stranger who's been thrust
upon us. D'you want the list?
PEER [bows]:
Please, by all means.
HUHU: Lend me your ear.
Look at the coasts of Malabar[50]
far to the east; its wreaths of flowers
clapped on the skulls of foreign powers.
The Portuguese, the Dutch, arrive.
Culture's merchandisings thrive.

Native Malabarians also
make their mark – that's something else tho'!
Portuguese, Dutch, Malibari
mix their languages like curry;
together, in some sort, proclaim
such lordships as God's paradigm.
Yet, in a lost primeval age,
the orang-outang was in charge;
child of the forest and its master;
fought and hunted; yawned at rest there;
screams of triumph, screams of pain,
reverberant in his domain,
primeval and primordial,
till Man conveyed his murder-deal.
Four hundred years of commerce-making[51]
gave darkness to the orang-outang;
little indigenous survives;
the forest closes on its lives,
the growls, the murmurations, all,
the language of the common soul.
If we're to speak of these, our tongues'
emancipation's fettered things,
compulsion must assign us freedom;
Portuguese, Dutch, pure bred, mixed race,
must self-dissolve in a grand Ur-dom,
the purest song of our distress.
I have endeavoured with truth's blade
to preach the aboriginal;
tried to resuscitate the corpse;
maintained the people's right to curse;
and, in my isolation, tried
variants of that ancient call.
We must revive the folk-song if
the truth of things is to survive,
but none will hearken. You may feel
now, your highness, why I grieve.
Thank you for listening. If you have
any suggestions I will listen.

PEER [*quietly*]:

   It is written, one must howl
   when wolves are running, just to live.
   [*Aloud*]
   My friend, I seem to recollect,
   Morocco had some bushes packed
   with orang-outangs: they appeared
   to be without a single bard.
   Their language, I've no doubt, is full
   of sounds on which your skills could fasten;
   to me it sounded Malabarian
   but I'm no expert. With your brain
   and expertise and colleagues, could
   you not arrange to take the Word
   to where such gifts might work great good?

HUHU: Words most persuasively precise.

   I'll act on your advice.
   [*With a grand gesture*]
   The bard
   rejected in his own land's heard
   by apes upon a foreign strand!
     He leaves.

BEGRIFFENFELDT: Was his the Nonself's selfhood? Could
    you understand?

   I say it was, in some remote kind.
   He is his Nonself's maestro, that alone,
   in everything he pours forth, Archimedean point,
   beside himself, both in and out of joint.
   Attend, please, for I have another patient
   who, since last night, has been indisputably sane.
   [*To a* FELLAH *carrying a mummy on his back*]
   King Apis,[52] how do you do, my noble lord?

FELLAH [*wildly, to* PEER]:

   Am I King Apis?

PEER [*hiding behind the doctor*]:

   I am obliged to confess
   that I do not possess the full details of your case;
   but, judging by your symptoms, I would diagnose . . .

FELLAH: You too are a liar!

BEGRIFFENFELDT: It would help us to achieve
   a diagnosis if, Your Highness, you could give
   a full account of things; perhaps relive . . .

FELLAH [*turning to address* PEER]:
   This fellow I'm here carrying,
   King Apis was his name.
   He's what they call a mummy.
   He's as dead as they come.
   Pyramids were his buildings.
   He chiselled the great Beast.
   As the Doc says, he battled
   those Turks from the east.
   So, by the whole of Egypt
   he was worshipped as a god.
   They stood him in their temples,
   an ox as he stood.
   Now I'm him with that power,
   I see it clear as day.
   If you are blind, listen;
   I'll tell it my way.
   King Apis he went hunting
   and he was caught short,
   went on great-grandad's property
   for to take a shit.
   The field that he manured,
   it has fed me with corn.
   If final proof's needed
   I've got invisible horns.
   Is it not most damnable
   no one speaks of my power?
   By rights I am King Apis
   though I'm damned poor.
   If you know any remedies –
   let's have no deceit –
   tell me how I might be becoming
   King Apis the great.

PEER: Your Highness must build pyramids

and sculpt a bigger Sphinx;
and battle, as the Doc has told you,
a Turkish phalanx.
FELLAH: Ah well, that's some fine talkin':
that's as far as it gets.
I've enough keeping my lean-to
free of rats.
Come up with something better
is my plea and desire,
to have me feel as good as
King Apis here.
PEER: What if you hanged yourself,
Your Highness, and then,
snug in that old coffin,
have a grand time on your own?
FELLAH: Yessir! A rope to take me,
both my skin and my bone.
At first I'll not look like him,
but later on . . .
    Walks away and prepares to hang himself.
BEGRIFFENFELDT: So there was one well stuck on himself,
    Herr Peer, *mit Methode.*
PEER: I suppose I must concur.
    But – he can't be going to hang himself from that hook?
    Oh, my God, he is! This is terrible!
    My thoughts are spinning beyond my self-will!
    I'm becoming ill!
BEGRIFFENFELDT: A very brief transitional phase of shock.
PEER: Transition to what, God help me? I have to be gone!
BEGRIFFENFELDT [*grasping him and speaking overbearingly*]:
    What? Leaving? Are you mad?
PEER [*quietly*]:
    That judgement's not yet made.
        A general agitation, people milling about. MINISTER
        HUSSEIN *forces his way through the crowd.*
HUSSEIN: An emperor's arrival's now officially made
    known.

[*To* PEER]
That is you, excellency?
PEER [*desperately*]:
Everyone seems agreed that I am he.
HUSSEIN: Very good. Here are some notes that need your
    immediate answer.
PEER [*tugging at his hair, in a kind of frantic gaiety*]:
                                High jinks at the nadir!
HUSSEIN: Will you honour me with a dip?
    [*Bows deeply.*]
                                                I am a quill.
PEER [*bowing even more deeply*]:
    And I have the honour of being a fully inscribed
    imperial parchment.
HUSSEIN: My history, Excellency, I shall briefly tell.
    I am used as a sand-shaker when in fact I'm a pen.
PEER: My history, Chief Minister Quill, appears to have been
        scrubbed.
    I am a sheet of paper on which nothing is written.
HUSSEIN: I have capacities that no one can comprehend.
    I wish to write well, and yet I scatter sand.
PEER: I was a book with a silver clasp[53] in a woman's hand.
    Whether sane or insane we are the same printer's error.
HUSSEIN: But pray bear in mind my debilitated life:
    I am a quill pen that has never tasted the knife.
PEER [*giving a high kick, as in the halling*]:
    Just think – to be that reindeer buck! He plunges
    into a void of air, exquisite terror,
    no hoof-print is ever found.
HUSSEIN: I am a blunt knife. My edge must be reground.
    The world will die for want of such changes.
PEER: That's a great shame for the world, which, like all
        other
    self-made things, our Lord believed to be sound.
BEGRIFFENFELDT: A knife, Freiherr!
HUSSEIN [*snatching it*]:
                                How I shall slather

myself with red ink! The ecstasy of that wound!
   He slashes his own throat.
BEGRIFFENFELDT [*turning sharply away*]:
  Don't splash! Tch!
PEER [*clearly appalled*]:
               Hold him!
HUSSEIN: Hold! A good word to have found!
  I am a dulled edge ground
  down. Put paper. Hold pen.
  Let there be a postscript, a 'last inscribed work'.
  You set it down:
  'He lived so that, through him, illiterates might leave a mark'.
PEER [*in a state of near collapse*]:
  What should I . . . ? What am I . . . ? Oh, Lord! Hold fast!
  Whatever You want me to be – Turk, sinner,
  or mountain troll – there was a thing that burst –
  I nearly became a trolls' dinner.
  [*Screams.*]
  Can't quite call You to mind, sorry!
  'Our Lord is the guardian of fools.' Some story.
    Sinks down unconscious.
BEGRIFFENFELDT [*with a wreath of straw in his hand sits
    down on top of* PEER, *straddling him*]:
  See how his filth becomes him now.
  Ausser sich.[54] A straw wreath for his brow.
  [*Crams the wreath – it looks obscenely rakish – on* PEER's
  head and proclaims:*]
  Long may he last – Self's emperor!
SCHAFMANN [*from the cage*]:
  Es lebe hoch der grosse Peer![55]

ACT FIVE

SCENE 1

On board a ship in the North Sea off the coast of Norway. Sunset. Stormy weather. PEER, *a sturdy old man with ice-grey hair and beard, is standing on the quarter deck. He is dressed partly in the manner of a mariner, with a pea jacket and sea boots. His clothing shows signs of wear. He himself is weatherbeaten, and his expression, over the years, has grown harder. The* CAPTAIN *is standing next to the* HELMSMAN. *The* CREW *are for'ard.*

PEER [*resting his arms on the ship's rail, gazing intently towards land*]:
  And there's the Halling ridge in his winter coat. He's putting on
  a display, the old fellow, using the last of the sun.
  Behind, at an angle, I see there's the Hardanger glacier, his twin.
  He's not yet shed his mantle of green ice.
  Folgefonn, now, she's always lain,
  looking virginal in the purest frozen linen.
  Don't dance about so, two old men with one old woman.
  Stand as you've always stood, granite peaks firmly in place.
CAPTAIN [*shouting to the crew for'ard*]:
  Two men at the helm! Make ready the signal-lantern.
PEER: It's a gusting wind.
CAPTAIN: Ay, there's a storm building.
PEER: Will I
  be able to spy Rondane from this far out to sea?

CAPTAIN: Unlikely, I would say; it stands behind Fonnen.
PEER: How about Blåhøi, then?
CAPTAIN: No, but from high in the rigging,
  in clear weather, you can just make out Galdhøpiggen . . .
PEER: And Hårteigen?[56]
CAPTAIN [*pointing*]:
                    Where my finger . . .
PEER: That's about right.
CAPTAIN: It seems you know the region.
PEER: When I shipped out
  I sailed past here but in the other direction.
  [*Spits and stares towards the coastline.*]
  There's a blueness of light in those black rifts, I've
      remembered,
  those deep valleys that are as narrow as trenches,
      embedded,
  and, at the base of it all, the open fjord –
  that's where folk in fact live,
  [*Looks directly at the captain.*]
                          their biggings scattered.
CAPTAIN: Aye, as they say, far between, far apart.
PEER: Think we'll be in before dawn?
CAPTAIN: Aye, thereabout,
  provided we don't get storm-force these next hours.
PEER: Cloud's thickening in the west.
CAPTAIN: So it appears.
PEER: When I settle up with you for my passage
  I have in mind a little something for the crew.
CAPTAIN: They'll appreciate that.
PEER: Nothing much to show,
  mind you. I've had gold but gold's disappeared,
  for I've enjoyed fate's kinds of usage
  more than once. You saw what I brought on board,
  reminders of lost wealth.
CAPTAIN: A more than adequate hoard
  to set you up in style when we arrive.
PEER: I've no kin,
  there's no one waiting for the ugly rich old man.

At least there'll be no welcoming committee
when we come alongside the quay.
CAPTAIN: Storm's here!
PEER: Hold on to what I've said.
If any of the crew is truly in need
I'll not grudge my cash.
CAPTAIN: That is handsome indeed.
Most are hard up, with wives and children at home.
The ship's wages, I fear, barely support them;
so that with a bit of extra cash in pocket
it could be such a homecoming as few would forget.
PEER: They've wives and children, have they? They're
    wedded!
CAPTAIN: Wedded, ay wedded, the whole crew,
though how could you be expected to know?
The one in the tightest corner is the cook.
Hunger in his house is well and truly at work.
PEER: So, there is always someone watching and waiting
and who rejoices when they come through the door.
CAPTAIN: Indeed, as is the custom among the poor.
PEER: And if they come towards evening, well, what more?
What manner of greeting?
CAPTAIN: Then, I imagine, the wife would bring out
something that's perhaps a bit tastier to eat,
and a bit more of it.
PEER: The oil lamp would be lit?
CAPTAIN: Two, even; and she'd fetch him a dram of aquavit.
PEER: They sit there, the two of them, side by side; for once
they've a decent fire; the children shout and prance,
they interrupt each other happily a lot?
CAPTAIN: Yes, thanks to your benevolence . . .
PEER [*bringing his hands hard down on the ship's rail*]:
They can forget that!
Not a single piece of my coin shall go to the sustenance
of other folks' children. I'll not be led that dance!
I've done bitter hard labour for the little I've got.
Let no man await Peer Gynt with his hand out.
CAPTAIN: But, sir, the money is indeed yours, still

to give or withhold. That is the owner's right.
PEER: And no one else's! As soon as we're berthed, I'll
give you what I owe: the money
due for my passage from Panama,
sole use of cabin. I'll grant each man on board
a shot of brandy, soon as the anchor's heard.
If I give more then hit me on the mouth hard.
CAPTAIN: It's a receipt you'll get, sir, not a beating.
Excuse me now: the wind's at storm-force as we feared.
He moves for'ard. It has become dark; lights are lit in the
cabin. The sea-swell increases. Thick clouds and fog.
PEER: Those beggars can work it, keeping a brat-pack in a
poor home;
they know how to stay in folks' minds as a joy to come
after so long a parting,
to voyage tugging the hearts of loved ones in their wake.
There's never a single soul that I've left waiting.
The lighted oil lamp – let it grow bleared,
the room darkening, a malodorous wick.
I'll think of something richly detrimental
to these wastrels one and all.
I'll make them drunk: not one of the whole boiling
but shall come home to his wife reeling and yelling,
calling on God to damn him and his heirs,
smashing fist on tabletop and hurling chairs,
driving wife and children out of their wits,
the woman in fear of death, clutching her bairns close,
stumbling out of the house.
[*The ship heels heavily;* PEER *lurches, then has difficulty*
staying upright.]
The ship has the staggers. The sea heaves as if it's
in somebody's pay.
It's always its old self, cussed and contrary,
in these northern shipping lanes. Now it hits
full across the bows! What's that I heard?
LOOKOUT [*for'ard*]:
Wreck ahoy! Wreck to leeward!
CAPTAIN [*amidships giving commands*]:

Helm hard a'starboard! Hard up against the wind!
HELMSMAN: Are there folk aboard?
LOOKOUT: Can see three through the spray.
PEER: Swing out the stern boat! Lower away!
CAPTAIN: Swamped almost before we'd launched her,
    she'd be!
    Goes for'ard.
PEER: Who'd have that on his mind
  at such a time? If you're human you do it –
  so what if you get a bit wet?
BOSUN: Can't be done, not in this swell.
PEER: They're screaming yet! I felt the wind, just now, abate!
  Cook, there! You'll dare? Do it, I'll pay you well.
  You need the funds.
COOK: Not if you gave me twenty English pounds!
PEER: Cowards! You fritted curs! You're all the same!
  These poor folk will have wives and children at home
  caught between hope and dread. Can't you think of them?
BOSUN: A bit of patience never did anyone harm.
CAPTAIN: Hold her off from the breakers!
BOSUN: The wreck's been
  swept somewhere astern.
PEER: And now I can hear nothing but wind and sea.
BOSUN: Well, if those poor fellows were wedded, as you say,
  there's three freshly baked widows on the shelf today.
    The storm increases. PEER *makes his way aft.*
PEER: No kind of bond exists between people any more,
  certainly not Christianity as it's now taught everywhere;
  little of practical value gets done; and, as for prayer,
  as for the 'everlasting arms', folk couldn't care less.
  In weather like tonight our Lord is dangerous.
  The brutes aboard this ship should consider that:
  it's risky to meddle with forces elephantine
  as if you were merely tying back a loose buntline.
  Instead they spit
  in the face of His commandments. I on the other hand
  have a clear conscience about these latest events.
  I can prove, if need be, that I pulled cash from my pants

and thrust it in their faces. Save those poor wretches, I cried!
'An easy conscience makes for an easy bed',
that certainly holds good while you're on land,
but it's not worth a fleck of foam on board,
where a good man is pitched among the thieves.
Privacy, at sea, is something that's unheard
of; you're with a rabble, deck to keel.
If God's judgement – anytime now – strikes down
bosun and cook, why, then, I also drown.
Who notices one sausage when there's scores to fill?
You go down with the rabble when the vessel dives.
My great mistake in life is that I've been
too ready to oblige, too pliable.
Brutish ingratitude repays my trouble.
If I were younger I'd review the course
of my whole life, change to another horse,
or briefly have a go at being boss.
Still time for that, I imagine; will not the word
fly round the village and up the fjord
that Peer's at last set down from his aery road
over and across the world's oceans? I'll
win back the farm by fair means or foul;
I shall rebuild it; it will gleam like a castle.
But no one who spurned me shall come into the hall.
Outside the gate they shall stand, twisting their greasy caps,
whingeing and pleading with their wretched hopes.
But none shall have a shilling of what's mine.
They saw that I writhed repeatedly under fate's goad.
There must surely be others whom I can goad in return.

  A STRANGE PASSENGER *appears beside* PEER, *out of the*
  darkness, and gives him a friendly greeting.

PASSENGER: Good evening!
PEER: Evening. Don't believe I've seen . . .
PASSENGER: I am the companion of your voyage.
PEER: I have been
 the sole passenger throughout the entire trip;
 the captain assured me of that.
PASSENGER: A slight misapprehension,

happily resolved between us. I should mention . . .
PEER: But how, then, did you keep
  for so long out of sight?
PASSENGER: I have walked only by night.
PEER: You've been ill, is that it?
  Even now, you're as white as a sheet.
PASSENGER: Thank you, but I am perfectly well.
PEER: And we have this terrible storm the while.
PASSENGER: I would call it more glorious than terrible.
PEER: Glorious?
PASSENGER: Yes, my friend; it makes my teeth drool
  with the ecstasy of it! The dwellings it could uproot,
  the carnage it will consummate this night,
  the blue-white corpses that it will fling ashore.
PEER: Heaven protect us!
PASSENGER: Three forms of death excite
  our gaze: by water, noose and garrotte.
PEER: Now you go much too far!
PASSENGER: The corpses grin but their laughter is contained;
  and most have bitten through their tongues, you'll find.
PEER: I want no more of this!
PASSENGER: One question, then:
  suppose we are wrecked this night and you drown
  while I bob up . . .
PEER: What rubbish!
PASSENGER: Just suppose;
  indulge me; if, while you're halfway down,
  you get frantically generous, start to disown,
  because of remorse . . .
PEER [clutching his pocket]:
  My money, ha!
PASSENGER: Your money, no. What I would wish of your
  largesse is your cadaver, highly respected sir.
PEER: This is disgusting.
PASSENGER: Merely the corpse, no more.
  It will inspire my scientific work.
PEER: Vile clown!
PASSENGER: But, my dear man, you too will gain.

I'll rip up to the light your secret seams;
perhaps in you I shall find the plexus of dreams
believed not to exist . . .

PEER: Get thee hence, I command!

PASSENGER: . . . analyse its contents.
Do please agree. With one so freshly drowned . . .

PEER: Blasphemous tempter, whipper-up of deluge,
or is that thought too wild? Wild winds at large,
towering waves, all among other portents:
you seem intent on bringing death upon us.

PASSENGER: You're clearly in no mood to discuss plans.
But, then, the whirligig of time's the thing.
[*Takes his leave in a most amiable manner.*]
Perhaps, when you're going down for the third time,
we'll meet again and do some bargaining.
Perhaps you'll then be in a better frame
of mind.
    Enters the cabin.

PEER: What weird blinkers
these scientists wear; self-obsessed Free-thinkers.
[*To the* BOSUN, *as he goes past*]
A word, my friend.
From what madhouse did he abscond,
my strangely disposed fellow passenger?

BOSUN: You are the only stranger here.

PEER: This is going from bad to worse, I fear.
[*To an* ABLE SEAMAN, *who is leaving the cabin*]
Who just entered through the cabin door?

SEAMAN: All I saw enter was the ship's dog, sir.
    Continues on his way.

LOOKOUT [*screams*]:
Breakers ahead!

PEER: My suitcase! My travelling chest!
All my belongings to be saved first!

BOSUN: We've worse things to think of. Out of the way!

PEER: Aye aye, bosun, just nonsense, harmless play,
my little joke. Of course I'll help the cook.

CAPTAIN: The jib's blown to tatters!
HELMSMAN: The foresail's in shreds!
BOSUN [*yelling*]:
  She's aground any minute!
CAPTAIN: The masts will be down on our heads!
  The ship drives on to the rocks. Terrible sounds. Dreadful
  confusion.

SCENE 2

Inshore amongst reefs half-covered in surf; the ship is wedged,
broken-backed. In the fog you can just make out a ship's
dinghy, which contains two men. A wave capsizes it; a scream
is heard; after that a brief silence. Then the keel of the upturned
dinghy can be seen. PEER's *head emerges near the boat.*

PEER: Ahoy, ashore! Row out and save me!
  The Good Book says you must! Believe me!
    Clings desperately to the dinghy's keel. The COOK's *head*
    emerges on the opposite side.
COOK: Lord, spare me for my starving band
  of little children! Help me safe to land!
    Clings to the keel.
PEER: Let go!
COOK: No, you!
PEER: I'll break . . .
COOK: . . . your neck!
PEER: I'll drub your bones, I'll stop your breath!
  Let go, this thing won't bear us both.
COOK: I know! Gerroff!
PEER: No! You gerroff!
    They struggle; one of the COOK's *hands is injured; with*
    the other he still clings desperately to the keel.
PEER: Let go, I say!
COOK: Sir, spare my life,
  I beg! My children! My poor wife!

PEER: My life's more valuable than yours,
   I haven't yet begotten heirs.
COOK: You've lived your life; I've mine to live; I . . .
PEER: Sink, damn you, sink! You're too heavy.
COOK: Oh spare me, sir, in the Lord's name.
   You've nobody to grieve at home.
   [*Screams and lets go.*]
   I'm going!
PEER [*seizing a fistful of hair*]:
                    While I've got your hair
   begin reciting the Lord's Prayer.
COOK: I can't recall . . . it's going black . . .
PEER: Recite the most important bit!
COOK: Give us this day . . . give . . . give . . .
PEER: No, that's not it.
   What you need you'll no doubt receive.
COOK: Give us this day . . .
PEER: Don't just repeat it.
   No need to tell us you were cook.
      Releases his grip on the COOK, *who sinks.*
COOK: Give us this day . . .
      He goes completely under.
PEER: Amen, my lad.
   You were yourself, *Sich selbst*[57] indeed.
   [*Swings himself out of the water and sits astride the keel.*]
   Well, where there's life there's hope. Whatever.
      The STRANGE PASSENGER *swims up and takes hold of
      the keel.*
PASSENGER: Good morning.
PEER: Aagh!
PASSENGER: I heard you shout.
   How pleasant it will be to chat.
   Well, my prediction hit the spot.
PEER: Be off. There's hardly room for one.
PASSENGER: Using my left leg I can swim
   or I can float just holding on,
   a fingertip stuck in a seam.
   But, apropos, sir, your cadaver . . .

PEER: Not now!

PASSENGER: It's all you can bequeath.
   The rest is gutted.

PEER: Shut your mouth.

PASSENGER: Just as you wish.
      Silence.

PEER: Well, what?

PASSENGER: I didn't speak.

PEER: What now?

PASSENGER: We wait.

PEER [*tearing at his hair*]:
                        The devil's trick.
   You'll drive me mad in time. So, *what*
   are you?

PASSENGER: Friendly.

PEER: What happens now?

PASSENGER: What do you think? Surely you know
   someone, some others, who are not
   wholly unlike me?

PEER: Well, there's Satan.

PASSENGER [*quietly*]:
   Is he the one who keeps the light on
   for life's long trek through dark and dread?

PEER: How about that! Misunderstood,
   have I? So you're a spirit lamp!

PASSENGER: In six months, say, have you known once
   the kind of fear that grips your bones?

PEER: I do get panicked a fair bit.
   Your words contort and also clamp.

PASSENGER: And have you once, in your long years,
   experienced victory *through* such fears?

PEER [*staring*]:
   D'you come to 'ope the narrow door'?
   A shame you weren't here earlier.
   This truly is a bad old time
   for arguing codicils to doom.

PASSENGER: Would victory seem more probable
   if you were tucked up in Gynt Hall?

PEER: Perhaps not; but you scathe and mock.
  D'you really think such tones will work?
PASSENGER: Where I reside, our practice rates
  smiling equivalent to pathos.
PEER: 'Time for all things' is a factor
  appropriate to a tax collector,
  not to a bishop.
PASSENGER: That great
  silent majority in their ash
  have no time for our vain panache.
PEER: Off, scarecrow, I'm not dying yet.
PASSENGER: You're safe for now, at any rate;
  I can assure you, you'll not die
  before act five's peripety.
    He glides away.
PEER: Well, he betrayed himself, at last,
  as just another moralist.

SCENE 3

A cemetery in the high mountain area. A funeral procession.
PRIEST *and* MOURNERS. *The last verse of a hymn is sung.*
PEER *passes by on the road.*

PEER [*at the gate*]:
  A man of earth proceeds to his long home.
  Again I must thank God that it won't be me in the tomb.
PRIEST [*addressing the* MOURNERS *at the graveside*]:
  Now that this soul is on its judgement road
  his body lies here like a bursten pod.
  So now, dear friends, before we shovel earth,
  we speak of his long journey here from birth.
  He was not rich, nor had he the right touch;
  his voice was weak, his posture deemed unmanly;
  when he dealt with ideas they stood ungainly.
  You could not call him master in the home.
  When he attended church he seemed to need

forgiveness from the priest for having come.
Hailing from Gudbrandsdalen, as you know,
when he moved here he'd not long ceased to grow.
From youth until the very day he died
there was a thing, of all the things he did,
we most remember: how it was he hid
always his right hand deep inside his jacket.
'Right hand in pocket' is what now commends
the final memory of him to our minds.
That, and the ever-awkward, ay, the naked,
expression of his face to those he met.
He chose to trudge along his path, a quiet
stranger among us to the very end.
And yet, that finger missing from one hand!
I well remember – many our Lord's years
since gone – that day of the conscription board
in Lunde. We were at war. You heard
talk of privations, common hopes and fears.
There was the captain sitting centre-table,
the sheriff, sergeants, looking stern and able.
Lad after lad was measured top to toe
and told 'that for a soldier he must go'.
The room was full; from outside, in the yard,
it was the larking of those lads we heard.
A new name was called out, and in he came,
pasty as snow gets when it's past its prime.
They told him to come closer; this he did;
his right hand wrapped in linen and well hid.
His Adam's apple retched, could not uncork
one word in answer to the captain's bark.
Then finally he croaked out – his cheeks aflame,
his tongue a-stumble – words that sealed his shame.
He mumbled something none of us believed:
a sickle slipping and a finger cleaved.
The room fell hushed: a miming theatre
of lips a-pursing, mass caricature.
They stoned the lad with their unspoken words;
invisible hail stung. That old grey man,

the captain, stood, spat, pointed and said 'Go!'
And the lad went. Crowd parted on both sides;
he ran the gauntlet back where he'd crept in;
fumbled the door; shot forth like bolt from bow.
Straight up he went, through grove and meadowland,
up through the stone scree staggering and falling.
Somewhere among the mountains was his home.
Six months later he was back again
with mother, babe-in-arms and the babe's mother.
And it was said he'd rented some rough ground
between the wilderness's edge and Lom.[58]
He made an honest woman of the girl;
built a cabin; did much heavy tilling;
and slowly made his way amid the weather,
as many a little field could testify
with good corn thrusting strongly through good soil.
He came to church, with his right hand concealed
as always, though at home I have no doubt
nine fingers did as well with what they wrought
as other people's ten. And fortune smiled
until, one spring, the floods swept all away.
They escaped with their lives, barely; day by day
he mured wild land, brought new fertility.
Ere long a pleasant hearth-smoke rose again
from a new farmstead; things stood true and plain.
Two years; and then the glacier's fresh moraine
buried in rubbled scree, deltas of silt,
his heart's investment. And he may have wept.
For the third time, as, doggedly, he built
their modest dwelling where rude fate had swept.
They had three sons, three bright boys who were schooled
by different stages on life's way (I mean
by way of a most arduous terrain).
To reach the district road – a different world! –
perilously stepped father and eldest son,
each roped to each, like practised mountaineers,
which they became, no doubt. He, on his back,
the father, bore the second son; his arms

carried the youngest. So they made their trek
overcoming nature and their own fears.
So he toiled on; the boys grew into men.
Here I must pause. I look around in vain.
Justice may here demand a just return.
Three prosperous gentlemen of the New World,
I do not see them here to meet the claims
he – oh so rightly – had on filial love.
A father, sons, the hard road: that is all.
He was a man near-sighted. Past the small
circle of those closest, he could not move
his range of vision. So for him the names
that resonate for us were not enscrolled.
Our blessed homeland, that ever-glowing term,
was but remote philosophy to him.
He was humble; humble indeed this man
who, from that far conscription day, had borne
his judgement, as he bore the branded shames,
the public scorn, four-fingered hand well hidden
yet known to all. He failed in what was bidden,
indeed he did; and broke his country's laws.
But there are laws, greater by far than these,
that utter their divine simplicities,
as Glittertinden,[59] round its topmost peak,
is crowned by heaven itself when the clouds break.
He was a hapless citizen, God knows;
in terms of state and Church a barren tree.
But back there, grafting order on wild ground,
in compass of the small diurnal round,
there he was great, to his own self was true;
his passage through this world a muted sound
plucked from the homeliest of instruments.
And therefore peace be with you, patient soul
who served, who fell, fighting a peasant's war.
We will not search his heart for its intents,
nor on his reins our pettiness obtrude.
That task is proper to the Lord of All.
Yet, free and frank, let us in faith declare:

this man's no cripple where he stands with God.
 The MOURNERS *disperse.* PEER *remains.*
PEER: Now that's what I call genuine Christian feeling.
 Nothing that could possibly leave a nasty taste in the mind.
 I also found the main text of the sermon appealing:
 being unshakeably for yourself is where I always stand.
 [*Looks down into the grave.*]
 Was this the very same lad, I wonder, who,
 all those long years ago,
 chopped off a finger that day I was tree-felling?
 Who can say? If I were not stood here with my pilgrim's staff,
 looking down at the grave
 of someone I truly feel was a kindred spirit,
 I could believe it was me lying peacefully there,
 hearing my praises sung, a roll-call of merit.
 It truly is a most charming Christian habit
 to cast a final glance, a totting-up as it were,
 back over the lifetime of the dear departed,
 but always in the most genial kind of way.
 I'd have not the slightest objection to being bade goodbye
 by this kind, fair-minded spiritual advocate
 when my time comes, which, I trust, is not quite yet,
 and when that honest sexton invites me to stay.
 For, as the scriptures say, best is still best,
 and, in the same vein, sufficient unto the day.
 Don't pay for your funeral in advance
 is another good one. All of life at a glance,
 the Church remains the one true comforter.
 Though I've not set great store
 by its precepts up to now, they stand the test.
 To be assured, by those who really know,
 that, as you sow,
 so shall you reap, is reinvigorating.
 Be true to yourself, they say,
 and keep a close eye on your property;
 look to yourself in matters great and small.
 If, then, from fate you get a final slating,
 even so, you know, you've lived life by that rule,

and none can steal that from you. Home,
here we come!
Although the way be steep and narrow, fate
at its most unpleasantly jocular,
treading his own path as always, here comes Peer
Gynt, who is, as he always was, poor
but never less than straight.

    He leaves the graveyard and returns to the road.

SCENE 4

*A hill with a dried-up river bed. The ruins of a mill by the
river. The ground is churned up; everything around is laid
waste. Higher up, a big farmhouse. Up at the farm an auction
is in progress. A crowd of common people has gathered; there
is drinking and much clamour.* PEER *is sitting on a heap of
gravel down by the mill side.*

PEER: Forwards, back, same length of trek.
   Out and in, you scrape your skin.
   Time corrodes, river abrades.
   'Around,' said the Boyg; the advice was sound.
A MAN DRESSED IN MOURNING: What's left is stuff to
     throw away.
   [*Catches sight of* PEER.]
   A stranger in our midst? God's blessing, friend.
PEER: Well met! The place is lively today.
   A christening is it? Or a wedding feast?
MOURNING MAN: You could call it a housewarming of
    a kind.
   The bride is lying in her bed of clay.
PEER: The worms competing among rags of breast.
MOURNING MAN: Let's end the ballad there. Over
    and done.
PEER: All the ballads end in the same way;
   they're ancient, too; I knew them as a boy.
A YOUTH [*with a casting-ladle*]:

Look, here's a fine thing I was lucky to buy.
Peer Gynt used it to cast silver buttons in.
SECOND YOUTH: And how about this? It's an old
        money-chest.
    Just a shilling it cost.
THIRD YOUTH: I paid a bit over four for this peddler's pack.
PEER: 'Peer Gynt,' you said; was that the name?
MOURNING MAN: Brother-in-law to death, to the smith
        Aslak,
    the two in one, that's how they tell it.
MAN IN GREY: Hey, I'm still here! You four can swill it!
MOURNING MAN: You've forgot Hæggstad and a
        locked door.
MAN IN GREY: You also, remember, came out of that
        game poor!
MOURNING MAN: Let's hope she doesn't wrangle
    so readily with the recording angel.
MAN IN GREY: Come now, brother-in-law, let's knock back
        a dram
    for old time's sake!
MOURNING MAN: I don't give a damn.
MAN IN GREY: What do they say? However thin
    the blood . . . Like it or not, we're Gynt's kin.
        They leave together.
PEER [*to himself*]:
    Well, old acquaintance is not forgotten,
    not in these parts.
A BOY [*shouting after the* MAN IN MOURNING]:
                        Our mother, may she rest in peace,
    will haunt you, Aslak, if you get spewing-drunk!
PEER [*stands up*]:
    What the rural economists say,
    'the deeper you dig the sweeter it smells',
    does not hold true of this particular clay,
    I think.
BOY [*with a bearskin*]:
    Here's the skin of the cat that chased the trolls
    one Christmas Eve!

SECOND BOY [*with a reindeer's skull*]:
                    Here's the great reindeer buck
    that bore Peer Gynt safely through mist and murk.
THIRD BOY [*carrying a hammer calls to the* MAN IN
        MOURNING]:
    Hey, Aslak, did you send him reeling –
    the devil – once? Knock him through the ceiling?
FOURTH BOY [*empty-handed*]:
    And here's the cloak that makes you disappear,
    Mads Moen, ere you can think twice.
    With it Peer Gynt and Ingrid flew through the air.
PEER: Let's have the brandy, lads, I feel so old.
    I'm thinking I might hold
    my own auction of odds and ends.
FIRST BOY: What priceless items would you have to hustle?
PEER: To start with, I have a castle.
    It stands in Rondane; and it's of solid build.
SECOND BOY: I bid one button.
PEER: You'll need to bid more.
    You must stretch to a dram.
    It would be sin and shame
    to let it go for less, even among friends.
THIRD BOY: Well, this old lad's a great character,
    I must say!
        They crowd around him eager for more fun.
PEER [*shouting like an auctioneer*]:
                    Lot two! Grane, my horse! Fine beast!
    Who'll bid?
ONE OF THE CROWD: Where is he?
PEER: Far to the west,
    towards the sunset, my lads. That steed can fly
    as fast
    as Peer Gynt, at the top of his form, could lie.
ONE OF THE CROWD: What more do you have to be rid
        of?
PEER: Some golden tawdry.
    It cost me too dear. I'm selling far below cost.
FIRST BOY: So, call the lots!

PEER: And be prompt to bid.
  A precious dream of a book with a silver clasp.
  That you can have for a hook without an eye.
SECOND BOY: To hell with all dreams.
PEER: Next the unsigned decree
  that claimed I was emperor. It's for free
  and you can scramble for it.
THIRD BOY: Can you throw in a crown?
PEER: Yes, of the finest straw. And it will fit
  the first person who tries it on.
  Hey, there's still more: an egg without
  its shell; a madman's hair (grey); a prophet's beard.
  You can have the lot if you're prepared
  to take me to the heath and set me right.
  The finger-post will read: 'here is your road'.
SHERIFF [accosting him]:
  The way that you're behaving, I don't doubt
  a spell in prison lies within your grasp.
PEER [with his hat in his hand]:
  That may be true. But tell me, who was Peer Gynt?
SHERIFF: Think you're cut out
  to be a comedian?
PEER: No, no, it's facts I want.
SHERIFF: They say he was a damnable fabricator,
  fabulator, whatever the right word is.
PEER: A teller of tall tales?
SHERIFF: Whatever was great or
  extraordinary,
  he invented a story
  claiming that he was the genius of such absurdities.
  But, look here, Grandad, I have other duties.
      Strides officiously away.
PEER: So where is he, this extraordinary creature?
AN ELDERLY MAN: He went overseas to some heathen land
      or other,
  and fared ill; he had a skewed nature.
  Whatever it was he did, he swung for it
  many years since.

PEER: Hanged was he? Well, he was that sort,
   true to himself.
   [*Prepares to be on his way.*]
                    My thanks, I've enjoyed this rather.
   [*Walks a short distance, then stops.*]
   But there again, I've – hey-ho, lads and lasses,
   would you like a tall story of high enterprises?
ONE OF THE CROWD: Yes, do you know any?
PEER: As it happens, this old man does.
   [*Comes nearer; he adopts a strange, vatic expression.*]
   In San Francisco, where I worked as a gold miner,
   everyone was putting on some kind of an act.
   If one of them played a violin with his toes
   another would dance the halling but – it's a fact –
   do it while kneeling, 'Spanish style'. Another shiner
   I heard about would compose verses extempore,
   'off the top of his head', I suppose you could say,
   while someone else was drilling through his skull.
   Well, at this charlatans' convention there arrived,
   on one occasion, the devil, just to try his luck.
   As it turned out, his one and only trick
   was to grunt like a pig and do it lifelike.
   He had a good sales pitch and so contrived
   to fetch in a fair crowd for his first and only appearance.
   Expectations ran high, and the theatre was full.
   So, on to the stage he strode, an enormous cloak
   billowing around him: '*man muss sich drapieren*',[60]
   as that German proverb says. Of all the confounded cheek!
   He's smuggled in a live pig, swathed in the folds.
   So, the performance starts: the devil gives a squeeze,
   and the pig gives voice, a bit like a bagpipe scolds.
   Its billing was 'symbolical fantasy
   depicting porcine existence bound and free'.
   The coup de théâtre was a kind of wheeze
   as though the pig had felt the butcher's knife.
   And that was that; the artiste took a bow
   and left the stage. Opinion was not wanting.
   Some found the range of voice too narrow,

others thought the death-squeal untrue to life;
but all were agreed: as a display of grunting
the whole performance was quite over the top.
You can all draw the lesson from that, I hope.
The devil got 'thumbs down' for his insolent stunt
because he did not take public sentiment into account.

    He takes his leave. An uneasy silence descends on the crowd.

SCENE 5

Whitsunday Eve. We are at the heart of the forest. Some way off, in a clearing, there is a cabin with reindeer antlers above the door frame. PEER *is on his knees in the undergrowth. He is gathering wild onions.*

PEER: If this is seeing things from a new angle, I can hardly
    wait for the next. The Good Book says to try
    all things, make sure you pick the best.
    Well, I've done all that, top to bottom, you could say,
    from Caesar to Nebuchadnezzar, the man who crawled,
    who 'from among his own people was made outcast'.
    The Good Book also says, make sure your guts are filled
    with things of the earth out of which you were pulled.
    Fill my belly with wild onions? Can't say I fancy them.
    Hang snares to catch thrushes
    among the high bushes?
    That's a much better scheme.
    There's plenty of nice fresh water in the beck;
    I shan't go thirsty. And if I have to live
    like an animal I mean to be lord of the pack.
    When I die – I can't live indefinitely
    however many japes I may contrive –
    I shall make my last hideout under a fallen tree,
    rake a great mound of leaves and crawl into it
    just like a bear when it's time to hibernate.
    And I'll carve somehow my epitaph for all to see:

'Here lies Peer Gynt; he was a decent fellow,
emperor of the forest creatures'.
[*Laughs quietly to himself.*]

                                        You old fool, though!
You're not an emperor; you're an onion,
in need of peeling, my friend Peer.
You can weep all you like; it still has to be done.
[*Picks an onion and begins to peel it.*]
Here is the outermost split layer.
Call it the shipwrecked man on the dinghy's keel.
Here's the skin I'll call 'Strange Passenger',
not yielding much, though with a whiffy scent,
somehow, of slick Gynt.
What do we have next as I continue to peel?
Inside here we have the gold-digger's spoil,
no longer worth tasting, if it ever was.
The tough part here, with a sharpish edge, must be
the fur-trader section up at Hudson's Bay.
Inside that again, a skin that looks like a crown.
Well, that's something I'm quite happy to disown.
The archaeologist: a strong taste still it has.
And here we uncover the prophet; the strongest taint,
I must say, of the entire peeling –
he stinks of wickedness, as the Good Book says,
so that an honest man can get tears in his eyes.
We're coming closer to the final unveiling.
This next layer, which is soft and self-infurled,
represents, I imagine, the wealthy man of the world.
The next, inlaid with black stripes, seems diseased,
black representing either Negro or priest.
[*Pulls off several layers at once.*]
What a tiresome quantity of the things!
When will I uncover the core within these rings?
[*Pulls the whole onion apart in a burst of irritation.*]
Well, I'll be damned! I've pulled the thing apart
and, what d'you know? it doesn't have a heart.
Nature is exceedingly witty, is she not?
[*Throws the mess away.*]

So, let the devil brood on what this means.
The introspective man who walks alone
can do himself some harm, but since I've gone
on all fours for some time, it should be safe
enough, I'd say, even to scoff.
[*Scratching his neck*]
Life's a strange business, though; rarely explains.
It has a fox behind its ear, but try
to grab it and the creature's pretty spry.
You're left with something else between your fingers
you'd be better without and which lingers.
[*He has been getting closer, during his onion picking, to the
cabin, which he now takes note of for the first time. He
appears disconcerted.*]
That cabin, there! House on the heath? It seems
like a vivid recollection of old claims.
The reindeer skull that stands out on the gable,
a mermaid formed like a fish below the waist,
what fantasies I spin myself! What trouble
I invent. There's no mermaid. But old planks nailed with rust,
yes, there are those; locks to keep out troll dreams.

SOLVEIG [*heard singing inside the cabin*]:
Now all is made ready for the Whitsun Eve.
And oh, my dearest boy, my blessèd one,
those logs that you have,
are they a great burden?
Take all the time you need.
Whether late or soon,
I shall wait as I said.

PEER [*gets to his feet, quiet and deathly pale*]:
Ah! One who remembered and one who forgot.
One who lost faith while the other did not.
Dire gravitational pull of things never to be reversed.
Here was my right true empire but I was self-deposed.
   He stumbles away along the forest path.

SCENE 6

Night. Among the pine barrens. The area has been devastated by a forest fire. Charred tree trunks as far as the eye can see. Clouds of grey mist here and there over the forest floor. PEER *hastens through this wilderness.*

PEER: Ash and fog and dust a-smother.
  Blighted plenitude to build on.
  Stench and rottenness together,
  whited sepulchre. Beholden,
  I, to dreams and stillborn knowledge,
  bad foundations mired in fullage,
  see a pyramid arising
  based on lies and false appraising;
  vacant truth and void repentance
  topping out my life's self-sentence,
  crowing like the Petrine rooster
  pinnacled upon disaster.
  Petrus Gyntus Caesar fecit.[61]
  [*Listens.*]
  There's a sound of children weeping
  might yet be their singing gladly.
  Self-projection, as I take it,
  of my guilty un-self-keeping.
  Balls of yarn, now, rolling madly
  at my feet . . .
  [*Kicks out.*]
           . . . troll thoughts a-gripping.
BALLS OF YARN [*on the ground*]:
  Thoughts we are not.
  You should have thought us;
  babes unbegot,
  you did not beget us.
PEER [*steps aside*]:
  Him I fathered was a troll-child,
  brain askew, his body crippled.

BALLS OF YARN: We should have risen
  as voices in song;
  we were not chosen;
  snarled here our wrong.
PEER [*tripping over them*]:
  Yarn ball, misbegotten cruddle,
  more like man-trap than cat's cradle.
    *He extricates himself and attempts to leave them
    behind.*
WITHERED LEAVES [*blown by the wind*]:
  We're a conundrum
  too long unsolved.
  We heard the wind drum
  while rain delved.
  Worms have reduced us
  to our small skeletons;
  when in right justice
  we are your laureate crowns.
PEER: I don't think you've done too badly.
  Make good compost; do it gladly.
A RUSHING IN THE AIR: We are the rhymes
  you did not sing us.
  A thousand times
  you chose to wrong us.
  In your heart's chamber
  we've lain, mute song,
  years without number.
  May your throat ever be wrung!
PEER: I should have stifled such complaining
  long years since; damned poetic whining.
    Attempts to take a short cut.
DROPS OF DEW [*dripping from the branches*]:
  We are the tears
  that were never shed.
  Ice-daggers through the years
  we would have melted.
  The deepest ice-wound
  is in your heart yet,

    though the flesh looks sound
    over the heart.
PEER: I was imprisoned by the trolls;
    wept; but no one came to my calls.
BROKEN STRAWS: We are the deeds
    you failed to deliver.
    Doubt with its many heads
    the sole receiver.
    We shall come in a swarm
    on Judgement Day
    and speak you harm.
    You will blench at what we say.
PEER: Nasty tricksters, adding the final sum
    to my account, but in the debit column.
        He hurries away.
AASE'S VOICE [*heard as though from a great distance*]:
    Shame on you, such dreadful driving,
    almost tipped me out you did, lad!
    There's been fresh deep snow arriving.
    Well, you've bruised me pretty bad.
    Driven me the wrong way, have you?
    Where's the castle we were close to?
    Devil's made you misbehave – you! –
    with that stick out of the closet.
PEER: Think it wise and think it needful
    for this lost soul just to vanish.
    Carrying the devil's spadeful,
    and your own, spells heavy finish.
        Runs off.

                    SCENE 7

Another part of the heath.

PEER [*singing*]:
    A gravedigger! A gravedigger! Where are you, curs?
    I must be one who hears

music in a sexton's bleat.
I need a mourning ribbon round the brim of my hat.
I have so many dead I must follow through the lychgate.

The BUTTON MOULDER *appears from a pathway to one*
side. He carries a tool chest and a large casting-ladle.

BUTTON MOULDER: Greetings to you, old sir!
PEER: And to you, friend.
BUTTON MOULDER: Gentleman's in a hurry. Whither does
    he wend?
PEER: To a wake.
BUTTON MOULDER: To a wake, is it? I don't see too well.
    Forgive the question; might your name be Peer?
PEER: Peer, yes. Peer Gynt.
BUTTON MOULDER: Peer Gynt. I call
    that luck! For I am to meet you here
    this very night.
PEER: Are you indeed? And why the need?
BUTTON MOULDER: You're to go in this ladle o'mine.
PEER: And to what end?
BUTTON MOULDER: To be melted down.
PEER: Melted?
BUTTON MOULDER [*shows the ladle*]:
                                      It's freshly scoured,
    ready, waiting; grave dug, the coffin ordered,
    the worms have whetted appetites for the feast.
    And I am bid to find you with all speed,
    and in the Master's name to fetch your soul.
PEER: And I must tell you that's not possible.
    To be called like this, at some stranger's behest . . .
BUTTON MOULDER: There is a quaint old custom in these
        parts,
    for christenings and for funerals
    to be somewhat arbitrary in their dates;
    these to be settled without due regard
    to diaries of those new born or newly dead.
PEER: That may be so, but – ach, my head!
    Tell me again; you are . . .

BUTTON MOULDER: You heard me the first time. A button
     moulder.
PEER: I suppose it hardly matters what one calls
     you: a cherished child has many names,
     the saying is. So, Peer, you'll not grow older.
     But look'ee here, my man, it's a low trick
     you've played me, with these sudden games.
     I deserve gentler handling; although some make
     out I'm a scoundrel, I have done much good
     during my time on earth. At worst a fool.
     My sins, I'd say, were unremarkable.
BUTTON MOULDER: And that's the nub of the problem, you
     see, squire:
     the fact that you're so middling. Worst kinds of torture
     you're likely to be spared, that's understood.
     Like most, your prize is my old casting-ladle.
PEER: Well, call it what you will; whether brimstone lake
     or your big spoon, it's nothing but a fiddle.
     Home-brewed and import are both kinds of beer.
     Get thee behind me!
BUTTON MOULDER: I'm quite shocked to hear
     such coarseness from your lips. No one believes,
     in these enlightened times, that where you've feet I've hooves.
PEER: Horse's hoof or fox's claw, be gone,
     pick your way back over stock and stone.
BUTTON MOULDER: Once more I have to say how sorry
     I am to hear you speak so. We must hurry,
     the pair of us, and take a few shortcuts.
     I shall but briefly reason with your doubts.
     You have, as you have said, not greatly sinned.
     In the judgement of your own mind
     you are somewhat of middling kind.
PEER: I approve your thoughts
     as here expressed.
BUTTON MOULDER: Be patient yet awhile.
     But to call you a minor saint would go too far?
PEER: I've no claim to the highest style

of conduct, that I accept.

BUTTON MOULDER: You are,
    then, we're agreed, a kind of entrepreneur,
    an opportunist, a middle man.
    Old monstrous heroic sinners one doesn't meet
    with, these days, on your average street.
    Their kind of sin demands high seriousness;
    great willpower, grand design.

PEER: That's near enough, I'd guess.
    With them it was full pelt, like the old berserkers.

BUTTON MOULDER: You, on the other hand, were among
    the workers
    of expedient things.

PEER: Yes, a quick dabble
    when chance allowed; tried to keep out of trouble.

BUTTON MOULDER: There we agree. The brimstone lake of fire
    is not for toe-dippers, such as you were and are.

PEER: That's very good to hear.
    Now may I go?

BUTTON MOULDER: No!
    It's been decreed that you'll be melted down,
    here, in my spoon.

PEER: So that's the trick you've come up with, you devils,
    while I've been on my travels.

BUTTON MOULDER: The process dates back to the first
    creation
    of living things; and is an essential link
    in the grand economy. You'll have a fair notion
    of what I mean: you could trim a button mould
    in your young days. Many castings are spoiled;
    sometimes a button is without its shank.
    What did you do with a spoiled button?

PEER: Tossed it as junk.

BUTTON MOULDER: Ay, so you did. You were Jon Gynt's lad.
    Everyone rooted around in his grand pile
    just so long as it lasted, with the ale-casks full.
    But the master I serve is economical;
    he doesn't throw out what can be reused.

You, dear sir, he meant for a shining button
on the world's waistcoat; but somehow a loop broke.
Even so, you were never forgotten.
You shall be fused
into the lump that he'll rework.
PEER: Re-smelt me, you mean? Not that, surely?
Like Askeladden's failed brothers,[62] and all?
BUTTON MOULDER: Upon my soul, you've hit the nail entirely!
It's happened to thousands. At the Royal Mint
in Kongsberg[63] they melt down and then re-coin
whatever's been defaced or has worn thin.
PEER: But this is torture, not economy.
I beg you, beg your master to relent.
One shankless button or one battered shilling,
what's that to him? What could he possibly want
from me? I won't be melted down for ready money.
I'm shocked that he so lacks all decent feeling.
BUTTON MOULDER: According to, dependent on, and by and
large,
all things considered, with appended clause,
just as the spirit takes you, tit for tat,
the metal in itself is worth a bit,
you must admit.
PEER: No, and again no! It's physical abuse!
With tooth and nail I'll fight my case.
You can't detain me without charge!
BUTTON MOULDER: But we must do the best with what
we're given.
You're not ethereal enough for heaven.
PEER: Obviously not. And I don't aim that high.
I hope I've my fair share of modesty.
But of my *Selbstgrundlage* I'll not yield
one farthing's worth to rivals in that field.
Let me be judged by the old rules of law.
I'll take my punishment – yes, that I vow!
I'll do my stretch with Old Nick, him with hooves,
a hundred years if need be. Modern thought believes
there's no real fire and brimstone, and that all

the torment's merely metaphysical.
So, things won't be too bad, more quarantine
than torture-chamber: 'transition', the fox said,
admittedly while being flayed.
But there we are. We wait and stand in line;
redemption's bell peals out. One doesn't thrust
ahead of others, waits one's turn in trust.
This other scheme, though, is ghastly: to be fused
into the beings of a thousand strangers
without distinction; *Selbstgrundlage* abused;
this utter travesty of the Gyntian Whole.
This is what angers,
this is what makes my innermost self rebel!
BUTTON MOULDER: My dear sir, you've no call
to make such protests. Never in the past,
even for a moment, have you been yourself,
so what does it matter? And on whose behalf
do you bewail this lost identity?
PEER: Have not *I* been? I weep with merriment.
Something else he has been – that's it? – this fellow Gynt?
No, button moulder, you stand in blind judgement
against me. Could you but see into my heart and soul
you would discover
Peer, Peer, the one and only Peer,
the irreducible entity
indissoluble to mere quantity.
BUTTON MOULDER: Such is not possible. I have my orders
set out in print.
Look, they're here; and I shall read them aloud.
'You must claim back Peer Gynt.
He has defied our determination for his road
through life. Into the casting-ladle with him; he is skint.'
PEER: Do they indeed say '*Peer* Gynt', those words you read?
Should you not truly have said 'Rasmus' or 'Jon'?
BUTTON MOULDER: It's a long while since they were
melted down.
Come along with you, now; you're trying to buy time.
PEER: I jolly well won't.

Suppose that someone else is meant,
and tomorrow you find that out, and it's too late?
Have a care, my good man!
Be slow to deliver this verdict as your own.
You'd be complicit in a crime.
BUTTON MOULDER: It is written.
PEER: Grant me some time of grace.
BUTTON MOULDER: How would you use it?
PEER: I shall get you proof
that I have been myself the whole of my life.
That's what we're wrangling over.
BUTTON MOULDER: What would the proof comprise?
PEER: Eye-witnesses, notarized referees.
BUTTON MOULDER: I say
that, even so, my lord's judgement will stand.
PEER: No, that's impossible; and, anyway,
sufficient unto the day!
Give me the chance to borrow myself against
my self remortgaged. I'll soon be back, you'll find.
You're born once only and, even if you're trounced,
you grow attached to yourself as you've been made.
Can we agree on that?
BUTTON MOULDER: It's so agreed.
You have until the next crossroads. Take heed.
     PEER *hurries away.*

SCENE 8

Another part of the heath.

PEER [*running hard*]:
Time is money, time is money, time is money, so it's said.
Where the next crossroads are, I do not know.
Near? Far? I register earth's heat
through the soles of my feet.
Witness! Must get a witness to show.
But how?

Surely not now, not on this desolate run.
The world is a botched job, the way things are done.
One's rights should be self-evident as the sun!

> *A bent* OLD MAN, *staff in hand, around his neck a bag, is*
> *shuffling along, slightly ahead of* PEER.

OLD MAN [*pausing*]:

Good sir, for charity! A shilling for the deserving poor.

PEER: Alas, I have no ready money.

OLD MAN: Prince Peer,

so we meet again, you see, after many a long year.

PEER: Who the devil are you?

OLD MAN: The old man of Rondane; you can't
have forgotten the Dovre King, even in his condition of want?

PEER: You're truly him?

DOVRE KING: On evil days though fallen, evil times.

PEER: Hard to believe . . .

DOVRE KING: And left to beg my way while hunger clems.

PEER: Witnesses like this don't grow on trees!

DOVRE KING: The prince also has grown grey since last
we met.

PEER: We both have cause to recall things with regret,
the wear and tear of the years.
But let us draw a line under private affairs,
the family feud.
Back then I was a footloose madcap lad.

DOVRE KING: That's true enough. The prince was young,
and youth is full of folly and does wrong.
But fortune smiled on him when he put aside
his bride.
In so doing he spared himself a lifetime
of grief and shame.
These many years she's run a dissolute course.

PEER: Is that so? You don't say?

DOVRE KING: Lives off cold water and lye;
what's as bad, or worse,
she's taken up with that Trond.

PEER: Which Trond?[64]

DOVRE KING: Why, him from Valfjeldet![65]
PEER: Once, he found
  I'd run three girls he thought were his to ground.
DOVRE KING: My grandson, though, has become tall and fat
  and is a stud. There's scores can vouch for that.
PEER: May we put by nostalgia for a while,
  I have something quite other to reveal
  about a trifling problem: I require
  a reference, a testimonial,
  which you could well provide, father-in-law.
  An honorarium or a *pourboire*[66]
  could be arranged.
DOVRE KING: If I can meet his wish
  the prince may care to offer me, in turn,
  a written affidavit duly signed.
PEER: With pleasure, as I'm slightly strapped for cash.
  I'll tell you now the thing that's on my mind.
  You must remember well my brief sojourn
  in Rondane when I came to claim my bride . . .
DOVRE KING: An unforgettable occasion, prince.
PEER: No need for titles here . . . and how you made
  an unprovoked attack on my eyeball
  in an attempt to change me to a troll;
  how resolutely then I fought,
  swore I would stand firm on my own two feet,
  abjuring love, renouncing power and glory,
  in order to retain my self and soul.
  I need you now to swear to that in court,
  there's an all-prying judge I must convince.
DOVRE KING: I'm sorry; can't be done.
PEER: Why on earth not?
DOVRE KING: The prince would not demand such perjury.
  He donned the nether garment of a troll,
  he will recall,
  and quaffed our mead.
PEER: While you all tried
  to lure me with troll arts which I rejected.

  I refused to deny
  my humanity:
  that's how you recognize a man, indeed.
  It's all there in the last line of that song.
DOVRE KING: Your lifetime's recollections heard it wrong.
PEER: What utter nonsense!
DOVRE KING: When you fled my hall
  you went with the troll's commandment stuck in your soul.
PEER: Commandment?
DOVRE KING: Strong and divisive that command
  which utterly divides our two worlds, trolls and men:
  'Troll, be to yourself sufficient!'
PEER [*taking a step backwards*]:

                                              Enough! No more!
DOVRE KING: And with your utmost strength of mind
  that is exactly how you've lived since then.
PEER: *I am Peer Gynt!*
DOVRE KING [*lachrymose*]:

                                        Oh, what ingratitude!
  You have lived like a troll but taken care to hide
  the debt. The motto, the commandment, that I gave
  has helped you to become a man of power.
  And yet you come along and toss your head
  at me and mine, who best deserve
  your thanks.
PEER: Enough, I said.
  You're but a mountain troll equipped with ego's goad.
  What you've been saying is a load
  of old rubbish.
DOVRE KING [*pulling out a bundle of old newspapers from
     his bag*]:

                              Do you suppose that in Dovre they lack
  news and newspapers? Here it all is, in black
  and red; so hearken. Hear the *Blocksberg Post* applaud,
  the *Heklefjeld Times*[67] resounding with your praises,
  all since the winter that you left us, Peer.
  Perhaps there's something else you'd want to hear.
  One writes under the byline 'Stallion-hoof'

and someone – here it is – outlines the thesis
'Concerning National Trolldom'. He offers proof
that trolldom, rightly understood, is not
a matter of horns and tails exactly, but
possession of a vital strip of skin.
The troll's motif 'Enough' can of itself donate
essential trolldom's powers to any man.
He cites you as an instance.

PEER: Me? A troll?

DOVRE KING: That's how it stands; and how things stand
    as well.

PEER: I could have stayed, then, where you had me,
  and, in a kind of peace, let you degrade me;
  spared toil and trouble, many pairs of shoes.
  Peer Gynt a troll? Your image I refuse.
  Here, take a shilling for a bit of baccy.

DOVRE KING: My dear Prince Peer – for prince I do still
    take ye –

PEER: Shog off, old man, you seem bewildered,
  confuse plain facts; you're in your second childhood.
  Some hospital for paupers may admit you
  and be more lenient with your vacant chat. You . . .

DOVRE KING: A pauper hospital is what I'm seeking.
  But, sad to say, my grandson's many offspring
  have gained such power in national politics;
  they claim that I exist only in books.
  'Kinsman to kinsman', as folk say,
  'is worst'; and that's a proverb few can deny.
  I've proved it, skin and bones. It's very hard
  to find yourself dismissed as tricks and trumpery.

PEER: Many can vouch for that, you will have heard.

DOVRE KING: And in Rondane itself we're much in need
  of charities and charitable aid,
  poor boxes and the like. I'm told they have no place.

PEER: Among your 'self-or-nothing' populace.

DOVRE KING: The prince can hardly disagree with that.
  Indeed he's sharp enough to follow suit.

PEER: Look, gaffer, you are wrong. Wrong track entirely.

I tell it fair-and-squarely.

I myself stand upon the barren scarp, or . . .

DOVRE KING: Surely this cannot be! The prince a pauper?

PEER: A pauper through and through. My princely ego
   long since pawned, though it still goes where I go.
   What's worse, I owe it all to you damned trolls.
   Bad precedents can't be soaped away like smells.

DOVRE KING: Well, there's another hope dropped off
    its perch.
   I'll limp on into town.

PEER: And when you reach
   town, what will you do?

DOVRE KING: Think I'll audition.
   They're putting on *The Character of the Nation*[68]
   in the theatre there; it's widely advertised.

PEER: Good luck go with you. I may do the same
   if I can solve my problem in good time.
   I have a farce in mind; crazy, yet deep;
   Sic Transit Gloria Mundi,[69] deep though crazed.
   Perhaps *Enough To Make the Angels Weep*?
    He hurries off along the path. The DOVRE KING *hobbles*
    after, shouting something unintelligible.

SCENE 9

At a crossroads.

PEER: Now things are urgent, Peer, as never before!
   The Dovrean 'enough' pronounces sentence.
   My vessel's wrecked, the flotsam drifts to shore,
   and I'll float with it; hope yet for remittance.

BUTTON MOULDER: So, Peer Gynt, present your affidavit,
   always supposing that you have it.

PEER: This is the crossroads then? It got here fast!

BUTTON MOULDER: I can read on your face, as on a
    'Wanted' fly-sheet,
   what your document says, even before I scry it.

PEER: I was hot and bothered and then lost.

BUTTON MOULDER: Quite so, quite so; and, after all, what's
    the point?

PEER: What indeed, stuck in this lousy forest.

BUTTON MOULDER: Here comes an old man trudging his
    poor stint.

  Let's call him over.

PEER: Pah! Let him go; he's squiffed.

BUTTON MOULDER: But yet, perhaps . . .

PEER: I've told you: squiffy, daft.

BUTTON MOULDER: Shall we proceed, then?

PEER: Just one question, please.

  To 'be oneself': I'm not sure what that is.

BUTTON MOULDER: Astounding, such a question, coming
    from one

  who only lately . . .

PEER: Answer me, if you can.

BUTTON MOULDER: To be oneself is to do away with oneself.

  That explanation, though, is wasted on you.

  So let's rephrase: it is to treat as pelf

  the master's treasures, and to smear with glue

  his best intentions, plaster them on the wall

  of your self-adulation and desire to sell.

PEER: But what if that man could simply never learn,

  however much he tried, the master plan

  of purpose and salvation?

BUTTON MOULDER: Why, then, he must

  'intuit' it.

PEER: But intuition-on-trust

  is enigmatic and our aims misfire;

  we find ourselves *ad undas*,[70] in despair.

BUTTON MOULDER: Ah yes, Peer Gynt, you strike exactly,
    there.

  Failure of intuition: there the bloke

  with the hoof finds the best bait for his hook.

PEER: A complex business, I think you'll agree.

  Say I renounce my right to autonomy,

  how do I find convincing evidence

that I have done so? I've lost it in advance,
I see that now. Stuck on this ashen heath
I felt my conscience like a catch of breath;
said, almost without thinking, 'I have sinned'.
BUTTON MOULDER: You seem to run round
  in circles the whole time.
PEER: This is different. I felt it as a web of crime,
  not in act only, in desire and word.
  I was a cunning, violent man abroad.
BUTTON MOULDER: It may be as you say; but, for the
    record?
PEER: I beg you for some further time of grace.
  I shall seek out a priest and, to his face,
  make my confession; return with my signed pass.
BUTTON MOULDER: Provided you do that, I think it's clear
  ordeal by casting-spoon will not occur.
  But the general order is not yet annulled.
PEER: The paper that you wave about is old;
  it must originate
  in those things of an earlier date,
  when I lived a life that was effete,
  and played the prophet and believed in fate.
  So, may I try to find the priest?
BUTTON MOULDER: But I . . .
PEER: You are not all that burdened with your duty.
  This district has an enviable atmosphere.
  The people live long lives who live round here.
  Remember him, the priest of Jostedal:[71]
  'Death's an infrequent visitor to our vale'?
BUTTON MOULDER: To the next crossroads; but then grace
  expires.
PEER: A priest I shall have, if I have to seize him with pliers!
  He departs hurriedly.

SCENE 10

A hillside clad in heather. The road winds, following the contours of the land.

PEER: *That* may come in handy for something,
    as the man said who picked up the magpie's wing.
    Who would have thought that volunteering your sins
    might buy you time on your last evening?
    Even so, it's touch-and-go,
    it's jumping out of the ash into the fire.
    'So long as there's life there's no call to despair':
    a decent old saying; it's so, I trust.
        A THIN MAN wearing a priest's cassock hitched up high
        and with a bird-catcher's net over his shoulder runs
        across the slope of the hill.
PEER: As if on cue, who is it that runs
    into the picture? Yes, a priest,
    a priest with a bird net over his shoulder.
    Ha! Fortune's favourite, aren't I, though?
    Good evening, Herr Pfarrer, the path is rough.
THIN MAN: One does not grudge it; there's a soul at call.
PEER: You're seeing someone off on the road to heaven?
THIN MAN: I pray that he's safely on the road to hell.
PEER: Herr Pfarrer, may I bring you on your way?
THIN MAN: I shall be grateful for the company.
PEER: There's something on my mind.
THIN MAN: So, shoot.
PEER: You see in me a decent man who's lost
    his way; not seriously; but
    needs to get back on track before he's older.
    Laws of the state he honestly has striven
    to keep in line with; has never occupied
    a prison cell. Sometimes a foot has slid
    where it should not have gone.
THIN MAN: I've often said
    'happens to the best people all the time'.

PEER: These peccadilloes, in no sense a crime . . .

THIN MAN: Peccadilloes? Is that all?

PEER: Why, yes,
  absolutely nothing gross.

THIN MAN: Then, my dear fellow, let me be.
  I'm not the one you took me for.
  You're looking at my hands. What is it you find there?

PEER: Quite extraordinary, your fingernails.

THIN MAN: My feet, too. Curiosity prevails.
  You'd better speak of what it is you see.

PEER [*pointing*]:
  Is that hoof natural?

THIN MAN: It certainly feels so to me.

PEER [*raising his hat*]:
  Well, well, well! I could have sworn
  you were a priest; but now, instead,
  I have the pleasure, honour indeed . . .
  If the hall door stands open, don't fret for a latch-key.
  If the king will see you, don't stop for the lackey.

THIN MAN: So good to find
  you keep an open mind.
  How may I be of service? I should warn
  you, nonetheless, that there are certain
  matters I cannot deal with: money, power.
  My sources have dried up and I'm quite poor.
  You'll scarcely credit how slack business is
  at the present time; our turnover is down.
  Souls are in short supply. Just now and then
  a suitable one shows up.

PEER: So, would you say
  the human race
  is in a state of grace
  for things to have shifted so disastrously?

THIN MAN: Quite the contrary. There is a vast amount
  of petty wickedness, but what I might term the saint
  of evil, the consummate sinner, has had his demise.
  It's the casting-ladle not the burning lake

for the vast majority of Christian folk.
PEER: The casting-ladle, now you mention it,
   has been on my mind lately, just a bit.
   It is, to be frank, the reason that I'm here.
THIN MAN: Speak freely.
PEER: If it's not presumptuous
   to ask, I should be grateful for the use . . .
THIN MAN: Of a spare room in which you can lie low?
PEER: You guessed my request, even before I made it.
   If, as you say, business is slow,
   then maybe you'd be willing to provide it.
THIN MAN: But, my dear man . . .
PEER: You wouldn't know I'm there.
   My needs are modest and I don't require
   financial support. Just the companionship.
THIN MAN: And a warm room?
PEER: Not too warm. And prior consent
   to take my leave of you without restraint,
   'free and saved', to speak it like the folk,
   when things start picking up.
THIN MAN: What I have to say will come as a shock.
   My desk is buried under applications
   from thousands such as yourself, soon to shake
   off, as you also must shake it off, this earthly yoke.
PEER: When I survey the scroll of my late conduct
   I am impressed by my high qualifications.
THIN MAN: But as you said yourself, the merest trifles.
PEER: There was some pettiness, I grant you, but
   I profited from the slave trade quite a bit.
THIN MAN: Some applicants have dealt exclusively
   with minds and wills,
   all at the highest levels –
   I speak, you must understand, allusively –
   but their logistics were shaky: we're not talking here
   of a blocked sin-duct.
   Well, they were turned down.
PEER: I plied a lucrative slave trade. I shipped to China

thousands of shoddy copies of some figurine, a
travesty of Buddha, as I recall.

THIN MAN: Profiteering in mock piety, not a big deal!
There are those who profit from much nastier habits,
sermons, belles-lettres, *objets d'art*, exhibits
of dubious kinds. And they haven't got in.

PEER: I've kept the worst till last. Listen to this:
I played at being a prophet . . .

THIN MAN: But overseas:
that's just as we expect.
The 'blue yonder' excites *'ins Blaue hinein'*,[72]
faith's mystery tour.
All candidates for the ladle; nothing more.
If this is what your evidence amounts to,
I have to tell you frankly, it discounts you.

PEER: No, wait – 'peril at sea'! I almost forgot:
I was sitting astride the keel of a capsized boat
and, as it is written, was grasping at a straw,
and, as it says also, was being 'intensely myself' –
well, I was half-
responsible for ridding a cook of his life.

THIN MAN: If you'd half brought a kitchen wench to grief
I'd be equally unimpressed.
What a species of half-gabble, now, is this?
What reason is there to light the furnaces,
turn up the heat, burning expensive fuel,
for such a bunch of mediocrities.
Please don't be angry: at the worst or best
your sins attract a sneering condescension.
Take my advice, abandon thoughts of hell,
become inured to thoughts of reinfusion
into the base metals of the ladle.
If I gave board and lodging what would you gain?
Think about it; you're a reasonable man.
True, you would keep your memory, some old saw
might be applicable; but passing in review
your lifelong mediocrity would not
be, in that Swedish phrase, 'a lot of fun'.

You've nothing over which to laugh or howl;
nothing to make you either cold or hot;
no joy and no despair squat cheek by jowl.
Your limbo would begin to irritate
and aeon upon aeon
would pass in a mild form of chagrin.
Read Revelation, three, sixteen.

PEER: 'The reasons why a pair of shoes
is agony, only the wearer knows.'

THIN MAN: More from the Good Book? And of course
it's true.
Praise be to Him of No Name,
it was my luck to come
into the world requiring only one shoe.
And that reminds me, I must hie abroad
to pick up the steak I've ordered, running red.
I can't waste further time in idle chatter.

PEER: And what, may I ask, did that steak feed on
to turn him out so juicy, a raw-red 'un?

THIN MAN: He fed on himself entirely, days and nights,
and, in the end, that set him in my sights.

PEER: *Selbstgrundlage*, that's what gives you entry
to hell's pantry?

THIN MAN: Well, yes and no; you could say the door is ajar.
You can be *Urselbst* in either of two ways
as you might wear
a coat
rightside – or inside out.
Or here's an analogy that might work better.
You'll know that, in Paris, they recently hit upon
ways to make portraits with the aid of the sun.
You can do either a positive or a negative one,
the latter having its light and dark parts reversed,
which makes it appear weird to normal eyes.
But nonetheless the likeness is inherent
and what they have to do is to draw it forth.
If it so happens that a soul from birth
has photographed itself, its acts recurrent,

but only in a negative likeness, its nature
is not the cause of the plate's being refused.
It is sent on to me, by me immersed
and steamed and soaked and scorched and rinsed –
sulphur and mercury (some might say 'censed') –
until the original likeness is sealed and held;
the positive, as it is rightly to be called.
But with a case such as yours, already mauled,
then neither sulphur, mercury, nor potash can
revive the sodden image of a man.

PEER: So one can't come, or be brought, here as a black raven
and issue forth as white as a winter ptarmigan.
Then may I inquire, reverend, whose name now stands
on that negative image which, in your hands,
will attain a positive value?

THIN MAN: Name's Peter Gynt.

PEER: Peter Gynt. Does this Herr Gynt affirm
that he's himself, beyond all argument?

THIN MAN: He does so affirm.

PEER: You can accept his claim.

THIN MAN: Your tone suggests that you're acquainted with
him.

PEER: Slightly, yes. One meets so many people.

THIN MAN: Time passes. Where did you see him last?

PEER: It was down at the Cape.

THIN MAN: *Di buona speranza?*[73]

PEER: Yes,
but he leaves there shortly; gives no new address.

THIN MAN: Then I must start immediately, travel fast,
and trust to arrive in time.
That Cape Province has always spelled trouble.
Stavanger missionaries[74] are there; they're a bad lot.
He sets off towards the south.

PEER: So, off he goes at a bound and a trot,
and with his tongue hanging out.
Well, he'll find he's been had!
I enjoyed cheating the idiot.
And him so jargon-proud.

All that fuss
pretending he's the boss.
He'll be out of business;
he'll fall off his perch with the whole caboodle.
Though I'm not all that secure in the saddle,
come to think of it.
The self-possessed gentry, of course, would say I don't fit.
[*A shooting star can be seen; he nods amicably towards it.*]
Greetings from Bror Gynt, brother shooting star!
To shine, to be put out, to be simply not there . . .
[*Hugs himself as if suddenly chilled with fear. He walks
deeper into the misty landscape. After a moment of silence
he cries out.*]
Is there none out there to respond? No one at all?
No one in the abyss? Nor under the heavens' shell?
[*Re-emerges from the mists at a point farther along the
path; he throws his hat on to the road and, as so often in the
past, tugs and tears at his hair. Gradually his mood becomes
calmer; finally he is still.*]
So unutterably poor a soul can return
to pristine nothingness in the dense grey.
Ah, dearest earth, do not be angry
that I have ravaged you so. Nor you, dear sun,
who gifted your radiance to a locked empty room
because he who owned it was always away.
Inviolable sun and you, dear, violated earth,
was it wise to bear and shed light on her who gave me birth?
The spirit is such a miser, nature so prodigal.
Life's held to ransom by what began it all.
If I could I would climb Glittertinden
to watch the sunrise as if for the last time,
gazing at what was promised and forbidden,
to have an avalanche drown me in its cry.
'Here lies no one' would serve to bury me.
Inconsolably the soul gathers where it is from.
CHURCHGOERS [*singing along the forest path*]:
O sacred morning light
when each appointing flame

raced from most holy Sion:
let us, our words made right,
re-gift the gifted Name
to whence it came, redeeming pain and sin.

PEER [*cowering, well-nigh prostrate with terror*]:
For you, now, Grace is the last wilderness.
Don't seek there some ease from your distress.
I'm so afraid I was dead long before I died.
*He tries to creep in among the bushes but finds that he
has stumbled upon a crossroads.*

BUTTON MOULDER: Greetings, Peer Gynt. So where's that
grand confession?

PEER: D'you think I haven't chased it hither and yon?

BUTTON MOULDER: Run across anybody on your trek?

PEER: A travelling photographer with his trade on his back.

BUTTON MOULDER: Your period of grace has now expired.

PEER: So's everything. The owl, that wise old bird,
can smell the slow-burning fuse. I heard,
just now, its call.

BUTTON MOULDER: That was the matins bell.

PEER [*pointing*]:
Whatever is it that can so transmit
such radiance?

BUTTON MOULDER: A lamp inside a hut.

PEER: That sound I hear so vibrant on the air?

BUTTON MOULDER: A woman's song as strong as any choir.

PEER: As well I know. She is my sins' recorder.

BUTTON MOULDER [*taking hold of him*]:
Go to her then. Set your own house in order.
*They have come out from among the trees and are stand-
ing in front of the 'reindeer' cabin. Dawn is breaking.*

PEER: My house in order, you say. Well, here it is. Be off,
man!
I tell you, if your ladle were as big as a coffin
it would still be too small for me and my sins to grieve in.

BUTTON MOULDER: Until the third crossroads, we agreed;
but then . . .
He moves away.

PEER [*approaching the cabin*]:
  Forwards, back,
  same length of trek.
  Both out and in
  you scrape your skin.
  [*Stops.*]
  But what I hear is a wild ceaseless lament
  for hearth and home, and dreadfully lost content.
  [*Walks a few steps; stops again.*]
  'Go around', said the Boyg.
  [*Hears singing from within the cabin.*]
                            No, this time arrow-straight
  however narrow the gate!
    He runs towards the cabin. At that moment SOLVEIG
    *appears in the doorway, dressed for church and carrying
    a psalter wrapped in a cloth. She has a staff in her hand.
    She stands erect and benign.*
PEER [*throws himself down on the threshold*]:
  If you've passed judgement upon me, speak it now!
SOLVEIG: He is here, he is here, I know.
    *She fumbles for him; it is now evident that she is almost
    blind.*
PEER: Put it on record how grievous have been the wrongs!
SOLVEIG: You have not wronged me in any way,
  my dearest boy.
    Fumbles again and finds him.
BUTTON MOULDER'S VOICE [*behind the cabin*]:
  Your sins are numbered.
PEER: Ay, numbered in wild throngs.
SOLVEIG [*sitting down beside him*]:
  You have made my life a sequence of love's songs.
  Blessed it is that, at the last, you are home
  and that 'the day of Pentecost is fully come'.
PEER: Oh, Solveig, I am lost.
SOLVEIG: But surely to be found
  in Him who holds all things at His command.
PEER [*laughing abruptly*]:
  Unless you can solve riddles I am done for.

SOLVEIG: So tell me what they are, and let us see.

PEER: What cannot I tell? So, what was I made man for?
  So where has Peer Gynt been since you and he
  last met?

SOLVEIG: Where been?

PEER: Ay, with the birthmark of his destiny
  stark on his forehead, as he first sprang out
  of some divine thought?
  Can you answer such questions? If you cannot,
  I must now gravitate to where I belong
  in the limbo of mists where there's no guiding song.

SOLVEIG [*smiling*]:
  Oh, that riddle is easy.

PEER: Then explain it to me.
  Where has it been, my true self, all this time?
  As though with 'the father's name
  written in his forehead'?

SOLVEIG: In my faith, in my hope, and in my love you have
      been carried.

PEER [*stepping back from her in his astonishment*]:
  I cannot believe what I hear.
  Are you saying it is I whom you bear,
  and have borne, within you, this many a long year?

SOLVEIG: That is what I am saying. And who might the
      father be?
  It is the one who answers his mother's plea
  with full forgiveness.

PEER [*as a gleam of light falls across him, cries out*]:
                    Mother, wife, dear maiden,
  keep me near your heart safe-hidden.
    *He clings to her and hides his face in her lap. There is a
    long silence. The sun rises in its full glory.*

SOLVEIG [*sings quietly*]:
  Sleep, my love, my own sweet child,
  I shall rock thee free from guilt.

  The child's safe in its mother's lap.
  The livelong day they play and sleep.

The child's at rest; his mother's breast
protects him; and in God they're blest.

The boy-child lay, close to my heart,
the livelong day. Now he is tired.

Sleep, my love, my own sweet child,
I have rocked thee free from guilt.

BUTTON MOULDER'S VOICE [*from behind the cabin*]:
Last crossroads, Peer? Our final meeting?
We'll see. Till then, I shall say nothing.

SOLVEIG [*singing more loudly in the clear light of day*]:
I have borne thee freed from guilt.
Sleep my love, my own dear child.

Afterword

Translating and Recreating Ibsen: An Interview with Geoffrey Hill

Kenneth Haynes

KH: *Brand* (1866) and *Peer Gynt* (1867) have often been taken as a complementary or contrasting pair. The critic and translator James McFarlane, for instance, whom you drew on when you were first working on Ibsen, wrote that the 'unbending, uncompromising, sternly self-disciplined Brand' was succeeded by 'the compliant, opportunistic, and self-indulgent Peer'; the one destroying illusion, the other living by it; one acting in a centripetal world, the other in a centrifugal one.[1] In your versions the contrast between the two plays is immediately striking in language and style. The characters in your *Brand* speak verse that is dramatically credible, that consistently maintains some relation to a speaking voice, while 'moving without incongruity between colloquialism and high poetry'.[2] *Peer Gynt*, on the other hand, exuberantly abandons this constraint and takes up the widest range of slang, elevated, archaic, fantastic and lyric languages. I wonder whether one source for this difference might be the nature of the commissions, *Brand* for the stage, *Peer Gynt* for publication by Penguin.

GH: My version of *Brand* was commissioned by the National Theatre, and it was performed there in April 1978. I was working from the literal translation, with extensive commentary and annotation, by Inga-Stina Ewbank. It was performed with cuts, and the first publication of the translation, by Heinemann, had those cuts also. A restored translation appeared in 1981 (Minnesota), and a revised and further restored translation came out in 1996 (Penguin). In the current edition there are further revisions, aimed at bringing it even closer to the literal. With *Peer Gynt*, I also worked from a literal annotated version, in this case by Janet Garton; you served as editor for it during revision and preparation for press, so that there was a difference in my working methods from *Brand*.

Perhaps misleadingly, I recall as my actual points of departure for the two versions some precise technical observations and suggestions. At an early meeting with Sir Peter Hall in 1975, I spoke of the challenge of resisting the pull of the English pentameter in coming to terms with *Brand*'s tetrameter; he suggested that I try something even shorter than tetrameter. That was the true genesis of my version of *Brand*, along with Ibsen's own remark that 'I wanted a metre in which I could career where I would, as on horseback.'[3]

In the case of *Peer Gynt*, I was blocked for two years, unable to proceed because unable to know which form to use; a chance reading – in late 2013 – of the fourteeners in Yeats' *The Green Helmet* provided a sudden sense of the possibilities of long lines for it. This was my initial point of departure; there is, I agree, a great variety of verse-forms in my *Peer Gynt*. I have faithfully attended to Garton's notes wherever she has indicated a change in metre.

KH: Did Yeats' subtitle, 'An Heroic Farce', for *The Green Helmet* help you to situate what you were doing, to get a sense in your mind's ear or eye of how to proceed?

GH: I think it may well have done. A sense of sublime doggerel, I trust, informs the many scenes of farce.

KH: Your *Brand* uses slant rhymes in short lines, sometimes shorter than the tetrameter; your *Peer Gynt* uses slant rhymes in lines of highly variable length, some quite short, sometimes of considerable length. In the first draft of your version, *Peer Gynt*'s lines were sometimes longer even than Ibsen's originals and included much internal rhyme and internal off-rhyme. I think that many of these lines have now been broken up, so that there are more short lines, and the rhymes and off-rhymes are made evident at the line-ending much more often.

GH: There was no perfect solution. Placing rhymes in the middle of lines risks obscuring the overall structure of the rhyming lines, which are sometimes quite elaborate – rhymes may be separated by half a dozen or more lines that are otherwise engaged. However, I have by no means abandoned internal rhyme altogether as a resource. For instance, where Ibsen uses a short line, it seemed to me possible to use internal rhyme as a kind of 'snap' effect, the verbal equivalent of the stage direction 'snaps his fingers'. This effect is present in the opening scene, and elsewhere.

KH: Did the difference in commission also affect how you handled issues of stage performance in the two cases? Ibsen wrote both as closet dramas, I believe.

GH: In the case of *Brand*, I was commissioned by the National Theatre to make a version that would justify the use of the big Olivier auditorium and its range of stage machinery. Having worked closely with the admirable 1978 cast and having witnessed the obstacles that the scenery presented, I came to feel that no elaborate stage machinery is needed. Around 1980, *Brand* was performed in the Theatre Workshop auditorium at Leeds University, with a seating capacity of fifty or sixty. It was played on a stage that was essentially bare by staff and student actors. Ewbank, who came up from London to see it, said that she was more impressed by it than by the National Theatre presentation.

The more claustrophobic the setting, the better. It is crucial that the fatal ambiguity of Brand's grandeur-grandiosity be perceived from his own words and actions, not from ice-fields and avalanches. I estimated in 1978 that the complex stage machinery added perhaps fifteen minutes to the production of a play which, in Ibsen's original and even in my reduced version, far exceeds the 'two hours' traffic of our stage'. Cutting for performance is probably inevitable; drastic cutting, however, destroys the integrity of the work.

Both plays have been called 'non-theatrical'.[4] Didn't some critic write that *Peer Gynt* seems to anticipate the medium of film? The distinction between closet drama and drama for the stage does not seem to matter much while actually writing them; either way, one always has a picture in one's head of some kind of human confrontation on the stage.

KH: In the preface to the 1996 edition of your *Brand*, you make a couple of remarks that I don't think I fully understand. For instance, you object to Ibsen's comment that he could as easily have written the play about a politician or a sculptor as about a priest.[5]

GH: Ibsen in that crass remark is betraying his own achievement. Such words reduce Brand, the character, to no more than the usual Romantic hero trapped in the usual dilemma. I have slightly heightened the Kierkegaardian streak in Brand to avoid this conflation.

KH: Would you give an example or explain more what you mean?

GH: Brand's decisions that vitally affect the crisis of the play (his eye-for-an-eye refusal to offer communion to his dying mother, his

decision to remain in the parish though he knows it will be the death
of his son) are vocational choices that pertain to the priest alone.
They are fundamentally different from the vocational choices of a
sculptor or even a 'visionary' reforming activist. I don't believe that
Ibsen had a theological cast of mind. To find it in drama, you would
have to consult George Buchanan's *Jephtha* of the mid-sixteenth century (which I have read in Robert Garioch's Lallans version of 1959);
or perhaps Milton's *Samson Agonistes*.

KH: You write in the 1996 preface: 'That [Brand] is so uncompromising and yet so available, as foil or reactive agent, is a technical
economy which may exact its own price: compromising both his
proper availability, his power of priestly mediation, and his more
contentious mediations of visionary certitude.'⁶ Do you mean that
Brand is lent a spurious appeal through his contrast with venal characters like the dean and the mayor? That his dubious and grandiose
vision is given too much credibility because we see him in his inter-
actions with caricatured figures?

GH: Yes; though delivered somewhat pretentiously, I think that is
what I meant. We ought to be careful, however, with the word 'caricature'. Raymond Williams, for instance, complains that the dean,
sexton, schoolmaster and mayor 'seem at times to be developed for
their own sake, as caricatures'.⁷ I demur: Ibsen is not thinking it
would be good to throw in a few caricatures for light relief but is
recognizing how grotesque such provincial pettiness can be in its
power to maim.

KH: Yes, as you put it in an old interview, Brand is circumscribed by
the 'canting, provincial, sanctimonious, murderously self-righteous
society' in which he acts.⁸

GH: It is a complex problem of balance. Brand's own sado-masochistic,
self-aggrandizing and perhaps lunatic vision is to be set against that
provincial context.

KH: At times you freely depart from the literal versions. Take the end
of *Brand*, for instance. In Ewbank's literal, it reads:

> BRAND [*shrinks under the approaching avalanche and calls out, upwards*]:
>   Tell me, God, in the jaws of death; –
>   Can not a scrap of salvation

Come through man's own will,
If it's *quantum satis* . . .⁹
   The avalanche buries him; the whole valley is filled.
A VOICE [*calling through the rolls of thunder*]:
He is deus caritatis!

Now your version:

BRAND [*shrinking under the approaching avalanche and crying out*]:
                                    Tell
me, O God, even as Your heavens fall
on me: what makes retribution
flesh of our flesh? Why is salvation
rooted so blindly in Your Cross?
Why is man's own proud will his curse?
Answer! What do we die to prove?
Answer!
   The avalanche buries him. The whole valley is filled.
A VOICE [*calling through the noise of thunder*]:
He is the God of Love.

GH: Ibsen situates us, appropriately enough, between a rock and a hard place. To have this exchange of Latin commonplaces between the protagonist and the Almighty as the last word in this drama of human expenditure seems flippant, almost like flicking away a cigarette butt. Some may say this would be an entirely appropriate conclusion. What must be avoided, however, is the impression that Ibsen has by this time exhausted his own imagination and is too drained to do more than conclude with a cracker motto. We need to feel that even if Brand is finished, the dramatist's inventiveness most certainly is not. There has to be something existential, desperate, in the voice. If someone says that I have perpetrated a psychological-dramatic howler in robbing Ibsen of his own meagreness of spirit at this point, that is something I must live with.

Working to my remit, that of making the unactable actable, I make further deviations from the literal. For example, at the beginning of *Brand*, Act Five, I introduce direct address, i.e., 'sexton' and 'schoolmaster', into the opening lines of the conversation for dramatic purposes, in order to establish stage identities immediately. I conflate or delete some of the sexton's and the schoolmaster's more stichomythic exchanges, again for the purpose of dramatic economy. I try to trim and condense stage-business where I can.

Furthermore, I heighten the lyric temper where it seems dramatically effective. In Act Three, Brand speaks in anguish to Agnes. In Ewbank's translation:

BRAND: In agony and tears I secretly bit
   The tongue with which I chastised . . .
   And if I raised my arm to strike,
   I longed for an embrace! . . .
   Go, Agnes, see to the sleeper;
   Sing him into bright dreams;
   A child's soul is clear and soft
   Like a tarn in the light of the summer sun;
   A mother can glide across it
   Like the bird which is beautifully mirrored
   In the deepest depth on its soundless flight.

In my version, I draw as much on Ewbank's notes as on her literal. She says of this passage, for instance, that 'Light, in every sense, is the main issue of the rest of this Act, right to the last line.'

BRAND: Everything that I speak
   is spoken in agony.
   I'm like a castaway
   crying in vain among
   the spars of a great wreck.
   I could bite out my tongue
   that must rage and chastise
   and with its prophecies
   strike terror where I crave
   the touch of human love.
   Watch over our child,
   Agnes. In a radiant dream
   his spirit lies so calm,
   like water that is stilled,
   like a mountain tarn
   silent under the sun.
   Sometimes his mother's face
   hovers over that hushed place,
   is received, is given back,
   as beautifully as a bird
   hovers, and hovering, is mirror'd
   in the depths of the lake.

KH: In both plays the main character is a man who consumes, devours a woman. Brand uses Agnes up, and the play is clear that this is what he is doing. *Peer Gynt*, on the other hand, to some extent seems to endorse Gynt's vicarious redemption by Solveig's lifelong sacrifice of her self to him.

GH: I agree with you about Brand, whose spiritual exploitation of Agnes is if anything worse than Gynt's treatment of women. However, Solveig's last words to Peer, the words that conclude the drama – 'I have borne thee freed from guilt. / Sleep my love, my own dear child' – I would hesitate to accept as the final statement of the play. The Button Moulder's final words are interpolated between the two last couplets of Solveig's song, and his words introduce a loaded ambiguity about the possibility of Gynt's future redemption; it keeps us from merely accepting Solveig's word as the happy resolution (happy, that is, for him). Still, it is a problem, I agree, one I imagine Ibsen inherited from Goethe's *Faust*.

KH: What in your version of *Peer Gynt* gives you the most technical satisfaction, if I can put it that way?

GH: The madhouse of Act Four, scene 13. There Ibsen steadily controls such a diversity of unstable, reiterative monomanias, partly through the astuteness of psychological characterization, partly through the variety of verse-form and language, such as ballad, *Knittelvers*, couplets, and so on.

KH: That makes an effective contrast with the world outside the madhouse. My impression is that the larger, cosmopolitan world that Gynt inhabits is often rather tedious, filled with nationalists, reformers or businessmen who are always repeating themselves in their variously stereotyped ways.

GH: The world's variety turns out to be monotonous; for Gynt, everything, any experience, can be exchanged for anything else. But that very monotony and monomania can in themselves be highly varied. I must qualify the generalization. Gynt's first soliloquy in Act Four, scene 5 is luminous in its realization of nature's beauty and bounty. It seems to me that Ibsen in this passage makes Gynt – who is loud in his disdain for 'Poetry' throughout the play – reveal that he might well have been a poetic genius (greater perhaps that Ibsen himself) if his creative imagination had not been so warped and misdirected from childhood on.

KH: I thought we might conclude with a passage near the end. Garton calls it 'one of the most moving and lyrical passages in the whole play, where Peer finally realizes how he has wasted his life', adding that it 'is a slow-moving passage, with dark vowels (*gaa, det taagede graa*) and enjambement which sustains the sense of regret'. It is a reminder how often you stay close to Ibsen's lines as rendered by the literal. Here is the passage in Garton's version:

> GYNT: So unutterably poor a soul can return
> back to nothingness in the misty grey.
> You beautiful earth, don't be angry
> that I trampled your grass to no avail.
> You beautiful sun, you have wasted
> your splashes of light in an uninhabited cabin.
> There was no-one inside to warm and console; –
> the owner, they say, was never at home.
> Beautiful sun and beautiful earth,
> you were foolish that you bore and shed light on my mother.
> The spirit is miserly and nature is prodigal.
> It is costly to pay for with your life for your birth. –
> I shall climb up high to the steepest peak;
> I want once more to see the sun rise,
> to look till I'm weary on the promised land,
> then I shall make a snow avalanche cover me;
> they can write on the top: "Here lies no-one";
> and after that, – then! Let things happen as they will.

And in yours:

> GYNT: So unutterably poor a soul can return
> to pristine nothingness in the dense grey.
> Ah, dearest earth, do not be angry
> that I have ravaged you so. Nor you, dear sun,
> who gifted your radiance to a locked empty room
> because he who owned it was always away.
> Inviolable sun and you, dear, violated earth,
> was it wise to bear and shed light on her who gave me birth?
> The spirit is such a miser, nature so prodigal.
> Life's held to ransom by what began it all.
> If I could I would climb Glittertinden
> to watch the sunrise as if for the last time,
> gazing at what was promised and forbidden,

to have an avalanche drown me in its cry.
'Here lies no one' would serve to bury me.
Inconsolably the soul gathers where it is from.

GH: You will see that Ibsen, in Garton's faithful version, does not name the 'steepest peak'. I had noticed, however, that Glittertinden *is* named elsewhere in the play as a metaphor for the highest reach or point of human aspiration; and it seemed to be pertinent rather than impertinent to name it in this elegiac summation. The internal rhyme ('inconsolably', 'soul') is deliberate. I wanted the melancholy to be aurally unmissable, while at the same time reaching forward with a tone of positive irony to the consolatory cadences of the imminent scene with Solveig. My deviation in this passage from the literal, in order to name Glittertinden explicitly, is an exception to my usual practice, not the rule. I try throughout both plays to remain faithful to the literal versions.

Notes

BRAND

1. *Brand:* Nordic male name, from the Norse *brandr*, meaning 'fire', 'torch' or 'burning wood' and 'sword'. Cf. English 'firebrand'.

2. *miles:* The original has one 'mil'. Before the metrical system was introduced in the 1870s, a Norwegian mile was 18,000 ell, or 11.3 kilometres.

3. *Hercules:* A demi-god and the greatest hero of Greek mythology. Son of Zeus and Alcmene.

4. *Samson in the harlot's lap:* See Judges 16.

5. *five loaves and three fishes:* See Mark 6, Matthew 14, Luke 9 and John 6.

6. *You built on sand:* See Matthew 7:24–7 and Luke 6:46–9.

7. *the God . . . of his father's faith:* See Genesis 22.

8. *good King Bele's:* King Bele is supposed to have lived in west Norway around 800–900 AD. He appears in the Icelandic *Fridthjofs Saga* (c.1300).

9. *Ulf and Thor:* Ulf and Thor are not historical or mythological characters. The name of the god Thor was used as a male name from the Late Middle Ages. Ulf means wolf.

10. *'An eye for an eye, a tooth for a tooth':* The law of retaliation; see Exodus 21:24.

11. *'Consummatum est!':* 'It is finished', Christ's final words on the cross in the Latin Vulgate; see John 19:30.

12. *our tree:* The Christmas tree was introduced to Norway in 1822 but was still a city and upper-class phenomenon in the 1860s.

13. *'The young shall see visions and the old dream dreams':* A reference to the last days, the end of the world; see Acts 2:17.

14. *new Zion*: Zion was the name of a mountain near Jerusalem, often used as a synonym for the city. The 'new Zion' refers to prophecies about the creation of a new Jerusalem.

15. *lex talionis*: The principle or law of retaliation. Cf. 'an eye for an eye . . .', note 10, above.

16. *pro bono publico*: Latin phrase meaning 'for the public good'.

17. *'Whoever looks on God shall die'*: See Exodus 33:20.

18. *A year and a half later*: This means that the action takes place around midsummer.

19. *Égalité*: French for 'equality'. From the national motto 'Liberty, Equality, Fraternity', associated with the French Revolution.

20. *The Tower of Babel*: See Genesis 11.

21. *That vision Jacob saw*: Jacob had a vision of a ladder reaching from earth to heaven; see Genesis 28:10–19.

22. *'The meek shall be exalted'*: See Christ's Sermon on the Mount, Matthew 5:5.

23. *Cain . . . Abel*: The two sons of Adam and Eve; see Genesis 4. Cain was cursed by God for killing his brother.

24. *Caudates*: The word 'Caudates' refers to creatures with a tail. The original has 'Halenegerlandet', 'the land of black people with tails'.

25. *the Ark*: The Ark of the Covenant, containing the Ten Commandments, also called the Ark of Testimony; see, e.g., Exodus 25:10–22.

26. *from Pilate, from Caiaphas*: The prefect of Judaea, Pontius Pilate, and the high priest Joseph Caiaphas are both associated with the death of Jesus.

27. *Dagon*: A Semitic fertility god, part of the pantheon of the Philistines. After the Philistines had captured the Ark of the Covenant, the statue of Dagon was found prostrate before the Ark; see 1 Samuel 5:2–7.

28. *manna from Heaven*: Manna was the food God gave to the Israelites in the desert; see Exodus 16:1–36 and Numbers 11:1–9.

29. *'Thou shalt not murder'*: One of the Ten Commandments; see Exodus 20:1–17 and Deuteronomy 5:4–21.

30. *Vox populi, vox Dei*: Latin for 'The voice of the people is the voice of God.'

31. *that old king of Norway*: A reference to Harald Fairhair, the first king of Norway, and his Sami wife Snæfrid.

32. *God is God and is for ever*: God's name in Hebrew, Jehovah, is commonly understood to mean 'I am that I am'.

33. *He is the God of Love*: The original has the Latin phrase 'deus caritatis', 'God of mercy'. See Afterword.

PEER GYNT

1. *Peer Gynt*: The first name, 'Per', is a version of 'Peter', and Ibsen uses the unusual spelling 'Peer' in line with the fairy-tale collections of Peter Christen Asbjørnsen and Jørgen Moe from the 1840s. Peer Gynt appears as one of the characters in the former's tale 'Reindeer hunting by Rondane'.

2. *seter*: A 'seter' is a Norwegian name for the hut(s) used for summer farming in the mountains.

3. *The Troll King*: The Troll King is called 'Dovregubben' in the original, literally 'the old man of Dovre', a high mountain in south Norway.

4. *Boyg*: The name 'Bøygen' is connected to the verb 'bøye', to bend, and characterizes something which is bent or crooked. The Boyg appears in the tale of Peer Gynt in 'Reindeer hunting by Rondane'.

5. *Lake Gjendin*: Large lake in the eastern part of the Jotunheimen mountain range, most often spelt 'Gjende'.

6. *Gjendin Ridge*: Mountain ridge between two lakes in Jotunheimen, Gjende and Bessvatnet, normally called Besseggen.

7. *Gudbrand Glesne*: A hunter mentioned in the tale 'Reindeer hunting by Rondane'.

8. *a Copenhagen man*: After more than 400 years of Danish rule, Norway had been in a union with Sweden since 1814. The official language remained Danish, however, and the class of civil servants were mainly of Danish origins. Until Norway got its first university in 1811, nearly all theologians were educated at Copenhagen University.

9. *Lunde*: A wealthy farm in Gudbrandsdalen, close to where the mythological Peer Gynt is supposed to have lived.

10. *the halling*: Norwegian folk dance, originally from the area of Hallingdal.

11. *Hedalen*: A western side valley of Gudbrandsdalen.

12. *the Rondane mountains*: A mountain region in the interior of Norway, between the northern parts of the valleys of Gudbrandsdalen and Østerdalen.

13. *Mount Ronden*: One of the highest peaks in the Rondane mountain range.

14. *Soria Moria*: The castle Soria Moria appears in two of Asbjørnsen and Moe's fairy tales, 'Soria Moria Castle' and 'East of the Sun and West of the Moon'.

15. *a Weltanschauung, echt und wahr*: German for 'Weltanschauung (world view or philosophy of life), real and true'. (Not in the original.)

16. *Ur-natur . . . Erhebung . . . Kreis . . . Krise*: 'Ur-natur' is German for 'original nature'. The German words 'Erhebung', 'Kreis' and 'Krise' mean 'elevation', 'circle' and 'crisis' (only 'Ur-natur' appears in the original).

17. *dolce far niente*: This Italian expression literally means 'sweet doing nothing', i.e., 'delicious idleness'.

18. *Selbst*: German for 'self'. (Not in the original.)

19. *Mein Selbst ist dies*: German for 'my self is this'. (Not in the original.)

20. *Lippe-Detmold's*: Lippe had been a German mini-state from 1836. Detmold was its capital.

21. *L'État c'est moi, c'est moi en bloc*: 'L'État c'est moi' is French for 'I am the state' or 'The state, it is I', often attributed to Louis XIV. The rest of the phrase means 'it is me altogether (or "all of it")'. 'But I want to be *myself*, en bloc' is a more literal rendering of the original.

22. *La belle Hélène, un grand désir*: French for 'The beautiful Helen (of Troy), a great desire.' The original has 'To possess the world's greatest beauty'.

23. *Johannisberger*: A wine from the Rhine region.

24. *Ne comprenez-vous pas?*: French for 'You don't understand?' (Not in the original.)

25. *Niente*: Italian for 'no', 'nothing'. (Not in the original.)

26. *Mon Dieu*: French for 'My God'. (Not in the original.)

27. *Sans honneur*: French for 'without honour'. (Not in the original.)

28. *Coup de tonnerre*: French for a 'thunderclap'. (Not in the original.)

29. *Machtübernahme*: German for 'takeover' or 'seizure of power'. (Not in the original.)

30. *Et alors*: French expression meaning 'and then?' or 'so what?'. (Not in the original.)

31. *A dam*: In the original Peer also uses the word 'Kanal', an allusion to the Suez Canal, which was being planned and constructed in the 1860s (it was officially opened in 1869).

32. *Mount Atlas*: Mountain in northwestern Africa.

33. *costa del sol*: Spanish for 'coast of the sun' or 'sun coast'.
34. *Abyssinia*: The historical name in English (now outdated) for Ethiopia. In the original Ibsen uses the Arabic term Habes.
35. *Atlantis*: A mythological island said to have belonged to Poseidon, the Greek god of the ocean.
36. *ab esse ad posse*: A principle from logic. The full phrase is *ab esse ad posse valet consequentia*, meaning that one can deduce a thing's possibility from its existence. The opposite is not the case.
37. *the simoom*: A scorching desert wind, particularly in North Africa and West Asia.
38. *Kaba*: The holy temple in Mecca, the goal of Muslim pilgrimage.
39. *'Das Ewig-Weibliche ziehet uns an'*: Peer slightly misquotes the ending of Goethe's *Faust II* ('ziehet uns an' rather than 'zieht uns hinan'), so that the meaning becomes 'the ever womanly attracts us' rather than 'draws us upwards' (to God).
40. *Babylon's gardens*: The Gardens of Babylon were known as one of the Seven Wonders of the ancient world.
41. *Becker*: Karl Friedrich Becker (1777–1806) was a German historian responsible for *Die Weltgeschichte für die Jugend* (World History for the Young) in twelve volumes. The first edition appeared in 1801.
42. *Leonidas*: Greek warrior king of the city-state of Sparta. He died in 480 BC.
43. *Ach, Sfinx, wer bist du?*: German for 'Oh, Sphinx, who are you?'
44. *Lebensfrage*: The German 'Lebensfrage' literally means 'question of life', a vital issue.
45. *was er ist*: German for 'what he is'. (Not in the original.)
46. *Selbstgrundlage*: German for 'the foundation of the self'. (Not in the original.)
47. *schnell*: German for 'fast'. (Not in the original.)
48. *as the fox leaps out of its pelt in Münchhausen*: The fox appears in the tales of the German officer and huntsman Karl Friedrich Hieronymus Münchhausen (1720–97). These were translated into English in 1786 by the German archaeologist Rudolf Erich Raspe (1737–94).
49. *in toto*: Latin for 'in total' or 'completely'. (Not in the original.)
50. *Malabar*: A district in Deccan, India. Used as synonymous with incomprehensible language, gibberish.

51. *Four hundred years of commerce-making*: An allusion to the time of the union with Denmark, by Norwegians often called 'The four hundred years' night'. The satire is directed against those who wanted another direction in the Norwegian language question than Ibsen, namely towards what became 'New Norwegian'.

52. *King Apis*: The Egyptian bull-deity Apis was considered the incarnation of the god Ptah.

53. *a silver clasp*: Hymnals were often shut with a clasp.

54. *Ausser sich*: German for 'to be beside oneself' (Not in the original.)

55. *Es lebe hoch der grosse Peer*: German for 'Hurrah for (or long live) the great Peer'.

56. *Halling ridge ... Blåhøi ... Galdhøpiggen ... Hårteigen*: Mountains in the interior of south Norway, Galdhøpiggen being Norway's highest mountain (2,469 metres). Hardanger glacier (Hardangerjøkulen) and Folgefonn, here also referred to as Fonnen, are large glaciers in the west of Norway. Some of the names have been slightly modernized.

57. *Sich selbst*: German for 'himself', as in 'to be himself'. (Not in the original.)

58. *Lom*: Small mountain village on the north side of Jotunheimen.

59. *Glittertinden*: The second-highest mountain in Norway (2,451 metres). Part of the Jotunheimen mountain range.

60. *man muss sich drapieren*: Not a set phrase in German, but meaning that one must dress up.

61. *Petrus Gyntus Caesar fecit*: The First three words are Latin for 'Emperor Peer Gynt'. 'Fecit' is Latin for 'he has made it', the signature or artist's name on a work of art.

62. *Askeladden's failed brothers*: Askeladden (The Ash Lad) is a character from Norwegian fairy tales. His brothers Per and Pål are failures, but he, the youngest, succeeds against the odds.

63. *Kongsberg*: The town of Kongsberg in south Norway was known for its silver mines. The Royal Mint was founded there in 1686.

64. *Trond*: Ibsen has taken the story of Trond and the three girls from 'Reindeer hunting by Rondane'.

65. *Valfjeldet*: A mountain.

66. *pourboire*: French for 'tip'.

67. *Blocksberg Post ... Heklefjeld Times*: Blocksberg is the mountain Brocken in northern Germany where witches were said to congregate, and Heklefjeld refers to the Icelandic volcanic mountain Hekla, also associated with witchcraft.

68. *The Character of the Nation*: Fictive play title. (Not in the original.)

69. *Sic Transit Gloria Mundi*: Latin for 'Thus passes the glory of the world'. The phrase was used during papal coronation ceremonies.

70. *ad undas*: Latin for 'to (or in) the waves', often used in Norwegian to mean '[to go] down the drain', 'to the dogs', 'to hell'.

71. *Jostedal*: A valley in the west of south Norway, below the glacier Jostedalsbreen. It is associated with the tale of Jostedalsrypa (a woman called the 'Jostedal grouse') during the Black Death.

72. *'ins Blaue hinein'*: Looking out into the blue, the sky. An allusion to *Either–or* (part two) by the Danish philosopher Søren Kierkegaard (1813–55).

73. *Di buona speranza*: Italian for 'of Good Hope'.

74. *Stavanger missionaries*: The first Norwegian mission association was founded in Stavanger in 1826. The town was associated with a strong missionary activity from this time onwards, particularly after the founding of Det Norske Missionsselskab (The Norwegian Mission Society) in 1842.

AFTERWORD: TRANSLATING AND RECREATING IBSEN

1. *The Oxford Ibsen*, vol. 3: *Brand, Peer Gynt*, ed. James Walter McFarlane, trans. James Kirkup and Christopher Fry (London: Oxford University Press, 1972), p. 22.

2. Michael Meyer, *Ibsen: A Biography* (Garden City, New York: Doubleday, 1971), p. 245, quoted by Hill in the Preface to his *Brand: A Version for the Stage by Geoffrey Hill* (London: Penguin, 1996), p. viii.

3. Ibsen made the remark to C. H. Herford, who recorded it in the introduction to his translation, *Brand: A Dramatic Poem in Five Acts* (London: Heinemann, 1894).

4. Raymond Williams, *Drama from Ibsen to Eliot* (London: Chatto and Windus, 1965 [1952]).

5. Ibsen, *Brand*, op. cit., p. viii. See Ibsen's letter to Georg Brandes of 26 June 1869 (Henrik Ibsen, *Letters and Speeches*, trans. Evert Sprinchorn (New York: Hill and Wang, 1964), pp. 83–4).

6. Ibsen, *Brand*, op. cit., p. ix.

7. Williams, *Drama from Ibsen to Eliot*, p. 55.

8. John Haffenden, 'Geoffrey Hill', pp. 76–99 of *Viewpoints: Poets in Conversation with John Haffenden* (London: Faber and Faber 1981), p. 97.

9. This is apothecary's Latin for a sufficient quantity of a particular drug.

THE MASTER BUILDER AND OTHER PLAYS
HENRIK IBSEN

The Master Builder / Little Eyolf / John Gabriel Borkman / When We Dead
Awaken

*'I couldn't believe there was a master builder in all the world who could
build such an enormously high tower. And then the fact that you were
standing up there yourself, at the very top! In person! And that you weren't
the slightest bit dizzy. That was the most - kind of - dizzying thought of all'*

Ibsen's last four plays were sensational bestsellers, performed in theatres
across Europe. These final works, exploring sexuality and death, the
conflict between generations, the drive for creativity and the frailty of the
body, cemented Ibsen's dramatic reputation, and continue to fuel debate
today on whether they celebrate freedom and love or are instead savagely
ironic studies of our shared human flaws. This new translation, the first
to be based on the latest critical edition of Ibsen's works, offers the best
version available in English.

A new translation by Barbara Haveland and Anne-Marie Stanton-Ife
With an introduction by Toril Moi
General Editor Tore Rem

A DOLL'S HOUSE AND OTHER PLAYS
HENRIK IBSEN

The Pillars of the Community / A Doll's House / Ghosts / An Enemy of the People

'Our home has never been anything other than a play-house. I've been your doll-wife here, just as at home I was Daddy's doll-child'

These four plays established Ibsen as the leading figure in the theatre of his day, sending shockwaves throughout Europe and beyond. *A Doll's House* scandalized audiences with its heroine Nora's assertion that she is 'first and foremost a human being', rather than a wife, mother or fragile doll. Ibsen's even more radical follow-up, *Ghosts*, exposes family secrets and sexual double-dealing, while *The Pillars of the Community* and *An Enemy of the People* both explore the hypocrisy and dark tensions at the heart of society. This new translation, the first to be based on the latest critical edition of Ibsen's works, offers the best version available in English.

A new translation by Deborah Dawkin and Erik Skuggevik
With an introduction by Tore Rem
General Editor Tore Rem